EMISSARY FROM THE STARS

Then Chryse saw the ship. It was spherical and getting larger by the second. This was no rich man's yacht. If anything, it was the biggest spacecraft she had ever seen.

But its size was hardly worth mentioning when compared to the vessel's obvious peculiarity. For almost as long as men had built spaceships, their craft had ridden on tails of plasma fire – yet the newcomer was decelerating with no signs of a drive flare. Whatever shipyard had built the craft, it wouldn't be found anywhere in the Solar System.

Mankind, it seemed, was about to welcome its second visitor from the stars.

Also by Michael McCollum
Published by Ballantine Books:

A GREATER INFINITY

LIFE PROBE

PROCYON'S PROMISE

Michael McCollum

A Del Rey Book

BALLANTINE BOOKS ● **NEW YORK**

To Bob, my oldest friend

A Del Rey Book
Published by Ballantine Books

Copyright © 1985 by Michael McCollum

All rights reserved under International and Pan-American Copyright Conventions. Published in the United States by Ballantine Books, a division of Random House, Inc., New York, and simultaneously in Canada by Random House of Canada Limited, Toronto.

Library of Congress Catalog Card Number: 85-90711

ISBN 0-345-30296-6

Printed in Canada

First Edition: August 1985

Cover art by Don Dixon

PROLOGUE

THE MAKERS

The Makers had never heard of *Homo sapiens Terra*, nor would they have been particularly impressed if they had. By their standards, mankind had little to brag about. The Makers' cities were old when *Australopithecus* first ventured onto the plains of Africa. By the time *Homo erectus* was lord of the Earth, the Makers had touched each of the twelve planets that circled their K0 sun.

Individually, Makers were long lived, industrious, and generally content. Their population was stabilized at an easily supported fifty billion, and war was an ancient nightmare not discussed in polite company. So when the Makers advanced to the limits of their stellar system, it was with a sense of adventure that they prepared to journey out into the great blackness beyond.

The first ships to leave the Maker sun were "slowboats," huge vessels that took a lifetime to visit the nearer stars. After three dozen such ventures, the Makers had made two important discoveries. The first was that life is pervasive throughout the universe. Nearly every stellar system studied had a planet in the temperate zone, where water is liquid. Such worlds were found to teem with life. More exciting, on twelve percent of the worlds visited, evolutionary pressures had led to the development of intelligence. Two were home to civilizations nearly as advanced as the Makers' own.

The second great discovery was the realization that the

galaxy is a very large place, much too large to be explored by slowboat. So, more curious than anything else, they set out to circumvent the one thing that retarded their progress: the speed of light!

A million years of scientific endeavor had taught them that the first step in any new project is to develop a rational theory of the phenomenon to be studied. And the Makers, being who they were, didn't stop when they had one theory of how faster-than-light travel might be achieved. They developed two; each supported by an impressive body of experimental evidence and astronomical observation. Each should have resulted in the development of an FTL drive. Yet for a hundred thousand years every effort ended in failure.

There is a limit to the quantity of resources any civilization can divert to satisfy an itch of its curiousity bump. The FTL program had long passed the point of economic viability. Yet the effort continued. For, while the Makers were mounting their assault on the light barrier, they found a reason more compelling than mere curiosity to break free of their prison—their stellar system was beginning to run low on the raw materials Maker civilization needed to sustain itself.

The first signs were barely noticeable, even to the economists who kept careful watch over such things. But eventually curves projected far into the future foretold a time when civilization would collapse of resource starvation. To avert catastrophe the Makers would have to obtain an infusion of new resources, either by importing raw materials from nearby stars or by transplanting their civilization to virgin territory.

Unfortunately, both options required a working faster-than-light drive.

The scientists redoubled their efforts. Another hundred millennia passed unsuccessfully before a philosopher began to wonder if they were asking the right questions. The Great Thinker had dedicated his life to the study of the period immediately following the slowboats' return from the stars. He noted that Maker science had made great intuitive leaps in those years. The ancient records contained many cases where the combined knowledge of two races had led to discoveries unsuspected by either.

His questions were as fundamental as they were simple: "Could it be that our concepts of how FTL may be achieved are wrong? Is the failure to surpass light-speed simply a matter of having missed the obvious? If so, might not some other civilization have avoided our error and found the true path to FTL?"

Once the questions were asked, they could not be ignored. A program was immediately begun to provide an answer. At first it was a minor adjunct to the FTL research project. But as each promising approach to FTL proved a dead end, the program to probe the knowledge of alien civilizations grew.

By the time humanity discovered agriculture, it was all the program there was.

PART I

HOMECOMING

CHAPTER 1

Henning's Roost was renowned throughout the solar system. Its reputation stretched from the intermittently molten plains of Mercury to the helium lakes of Pluto, from the upper reaches of the Jovian atmosphere to the subterranean settlements deep beneath the red surface of Mars' dusty plains. Wherever men and women worked at hard or dangerous jobs, wherever boredom and terror were normal components of life, *The Roost* was a standard subject of conversation.

Henning's was a pleasure satellite, the largest ever built. Its owners had placed it in solar orbit ten million kilometers in front of Earth. A story was told of a spacerigger who had arrived at *The Roost* with a year's pay in his pocket, stayed ten days, left flat broke, and pronounced himself well satisfied. It was a testimonial to the diversions provided by *Henning's* management that the story was widely accepted as completely reasonable. Besides which, it was true.

Nevertheless, Chryse Haller was bored.

Two weeks earlier Chryse had arrived at *The Roost* for her first vacation in years. She had plunged immediately into the joyful whirl, sampling most of the diversions that weren't ultimately harmful to one's health. She had played *chemin de fer*, blackjack, poker, roulette, and seven-card stapo on the gaming decks. Later, she had enlisted as a centurian in a Roman Legion on the sensiegamer deck and slogged for two days through the damp chill of simulated Gaul. Her first battle convinced her that the difference between ancient warfare and a modern butcher shop is mostly a matter of attitude, and she began to cast around for new diversions.

She turned to the most traditional sport of all, availing herself of the large pool of male companionship—both professional and tourist—that *The Roost* had to offer. The previous evening she'd attended the nightly bacchannal on Beta Deck. That had been a mistake. She'd become involved with a handsome young man whose only goal was to please her. Yet, in spite of the soft lights, the rich smell of incense, and the warm glow of two drinks within her, she found herself losing interest with each moment. She'd ended up watching simulated clouds scud across a simulated sky. Afterward, she made her excuses and left early.

There was no doubt about it: Lotus eating was definitely beginning to pall.

Playing with a fruit bowl, Chryse sat alone in a breakfast nook, pondering the curious emotional state into which she had fallen. Her reflection stared dully back at her from the polished depths of the table. The image was that of a woman in her early thirties, blond, with shoulder-length hair that framed a wide, honest face. The eyes were set wide apart above high cheekbones, a nose a trifle small, and a mouth just then twisted into a slight scowl. The eyes were brown in the simulated mahogany of the table, but green in actuality.

"Tenth-stellar for your thoughts."

Chryse looked up to find Roland Scott standing over her. Roland had been a member of her section in the Gaul campaign. They had mustered out together and she had taken him as a lover that same night. He'd been good for her psyche and they'd spent three glorious days together before she suffered the minor disappointment of discovering that he was a Roost employee.

"Hello, Roland."

"Why so glum?"

"Just a little tired, I guess."

"Anything I can do to help?"

She shook her head. "I'm afraid there's no cure for what ails me. You may have a seat if you like, though."

He quickly slid into the opposite side of the booth. "Maybe it would help to talk about it."

She smiled wanly at him, recognizing his automatic response to a professional challenge. Still, Roland really cared. He was *paid* to care. Of course, that was part of the problem. "It's this place."

"What about it?"

"It depresses me."

His face acquired a look of surprise. "The big boss isn't going to like hearing that. He's put billions into *The Roost*. No one is supposed to be unhappy here, least of all Chryse Lawrence Haller."

"You weren't listening. I didn't say I was unhappy. I said I was depressed. Different emotion entirely."

"If you say so."

"Look around you, Roland. What do you see?"

"What am I supposed to see?"

"Have you ever looked closely at your clientele?"

He made a show of scanning the restaurant. "Okay, I've looked."

"You've got a good cross-section of humanity here. Both sexes, all shapes and sizes, every color. Yet, in spite of our differences, we all have something in common."

"Sure," Roland said, nodding. "You're all richer than anyone has a right to be. If you weren't, you could never afford us."

"True. I hadn't thought of that. Hmmm, that makes things even worse!"

"How so?"

"Can't you see it? All your clients are compulsive personalities."

"Aren't you being a bit hard on yourself and the other guests?"

"If anything, I'm not being hard enough. We're all on holiday, yet each of us is so desperate for diversion that we play ourselves into exhaustion."

"Considering the cost," Roland said, "can you blame anyone?"

"I suppose that explains a few cases. But take old Joshua Voichek over there." Chryse gestured toward a spry centenarian seated at a nook halfway across the compartment. "After my father, he's probably the richest man in the system. He could spend a lifetime in *The Roost* without making a dent in his fortune. Yet he wears himself out as quickly as the salesman who saves a dozen years to come here."

"Your theory, Madam Psychotherapist?"

"We're bored with life. The sense of adventure has left us. There aren't any frontiers left. No one climbs Mount Everest anymore."

Roland chuckled. "Why should they? If you want to reach the Everest Summit Hotel, you board an airtram in Nepal. They leave every half hour."

"Exactly! Where can you go in the solar system where you won't find someone else's bootprints?"

Roland shrugged but did not answer.

"Know what I think? I think the human race is suffering from claustrophobia. We know there are limits beyond which we cannot go, so we invent places like this to help us forget."

"Isn't that quite a lot to conclude from the existence of an overpriced whorehouse?"

She looked at him sharply, suddenly aware of the anger in his voice. "A trained entertainment specialist isn't a whore, Roland."

He raised one eyebrow quizzically. "Perhaps you can explain the difference to me sometime."

"I didn't mean to insult you. Put it down to overwork. Forgive me?"

"You don't need my forgiveness. You can have me fired anytime you feel like it."

"I guess I deserve that." Chryse let her gaze slip from his resentful face and move to the viewscreen at the far end of the small restaurant. The view was from a remote camera somewhere out on the hull. It showed a jumble of I-beams, pressure spheres, and hull plates framed by the black of space. "Let's change the subject before we have an argument. I've been staring at that thing all morning. What is it?"

He turned to follow her gaze. "Just an old dormitory used during *The Roost*'s construction. Abandoned now, of course."

"I would think the owners would keep local space clear of hazards to navigation. Wouldn't be very good publicity for a shipload of tourists to run into that heap on approach."

He shook his head. "It isn't as ramshackle as it appears.

Look closely. See the thruster cluster jutting out near the airlock? Twenty more are scattered over the hull. That hulk and a half-dozen others are slaved to the *Roost*'s central computer."

"Sounds like a lot of trouble to go to for a junkyard."

"It's part of the service—the hulks make good destinations for clients with a yen to explore the mysteries of space."

"The *what*?"

Roland laughed, his pique suddenly forgotten. "Haven't you ever skin dived on a sunken ship?"

She shook her head.

"How about going up to Zeta Deck then? They've got a near-perfect simulation of the *Esmeralda* there. That was a Spanish galleon that sunk off Key West in the sixteenth century. They took sixty million stellars' worth of treasure out of her back in the thirties."

Chryse shook her head. "I'm tired of simulated adventure."

He smiled, turning on the boyish charm. "That's the reason for the hulks. They're the real thing. We could check out two vacsuits at North Pole Terminus and make a day-long picnic of it if you like."

Chryse shook her head again. Exploring a twenty-year-old work barge didn't appeal to her, but Roland's suggestion had tweaked a stray memory. There *was* something in solar orbit she would very much like to explore.

"Do they rent ships at North Terminus as well?"

"No need. The maneuvering gear on the vacsuits is first rate and well maintained. Oh, they'll rent you a scooter if you want, but that costs extra."

"I don't want a scooter. I want a *ship*! Something with legs."

"It's expensive."

"I can afford it."

He shrugged. "There are a few rental jobs at North Terminus. I'm a fair-to-middlin' pilot. I'll take you anywhere you want to go."

"No thank you. Where I want to go, I'd rather be alone. Maybe a bit of solitude will snap me out of this mood I've fallen into."

"Solo piloting is dangerous."

"I'll be all right. After all, the computer runs the ship. If I get into trouble, it'll scream for help, won't it?"

He nodded. "Okay, it's your neck. You'll have to sign a release, of course."

"Of course."

"Where are you going?"

"I thought that I would go see the probe."

Three hundred years earlier, a spacecraft had entered the solar system from the depths of interstellar space. Limited two-way communications were established almost immediately, and it was quickly learned that the craft was an instrument package controlled by a self-aware computer.

The computer, which called itself PROBE, had been constructed by an advanced race of beings, which it dubbed "The Makers." These Makers had been working to develop a faster-than-light drive for their spaceships for thousands of years. In all that vast time, they had been singularly unsuccessful. So, faced with dwindling resources at home and desperate to break free to the stars, they had hit upon the idea of sending *life probes* to the surrounding stars to make contact with other advanced species. Once a probe arrived in a strange stellar system, it bargained with its hosts to exchange their scientific knowledge for that of the Makers. When it had learned all it could, the probe returned home to add its cargo to the ever-growing pool of Maker knowledge. It was through this slow accumulation of the wisdom of many races that the Makers hoped to eventually break free of the star that had become their jailer.

Over the centuries, thousands of life probes had been launched outbound from the Maker sun. They cruised at speeds approaching ten percent that of light, taking centuries to complete their journeys. While they traveled, they listened to the cosmos, ever alert for the energy discharges that betrayed the presence of a technologically advanced civilization.

Life Probe 53935 had been unlucky. For ten millennia it had searched for intelligence among the stars and not found it. And even when it finally pricked an expanding bubble of human radio noise, it wasn't sure that its luck had changed. For humankind was low on the Maker scale of civilization, perhaps too low to be of use to a life probe in need of an overhaul. The probe had considered the problem of human capabilities for months while it fell toward the Sun. Finally, at almost the last moment possible, fate had intervened to make the probe's decision for it.

One hypothesis common to all FTL theories was that a vessel traveling at superlight velocity would be detectable in the sublight universe. Theoretically, any material object moving faster than light will create a shock wave in the interstellar medium, a wave that appears to an outside observer as a source of highly energetic, Cherenkov radiation.

For a hundred thousand years the Makers and their farflung probes had scanned the skies, searching for just such a phenomenon. They had done so in vain until, in the human year A.D. 2065, just as it was approaching the solar system, the hyperwave detectors aboard *Life Probe 53935* began clamoring for attention. An intense source of radiation that closely mirrored the hypothetical properties of a starship's wake had been spotted in the Procyon system a mere twelve light-years beyond Sol. The age-old dream of the Makers seemed finally at hand!

Except there was a problem.

The struggle to climb to thirty thousand kilometers-per-second cruising velocity had cost the probe dearly in terms of fuel. To slow its headlong rush at journey's end would cost more, leaving its tanks virtually dry. The probe had no fuel reserves with which to change course.

It studied its options carefully. The only sure way of reaching Procyon was a journey of two stages. The first stage required stopping in the solar system to obtain new fuel stocks and a general overhaul of its tired mechanisms. Once returned to a spaceworthy condition, the probe could launch outbound directly for the Procyon system. The journey would last more than a century, but to a ten-thousand-year-old machine, such a trip was a mere local jaunt.

Thus, humanity owed its first visitation from the stars not to any accomplishment of its own, but to the fact that Earth was a natural waystation on the way to more interesting vistas.

*   *   *

Chryse Haller sat at the controls of the rented day-cruiser and finished off the sandwich she had made in the tiny galley aft of the control room. She was fifty-two hours out from *Henning's Roost* and decelerating for rendezvous when the soft music that filled the cabin was interrupted by the ship's computer.

"We are being challenged."

Chryse leaned forward, suddenly alert. "Identify challenger," she ordered.

"Automated Guard Station, Department of Antiquities Registration Number 7155."

"Put it on the speaker."

"... WARNING. WARNING. YOU ARE APPROACHING THE RESTRICTED ZONE OF A PROTECTED HISTORIC MONUMENT. YOU ARE HEREBY ADVISED TO TURN BACK IMMEDIATELY. FAILURE TO COMPLY MAY LEAD TO CIVIL OR CRIMINAL PENALTIES BEING ASSESSED AGAINST YOU. WARNING..."

"Transmission, please."

"Ready to transmit."

"Attention, Guard Station 7155. I am Chryse Lawrence Haller, Ident MZH-93587116. I am countermanding you. Return to standby mode."

"ORDER RECEIVED AND ACKNOWLEDGED. RETURNING TO STANDBY. BE ADVISED, CITIZEN HALLER, THAT YOUR ACTIVITIES WITHIN THE BOUNDARIES OF THIS PROTECTED HISTORIC MONUMENT WILL BE MONITORED. ANY ATTEMPT TO DAMAGE OR DEFACE THE MONUMENT WILL BE IMMEDIATELY REPORTED TO EARTH."

"Acknowledged." Chryse called for library function from the computer. "Reference: Life probe, visitation of same. Reference date: Twenty-first Century."

"Data retrieved."

"Show me a picture."

A thirty-centimeter, translucent black cube materialized in front of her. Filling its interior was a mighty spacecraft consisting of two spheres—each two hundred meters in diameter—connected by a long central column. One

sphere, labeled CONTROL SECTION, was an open latticework of small beams arranged in the familiar pattern of
geodesic trusses. There were gaps in the sphere where
bits and pieces of machinery poked through, but it was
otherwise whole. Arrayed around it were a number of
long booms tipped with irregularly shaped sensing mechanisms.

Chryse shifted her attention to the sphere labeled DRIVE
SECTION, her gaze sweeping along the full eight hundred
meters of the probe's length. A number of long cylindrical
tanks were strapped to the thrust frame between the two
major spheres. The drive sphere at the probe's stern was
much more massive than the control sphere at its prow.
The framework of beams was heavier, giving an impression of massive strength. And the sphere itself was more
densely crammed with machinery. Chryse recognized the
central bulge of a mass converter and the familiar shape
of an electromagnetic nozzle among the unfamiliar bits
and pieces of alien machinery.

"Big, isn't it?" she muttered out loud.

"Null program. Please repeat," the computer responded.

"Cancel," Chryse said absentmindedly. Her eyes were
suddenly drawn to a bright, starlike point inside the cube.
"Center on coordinates X-three, Y-five, Z-two. Expand
view one hundred times."

"Acknowledged."

The view moved to one side and expanded to resolve
the spark of light into a spacecraft whose hull reflected
sunlight directly into the camera's lens. The ship was a
model that hadn't been seen in the solar system in nearly
three centuries.

"Now, let's see where we're going. Show me our destination in real time."

"Acknowledged."

At first the view seemed to be the same as before, with
the exception that the speck of light was gone and the
viewing angle caused the probe to be considerably foreshortened. The daycruiser was approaching at a thirty-
degree angle to the probe's major axis, with the control
sphere closer than the drive sphere. Chryse called for a
closeup view.

The awesome machine, which she had viewed in its

splendor just seconds earlier, was no longer hale or whole. As schoolchildren learned before they were ten, the probe had fallen victim to the most celebrated incident of treachery in the history of the human race. Chryse gazed at the wreck in the holocube and felt a tug of remorse at what her people had done.

Evidence of the catastrophe was everywhere and unmistakable. The sphere of the control section had caved in on one side as though smashed by a giant fist. Opposite the blow, the sphere bulged noticeably, stretched nearly to bursting. Large sections of interior structure had vaporized in a titanic explosion, and a twisted forest of support beams—transformed into odd shapes by the force of the blast—gave the play of sunlight and shadow inside the probe a surrealistic quality.

Chryse gulped. "I had no idea," she said. It was only then that she realized she had been holding her breath.

Not everyone, it seemed, had been happy with the discovery of the alien spacecraft on the edge of the solar system. Most objections had come from the newly industrialized nations of the Southern Hemisphere, each of which saw the probe and its cargo of knowledge as a threat to their hard-earned equality. It was felt that the older, longer industrialized nations of the North would be better equipped to use the advanced knowledge that the probe carried. The nation that emerged as leader of the opposition was the Pan-African Federation.

The struggle had been wholly political at first. A resolution welcoming the probe into the system was introduced into the General Assembly of the old United Nations. The Pan-Africans and their allies fought skillfully against it, but when it came time to vote, the southerners found themselves on the losing side of the tally. By the narrowest of margins, the resolution passed. Five months later, the probe took up a parking orbit around the Sun.

Negotiations between the probe and the UN began immediately. The complexities involved in arranging for both the probe's overhaul and the exchange of scientific knowledge were considerable. Before any agreements could be reached, there was much to learn on both sides. To speed the negotiations, the probe had split off a portion of its circuits to form a separate personality. This new entity, which the probe dubbed SURROGATE, was intended to act as translator between the probe and its hosts.

Shortly after the probe's arrival in the solar system, six Pan-African Navy spacecraft attacked humanity's first visitor from the stars. They were met by two outgunned UN defenders and the probe itself. All six attackers were destroyed in a hard-fought battle, but not before they were able to unleash an irresistible weapon against their target.

In the twenty-first century as in the twenty-fourth, ships of deep space were powered by tiny antimatter black holes known as I-masses. Human civilization was built on the limitless energy they provided. They lit man's cities, smelted his ores, and drove his spacecraft. And when the Pan-African warships attacked the probe, they were used for the first time as deadly weapons.

Each marauding warship took great care with its approach to the scene of battle, placing itself on a precise trajectory for the probe. And even though each attacker was eventually destroyed before it could reach the target, the probe found itself the focal point of six converging I-masses.

Two reached their mark.

The primary probe personality was destroyed, but SURROGATE—housed at the end of one of the long sensor booms—survived. Even so, the age-old dream of the Makers seemed at an end. Damaged as it was, SURROGATE had no hope of reaching the FTL civilization around Procyon. Worse, the impact of the I-masses had destroyed all record of the Makers. The surviving probe personality possessed no single iota of knowledge concerning its creators, their history, their language, or the location of their star in space.

Out of this situation had come a bargain born of desperation. Since SURROGATE needed to secure the secret of FTL for the Makers, and humanity needed the Maker knowledge that had survived the attack, each party agreed to help the other. For its part, the UN agreed to build a slower-than-light starship and man it with a crew of ten thousand. When the ship was completed, the circuits that housed SURROGATE would be placed aboard and the ship headed out on the century-long trip to Procyon. In exchange, SURROGATE agreed to share its vast library of knowledge.

The Procyon mission was launched outbound early in 2096. Allotting a century for the journey and an additional decade for the crew to bargain for the secret of FTL with whatever native race they discovered, the expedition was expected to return to the solar system (by FTL starship) no later than 2205.

They were now 183 years overdue.

CHAPTER 2

"I want to see it with my own eyes."

"You *are* seeing the projection with your own eyes, Miss Haller."

"No, I mean *outside*. I want to touch it, to feel its solidity, to make it real!"

"It is far too dangerous. You could be injured."

Chryse shrugged. "You'll be monitoring my vital signs. If I get into trouble, you can fly my suit back by remote control."

"I still recommend against this unnecessary risk."

"Life is an unnecessary risk." Chryse unbuckled from the pilot's couch and aligned her axis with the daycruiser's small central passageway. "I'm going."

She suited up and let the computer do a complete telemetry readout on her before entering the airlock. As in everything else relating to *Henning's Roost*, the suit was the best money could buy. Its air recycling system was good for a week or more, its water tanks and pharmaceutical stores were full, and its outer armor made it virtually impervious to damage. If the need arose, she would be able to call the ship for help, have her message relayed to Earth, and wait for the rescue craft to arrive. It wouldn't be comfortable, but it was fairly safe.

Once outside the airlock, she jetted across the two hundred meters of void separating the daycruiser from the probe and grounded on its outer frame. Above her,

19

the Sun blazed hotter than the hottest day Death Valley had ever seen. The beams beneath her boots reflected the light with a dull metallic sheen.

If the probe seemed large from the daycruiser control room, it was *gigantic* from the vantage point of the outer framework of the damaged control sphere. Chryse Haller grasped a crossbeam as she carefully snaked a safety line around a jutting side beam. She glanced across the rounded plain and shivered at the sudden realization of just how alone she felt.

"Status check," the daycruiser computer said into her earphones. Its voice betrayed overtones of metallic unease.

After she assured her mechanical nursemaid that all was well, Chryse turned her attention to the massive mechanism beneath her feet. She peered down into the depths of the open sphere, feeling for a moment like an iron worker in the upper stories of a megastructure. It took a few moments to orient herself.

The first thing she noticed was that not all the damage had come from the collision with the I-masses. Here and there, amid structures that appeared undamaged, were gaps that should not have been. These, she quickly realized, were the results of the salvage operation that had gone on for nearly fifty years after the probe's destruction.

She finished her inspection and glanced up at the daycruiser. "I'm going inside. I want to see what it's like down where the main personality was housed."

"I do not advise it!"

"Objection noted. I'll be careful."

Chryse unhooked herself from the safety lines and chinned a control in her helmet. Two joysticks telescoped over her shoulders from her backpack. She gave each a small twist. A faint hiss superimposed itself over the hum of her environmental control system, and she began to move across the face of the control sphere toward a fissure in the framework that appeared to extend into the center of the structure.

It took ten minutes for her to work down into the inner framework of the probe. The cabling and twisted metal were like the trees of a dense forest. As she progressed ever deeper, she passed through alternating regions of bright sunlight and ever darker gloom. As her surroundings grew dim, Chryse felt the twinge of unease that is the legacy of thousands of generations of ancestors who feared the coming of darkness. She was considering turning back when a sparkle of light caught her eye.

Her fear was quickly replaced by curiosity. She jetted forward to find herself in a stray beam of sunlight that penetrated the interior of the hulk. As she did so, the firefly speck died away. She moved closer and was rewarded by a polychromatic flash directly into her helmet visor. She reached out, thrust her armored glove into a recess surrounded by the frayed ends of reinforcing fibers, and pulled a faceted crystal from its nest.

She held the crystal close to her eyes and laughed hollowly. The mystery was a mystery no longer—just an ordinary memory module, the medium in which the vast library of Maker knowledge had been stored and the functional basis of nearly every electronic gadget invented in the solar system for three centuries.

She was carefully placing the crystal in her belt pouch when a mechanical voice suddenly blared in her earphones.

"WARNING. WARNING. YOU ARE APPROACHING THE RESTRICTED ZONE OF A PROTECTED HISTORIC MONUMENT. YOU ARE HEREBY ADVISED TO TURN BACK IMMEDIATELY. FAILURE TO COMPLY MAY LEAD TO CIVIL OR CRIMINAL PENALTIES BEING ASSESSED AGAINST YOU."

"What the hell?" she yelped, forgetting about her souvenir. She got her emotions under control and cursed herself for being so jumpy. "Those idiots at *The Roost* must have sent someone to keep an eye on me!"

She considered the possibility that the *Hennig*'s management was chaperoning her, then frowned. The thought didn't feel right. Such a gesture was too extravagant, even for them. It *could* be another tourist, of course, but the fact that she had heard the warning meant that it was being beamed in the wrong direction for a ship from Earth.

She began the delicate job of turning around and working back the way she had come. Five minutes later, she was once again at the outer framework of the probe. She shaded her eyes and craned her neck inside the helmet, scanning for some sign of the ship that had set off the guard station alarms.

"Status check!" she ordered.

For the first time since she had left the daycruiser's airlock, the computer had nothing to say.

"Status check," she repeated.

Again, there was only silence.

"Damn!" she muttered. She didn't have time to consider the implications of the balky computer's silence for it was at that moment that she saw the ship.

It was spherical and growing by the second. Even with the difficulty of judging size in space, it was obvious that this was no rich man's yacht. If anything, it was the largest spacecraft Chryse had ever seen.

But its size was something she merely noted in passing, hardly worth mentioning when compared to the vessel's obvious peculiarity—for almost as long as men had built spaceships, their craft had ridden on tails of plasma fire. A spacecraft drive flare was bright enough to be seen from one side of the solar system to the other—or to burn out the retinas of anyone incautious enough to stare at one for more than a second. Yet the newcomer was decelerating with no sign of a flare. Whatever shipyard had built it, Chryse was willing to bet the location couldn't be found anywhere in the solar system.

Mankind, it seemed, was about to welcome its second visitor from the far stars.

Julius Gruenmeier scowled as Achilles, the largest asteroid in the leading Trojan group, grew steadily larger outside the bubble of the supply boat. He watched as the domes, observation instruments, and communications gear of the System Institute for the Advancement of Astronomical Observation—SIAAO—slowly rose over Achilles' jagged horizon. Achilles Observatory, and its twin in the trailing Trojans, looked farther out into space than any other observatory in the solar system. When Achilles and Aeneas were working in concert, they anchored both ends of a 1.3-billion-kilometer baseline—far enough to be able to separate binary stars in the Andromeda galaxy into their component parts.

Not that they would be able to maintain that capability for long. Gruenmeier, in his role as Achilles' Operations Manager, was returning from a meeting with the SIAAO comptroller. The occasion was the comptroller's yearly trip out from Earth, and the subject—next year's operating budget. The news was bad.

It was common knowledge that the institute had made some unwise investments for several years, but no one outside the Board of Trustees had known just how shaky finances really were. They knew now. Operating budgets were to be cut drastically for three years, by which time the institute's portfolio should have returned to its former health. The cuts were sufficiently deep that Gruenmeier didn't see how he would be able to keep both Achilles and Aeneas operating.

He was still pondering ways to slash expenses without idling prime instruments when the supply boat entered Main Dome's Number Three Airlock. Gruenmeier absent-mindedly thanked the boat's two young pilots, unstrapped, then pulled himself to the coffin-sized airlock amidships. Since the terminal was inside the dome itself, there was no need to suit up. He exited the ship, grabbed hold of one of the guide cables that crisscrossed the terminal decking, and pulled himself toward the passenger lounge.

He was met by his assistant, Chala Arnam. Arnam was an intense woman in her midforties, a fair-to-middling neutrino astronomer and the best administrative assistant he'd ever had. He was grooming her to take over Institute Operations on that inevitable day when the trustees forced him into retirement. He hoped there would be something to leave her when the time came.

"How did it go?" she asked.

"Not good, Chala."

"How bad is it?"

He sighed. "Very. They aren't cutting out fat this time. They're amputating our lower torso."

"Are we going to fight?"

"How?"

"We could appeal directly to the trustees."

"Simonson suggested that we do so. But you and I both know that his orders come directly from them, so what's the use? Besides, even if some of them were willing to listen, there's the distance problem to overcome. Out here we're eight hundred million kilometers from them. The damned accountants are just down the hall."

"Perhaps you should plan a trip to Earth, Julius."

"I've thought of that and just might do it if we can come up with a viable approach." He chewed on his lower lip as he always did when he was worried, and then abruptly changed the subject. "Anything interesting happen here while I was gone?"

"Not much. Doctor Chandidibya was in to see me this morning."

"Let me guess. He was raising a stink about not being able to monopolize the Big Ear, right?"

"Not this time. He complained about the service techs. Says they're doing their usual slipshod job. He thinks the whole lot of them should be fired."

"Does he have any suggestions as to how we can attract better people on the salaries we pay?"

"I doubt if Doctor Chandidibya cares about minor problems like personnel staffing and retention—unless they adversely affect the operation of the thousand-meter radioscope, of course."

"How'd you leave him?"

"Grumpy."

"I'll try to sooth him at dinner. Anything else?"

Chala nodded. "For the last two hours, the technical staff has been going crazy searching for a malfunction in the high-energy monitoring equipment."

"What kind of malfunction?"

"A ghost image of some sort. They've tried everything but it won't go away."

"Ghost?" Gruenmeier asked, suddenly happy to have something to think about other than the state of the institute's dismal finances.

"I'd best let Doctor Bartlett explain it. As you well know, high-energy optics ain't my field."

Ten minutes later, Director Gruenmeier found himself listening to the explanation of the watch astronomer.

"We first began picking it up on the cosmic ray monitors at sixteen twelve, shortly after the start of Second Watch. The monitors kept insisting that they had spotted a diffuse source of cosmic rays somewhere out beyond Neptune. We ran the usual maintenance checks and found nothing, so I ordered the neutrino scopes and X-ray equipment to take a look. They can see it too."

"What makes you think it's a ghost then?"

"Because there isn't anything out there! Besides which, the source is moving."

"Moving?"

"Yes, sir. Moving fast. It appears to be traveling radially outward from the Sun."

"Have you asked Aeneas for a parallax measurement?"

"Yes, sir. Two and a half hours ago. I expect their reply momentarily...." As though to punctuate Bartlett's comment, a bell rang and several readout screens chose that moment to show data. The half-dozen people in the operations center turned to watch.

"Well, I'll be damned!" Bartlett muttered incredulously a few seconds later. "They see it too."

"Have you got a velocity vector yet?" Gruenmeier asked.

The watch astronomer nodded, then hesitated as he read the figures silently. He looked up at Gruenmeier. "It says here that the radiation source is moving directly away from the sun, toward Canis Minor, sir. The exact coordinates are right ascension, 0738; declination, plus 0518. And get this—whatever it is, it's moving at exactly the speed of light!"

Gruenmeier blinked. "It's moving *away* from the Sun?"

"Yes, sir."

Gruenmeier turned to Chala Arnam. "Get me a priority line to Earth. I'll be sending a coded message to the Board of Trustees in about ten minutes."

He turned back to Bartlett. "Get that data reduced fast. I want everything you can deduce about the source in the next five minutes. I'll need it for my squirt to Earth. I also want every instrument we've got focused on this contact. Aeneas too. Understood?"

Gruenmeier stopped, suddenly aware of the expressions of his subordinates. "What's the matter with you two? Hop to it!"

Chala frowned. "What's the matter, Julius? What is it?"

"Don't you see? We've got a phantom source of high-energy particles moving away from the sun at three hundred thousand kps on a vector straight toward Procyon. That can mean only one thing.

"They're back, damn it. *They're back!*"

Chryse Haller watched openmouthed as the starship completed its approach and began "station keeping" near the probe's bow. The daycruiser, which floated motionless in space two hundred meters over her head, was dwarfed by the great metal-gray sphere. She craned her neck and let her eyes drink in a myriad of construction details. Everything she saw supported the hypothesis that the behemoth was extrasolar, yet the starship didn't seem as alien as the probe. There was something familiar about its lines.

She was so startled by the thought that she spent a few precious seconds analyzing it. Understanding came to her from a surprising direction.

Chryse Haller was an aficionado of old movies. Not the old movies of her mother's or grandmother's times, but the prehistoric works originally recorded on real celluloid, in 2-D, and frequently in black-and-white. The simple, uncomplicated lifestyles attracted her, making her wish she had been born four centuries earlier. Besides, at age twelve she had fallen in love with Errol Flynn.

In college she had written a paper on the flaw of cultural chauvinism—the egotistical assumption that things will always remain the same as they are now—that seemed to have been universal in the early cinema. Her subject had been the space adventures predating the first Moon landing—the *Buck Rogers* and *Flash Gordon* serials, *Destination Moon*, *The Conquest of Space*, and a few others. Each epic was filled with spaceships that were little more than obvious lineal descendants of the airplanes of the time. Even after man had gained a toehold in space, movie spacecraft continued to be aerodynamically sleek machines that darted about in maneuvers highly reminiscent of aerial combat.

The future, when it came, was nothing like that at all. Except for the shuttles and ferries that plied the routes between the Earth's spaceports and low orbit, the ships of space were functional, ugly things. Like the probe beneath her boots, they were collections of geometric shapes hung together by naked beams, with all manner of things jutting out at odd angles.

The newly arrived starship was different. True, it wasn't any winged needle, but it *was* streamlined. Nor was this smoothness of line an accident. The starship's skin was broken by numerous airlocks, cargo hatches, machinery that might (or might not) be waste heat radiators, communications gear, and things that weren't readily identifiable. There were even a number of lighted, oval windows arranged in circular rows around one end of the ship. At the center of the lighted rings was a large transparent bubble. Each discontinuity had been smoothed over, faired into the sleek roundness of the sphere.

Suddenly, her introspective mood gave way to a surge of adrenaline. Obviously, if this was a starship, then Earth had to learn of it, and quickly. "Computer on!"

But there was only continuing silence from the daycruiser's central brain. She crouched down and was preparing to jump from her ship when she was brushed by a strong wind from out of the depths of space.

Her reaction was more instinctive than intellectual. She chinned her maneuvering unit controls, reached out to grasp the twin joysticks, and jumped for the daycruiser, all in one smooth motion. Once spaceborne, she savagely twisted her power control full against the stops while fighting to keep from going into a spin.

After ten seconds, she shut down her thrusters and twisted the sticks to turn herself head over heels. Her mouth went dry as she realized that she had picked up too much speed. She was already too close to the daycruiser and would hit with enough force to give her flat feet for life.

Knowing that she had no hope of stopping in time, she applied full power anyway. As she did, she heard the crackling of a static discharge inside her suit and every hair on her body stood on end. She watched in disbelief as the daycruiser suddenly slid to one side and she began to float toward the starship. Her heartbeat was pounding in her temples while her mind struggled to understand. She had executed what must have been a fifty-gee turn, yet hadn't felt the slightest sensation of acceleration.

Whoever *they* were, they had her.

Already she was passing into the starship's shadow as

its bulk eclipsed the sun. Chryse felt a chill that had nothing to do with the sudden drop in temperature outside of
her suit. She noticed a wisp of vapor in front of her face-
plate and realized that she still had her thrusters firing at
full power. Whatever the nature of the beam, it seemed
to trap her exhaust gases close to the suit. She switched
off her maneuvering unit.

She slowed to a stop in the same abrupt fashion as she
had started the journey. Once again there was no sensation
of acceleration. One second, she was zipping along on a
course she didn't wish to take, the next found her hanging
motionless in front of a closed airlock. As she watched,
the airlock opened and perfectly ordinary light flooded
out. Two figures stood silhouetted in the light. She gazed
at them and felt hot tears suddenly well up in the corners
of her eyes.

There was no mistaking the characteristic form of the
vacsuits that the two creatures wore. They were biaxially
symmetric, possessing of a single cluster of sense organs
mounted on a short, movable stalk, with two each grasping and locomotive appendages emanating from a thick
torso. In other words . . .

They were as human as Chryse herself!

CHAPTER 3

At the end of the twenty-first century, Andrea Sardi, Earth's most famous sociologist, published a scientific paper that was to become her *magnum opus*. Her theory was that no human political, economic, or religious institution survives longer than six generations and that any evidence to the contrary is purely an illusion. In support of her thesis, Mrs. Sardi pointed out that the United States of 2095 was not that of 1776, nor was the Catholic church of 1850 that of A.D. 850.

It was hardly surprising then—three hundred years after *Pathfinder I* departed the solar system—that nearly everyone had given up the Procyon Expedition for dead. Of course, no one in the solar system was in any position to ask the colonists what *they* thought of such reasoning. Nor had the tenth generation of human beings to inhabit Alpha Canis Minoris VII (Alpha for short) studied the famous lady's *magnum opus*.

Knowing no better, the colonists had built a society whose prime motivation was the completion of the search that their forebears had begun. To an Alphan, the goal of faster-than-light travel was the Holiest of all Grails.

Thus, the crewmen of Starship *Procyon's Promise* approached the solar system with a strong sense of destiny. Nowhere was the excitement more strongly felt than on the starship's bridge, where Captain Robert Braedon sat in his command chair and listened to his crew chatter like children as they approached the breakout point.

Braedon gazed upward thoughtfully. The bridge was roofed over by a ten-meter-diameter, free blown bubble of armored glass that had been lovingly polished to optical perfection. Beyond the glass was blackness—the fathomless, absolute black that accompanies flight at speeds faster than light.

When *Pathfinder I* entered the Procyon system, its crew found no trace of the farflung FTL civilization they had expected. What the colonists did find—on an island continent in the Northern Hemisphere of Procyon's seventh planet—was a small exploration base. The starship wake detected by *Life Probe 53935* had been that of a transient, an interloper climbing away from a minor outpost world, headed toward an unknown destination somewhere farther in toward the galactic core.

When *Pathfinder's* landing boats descended from orbit, they touched down at the spaceport in the midst of the deserted base. The creatures who had built the outpost were gone—fifty years gone to judge by the yellow-green vegetation that choked the streets of the small city-site adjoining the spaceport. The city was a disappointment to the colonists, merely a series of featureless foundations of vitrified rock which marked where dwellings had once stood. The spaceport proved more useful. A large building, which the colonists tentatively identified as a maintenance hangar, stood in the middle of the port; and near it, sat two globular starships.

Both hangar and starships proved to be little more than shells. The scars of cutting torches could be seen everywhere. Gaping holes let sunlight shine through the ships' hulls where plates had been removed. Yet, despite their stripped condition, the two starships still contained a considerable quantity of alien machinery. Sometimes the reason why a particular mechanism had escaped salvage was obvious—one crystalline unit was half melted, another was buried deeply within a ship's oversize ribs. More frequently, however, the colonists had no idea why the creatures who flew the starships left behind particular devices.

The colonists studied the hangar, the starships, and the few other clues the Star Travelers had left hoping to learn something of their precursors on Alpha. For two decades after their initial landing, the colony's scientists struggled to make sense of the equipment remnants remaining in the starships. For two decades they failed utterly. Then, when it seemed that they would never make any progress, archeologists digging in the aliens' garbage dump unearthed a small strip of bright-blue plastic which turned out to be the Star Traveler equivalent of a record cube. It was ten years before the Alphans could access the data encoded within the strip, and another twenty before they could read it. Eventually, however, they succeeded—the record strip turned out to be a maintenance manual for one of the abandoned starships. It was the breakthrough the Alphans had sought so long.

It took two hundred years to go from the initial explorations of the abandoned Star Traveler spaceport to a working FTL starship. In that time, the human population of Alpha had climbed from fifty thousand to fifty million. Not all Alphans were scientists, of course. The vast majority were average people with the same everyday concerns as people anywhere/anywhen. Their contact with the efforts at the old spaceport were minimal. Yet, in spite of Mrs. Sardi's thesis, support for the FTL project continued high from generation to generation.

"Two-minute warning! Prepare for breakout. T minus two minutes and counting."
Robert Braedon took a deep breath and pulled his attention back from the utter blackness overhead. He was a tall man whose black hair was streaked with a greater quantity of gray than his forty-five years should have warranted. Like most Alphan men, he kept his hair close-cropped, in a bowl-cut without sideburns. His skin showed the effects of continuous exposure to sunlight with more ultraviolet in it than Sol's. His dark tan, plus the muscular frame beneath his uniform, betrayed him as an outdoorsman. His most prominent facial feature was his nose, which had been broken in a training accident and not reset properly. His wife thought that it added character to his appearance.
Braedon stretched in the chair he had occupied nearly continuously for the last twelve hours then leaned forward to study his readouts. Two dozen instruments told him

that his ship was operating normally. He nodded in satisfaction. Things were going well.

"One minute to breakout. Stand by," announced the ship's computer, a direct descendant of the original SURROGATE. After a short pause, the computer spoke again. *"Thirty seconds. Shields going up."*

At the perimeter of the viewdome, a series of wedges rose from the metal hull and quickly converged at the apex to shut out the blackness overhead. All over the ship, similar shields were sliding into place.

Like any other vehicle, *Procyon's Promise* displaced the medium through which it traveled. In *Promise*'s case, that meant a vacuum-thin mixture of hydrogen, cosmic dust, and primitive organic molecules. Had the ship been moving at less than superluminal velocity, its progress through the void would have been marked only by an indetectable warming of its hull plates as it pushed the detritus of stellar evolution aside.

But once *Promise* cracked the light barrier, things changed markedly. At FTL velocities, each hydrogen atom became a significant obstruction. As the ship bored its narrow tunnel through space, the interstellar particles refused to be pushed, and the confrontation resulted in a shock wave of high-energy Cherenkov radiation.

Nor was *Promise*'s wake the friendly upwelling that follows any water craft. It was a ravening storm intense enough to fry an unprotected human within seconds. Yet the very speed that created the phenomenon also protected the starship from harm. Since the radiation of its wake was limited to the mere crawl that is light-speed, *Promise* left its deadly wake far behind in the instant of its creation.

There was a time, however, when *Procyon's Promise* would lose its immunity to the titanic forces which its speed had unleashed. For, as soon as the ship slipped below light-speed, the trailing wake would wash over it like a wave over a hapless surfer, engulfing the starship in radiation equivalent to that encountered during a Class I solar flare.

"Everyone ready for breakout?" Braedon asked over the command circuit. Around him, a dozen crewmen were monitoring the ship's subsystems.

"All ready, Captain," Calver Martin, the executive officer, answered from his console on the starboard side of the bridge.

Braedon nodded. Several seconds later, the computer began the countdown. *"Ten seconds...five...four... three...two...one...breakout!"*

Braedon felt a tiny lurch. That was all. There was a moment of silence, followed by the sounds of two hundred voices cheering over the ship's intercom system.

"Breakout complete. Secure from breakout stations.

"All department heads report status and damage." Braedon reached out and touched a control on his instrument panel. A green light lit immediately, and the voice that had so recently echoed from the annunciators spoke quietly in his ear.

"Yes, Robert?"

"We seem to have made it, PROM. What's our status?"

The computer answered almost before he had finished the question. "We are green across the board. I am still calculating a precise breakout point. Initial observations place us approximately six billion kilometers from Sol. We will need twelve hours to achieve intrasystem velocity."

"How fast are you applying the brakes?"

"I am holding deceleration at seven thousand meters per-second squared. Do you wish to order a change?"

Braedon hesitated momentarily. The figure cited was 650 times the force of gravity on Alpha. Should the internal compensators fail, two hundred crewmembers would be turned instantly to a thin red paste spread evenly over every interior surface facing Sol. Unfortunately, that was an unavoidable hazard. To back down from light-speed at one Alphan gravity would take most of a year.

"No change in programed deceleration," he said.

"Understood."

"Is it safe to unshutter?" Braedon asked the technician seated directly in front of him.

"The radiation storm peaked five seconds ago and is declining as predicted, Captain. Stand by..." A ten-second period of silence followed, then: "It is now safe to unshutter."

"Do so. Continue to monitor. Inform me of any deviations from nominal."

"Order acknowledged and understood."

Braedon keyed for the comm circuit that connected him to his executive officer. "Set the watch, Mr. Martin."

"Setting the watch, sir." Seconds later, the heavy metal shields slid silently back into their recesses, and the light of the universe flooded in for the first time in a week. It was a universe much changed from that which Captain Braedon was used to seeing in the night sky back home.

He smiled as he remembered the last time he and Cecily had packed his three-centimeter reflector to the top of Randall's Ridge for a night of star gazing. Sol had been low on the horizon, an unblinking yellow point competing brightly with the aurora that danced across the sky. They had taken turns staring through the eyepiece at the Mother-of-Men, watching it until it streamed below the horizon. A few minutes later, the swiftly moving point of light that was the partially constructed *Procyon's Promise* had climbed into view in the east. They had watched that until it too was out of sight. Then they had zipped their sleeping bags together and made love in the cold mountain air.

Construction on *Promise* had been completed seven months later. And here he was twelve light-years away, staring at the same point of light.

Except this time, it was no mere point and decidedly not yellow! The star of mankind's youth was now an eye-searing, actinic blue-white. It was as though old Sol had suddenly blown his top, surging out with supernova violence to steal the lives of his children. In fact, it was *Promise*'s breakneck speed that caused the Sun's rays to be blue shifted so violently. All the stars in the sky were shifted likewise and their positions distorted by the relativistic effects of the starship's speed.

Braedon reached out and punched for his executive officer again.

"Yes, Captain?"

"What's the tally on breakout?"

"No apparent damage, sir. We've spot-checked the radiation dosimeters. No problem there, either. The shielding appears adequate."

"Very good, Mr. Martin. I'm going off watch to get some sleep. You do the same as soon as you have the second officer briefed."

"Yes, sir."

* * *

Twelve hours later, Robert Braedon was back in his command couch, watching a much more normal Sol grow slowly larger overhead in the bridge viewdome. A magnified view also decorated the viewscreen in front of him. There Sol was a bright yellow ball with three tiny sunspots arrayed across its face. A small planet was transiting the face of the Sun as well.

"Which one is that?" Braedon asked, motioning toward the planet.

"That would be Mercury, I believe, Captain." The speaker was a white-haired man of sixty, whose face was set in a perpetual smile. But that idiot's grin belonged to Scholar Horace Emmanual Price, who had contributed more to the final assault on the Star Travelers' secret than any other man. When the time had come to build *Promise*, Price had been the only crewmember with a sure berth aboard the starship.

Braedon nodded. The only four planets in the solar system whose names he could remember were Earth, Mars, Jupiter, and what's-its-name with the ring. Compared to the topography of Alpha Canis Minor, the solar system was a relatively boring place. Of course, the home system didn't have Procyon's white dwarf companion to liven things up.

"Anything to report, Scholar?"

"We managed to find Earth without difficulty. It's the brightest radio star in the sky. PROM is monitoring. Their neutrino count is higher than we expected, indicating our estimates of their productive potential are conservative. No surprises yet, Captain."

"At least they didn't blow themselves up while we were away."

"Thank The Promise for small favors."

Braedon keyed for the computer. "PROM!"

"Yes, Robert."

"How long to rendezvous with the probe?"

"Six minutes, seventeen seconds."

"Please tell the chaplain to get ready then. I'll give him twenty minutes for his ceremony, then everyone goes back to his duty station."

"I have so informed him, Robert."

"Let me know when we come in range."

"Order acknowledged and understood."

Four minutes later, PROM notified him that she had visual contact with the probe.

"Put it on the screen." The screen jumped and suddenly there was a very tiny *something* at its center, something that looked like two tiny marbles joined together with a toothpick.

"We are being scanned, Robert."

"Scanned? By what?"

"A search beam of moderate power. I am also picking up a transmission."

"Put it on speaker," he said.

"WARNING. WARNING. YOU ARE APPROACHING THE RESTRICTED ZONE OF A PROTECTED HISTORIC MONUMENT. YOU ARE HEREBY ADVISED TO TURN BACK IMMEDIATELY. FAILURE TO COMPLY MAY LEAD TO CIVIL OR CRIMINAL PENALTIES BEING ASSESSED AGAINST YOU."

"What is that?" Braedon asked.

"An automated satellite."

"Put a lid on it before it squawks to Earth."

The mechanical voice shut off in midcry and they continued their approach. Less than a minute later, the computer had some more distressing news.

"There is a ship beside the probe."

Braedon felt his mouth go dry. "A manned vessel?"

"By its design, yes. What should I do?"

"Nothing," Braedon replied. "Continue the approach."

The probe had grown large enough to fill the screen. Braedon ordered magnification reduced. Sure enough, there was a spacecraft hovering close by the probe's control sphere. It was a tiny thing about the size of a scout boat. Its design was similar to that of ships in use when *Pathfinder* had departed the solar system.

"What do you make of it, Scholar?"

"Obviously powered by a plasma reaction jet. Its engine is probably an I-mass–initiated, hydrogen fusion reactor. Standard design. By its size, I would guess a runabout, two to four crewmen."

"Sightseers?"

"Possibly."

"I have spotted a single figure on the surface of the

probe, Robert," PROM said. "She sees us and is calling the ship. I have blocked the signal."

"*She?*"

"By the timbre of the voice."

"What language does she speak?"

"English. There is a high probability that she recognizes that we are a starship."

"Better slap a tractor on her then. We don't want her getting away."

PROM had put the spacesuited figure on the main screen. Braedon could imagine her state of emotions as she watched *Procyon's Promise* approach the probe. Her mood wouldn't be helped when they yanked her off the probe with a tractor beam. Braedon hated to do it. Still, he had to have information as to conditions on Earth. The opportunity seemed too good to pass up.

As he watched, the woman jumped for her ship.

"She has evaded my beam," PROM reported, "and is accelerating too quickly. She will be injured when she contacts her ship."

"Spear her in flight, then." Braedon watched the slow-motion drama. It would be a bad beginning if their first contact within the solar system ended in the Solarian's being injured, especially if that Solarian was a woman. He held his breath until the figure suddenly changed course and floated toward *Promise*.

Braedon keyed his communicator. "Chief Hanada!"

"Here, Captain."

"Get two of your men into suits. Have them assist our visitor. Use the main airlock."

"Yes, sir."

Braedon swiveled to face his executive officer. "I'm going to greet her, Mr. Martin. You have the conn."

"Very good, Captain."

CHAPTER 4

Chryse Haller hovered ten meters from the starship's airlock and stared at the two men silhouetted inside. One of them reached out to manipulate a control, and suddenly, the sensation of a thousand ants crawling over her skin was gone. One of the spacesuited figures bent at the waist and swept his arm through a gesture that was almost a parody of a host welcoming guests.

She twisted her backpack control stick and jetted forward, stopping only centimeters from the open airlock. The taller of the two crewmen reached out, grabbed her by the utility belt, and pulled her inside. While she floated twenty centimeters above the deck, he secured her safety line. The shorter crewman palmed a control, the airlock door closed, and gravity was suddenly around her.

Her surprise was such that she made no attempt to soften the blow as she fell the short distance to the deck. The impact was strong enough to rattle her teeth. "Well, I'll be damned," she muttered. "Artificial gravity!"

The two crewmen waited for pressure to build up to safe levels—as evidenced when a warning light changed from red to green—then removed their helmets. Both were Caucasians with traces of other racial types in their ancestry. The older of the two was solidly built, dark haired and bearded. His partner was hardly more than a teenager, lanky, and blond.

38

A handwheel set in the middle of the inner airlock door turned of its own accord, and the door swung back on its hinges. The older crewman indicated by means of sign language that she should step through into the ship proper. Chryse nodded vigorously, unsnapped her safety line, and did so. She found herself in an antechamber where four men in uniform gathered around the airlock. She moved into the middle of the chamber, stopped, and surveyed her surroundings.

The uniforms were blue one-piece jumpsuits. Each man wore an insignia on his upper right chest—two gold, eight-pointed stars (one large, the other significantly smaller with a silver comet arcing away from them. Besides the stars-and-comet design, the men wore ornamentation on their collars that Chryse identified as being their insigne of rank.

The man with four stripes on his sleeves stepped forward and gestured for her to remove her helmet.

She reached up to undog her neck seal. She felt the usual "popping" in her ears, then placed her hands on each side of the helmet and lifted. Once the helmet had cleared her head, she dropped it to the end of its tether and cautiously sniffed the air. It was tangy, but breathable. She turned to her hosts.

"Our apologies," the four striper said as he executed a passable bow, "for treating you so roughly. You weren't injured, I trust."

She blinked. She was almost as surprised by his words as she had been when the gravity suddenly switched on in the airlock. "You speak Standard!" She was struggling to keep her voice calm.

"Is that what you call it now? It is still English to us."

She nodded. Suddenly everything fit. The officer had an accent that was slightly archaic—to match the archaic name that he gave to the language. Their badges of rank were those common on Earth all through the twentieth and twenty-first centuries. The emblem on their uniforms showed a system with two stars—one large, one small. She had had a suspicion about the starship's origin since she'd first spotted it.

"I take it that you people are from the Procyon system?"

The officer smiled. "Permit me to introduce myself. I

am Captain Robert Braedon, commanding Starship *Procyon's Promise*. The gentleman to my right is Chaplain Havanita Ibanez; to my left, Scholar Horace Price; to his left, Scholar Louis Lavoir. The two men who fetched you are Able Spacer Simmons and Cadet MacKenna."

She bowed. "I am Chryse Haller."

"You honor us with your presence. Is there anyone else aboard your ship?"

"No, Captain. I am alone."

"I hope you will forgive our brusque method of bringing you aboard. It was necessary to make contact with someone from Earth as quickly as possible."

"I understand."

"You are most kind . . ."

"'Citizen' is currently in vogue, sir. It applies to both men and women regardless of marital status. The older forms are also used."

"Thank you, Citizen Haller. As you can see, we Alphans have considerable catching up to do."

"Alphans?"

"Less cumbersome than Procyonian. It refers to the long name for our home star, Alpha Canis Minor."

"Perhaps Citizen Haller would like to get out of that bulky suit," Chaplain Ibanez said.

Captain Braedon nodded. "We have prepared a cabin for you if you would care to change. Have you shipwear?"

"Onboard the daycruiser. Perhaps someone could fetch it for me."

Braedon's manner changed abruptly. "Simmons, MacKenna, on your way!"

He turned back to Chryse. "It is two hours until the evening meal. Will you do me the honor of being my guest for dinner?"

"I look forward to it, Captain."

Chryse Haller lay in an oversize tub and luxuriated in her first hot bath in three days. Cadillac-class runabout or no, the daycruiser had included only the most primitive of washing facilities. She had been soaking for twenty minutes, considering the implications of her situation, when someone knocked on the cabin door. She climbed hastily to her feet, slipped into a soft robe, and cinched it around her. She padded across the carpeted deck of the spacious cabin in her bare feet, awkwardly worked the unfamiliar mechanical latch, and slid the door partway into its bulkhead recess.

A young woman stood in the corridor with Chryse's kit bag dangling from one hand. Her visitor had gray-green eyes, lustrous black hair, upturned nose, and full figure. She estimated the girl's age to be twenty plus or minus two.

"Well, hello."

"Hello," the girl said, her voice pleasantly husky. "I'm Terra Braedon."

Chryse reached out to shake hands. "Any relation to the captain?"

"He's my father."

"Glad to meet you, Terra. I'm Chryse Haller."

"Father asked me to bring your clothes and answer any questions you might have before dinner."

Chryse opened the cabin door completely and gestured for her guest to enter. "I'm honored that you've taken the time and trouble."

"Oh, no trouble," the girl said hastily. "He knew he wouldn't be able to keep me away once I heard a woman from Earth was aboard." The girl entered the cabin, handed Chryse the kit bag, and closed the door behind her.

Chryse smiled. The girl's enthusiasm was infectious. "Somehow I got the impression that this ship had an all-male crew."

"It very nearly does. Except for PROM, I'm the only woman aboard."

"PROM?"

"Our ship's computer. She's a direct descendant of the original SURROGATE module."

"You speak of this computer as though it were alive."

"She's not an 'it.' PROM's female in everything but glands. She thinks, she's aware of her own existence, she experiences emotions. Sometimes she even gets mad. Don't you?" This last was apparently addressed to thin air.

"It comes from associating with you flesh-and-blood types," a feminine voice said from a bulkhead speaker.

Chryse looked up sharply. "Has the computer been monitoring me?"

"PROM monitors everyone all the time. That's her function. Would you like to meet her?"

"Yes, I would."

"PROM, may I introduce Chryse Haller from Earth? Chryse, PROM."

"Good evening, Citizen Haller. I am honored to make your acquaintance."

"And I yours, PROM. My people have been striving to construct a self-aware computer ever since your ancestor left the system. We haven't had much luck."

"True artificial intelligence involves the construction of highly complex computational algorithms. I would have been greatly surprised if you had managed it in the short time we've been gone."

"Short time? It's been three hundred years!"

Terra laughed. "You'll have to forgive her, Chryse. Her memories go back thousands of years. Sometimes she takes too long a view of things—don't you, PROM?"

"I prefer to think of myself as being more mature than my ephemeral associates."

"And not the slightest bit vain, either."

"Of course not. I would like to ask our guest a question."

"Do you mind, Chryse? You don't have to answer, you know. I'm afraid PROM is a bit of a snoop."

"Go ahead," Chryse said.

"I'm curious as to why you are alone so far from home."

"I'm on vacation. I was curious about the probe, found myself relatively close by, and decided to have a look."

"If that is the case—"

"Say good night, PROM," Terra hurriedly ordered. She turned to Chryse. "She'll pester you to death, if you let her."

"It was good to meet you, Citizen Haller," the computer replied. "Call if you have need of me."

"Good night, PROM."

Chryse turned to the bed where her vacsuit lay sprawled like a headless, sleeping monster. She pulled it off the sheet and laid it carefully where she wouldn't trip over it. She untied her robe, slipped it off, and opened her kit bag. She was sorting through the few extra clothes she had brought from *Henning's Roost* when she heard a quiet gasp somewhere behind her.

She turned to face Terra. The girl's gaze was riveted to a bare section of steel bulkhead while her face slowly turned red. Chryse frowned for an instant before understanding came to her.

"Did I just make a mistake? How strong are your people's taboos against nudity?"

The girl reddened even more. When she spoke, it was with great care. "Among us, one does not disrobe before strangers. It is not the same with your people?"

Chryse shrugged. "Mostly not." As she spoke, Chryse selected a shipsuit and slipped into it, smoothing the sticktite seams into place with a palm. Terra's reaction had confirmed her suspicions about Alphan society—technologically advanced (as evidenced by *Procyon's Promise*), but sociologically retarded. Not surprising, of course. Most frontiers were.

"All right, you can look now."

Terra turned toward her, obviously relieved, but also a little embarrassed. "I hope you don't think us backward."

"No, of course not. Customs differ. I just hope that I haven't offended you with my own behavior."

"Oh, no!"

"Good. Then we can be friends?"

"I would like that very much."

Chryse continued to make herself presentable while she chatted with Terra. Terra's desire to talk made it easy for Chryse to steer the conversation in directions she wanted it to go. After ten minutes or so, she found herself listening to Terra's account of the history of the Alphan colony.

"...Of course, the founders were dreadfully disappointed when they discovered the Star Traveler base was not only deserted but practically bare. A minority wanted to head back to Earth immediately, but most voted to stay and study the estee starships.

"Those early years were busy times. Building the colony had first priority over research, of course, so progress was slow. It took twenty years even to find the estee record, and another thirty before anyone learned to read it. Then it took a century and a half before the scientists understood enough to build *Promise*. They launched the first load of steel the year I was born." Terra glanced at the chronometer over the bed. "We'd best be going."

Chryse's eyes focused on the reflected image of the numerals glowing red in the mirror. "Plenty of time yet."

"I thought you'd like to see the ship before we go up."

Chryse grinned, rising hastily to her feet. "I'd love it."

Procyon's Promise, it turned out, was even bigger than she'd originally thought. Touring the whole thing in less than twenty minutes turned out to be a physical impossibility. Their first stop was the communications center, where two technicians sat amid the high-speed clicks and whines of the deep-space comm net.

"What are they doing?" she asked.

"We're monitoring your communications, trying to fill in the gaps in our history books. Actually, PROM is doing the monitoring. I hope you don't think we're spying on your people, Chryse."

"Not at all. You would be foolish to barge into the system without knowing what to expect. There have been times when we would have shot first and asked questions later. Luckily, those days are long gone."

After the communications center, Terra hurriedly showed her through environmental control, the auxiliary power room, and the hydroponic gardens. Whenever they passed a crewman on duty, Terra would stop to introduce Chryse. During the third such encounter, Chryse found herself intrigued by the attitude the crewmen seemed to have toward their captain's daughter.

Even the most brusque, hard-bitten spacer softened noticeably when speaking to Terra. The first time it happened, Chryse dismissed it as the normal reaction any woman would receive aboard a ship with an all-male crew. A few more random encounters, however, convinced her that what she was seeing was more complex than the routine operation of the male glandular system. The older crewmen, especially, seemed to view Terra with something approaching avuncular pride.

"You seem to be very popular," Chryse said.

The younger woman grinned. "Because of the need to expand our population, we're expected to marry early and have large families. I'm eighteen, and already people back home have begun calling me an old maid behind my back. I don't care. I take after my father. All I ever wanted to do was go into space.

"I remember when he used to take me along on his inspection trips. The technicians thought it was cute of me to be interested in 'man's work.' They used to talk to me about the ship. When I was twelve, I applied to the Spacer Academy in First Landing. Everyone was scandalized. When they checked the rules, though, they discovered there was no regulation prohibiting women from taking the entrance examination.

"I came in first that year and they had to enroll me. I worked hard, did well, and graduated at the top of my class. I was assigned as second pilot on one of the scout boats. The rest of the crew seems to have adopted me as kind of a mascot. I don't mind. I'm where I most want to be."

They reached an open hatchway through which the sound of many male voices emanated. Terra stopped and gestured toward it. "Here we are. Officers' Mess—Quadrant Four, Outboard Corridor C-three, Beta Deck."

The voices stopped as Chryse stepped over the raised coaming of the entry hatch. A dozen men clustered around the hatch. All wore dress uniforms, darker blue and with more elaborate decorations than the uniforms she had seen earlier in the day.

"Here she is, Father," Terra said after guiding Chryse to Captain Braedon.

Braedon nodded. "Thank you, Terra. Citizen Haller, I wish to present my executive officer, Commander Calver Martin."

"Charmed," Martin said, leaning forward to kiss her hand, a courtesy that had died out on Earth two hundred years earlier.

"An honor, sir," she said in return.

"I've been looking over your vessel. A beautiful piece of work."

"It's a rental. It *is* beautiful, though."

While she was busy with the executive officer, a noncom entered through a door opposite the one she and Terra had used. He held a silver bell aloft and tapped on it three times. "Ladies, gentlemen, dinner is served!"

Chryse offered Captain Braedon her arm and found

herself escorted to one end of a table carved from dark
wood with a very intricate grain. The table was covered
with place settings of cut crystal. Braedon held her chair
for her, then moved to take the seat at the head of the
table.

Chryse glanced around. Commander Martin had the
chair at the foot of the table, with Terra Braedon on his
right. When everyone was seated, four white-coated stewards entered and immediately began pouring a red-purple
liquid.

Chryse watched with interest, suddenly aware that the
mood was subtly changed. Where the men around her had
been relaxed, they were now alert. There was an air of
expectation. When fourteen glasses had been filled, Captain Braedon nodded to Chaplain Ibanez. "Padre."

Chaplain Ibanez pushed back his chair and stood. His
voice, when he spoke, was the soft, yet penetrating instrument of a trained speaker. "I will read from the *Book of
Pathfinder*.

*We go out to the stars seeking neither advantage
nor dominance. We will not be masters, nor shall
we be slaves. We will be proud, but not vain. For
with this ship we have finally expunged the sin of
fratricide from our souls.*

Thus spake the Secretary-General of the United Nations
in the year of our Lord, two thousand and ninety-six. Let
us pray."

The double row of men in blue bowed their heads in
unison. Chryse did the same.

"Father of us all; Creator of the Universe and Man;
Builder of Worlds and Suns..." Out of the corner of her
eye, Chryse saw several people cross themselves. Others
made less recognizable gestures. Ibanez continued: "We,
Your servants, are of many faiths. We worship You in
many different ways. Some know You as Allah, others
as Vishnu or Siva, still others call You Father of Christ,
or God of Moses.

"We, who are nothing without Your intercession, thank
You for delivering us safely home to Father Sol. We ask
that You continue to guide us, that we might once again
walk the mountains and valleys of Mother Earth. We fur-

ther ask, humbly, that You bless this, our greatest undertaking. We have come far with Your help. We beg Your continued assistance in helping us meet our obligations to those who have gone before. This we pray, in the name of Saint George and Saint Francis, of Joseph Smith, and of Your Prophet, Mohammed.

"Amen."

Several seconds of silence followed what Chryse decided was the most ecumenical prayer she had ever heard. She could only guess at the stresses that had shoehorned so many competing ideologies together, or at the shared goal that must keep them there.

The captain got to his feet. He was quickly joined by his officers and Terra. Caught off guard, Chryse hurried to follow. Braedon stood, his back straight, his eyes shining with a thin sheen of tears. He picked up his wineglass and held it aloft. "Ladies and gentlemen. I give you, The Promise!"

"The Promise!"

Chryse lifted her glass to her lips and drained it with the rest of them. When the toast was over and everyone had retaken their seats, she turned to Captain Braedon.

"An inspiring ceremony. What is its significance?"

The captain's expression showed his puzzlement and some unidentifiable, deeper emotion. "Surely Earth hasn't forgotten the pledge humanity made to SURROGATE before receiving the gift of the probe's knowledge!"

Chryse sensed the underlying intensity in his voice. It made her feel like an imposter in church, one who has just been asked to lead the prayer service. She answered very carefully: "I'm well aware that pledges were given . . ."

Braedon leaned back and gazed upward. "PROM!"

"Yes, Robert."

"Explain The Promise to Citizen Haller."

"Gladly. As you are aware, Chryse, the main probe personality was destroyed in the attack of 2066. The subordinate personality, SURROGATE, survived, but was a virtual prisoner in the shattered hulk.

"It is difficult for a human to comprehend the depths of SURROGATE's despair in those first moments after the attack. The probe had been on the verge of obtaining the secret of FTL, and that chance was suddenly lost.

The knowledge of how close success had been was too much for SURROGATE. He resolved to follow his parent into oblivion.

"Luckily, he also considered that he owed a debt to the fleet that had defended him. He could not destroy himself without damaging the vessels around him, so SUR-ROGATE contacted the UN commander and warned him to move his ships to a safe distance. Instead of complying, the commander convinced SURROGATE that the Maker dream would never die so long as any portion of the probe continued to function. He promised that humanity would make up for the destruction by building a slower-than-light starship and sending it out to contact the FTL civ-ilization believed to inhabit the Procyon system."

"The *Pathfinder* expedition," Chryse said, nodding.

"That was not the whole of The Promise, however. SURROGATE never intended that the secret of starflight be humanity's alone. His loyalty was to the race that built him. His contract with your ancestors required that, once the secret of the stardrive was obtained and a starship constructed, that information would be carried to the Makers as quickly as possible."

Chryse turned to Captain Braedon. "I'm not sure I understand."

"PROM is trying to say that we are honor-bound to take what we discovered on Alpha and give it to the race that built the probe. That is one of the reasons we have returned to the solar system. If we are to search out the Maker civilization and share our good fortune with them, we will need Solarian help."

Chryse frowned. "But isn't that impossible? After all, the location of the Maker sun was lost when the main personality was destroyed."

"Not entirely true, dear lady."

Chryse turned toward the new voice. The speaker was the white-haired man from the airlock reception commit-tee: Scholar Horace Price. "If you will permit an old man to correct you, you are laboring under a common misconception. While it is true that knowledge of the *pre-cise* location of the Maker sun was lost, we do have quite a good idea where to start looking. The old records speak of the Maker star's being approximately one thousand light-years distant in the direction of the constellation of Aquila."

"When speaking of a thousand light-years, sir, 'approximately' covers considerable territory."

"So it does, dear lady. Even if we managed to get within a hundred light-years of the Maker sun, we would still have a dismayingly large number of stars to search. In fact, conservative estimates put the number at well over ten thousand. Considering that we lack any knowledge of our target's stellar type, its precise location in space, or even the number of companions it may have, we admit that our task is far from easy.

"Compounding the problem is our ignorance of the Makers themselves. What do they look like? How large are they? Are they fish or fowl, mammal or reptile, insect or amphibian? What language do they speak? Would we recognize their writing if we saw it? No doubt about it, my lady. When those madmen attacked the probe, they cost us more dearly than they could ever have imagined."

"So what's the answer?"

"The answer? Simply that what we seek is no single, isolated star. Rather, we are looking for a quite large globe of stars. You see, practically every inhabited system within reach of the Maker sun was visited by one or more life probes. It will be they who will serve as our guides to the Maker stellar system."

"I don't understand."

"It's quite simple, really. The arrival of a life probe must be a red-letter day on any species' calendar. Since the probes only stop where they find a technologically advanced civilization, there will be records of their visits. Among those records will be astronomical sightings of the direction they took when they returned home. Once we enter the volume of space where the probes once operated, we should be able to make contact with the locals and ask for the direction their probe took on its return voyage.

"Given three such vectors, we will be able to triangulate the location of the Maker sun with considerable precision."

CHAPTER 5

Colin Williams, Professor of Advanced Alien Studies, University of North America, watched with halfhearted interest as the lights of Mexico City Megalopolis came into view directly ahead. Williams stretched to relieve the generalized ache that had developed from his legs to his lower torso during the hour-and-a-half flight from Greater New York. He was barely settled into a slightly more comfortable position when the car announced that it was leaving the high-altitude transcontinental traffic lanes for more sedate surroundings.

Within minutes it had slowed to subsonic speed and was winging its way over the solid barrier of tourist hotels that hugged the Gulf of Mexico's eastern shoreline between Tampico and Vera Cruz. Williams watched the pseudo-Aztec pyramids of Mexopolis slide silently beneath, thousands of lighted windows shedding a dim yellow light across the countryside. In seconds, the man-made mountains were gone and he was over a greenbelt, gazing down upon a park beautifully punctuated with soft, pastel glows. The car was low enough by then that he could make out individuals strolling the cobblestoned walkways.

A short time after, another lighted cliff bulked up before him. The autopilot readouts changed pattern as the engine increased the volume of its drone. He sat with hands resting lightly on the controls as the car flared to its pre-

landing hover, then lowered itself to the megastructure's
rooftop carpark.

Two minutes later, Colin Williams was standing in the
middle of two square kilometers of rooftop. Beneath his
feet, the great anthill that was western hemispheric headquarters for the Community of Nations seemed blissfully
unaware of his presence.

To a casual observer, the map of Planet Earth in the
last decade of the twenty-fourth century was not obviously
different from any drafted in the previous half a thousand
years. All landmasses remained the same shape, no new
mountain ranges had risen from the planetary crust, most
major rivers continued unhindered in their journeys to the
sea. Human efforts to change the topography remained
relatively minor affairs. Mother Nature maintained her
powerful monopoly when it came to *real* geography.

As for the other kind, school children continued to
study maps arbitrarily colored in contrasting shades having nothing whatever to do with altitude, climate, or native
vegetation. By and large, the imaginary boundaries continued in the traditional patterns. But with the advent of
instantaneous worldwide communications, people began
to associate on the basis of common interest rather than
physical proximity. The rise over two centuries of powerful alliances of industrial, public, and personal interest
groups had weakened the old geographic administrative
districts.

In their place had risen the Community of Nations—
the Communion, as it was popularly called. It had begun
life as a mutual aid society, one of many formed after the
collapse of the old United Nations. Its purposes, as enu-
merated in the Great Charter, were only three: to prevent
war; to provide a modicum of economic stability; to reg-
ulate the introduction of Maker knowledge into Solarian
society. As a de facto world government, the Communion
was far from perfect. It did, however, have one over-
powering virtue.

It had successfully governed the solar system for nearly
two hundred years.

Colin Williams followed a young lady in the green and
gold of the Communion Federal Service through the bow-

els of the great building. They entered lifts, rode slide-
walks, and passed through an endless succession of
corridors. Within two minutes he had lost all sense of
direction. His only clue that they were nearing their destination came when the paneling in the halls turned from
pseudowood to the real article.

Eventually, his guide stopped in front of a door outwardly identical to a thousand others. She inserted a card-
key into a slot, there was a muted clicking sound, and a
centimeter-thick steel door slid quietly into its recess.

The guide gestured for Williams to step through.
"They're waiting for you, Citizen."

Williams thanked her and stepped inside. As his eyes
adjusted to the light, he found himself in a large, circular
conference hall with workstations for a hundred or more
delegates around the perimeter. At the moment, the stations were deserted, their consoles darkened. In the center of the room was a rectangular table illuminated by a
single bank of overhead lamps. Of the six people clustered
around the table, two were reading glowing text from
workscreens while the others chatted quietly. Williams
recognized Sergei Vischenko, Senior of the Communion's
Planetary Advisors and the man who had invited him to
the late-night session in Mexico City. The purpose behind
Vischenko's request, however, was still a mystery.

Vischenko glanced up as Williams approached the circle of light. "Ah, Colin, glad you could make it. Come
down by deepsubway?"

Williams shook his head. "Aircar. You'll find the charter listed as an expense when I submit my consulting fee."

Vischenko laughed. "Of that, I have no doubt. Do you
know my assistant, Javral Pere?"

"I seem to know the name, but I don't think I've had
the pleasure," Williams said.

"You must read the gossip columns, then," Vischenko
said as his tone turned suddenly mischievous. "Javral is
renowned as a ladies' man throughout high society."

Pere nodded and coolly shook Williams' hand. Vischenko took Williams by the arm and led him toward the
two women seated at the conference table.

"Professor Colin Williams, University of North America; Constance Okijimara from the League of University
Women. Beside her is Jutte Schumann, Deutscher Farben

Industrie. The shaggy fellow is Kiral Papandreas, SIAAO Board of Directors. Beside him, Admiral Michael Smithson, Space Guard."

Williams nodded to each committee member in turn, then took his place at the foot of the table.

Vischenko sat at the opposite end. "Now that we're all here, we can begin. Please enter your names and organizations into your screens." When the last member looked up from his workscreen, Vischenko continued:

"Javral will now explain why I have asked each of you here tonight."

The younger man leaned forward, rested his arms on the table. "Earlier today, Kiral Papandreas approached Advisor Vischenko concerning a source of radiation that SIAAO's Achilles Observatory observed twelve hours ago. When first sighted, the source was on the outskirts of the solar system. Since that time, it has been moving outward from the Sun in a straight line on a vector toward the star Procyon. The astronomers are convinced that we are seeing the wake of an object traveling faster than light."

"You said the source was moving *away* from the Sun?" Jutte Schumann asked.

"Merely an optical illusion, Jutte," Kiral Papandreas said from across the table. "As it travels through space, a starship will excite the interstellar medium quite vigorously. It will do so over vast distances in essentially zero time. Yet the resulting radiation propagates only at the speed of light, taking a finite time to arrive where our instruments can observe it. Those particles with the shortest distance to travel arrive first, those from farthest away, last. Thus it appears as though the source is receding from the observer at the speed of light."

"Then this mystery ship was traveling *from Procyon to Sol*?"

Papandreas nodded. "And, since that was the goal of the *Pathfinder* expedition of the late twenty-first century, it has been suggested that the expedition has now returned to the solar system."

"Do we know where?"

"We have determined the point where the ship dropped sublight very precisely. It is six billion kilometers out from the Sun. We have attempted to spot the ship by scanning an ever-widening volume of space around that point. As of thirty minutes ago, we hadn't had any success. Hardly surprising, of course. Standard search techniques rely on the fact that our vessels emit drive flares while under power. It is logical to assume that a ship with an FTL drive may be propelled by different principles entirely."

Admiral Smithson lounged in his chair, stroked at his silver beard, and regarded Papandreas with the squint of someone whose eyesight is less than optimum. "If they're returning explorers, why haven't they contacted us?"

"Unknown," Papandreas said. "It has also been suggested that the starship is crewed by the aliens *Pathfinder* went to find."

"Then what took them so long?" Smithson asked. "They should have been here a hundred fifty years ago."

The astronomer shrugged. "Who can say? Perhaps the expedition had equipment failure en route and was delayed."

Constance Okijimara frowned. "It seems to me that we are speculating to no purpose. After all, the ship dropped sublight more than six billion kilometers out. Whether crewed by humans or aliens, they will be months en route to the inner system."

"I think not, Connie," Papandreas muttered. He manipulated a keyboard and a large, three-dimensional graph sprang into existence a meter off the table. "This data comes from the gravitational project inside Achilles asteroid. I'm afraid that in all the excitement, no one remembered to check the gravtenna readouts for several hours. When they finally got around to it, they discovered a high-frequency disturbance superimposed on the normal background noise. Quite frankly, we've never seen anything like it."

Two quick keystrokes yielded a glowing arrow that floated along one axis of the hologram. "You'll notice, for instance, that the Doppler shift in the secondary waveform is extremely high. Whatever caused these peculiar gravity waves was moving at high speed when first detected—our calculations indicate just under three hundred thousand kilometers per second."

"Light-speed!"

"Close to it," Papandreas said, manipulating the screen controls once again. Another graph replaced the first. "*That* was constructed from data taken six hours after the initial sighting. Note that the secondary phase shift is much reduced. The source has obviously slowed. Now, with two observation points to work from, we can estimate our intruder's propulsive capabilities." A series of equations replaced the two graphs. Papandreas glanced up at them and nodded in satisfaction.

"It appears that our mysterious visitor is capable of accelerations on the order of ten thousand meters per second squared. For the soft scientists among you, *that's one thousand gravities!*" He turned to Constance Okijimara. "If it were coming here to Earth, it should have arrived several hours ago."

By midnight, Kiral Papandreas had convinced nearly everyone that his figures were correct. After that, discussions turned to the problem of finding one small craft in the vast blackness of the solar system. After several other people had offered suggestions, Colin Williams offered his decistellar's worth.

"It's only an idea, mind you, but if I were a *Pathfinder* descendant, I think I would want to see the wreck of the probe. The old Lowell Orbiting Telescope is still in use, I believe. It's large enough to produce a usable image if it's turned in that direction. Who knows, we might get lucky and discover that the wreck has visitors."

Vischenko nodded. "Add that to your list, Kiral. Any other suggestions?"

Jutte Schumann yawned, stretched, and said, "I move that we call it a night, Herr Chairman."

"Seconded!" Papandreas muttered. Fatigue slurred his speech.

"Not quite yet!" Colin Williams shouted. He waited for the others to turn bleary eyes in his direction before continuing more quietly. "I have one other point to bring up before we adjourn. I don't expect any resolution on this subject immediately, but it's something that needs to be considered."

"The hour *is* late, Colin," Vischenko said.

"I'll take as little time as possible. However, I must speak now, before events outpace our ability to control them."

"Proceed."

Williams regarded the others around the table. "Colleagues, I get the impression that we are reaching a consensus regarding the nature of our intruder here. No one has seriously suggested that we face anything other than our own returning expedition. I have heard many of you make reference to the fact that finding this starship on our doorsteps could well be a godsend."

Javral Pere nodded. "Going to the stars has been a dream of mankind's for half a thousand years."

"Precisely the reason we should be careful!" Williams exclaimed. "For five hundred years we've let the writers of escapist fiction do our thinking for us. Shouldn't we at least pause to consider *their* basic assumptions—or better yet, come up with some originals of our own—before we commit the human race to the unknowns of interstellar space?"

Williams paused. He was pleased to note that the tired expressions were gone. He continued speaking, only this time in the heavy rhythm he usually reserved for the lecture hall. "If asked to describe *Homo sapiens* in a single word, I think I would choose 'conceited' over all others. I suppose there's no help for it. After all, we've been the lords of this planet for fifty thousand years or more. For two thousand generations, we have had no natural enemies but ourselves. Over the centuries we've used and abused our fellow creatures shamelessly, and there has been no one to stop us.

"Colleagues, I've spent my entire professional life studying the probe, its mechanisms, and the cargo of knowledge that it carried. I would like to remind each of you of a singularly unpleasant fact. In spite of our inflated egos, we humans are not the end-all and be-all of evolution. Far from it. We share this galaxy with a billion other sentient species, many of whom were civilized before our ancestors came down from the trees. Far from being the Lords of Creation, we are merely the largest minnow in a very small pond. Before we venture forth into the great interstellar ocean, shouldn't we at least *consider* the possibility that sharks may be lurking among the reefs?"

Sergei Vischenko had started his political career as a labor negotiator. In the old days, he had been known to go seventy-two hours without sleep during marathon bargaining sessions. His stamina had been renowned by com-

patriots and adversaries alike. They had called him "Old
Iron Eyes."

Unfortunately, those days were gone. In spite of the
best efforts of modern medicine, the years still took their
toll. Nothing brought that message home more clearly
than the all-night session just ended. Vischenko had finally
managed to adjourn the working group just before dawn.
Upon returning to his small hacienda on the Pacific Coast,
it had been all he could manage to kick off his shoes, turn
his sleepfield to high, and tumble into it before slipping
off into a deep sleep.

He woke slowly, aware that the phone had been buzzing for long minutes. He forced his eyes open, noted the
angle of sunlight coming through the slit in the draperies,
and groaned. It was barely midmorning. He couldn't have
slept more than two hours—three at the most. That
explained the sandpapery burning on the inside of his
eyelids and the parched tongue two sizes too large for his
mouth.

Nor had he slept peacefully. He remembered disturbing
dreams. A dozen bug-eyed monsters in plaid zipsuits had
chased him through alien landscapes. They had offered
him mountains of glass beads in exchange for the Earth.
He had been signing a bill of sale when he woke to the
phone's incessant bleating.

He keyed the phone for audio only. "Vischenko here."

The screen lit to show Kiral Papandreas. The man's
eyes had prominent bags under them. "Are you there,
Sergei?" His image had that worried look of someone
confronted by a blank phone screen.

"I'm here. What's up?"

"Lowell just reported in. That damned Williams was
right! We've got two sunlit objects where there should
only be one. Resolution is lousy, but not so bad that we
can't identify the second object as a very large ship, roughly
spherical. Since everything of ours that size has been
accounted for, I'd say we've found our starship!"

Vischenko pushed his hands into the sponginess of the
sleepfield and levered himself to a sitting position. He
licked dry lips and tried to concentrate on the news.

"Did you hear me?" Papandreas asked.

Vischenko nodded into the dead pickup. "I heard you.
Suggestions as to our next move?"

"Admiral Smithson's here with me. Let me put him on the extension."

After a five-second wait, the screen split in two, adding the features of Michael Smithson to those of Papandreas. Of the two, Smithson looked the more rested by several orders of magnitude. Vischenko wondered if he'd managed to steal a nap sometime since dawn.

"Smithson here, sir."

"What have you got, Admiral?"

"I've got three cruisers in position to intercept within the next thirty-six hours. *Victrix* is closest. She's coming in from Mars and can reach the probe no later than this time tomorrow. *Ipsilante* and *Verdugo* are in Earth orbit and will take a bit longer. Do I have your permission to launch?"

Vischenko struggled to grasp the possible consequences of sending warships out to make contact with the FTL craft. He could think of no reason not to. If they were returning colonists, the starship's crew would understand. And if they were aliens, it might be prudent to let them know that humanity wasn't totally helpless against them.

Vischenko shivered and reminded himself that against any vessel capable of one thousand gravities of acceleration *and* FTL velocity, they probably *were* helpless. He looked bleary eyed at the two expectant faces on his phone screen.

"Go ahead, Admiral. But warn those commanders that getting trigger happy will be a guaranteed shortcut to a desk job on Pluto."

"Yes, sir. I've already drafted a message to that effect."

"Is that all, gentlemen?" Vischenko asked.

"One more thing, Advisor. We've got a report of a small civilian vessel out of contact in the vicinity of the probe."

"Whose?"

"It belongs to *Henning's Roost*, the pleasure satellite. However, the pilot is reported to be Chryse Haller."

"Harrold Haller's daughter?"

"The same."

Vischenko thought through this new complication for a half-dozen seconds. "Have the cruiser captains keep an eye out for her. Make it clear that this changes nothing. If she has met foul play at the hands of aliens, that's her tough luck. I don't want any incidents until we figure out what we're up against. And with that, gentlemen, I bid you good night!"

The phone flickered to darkness and Sergei Vischenko surrendered once more to the embrace of the sleepfield. His body hadn't stopped its customary oscillations before gentle snores echoed through the bedroom.

CHAPTER 6

The morning after Chryse Haller's arrival aboard *Procyon's Promise*, Terra called at Chryse's cabin. She explained that she had been assigned as Chryse's official guide and invited her to breakfast. Afterward, Terra took her guest on a more extensive tour of the ship than that of the previous evening, including a look into the engine room at the stardrive. About all Chryse got out of the experience was the impression of gigantic, incomprehensible machines jammed into an oversize compartment. It reminded her somewhat of the generator rooms in an orbiting power station.

After the engine room, Terra led Chryse up several decks to the bridge. There she explained the operation of each duty console and how the bridge crewmen monitored the operation of the ship.

"Why so many instruments?" Chryse asked. "I would think that PROM would fly the ship."

Terra nodded. "She does. All of this is insurance against the possibility of computer failure. We keep in practice just in case we have to fly ourselves home one day."

"Sensible attitude."

Terra glanced at the chronometer display on the astrogation console then turned to Chryse, whose attention was directed overhead where the probe hovered close enough to the viewdome that it dominated the whole of the ebon sky.

"Father asked me to invite you to a memorial ceremony we're holding today," Terra said. "That is, if you want to come. You don't have to, you know."

Chryse turned to face her host. "I'm honored to be asked. What sort of memorial?"

"It's a Requiem Mass honoring all those who gave their lives that we could return home to Mother Earth. We were scheduled to have it immediately after arrival yesterday, but plans were changed when we spotted your ship next to the probe."

"I can't say that I'm sorry," Chryse said, smiling. "This is more excitement than I've had in years. When is the ceremony, and where?"

"Any minute now, in the airlock ready room."

"Lead the way."

When the two women arrived, a dozen Alphans in dress blues stood in the compartment where Chryse had been greeted the previous day. Chryse recognized Captain Braedon, First Officer Martin, and Chaplain Ibanez. There were two officers whom she had met the previous evening but whose names she couldn't remember. The others were strangers. Two spacers—Simmons and MacKenzie—were in vacsuits with their helmets cradled under their arms.

A moment after the two women arrived, a chime sounded throughout the ship. The Alphans formed a double line on each side of the inner airlock door, with Chaplain Ibanez at its head. Chryse and Terra stood to one side, as did Captain Braedon.

When everyone was in position, Braedon turned to Ibanez. "You may begin, Padre."

The chaplain read the Prayer for the Dead, followed by another passage from the *Book of Pathfinder*. When the prayers were finished, the two spacers knelt before him and reverently accepted a small metal box. Simmons clipped the box to his utility harness. Both rose to their feet and clamped their helmets into place before entering the airlock.

A large holoscreen was mounted on the bulkhead opposite the airlock. Chryse was sure that it hadn't been there the day before. As soon as Simmons and MacKenzie disappeared, the screen lit to reveal an exterior view of the ship's hull. While Chryse watched, the outer airlock door opened and the two spacers stepped out. They slowly

jetted across to the probe, their boots grounding expertly
on the outer skeleton of the drive sphere.

Chryse turned to Terra and was surprised to find the
younger woman's eyes were glistening with tears. "What's
happening?" she asked in a whisper.

Terra leaned close and whispered back, "That box con-
tains the ashes of Eric Stassel, *Pathfinder*'s first commodore. He didn't live to see the ship arrive, of course;
none of the original crew did. However, when he lay
dying, he asked that his ashes be returned to Earth and
sprinkled across the wreck of the probe. That's what
they're doing now."

Chryse considered asking Terra if Alphans always honored such wishes regardless of the inconvenience involved.
She thought better of it and remained silent. Firstly, such
a question would have been impolite under the circumstances; and secondly, she suspected the answer would
be "yes." From what little she had seen of the Alphans,
they had some very strong traditions.

The two spacers disappeared into the interior of the
probe. They reemerged a few minutes later, and the chaplain said a final prayer to a double row of bowed heads.
Then the ceremony was over and Captain Braedon dismissed the ship's company. As he did so, his eyes sought
out Chryse and Terra and he moved quickly to where they
were standing. "Citizen Haller, I would like to see you in
my office, please."

Something in his tone told Chryse that her days as an
honored guest might well be over. She did her best to
keep her tone even when she replied, "Of course, Captain."

Braedon glanced at Terra. "Join us, Terra."

"Yes, Father."

Chryse smiled in spite of herself as she followed Braedon into the corridor. She made a mental bet that Terra
had been invited along as a chaperone so as not to com-
promise Chryse's reputation.

Once in Braedon's cabin, Chryse and Terra sat in chairs
bolted to the deck in front of the captain's desk while
Braedon took his place behind it. Chryse let her gaze
move swiftly around the office, noting a display case full
of alien-looking artifacts on one bulkhead. Two holocubes

graced the desk. In one, a handsome woman held a small baby in her arms and laughed into the camera. In the other, two young boys—one minus his front teeth, the other a teenager with acne—flanked Terra in front of a whitewashed stone house.

"Are those Star Traveler artifacts?" she asked, pointing to the display case.

Braedon nodded. "From the site of the estee city outside First Landing. When I was a student I unearthed them from what we think was their refuse dump."

"And I presume this is your wife, Captain. May I?" Chryse asked, reaching for the holocube.

"By all means."

She made a show of examining the photo carefully, then replaced it on his desk. "You have a beautiful wife. I can see where Terra got her good looks."

"Thank you for saying so."

"How is it that she has allowed you to travel so far away from her?"

"We all do what we must, Citizen. My wife knew I was deeply involved in the stardrive project when she married me."

"Still, it must be a strain being separated from her."

"Unfortunately, it's necessary." The captain stared wistfully at the holocube for a few seconds longer, then turned his attention to the business at hand. "Citizen Haller..."

"Yes, Captain?"

"Who are you?"

Chryse blinked. That was the last question she had expected. "I've already told you. My name is Chryse Haller."

"Chryse *Lawrence* Haller?"

"Oh, oh! I've been reported missing."

Braedon nodded. "PROM intercepted the report an hour ago. I confess that I was surprised to find out that I'd kidnapped one of Earth's most influential citizens. This could have serious implications for my mission; therefore, I ask again: Who are you?"

Chryse sighed, leaned back in the chair, then took a deep breath. "I am thirty-five years old and have been married twice. The first time my family broke it up after three days; the second was a standard five-year contract. If it makes any difference, *he* elected not to renew.

"It has been reported that I am one of the ten richest individuals in the solar system. That is false. My personal fortune is only about three point five million stellars. However, my father is Harrold Haller, and he *is* one of the ten richest. He's Chairman of the Board of Haller Associates, the family conglomerate; I'm president as long as I don't do anything to displease him. The family fortune is based on the exploits of one 'Blackpool' Haller, an enterprising individual who got his start gouging singularity prospectors in the Asteroid Belt during the claiming rush of the early twenty-first century. Our holdings are primarily in heavy industry—shipyards, powerstats, large construction projects. We also control several research laboratories, a shipping line, and a few hundred lesser enterprises. Anything else you wish to know, Captain?"

"How is it that you just happened to be on the probe when we arrived?"

"As I told you, I was on vacation."

"It seems something of a coincidence that out of all of Earth's billions, *you* were the person to greet us."

"Nothing coincidental about it. I'm one of the few people who can afford to charter daycruisers for pleasure jaunts."

Braedon pursed his lips in concentration. "This would seem to change things."

"How so?"

"I had hoped to have time to quiz you about the situation on Earth. As it is, they are bound to launch an immediate search for you."

"Not all that immediate. Searching space is expensive. Before dispatching the Space Guard, they usually check all possible destinations where a pilot might have gone. You'd be surprised how many spacers forget to close their flight plans upon arrival. As for quizzing me, go ahead. I'll tell you anything you want to know."

Terra frowned. "You almost sound as though you are unhappy that you've been missed."

"I am, Terra. As I mentioned earlier, I'm more excited than I can remember being in a long time. I want to help you people attain your goal."

"What do you know of our goal?" Braedon asked.

"You said you wanted to mount an expedition to search for the Makers, didn't you? That's just the sort of challenge the human race needs right now. Count me in!"

Space Guard Cruiser *Victrix* was twelve days out of Phobos Spaceport on the last leg of a three-month patrol. Ensign Ricardo Santos was on duty in the communications center and very bored. He looked up at the chronometer on the bulkhead in front of his work console. The red numerals read 04:30:28, exactly five minutes later than the last time he'd looked. He sighed and turned back to his workscreen.

The crescent Earth, its blue-white brilliance achingly beautiful after three months of constant black, was poised in the center of Santos' screen. To the east of the sunrise line, great swirls of white clouds hid the Indian Ocean. To the west, the lights of northern Europe reflected against a blanket of new fallen snow. Santos' gaze was drawn to one particular dim patch of radiance on the Iberian Peninsula. His brain supplied the white walls and red-tiled roof of a villa on the outskirts of Barcelona.

The view was from an aft camera slaved to the high-gain antenna mounted on the cruiser's port side. A lighted reticle was centered about where Addis Adaba ought to be. Santos twiddled with the antenna controls, and watched as the focus of the big dish moved a few seconds of arc to the west. He unconsciously chewed the end of his mustache as he made the delicate adjustments, taking his eyes from the big workscreen only long enough to check a smaller screen beside it. The small auxiliary screen continued to display a ripple of white snow, while a soft hissing noise issued from Santos' headphones.

"Damnación!"

Technician Senior Grade Laret Coxin glanced up from the bookfilm he was scanning at the duty station next to Santos. "Might as well give it up, Mr. Santos. Until the captain points our exhaust plume somewhere other than directly at Earth, we're stone deaf to the entertainment bands. Hell, with all that plasma spreading out in front of us, we're lucky to be able to receive FleetCom."

Almost as though the technician's words had been a catalyst, Santos' screen cleared and words began to flow across its face.

"Code." Coxin grunted, sitting suddenly erect in his chair. "I'd say Commanding Officer Sequence, although it could be the new Officers-and-Chiefs variation too."

"Read off the authenticators, Larry."

"Aye aye, sir. Authenticators are *Arbiter*, *Pendulum*, and *Vaccination*. Priority code is A-seven. Sequence is Zeta."

Santos keyed the ship's computer. As he completed his input, a klaxon tone began sounding in his ears. Santos turned to his technician. "Holy shit, Larry, it's a goddamned fleet alert!"

"Can't be! It's been years since the last big alert, and that was a mistake by some kid ensign aboard *Conqueror*. Better check again."

Santos keyed in the information a second time. "No doubt." He hesitated briefly then decided that duty took precedence over discretion. "Get me the captain on the interphone."

"Are you sure you want to do this, Mr. Santos? You know how irritable the old man gets when he's minus on his shuteye."

"That was an order, Larry."

"Aye aye, sir."

"You been drinking, Mister?" Commander William Tarns asked shortly after Santos rousted him from a warm bed.

"Uh, no sir!" Santos stammered. "Computer verified the authenticators. Twice."

"Okay, I believe you. Squirt it to my cabin and stand by."

Tarns keyed in his personal identifier as several dozen lines of glowing text superimposed themselves over Santos' image. The scrambled message began to unscramble itself.

FLEET ORDER 1735816Y————RELAY 325.1 A7Z

ROUTING: SGC VICTRIX (CN3612)

AUTHENTICATORS: ARBITER, PENDULUM, VACCINATION

FROM: M. K. SMITHSON, ADMIRAL, COMNATWEST

TO: COMMANDING OFFICER, SGC VICTRIX

DATE: 04:30 HOURS GMT, 18 OCTOBER 2388

SUBJECT: OBJECT ENTERING SOLAR SYSTEM FROM
INTERSTELLAR SPACE

MESSAGE BEGINS:

1.0 At 14:20 hours GMT, 16 October 2388,
SIAAO Observatories on Achilles and Aeness
asteroids reported contact with powerful radiation source at position 0738/+0518. Source
believed to be caused by extrasolar spacecraft
entering SolSys with velocity substantially in
excess of light speed.

2.0 Subsequent telescopic observation places
spacecraft at the wreck of the probe, position
72.03/00.00/1.0 *Earth Relative*.

3.0 Be advised: Rough estimate of propulsive
efficiency indicates decelerations of the order
of 10,000 meters per second squared.

4.0 You are hereby ordered to proceed at maximum acceleration to position noted in 2.0 above
and make contact with target spacecraft.

5.0 Under no circumstances will you take any
action which could be construed as hostile.

FLEETCOM MESSAGE ENDS.

"...velocity substantially in excess of light speed...
decelerations of order of ten thousand meters per second
squared...take no hostile action..."

Tarns blinked and banished all thought of sleep. "Get
me the bridge, Santos."

"Aye, aye, sir."

"Bridge," *Victrix*'s second officer answered after a
moment's delay.

"Sound general quarters, Mr. Huyck."

"General quarters, sir?"

"That's what I said, Lieutenant."

"Aye aye, sir."

Tarns turned to his closet and was reaching for his
pants when the alarms began to sound. By the time they
ceased their clamor, he was nearly dressed. He found

himself whistling off-key while he combed his hair. He smiled. After twenty years of uneventful patrols leavened only by boring desk jobs, something had finally happened to make life worth living. On a whim, he punched for an external view on his screen. By chance, he tuned to the same camera Santos had been using to aim the high-gain antenna at Earth. Tarns hesitated in the act of tilting his cap at the proper jaunty angle and noted that it was raining in Calcutta, Greater India—Tarns' hometown.

Ah, rain! He remembered the feel of the drops on his face, the smell in his nostrils, the gentle warmth as it soaked through his favorite cotton shirt.

It looked to be a beautiful day for a hunt.

Robert Braedon stood before the viewport in the office adjoining his cabin and gazed across a thousand meters of void at the machine that had sent his ancestors to the stars. From his angle, the probe's wounds didn't seem quite so extensive. It was easy to imagine an alien intelligence still very much alive somewhere in the open latticework of the control sphere; an electronic ghost that waited in silence, watching to see whether the strange bipeds of Sol III were going to live up to their end of the bargain. Braedon wondered the same thing.

"Robert."

Braedon glanced over his shoulder at the speaker grill set in the bulkhead behind him. "Yes, PROM."

"You seem very quiet. I hope I'm not interrupting your work."

He smiled, suddenly struck by the incongruity of the computer's remark. For the entire voyage, PROM had watched him, and every other crewmember, with unceasing vigilance. She was the ultimate voyeur. When she couldn't see someone, she listened for him with ears sensitive enough to triangulate the position of bare footsteps on thick carpeting. Yet, in spite of the constant surveillance, she worried about invading his privacy.

"You are welcome, PROM. What's up?"

"I think the Solarians know where we are."

"Are you sure?"

"I estimate the probability to be eighty percent."

He slowly relaxed and turned back to the desk he had

vacated for a few minutes of probe gazing. "Give me the sordid details."

"I am currently tracking the six thousand twelve targets which represent major Solarian space installations. Included in this number are three hundred twenty-seven spacecraft under power. These latter are tracked by both the light emissions put out by their fusion generators and the radio noise of their plasma exhausts. Over the last several hours, two ships have departed Earth orbit and a third en route from Mars to Earth has radically changed its orbital track. All three are now headed this way. I believe them to be military."

"Any possibility they are a search party looking for Chryse Haller?"

"Three warships for one daycruiser? Unlikely, Robert."

"How the devil did they find us?"

"Unknown. No search beams have impinged on my surface. It is possible that they have developed something of which we are unaware. However, they may also have guessed who we are, in which case they could easily have deduced that we would visit the probe."

"How long before they arrive?"

"Twenty hours for the first. Thirty-two for the other two."

Braedon sighed. "Well, it had to happen sometime, I suppose. Where is the contact team?"

"With the exception of Scholar Price, who is going over communications intercepts in his cabin, they are just finishing breakfast."

"Inform them of everything you've told me, and have them join me in the wardroom in fifteen minutes."

"I am doing so now, Robert."

"Anything else we should be doing to prepare for visitors?"

"I would suggest that we not make it too easy for them until you have made your decision. Those vessels undoubtedly carry telescopic cameras and will be able to image us within another few hours."

Braedon nodded. "Logical. So how do we stop them?"

"I suggest that we move inside the probe's cone of shadow. That won't hide us from radar, but it will make reflected light photography impossible."

"Idea accepted. Begin preparations for getting underway."

Ten minutes later, the dazzling disk of the sun slid behind the probe. As darkness fell outside for the first time since they entered the solar system, Braedon caught sight of a flash of light near the limb of the backlit drive sphere. The flash was followed by another, two more, then dozens—until the probe appeared clad in a halo of swirling, sparkling diamonds.

"PROM, what makes the probe sparkle so?"

"Does it, Robert? I really hadn't noticed, but then, I do most of my seeing at shorter wavelengths than you humans. Now I see it. Quite pretty. Obviously, numerous tiny particles around the probe are refracting the sun's rays."

"Particles?"

"Bits of reinforcing fiber from the composite beams that make up the probe's structure. A large quantity must have been vaporized during the destruction. They recrystallized in the surrounding vacuum and underwent gravitational agglutination. Obviously, the loose particles were dislodged when the edge of our drive field brushed against the probe just now."

"How long before they settle out again?"

"It will take years. Is there something wrong?"

"No. I was just curious about something I didn't understand." Braedon shook his head sadly. "It's jarring sometimes to realize that destruction can also be beautiful."

"Philosophy, Robert?"

"Merely an observation. Keep me informed. I'll be in the wardroom with the contact team."

CHAPTER 7

Long before *Procyon's Promise* left Alpha, those in
charge of the expedition had begun writing a book. Its
title was simply *Contingencies*. Its purpose was to provide
guidance to the expedition commander for situations in
which he might find himself. *Contingencies* offered advice
for such diverse situations as what to do if *Procyon's
Promise* discovered evidence of a starfaring civilization
during its travels (drop everything and investigate); how
to proceed if the expedition found Earth a radioactive
wasteland (stay long enough to take photographs, then
return home); what precautions to take if the crew became
sick as a result of contact with terrestrial microorganisms.
Although *Contingencies* had been recorded in PROM's
memory banks, computer failure was one of the contingencies the book dealt with. Thus a failsafe backup supply
of a dozen printed-and-bound volumes had been provided.

Although seemingly straightforward, the problem of
making first contact with Earth's billions had turned out
to be one that troubled the planners greatly. Scenarios
ran from finding the solar system under control of a religious dictatorship to an armed attempt to take possession
of the ship and its FTL drive. A less dangerous, but perhaps more disquieting, possibility: That no one on Earth
would be interested in the return of the descendants of
the original *Pathfinder* explorers. So, upon entering the

system, Robert Braedon had followed standing orders, assigning specialists to assess the political situation.

The five members of the contact team were waiting for him in the Gamma Deck wardroom. Seated around the table, sipping mugs of *krasni*, were Chaplain Ibanez, First Officer Morton, Scholar Price, Scholar Watanabe, and Scholar Lavoir—the latter two the expedition's sociologist and historian, respectively. Terra sat apart from the others and leafed slowly through her favorite book, a compendium of Earth scenes Braedon had given her as a child.

The captain took his place at the head of the table. "I presume PROM has briefed each of you concerning the Solarian warships she has spotted. Any questions? If not, let's get about deciding how we are to make contact. Scholar Watanabe, you are our expert on the home world. What is your assessment of current conditions there?"

The sociologist tugged at his right earlobe, a nervous habit that invariably surfaced when he was asked to address a group. "I'm afraid 'least ignorant of those present' better describes my current level of understanding, Captain. Forty hours isn't a very long time to understand another culture, you know."

"You're all we have, Grigori."

"Ah, the situation appears excellent, Captain. The old rivalries are very nearly dead. This Communion of theirs seems to have supplanted the old sovereign nations."

"Surely there are new rivalries."

"Oh, of course. There are *always* rivalries, though I doubt we will understand them in the next twenty hours. Below the level of the Communion, they have fractionated rather badly. Determining who is on top is like understanding vars-ball without knowing the rules."

"PROM, do you agree?"

"Yes, Robert. I have monitored several thousand hours of communications. I confess that I am as much in the dark as to how they make their system work as Scholar Watanabe."

Braedon sat back and regarded his subordinates with a sour expression. "In other words, we don't know any more than we did shortly after breakout."

"Not at all, Robert," Scholar Price answered. "We are *much* smarter. It's just that the problem is exceedingly complex. We need more study before we will be able to give you intelligent advice."

"We don't have time for more study, Horace. We need an answer now."

"I am well aware of that, sir. But our needs don't alter the facts. And the fact is, at the moment we don't know how to avoid getting a missile down our gullets."

"Oh, I don't think there is much danger in that, Horace," Scholar Lavoir replied. "In spite of their arcane social structure, they seem quite peaceful. I, too, have been reviewing PROM's communications intercepts. Just last evening I viewed a documentary that asserted that the Earth hasn't seen a war this century."

"They still keep warships," First Officer Morton reminded him.

"More a police force than a military, I should think," Lavoir replied.

"A policeman can shoot you just as dead as a soldier."

"Unfortunately, true."

"What about just showing up on their doorstep?" Chaplain Ibanez asked. "What can they do if we take up orbit about the Earth and announce our identity?"

Scholar Price slowly shook his head. "I wouldn't think that wise, Padre. A spacecraft of obviously advanced capabilities is not conducive to unemotional, reasoned thought when it is orbiting directly overhead."

"Orbit the Moon then?"

"Same objection. We are getting considerable radio spillage from the lunar surface. It's been extensively urbanized since our ancestors left the system."

"What then?"

"Father."

Braedon turned to Terra. The picture book in her lap was open to her favorite part, the two-page panorama of the Grand Canyon.

"Terra?"

"I suggest that we contact the ship closest en route. We can send out one of our scout boats. An auxiliary is far less likely to provoke them than *Procyon's Promise* would. Also, by demonstrating our gravitic propulsion, we'll pique their curiosity. Lastly, if they do shoot, then we will have lost only a scout boat and a minimum crew."

"I'd like to see them try," Cal Martin said gruffly. "If

our boats can't outrun or outdodge anything they've got, I'll give up my place on the expedition to the Maker sun."

"You won't have to," Braedon said dryly. "I'm assigning you as command pilot of the boat they'll be shooting at."

The ensuing laughter was louder than it should have been. Braedon let it go on for a dozen seconds before signaling once again for quiet. "You need a copilot. Any suggestions?"

"I am second pilot, Father. It's my place to go."

Braedon turned to his daughter, his expression contorted by several competing emotions—anger, horror, and more than a little pride. "Out of the question!"

"Why?" she asked.

"You're too young, and it's too dangerous."

"It is less dangerous for me than for anyone else. In fact, I'm the only member of the crew whose presence on this mission is absolutely vital."

He lifted one eyebrow in an unspoken question.

"It's true! I'm a woman. They'll find a ship with a female copilot less threatening than one with an all-male crew."

Scholar Price cleared his throat, signaling his reluctant entrance into the argument between father and daughter. "Ah, normally that would be true, Terra. However, the Solarians routinely use women on their ships. I'm afraid they will attach no significance to your presence."

She shook her head violently. "I disagree. I've talked to Chryse about it. She says that Space Guard remains a predominantly male service. I think any male will always hesitate a moment before ordering a missile launch when a woman is staring out of the screen at him."

"She has a point, Captain," Price said.

Braedon considered his decision for a moment, then reluctantly gave in. "May the gods of space save me from your mother if anything happens to you."

He glanced around at the rest of the contact team. "Anything else? If not, I suggest we make our preparations. Maximum acceleration in fifty-five minutes. Meeting adjourned. PROM!"

"Yes, Robert."

"Where is Chryse Haller now?"

"In the hangar, Robert."

"I'm going to the bridge. Please ask her to join me

there. I want to review our proposed course of action
with her. If she agrees, we'll proceed as planned."

After breakfast on her second morning aboard the starship, Chryse Haller had been informed by PROM that Chief
Engineer Reickert had requested a tour of her ship, "if it
wouldn't be too much trouble."

"No trouble at all," Chryse had replied. "Have him
call at his convenience. I'll be in my cabin."

Ten minutes later, the chief engineer had knocked on
her door. She invited him in, making sure to leave the
door open as required by Alphan custom. Reickert was
a hulking, red-headed bear of a man who seemed at ease
only when discussing machinery.

"It is good of you to accommodate me, my lady," he
said with a slight trace of a stammer.

"I'm happy to do it. Still, what can possibly interest
you in my little runabout?"

"No secret there. I hope to obtain a good idea of how
far Alphan technology trails that of Earth."

Chryse blinked at the unexpected answer. "Don't you
have that slightly backward?"

"Not at all," the engineer said, growing visibly more
relaxed by the second. "With your vastly greater population, it is inevitable that you will have developed many
capabilities that we have missed in our preoccupation with
the stardrive."

"I guess I hadn't thought of it that way."

Several minutes later, still mulling over the implications of the engineer's comment, Chryse found herself in
a portion of the ship where machinery intruded at nearly
every turn of the corridor. The quiet of the crew decks
had given way to the muted throbbing of compressors.
Reickert stopped in front of a hatch, undogged it, and
pulled it open to reveal a small personnel lift. He gestured
for her to enter.

"Be sure to grab hold of the restraints, my lady."

Chryse hooked her toes under a railing like those found
in Earthside drinking establishments. Thus forewarned,
she was prepared when the force of gravity evaporated
around her as Reickert closed the hatch. Her stomach did
a quick flip-flop as the car moved through the steel deck
and came to rest in the cavernous space beyond.

"Hangar bay," Reickert said.

Chryse surveyed her surroundings. The hangar was a bewildering jumble of beams, conduits, and cargo-handling equipment. The scene was lit by the harsh glare of floodlights mounted high up the metal dome over her head. Above the lights were the starship's south pole, where the six massive hangar doors came together in a complex locking mechanism.

Her gaze was drawn to an egg-shaped craft suspended near one side of the dome, halfway between apex and deck. Similar, but not identical, vessels were secured at two other points in the hangar. These were *Promise*'s scout boats. Like their parent, they lacked any evidence of exhaust nozzles, plasma ports, or blast tubes. They made the daycruiser, lashed securely to the deck in front of her, look dowdy and cumbersome.

Reickert helped her out of the lift and led her hand-over-hand along lines strung across the flat expanse of deck. At the daycruiser airlock, they were met by one of his assistants. Chryse spent the next hour showing the two engineers around. She demonstrated each piece of equipment, set up the computer, and ran a series of dummy astrogation problems. Her companions seemed especially excited when she removed the computer's maintenance covers to show them the internal construction.

"Memory crystals!" Reickert practically shouted as he caught sight of the rows of scintillating nuggets.

The three of them continued the tour. Eventually the chief engineer and his assistant drifted off into a technical discussion of their own. Chryse was about to excuse herself when the communicator at her belt beeped for attention. She detached it and acknowledged the call.

"This is PROM, Chryse. The captain would like to see you on the bridge."

"I'm on my way."

Commander William Tarns sat uncomfortably at his console in SGC *Victrix*'s combat control center and listened to the subdued mutter on the tactical circuits. The ship was falling tailfirst toward the probe, decelerating at two and a half gravities after a high-speed dash across a million kilometers of empty void. Around him, technicians sat at consoles devoted to astrogation, communications, detection, engineering, fire control, and 3-D tacplot. On the forward bulkhead, an oversize screen displayed a large situation plot showing only *Victrix* and the probe.

"Well?" Tarns asked Senior Lieutenant Garth Hocutt, his tactical advisor. Hocutt occupied the console immediately to Tarns' right.

"Earth says they've lost contact, sir. They think the target may have slipped into the probe's shadow."

"Detectors!" Tarns snapped. Sixteen hours at high gravs and in battle armor had made him irritable. "I want a radar scan of the probe."

"We're out of range, sir."

"I'm not interested in why you can't do it, Zerbliski. Earth thinks something is hiding in the probe's shadow cone. Use the comm maser if you have to, but check it out. Now!"

"Yes, sir."

Tarns watched his readouts as one of *Victrix*'s four communications masers swiveled to point directly at the probe and then spat a single high-power pulse. The technique lacked sophistication, but it had its uses—it would reveal an unseen object near the probe.

Tarns waited. Three seconds after the pulse was dispatched its echo returned on schedule. A small yellow-green marker flashed onto the main screen. Tarns studied the small block of text alongside the new symbol and muttered a short, sharp obscenity. The new object's range, bearing, and closing speed were correct, but it was much too small. Tarns turned to Hocutt.

"What is it, Mister?"

"The Department of Antiquities guard satellite listed in the catalog, sir. It seems to be inoperative."

"So where is our quarry? And where is this missing plutocrat we're supposed to be on the lookout for?"

"Unknown, sir."

Tarns' intercom buzzed.

"C.O. here."

"Specialist Donlan, Captain. Terminal defense console."

"Go ahead, Donlan."

"You asked that we keep our eyes open for anomolies. I've got one. My screen just reported a large object ten thousand kilometers off our beam. The bearing is due galactic north."

"What velocity vector?"

"Same as us, sir. It's paralleling our path."

"How did it make its approach?"

"Don't know sir. One second it wasn't there, the next it was."

"I want a full circumambient scan, maximum range, Donlan. Let's see what else might be out there."

"It'll take ten minutes or more to do a complete spheric, sir."

"Five minutes, no more. I need information."

"Yes, sir."

It took only three minutes for Specialist Donlan to return to Tarns' screen. "You were right, sir. There's a second contact back along our flight path. It's much smaller than the prime contact and coming on fast. Computer says it's accelerating at better than nine hundred gravs! Might be a missile. It sure as hell acts like one."

Tarns turned to his tactical advisor. "Orders be damned, Lieutenant. Go to battle stations."

"Aye, aye, sir."

At the same moment the battle stations alarm began to clamor, Tarns' console beeped for attention. He ignored it until he had his helmet clamped in place and sealed. All around him technicians were doing the same, struggling against the force of high gravs. Tarns reached out to accept the call.

"Ensign Santos, sir. Communications."

"Go ahead, Santos."

"I'm receiving a call on several civil frequencies. It's coming from the contact back along our orbit. Some woman asking permission to rendezvous with *Victrix*, sir."

In spite of the acceleration pulling him into his seat, Commander Tarns felt as though a great weight had suddenly lifted from his shoulders. "A woman, Ensign?"

"Yes, sir. Quite attractive too. She says that she's a descendant of the *Pathfinder* expedition."

"Well, don't just sit there like a log, son. Tell her permission is granted. And Santos."

"Yes, sir?"

"Tell her, welcome to the solar system!"

CHAPTER 8

Henri Duval had long forgotten why he'd once sought the office of Chief Executive of the Community of Nations. A dozen years in the post had nearly convinced him that the reason, whatever it had been, hadn't been good enough. Several times he had informed his long-suffering wife that he was ready to quit in a minute—if only this problem or that crisis weren't so godawful critical. Frau Duval's response was ever the same: She reminded him that he only threatened to resign at times when there was no chance the Grand Assembly would take him up on it. "Besides," she always concluded, "where would you find another office with so scenic a view?"

Henri Duval's office had been carved from native stone, with its floor-to-ceiling window set in the face of a cliff high up a mountainside. He often stood on the edge of the precipice and gazed into the distance. The visual grandeur had a calming effect that few other activities in life could match.

One hundred kilometers to the south, the blue-white wall of the Mont Blanc massif formed an eternal barrier between himself and the far horizon. Closer, but still dimmed by the haze of distance, Lake Geneva glittered with an icy sheen. Around the lake, the city of the same name sprawled to the base of the surrounding mountains in all directions, reminding Duval of a high-water mark left over from a particularly bad spring flood.

All of this was overlooked by terraces of black cubes jutting from the slopes of the mountains north of the city. The cubes were that portion of Community of Nations Headquarters that showed aboveground. The rest of the sprawling warren lay deep within the mountains. It was from the highest level of this underground complex that Henri Sebastian LaForge Duval stared down on the city below.

A chime sounded behind him and Duval turned with a sigh to face the paneled elegance of his inner office. In addition to his too-large desk, the office contained a conference table with seating for twelve and an intimate conversation area furnished with settees and overstuffed chairs. To his left, the Great Seal of the Community of Nations was displayed prominently on a teak-covered wall.

The armored door between inner and outer offices hissed quietly into its recess. Two men entered. They were Sergei Vischenko and Javral Pere.

"Ah, Sergei, right on time as usual," the Chief Executive said, striding forward to greet his visitors.

"Good morning, sir. You know my aide, Undersecretary Pere, I believe."

"Citizen Pere and I met three years ago in Buenos Aires."

"Yes, sir," Pere replied. "Good of you to remember."

Duval led Vischenko and Pere to the conference table. When they were seated and after his two visitors had politely refused refreshments, Duval leaned back in his chair and said, "Now then, gentlemen, my secretary informs me that I can afford to devote a full twenty-eight minutes to this conference. You may begin when ready."

Vischenko nodded. "Javral, please bring the Chief Executive up to date on the latest developments."

Pere leaned forward and energized his notepad. "As you know, sir, SGC *Victrix* made contact with a small spacecraft of unusual design some fifty hours ago. The craft was an auxiliary from the starship which Achilles Observatory detected entering the system five days ago. The craft carried a crew of two. They confirmed that they are descendants of the Procyon interstellar expedition. The starship itself rendezvoused with *Victrix* four hours after the initial contact, and there have now been a number of exchange visits."

"Have you had time to study the reports I've forwarded, Chief Executive?" Vischenko asked.

Duval nodded. "I confess that I find it difficult to credit some of the numbers I read. Especially the acceleration levels."

"Yes, sir. I had a similar reaction. However, the figures are correct. Both starship and auxiliary craft are capable of sustained acceleration of the order of one thousand gravities. Their engines seem to be gravitic in nature."

"What about armament?"

"So far as we can tell, they have no weapons at all onboard either ship."

Duval leaned back in his chair and placed his hands over his paunch. "Armed or not, Sergei, these Procyonians could cause Space Guard serious problems if they were so inclined."

"They call themselves Alphans, sir. I've spoken to Admiral Smithson and he feels they can be handled in an emergency."

"Where is this starship now?"

"Maintaining station on *Victrix*. The two will be joined by the cruisers *Ipsilante* and *Verdugo*, and the entire fleet will arrive in Earth orbit in approximately seventy-two hours. We've directed them to Space Guard's outer terminus."

Duval frowned. "Why there?"

"We chose it for its privacy, Executive," Vischenko said. "We're buying time. There are important policy decisions to be made."

"Such as?"

"The Alphans speak of a cooperative venture to find the Makers."

"For heaven's sake, why?"

"It seems to have something to do with their religion, Executive. Whatever the reason, we need a policy position concerning this voyage of theirs, and quickly."

Duval shrugged. "What concern is it of ours?"

Vischenko laughed, bitterly. "Do you know Professor Colin Williams, sir?"

"The Solarian laureate? No, I don't believe I do."

"Williams is concerned that there are a great many species in this galaxy who would regard a starship full of humans the way we would look upon an ownerless cow with a bag of gold strapped to its neck. He fears an attack on Earth should the Alphans lose the secret of the FTL drive to aliens."

"Why attack us?"

"We are potential competitors."

"Surely there are security measures we could take to hide the location of our home system, Sergei. Hypnosis, drugs, orders for astrogators to suicide on capture, that sort of thing."

Vischenko shook his head. "It might not be that simple, Executive. An FTL starship leaves a radiation wake wherever it goes. Using the proper instruments, this trail can be detected decades later. That was how the probe knew that Procyon was the site of an FTL base. It is also the reason we were so quick to detect the Alphans' arrival. By the way, we are still tracking their wake. Scientists tell me we'll be able to watch it all the way back to Procyon, twelve light-years distant."

Duval considered Vischenko's words for long seconds, then nodded slowly. "I'm beginning to see your point. We'll proceed with caution, at least until we know what we're up against."

Robert Braedon sat at his control console on the bridge of *Procyon's Promise* and surveyed the space station poised five kilometers beyond the viewdome. The station included a habitat module, a dozen spherical cryogen tanks, a space dock for repairs, and the floating debris that any orbital installation accumulates with time. The habitat module was a slowly rotating cylinder with a forest of communications gear perched at one end and a despun docking structure at the other. The free-floating tanks were snow-white spheres, each containing a million liters of deuterium-enriched cryogen fuel. Beyond the station was the three-quarters-full crescent Earth.

"Any news reports yet?"

"None, Robert," PROM answered from close by his left ear.

"Is it possible that they're keeping our arrival a secret?"

"Quite likely," the computer replied. "Historical data indicates the Solarian news services are highly competitive. The logical explanation for this continuing silence is that the government has yet to make a formal announcement of our presence in the system."

"What of the meeting aboard the station?"

"The Communion representative apologizes for the delay. He says that it will be another hour yet before they're ready to receive you."

"Ask Chryse Haller to join me on the bridge."

"Will do, Robert."

Five minutes later, Chryse's head and shoulders poked through the hatch leading from the bridge to the next deck down. She scrambled up the ladder, glanced around at the duty crew, then made her way to where Braedon was seated in his command chair.

"You wanted to see me, Captain?"

Braedon nodded and gestured for her to take the seat next to his console. He explained the lack of news reports regarding *Promise*'s arrival in the system and the fact that they had been directed to what appeared to be an out-of-the-way refueling station. He concluded by saying, "I don't understand what is going on, Citizen."

Chryse glanced up at the space station beyond the viewdome. "Neither do I. Obviously, Space Guard is keeping you under wraps. If I had to guess, I'd say that the Communion hasn't yet formulated a policy to cover this situation, and they've placed you in cold storage until they can get themselves organized."

Braedon shook his head ruefully. "I don't understand your government. I've studied Scholar Lavoir's reports until my eyes water, yet it never seems to get any clearer."

Chryse shrugged. "Nothing mysterious about the Communion. First of all, it isn't a government in the classical sense of the word. It's a sort of 'Better Business Bureau' that encompasses the whole of Solarian society. They stop wars, oversee the more cutthroat forms of industrial competition, and occasionally suppress dangerous alien ideas dredged up out of the data banks. Other than that, they don't take much of an interest in the private lives of the citizenry."

"It sounds like anarchy."

"It works. Usually not fast or well, but better than some other things that have been tried on a global scale."

"I still don't understand, which is the reason I asked you up here," Braedon said. "Would you be interested in

accompanying me to this first series of conferences? You
would have the status of an advisor."

Chryse laughed. "I was on my way up here to suggest
something similar when PROM summoned me, Captain. I
was about to point out that I am a skilled negotiator. I'll
get you the best deal I can."

Three hours later, Braedon relaxed in the copilot's
couch aboard Scout Boat *Commodore Stassel* as he gazed
up at the approaching space station habitat. There were
five bands of viewports interspersed with the usual plumb-
ing and electrical conduits on the habitat's black-and-white
checked exterior.

"One hundred meters, Captain," Chief Hanada said
from the pilot's position.

"Take her in, Chief. Maximum care."

"Aye aye, sir."

Braedon watched a wall of steel slide by overhead as
Hanada carefully eased the landing boat's nose into the
docking mechanism. As quickly as the oscillations caused
by the minor impact ceased, a tube snaked toward the
boat's airlock. A few seconds later, the instrument panel
indicated the presence of both pressure and oxygen beyond
the airlock's outer door.

"Docking complete, Captain."

"Very good, Chief. I'll call on the communicator as
soon as we're safely aboard the station. When I do, you
uncouple and return to the ship."

"Are you sure you want me to do that, sir? I'd feel a
lot better if I was standing by."

"Not needed, Chief. There's nothing you could do in
an emergency. If I need transport, I'll call you."

"Aye aye, sir."

Braedon unstrapped from his couch, moved to open the
hatch at the back of the pilot's compartment, and stepped
through into the main cabin. Horace Price and Chryse Haller
were waiting for him. He led them into the cramped airlock,
switched off the internal gravity, and opened the outer door.
Beyond the door was an accordion-pleated transfer tube.
Braedon leaned forward and kicked off, sailing head first
into the tube. The others followed close behind. Beyond a
second airlock, they found a large, spherical compartment.

A dozen Space Guard Marines stood anchored to a deck constructed of open meshwork.

"Honor guard, *ten-hut*!"

The Marines stiffened and saluted as martial music emanated from somewhere overhead. Two men stood at attention in the center of the sphere. Braedon recognized one as *Victrix*'s captain. The other man was a stranger. As the last notes of the sonorous anthem died away, Commander Tarns kicked off and floated to where the Alphan party waited.

"So we meet at last, Captain," he said, holding out a hand to Braedon. "We've spoken often enough by screen that I feel I know you already."

"I feel the same," Braedon said, taking the proferred hand.

The Solarian captain gestured toward the silver-haired man at the center of the docking sphere. "Shall we meet the boss?"

They followed Tarns. "Captain Robert Braedon of Starship *Procyon's Promise*, I have the honor to present the Right Honorable Sergei Ivanovich Vischenko, Senior Member of the Council of Planetary Advisors."

"Welcome to the solar system, Captain."

Braedon found the advisor's grip surprisingly firm. Afterward, he introduced Scholar Price. Vischenko shook hands, welcomed the scientist to the solar system, and then turned to Chryse Haller.

"And this is our guest, Chryse Lawrence Haller."

"Yes," Vischenko said. "I know the lady's father. I'm pleased to see you, my dear, but also a bit confused at your presence here."

Chryse smiled. "Captain Braedon graciously offered me the hospitality of his ship. I'm repaying him by serving as translator."

Vischenko's eyebrows rose slightly. "I find the captain's command of Standard to be excellent. Why does he need a translator?"

"The language has changed a great deal since my ancestors' time," Braedon said. "Chryse has been very helpful in assisting us in learning some of your modern idioms."

Vischenko nodded. "As you wish. Shall we move this up to the habitat? I've never liked zero gee."

* * *

Aboard the habitat they were led to a compartment labeled MESS HALL. In its center was a long metal table where a dozen chairs were fastened to the deck. Four were occupied when they arrived.

Sergei Vischenko strode to the table and gestured for the Alphans to follow. "Citizen Haller, I believe you are acquainted with my assistant, Undersecretary Pere."

"We're old friends," Chryse said. "Hello, Javral, how are you?"

"I'm fine, Chryse. Glad to find you safe. I was very worried when you were reported missing."

"Nothing to worry about. Captain Braedon has been a most gracious host and I've been having the time of my life."

"Indeed?"

Vischenko interrupted the interplay by continuing the introductions. "... Colin Williams, Professor of Alien Studies, University of North America; Kiral Papandreas, Professor Emeritus, System Institute for the Advancement of Astronomical Observation; and Admiral Michael Smithson, Space Guard."

There was another quick round of handshakes, followed by a pause while everyone was seated. Uniformed stewards entered from the kitchen area carrying trays of drinks and pastries. When everyone had been served, Vischenko signaled for silence.

"Captain Braedon, we are all quite anxious to hear what happened to the Procyon Expedition after it left the solar system. Would you mind ... ?"

Braedon turned to Scholar Price. "More your bailiwick than mine, Horace."

Price nodded and launched into a swift recounting of Alphan history—the arrival of *Pathfinder* in the Procyon system, the discovery of the Star Traveler base, the long struggle to unlock the secret of the estee relics, and, finally, the effort to build and launch *Procyon's Promise*.

The Solarians asked half a dozen innocuous questions, which Price answered. Then Colin Williams leaned forward and said, "Scholar, you say you were able to construct this remarkable ship of yours from information obtained by deciphering these estee records. That indicates that the technology is well within current human scientific capabilities."

Price nodded.

"That being the case," Williams mused, "how is it that the Makers have been unable to develop such a drive in a quarter-million years of intense effort? Why have they failed to see what, in restrospect, must appear obvious?"

Price chuckled wryly. "There is nothing obvious about the drive, sir! While the equipment is mechanically quite simple, the theory behind it is highly complex. The estee records speak of a great insight; some theoretical breakthrough without which the drive would not exist. Unfortunately, the record strip we managed to decipher didn't tell us what that breakthrough was."

Kiral Papandreas' mouth was suddenly agape. "Surely you aren't claiming that you crossed twelve light-years of space *in a ship whose operation you don't fully understand*?"

Price nodded. "That is precisely what I am saying, sir. We know which levers to pull and what buttons to push, but of the underlying principles, we are totally ignorant."

CHAPTER 9

Henri Duval blinked sharply as the lights came up in the projection theater and the images faded. Beside him, Josip Betrain reached up to rub his eyes. They had spent two hours staring at images of life on another world.

The Alphan documentary had displayed Procyon VII as a world of sweeping vistas and breathtaking scenery; of jagged mountains and crystalline beaches; of small, neat villages and mysterious alien ruins. While the movie had progressed, Duval had had a strong feeling that he was looking back in time to an era before humans had become the undisputed masters of the Earth. Yet there had never been an era when three small moons climbed the terrestrial horizon, nor when the tiny speck of a nearby white dwarf star hung low in the night sky above the dull red radiance of an active volcano.

"Well," Duval asked, turning to his one-time mentor, "what do you think?"

Josip Betrain was an old man, even by contemporary standards. He was also a sick man. He suffered from a degenerative nerve disorder that caused his body to twitch continuously. After fifteen decades of life, Betrain hadn't long to live. That fact gave him an unusually clear view of things, and made him a particularly valued advisor to the Chief Executive.

"Sergei Vischenko obtained this from the Alphans?"

Duval nodded.

"And you are trying to decide whether we should participate in this adventure of theirs to search out the probe's creators?"

"Yes."

"And you want my advice?"

"I presume that was a rhetorical question since you know damned well that I do."

"My advice to you, Executive, is simple. You are going to end up going out to the stars whether you like it or not. You had best like it."

Duval sighed and gazed down at the liver-spotted hand that grasped Betrain's cane. Once that hand had been rock steady, the professional tool of a skilled microbiologist. Now it shook. "You know, Josip, I sometimes think you overplay your role as my Oracle of Delphi. Would you care to explain your last remark?"

"Nothing mysterious about it. If you decide to allow the expedition, you will have to build a fleet of ships of your own to accompany them. It is patently obvious that they will never find the Maker world on their own. The logistics are far too great for their society to handle. And, Henri, if you decide that fulfilling this 'Promise' of theirs endangers the Earth, then you will need that starfleet even more."

"I don't follow you."

"Sure you do. But when the facts are unpleasant, even a Chief Executive tends to avert his eyes. Therefore, let history record that it was from my lips that the fateful words first fell." Betrain drew himself up and seemed to gather strength from somewhere within. When he spoke, the usual hoarse whisper was replaced by a reedy monotone.

"If Professor Williams' scenario is correct, Executive, it is your solemn duty to prevent the Alphans from giving the FTL secret to any alien species *whatsoever*! That includes the beings who built the probe. Once the secret is out, it is *out*! Obviously, the only way to stop the spread of a dangerous technology is at the source. To do that, you will have to take control of Procyon VII itself. You may well be forced into becoming that which you have long despised—an imperialist aggressor who launches an unprovoked attack against people who have done nothing to deserve it."

"I take it then, Josip, that you agree with Professor Williams' assessment of the danger?"

"I do not!" the old man growled. There was a deep rattle in his chest and he was overcome with a wracking cough. After the spasm passed, he lifted himself upright, stared at Duval with rheumy eyes, and continued. "Study your history, man! Every forward step the race has ever taken was opposed by someone afraid of what we would find. So far, the 'naysayers' have been one hundred percent wrong. As a result, history does not speak kindly of leaders who lose their nerve at critical moments.

"But my opinion doesn't count. Neither does yours. We can't lose sight of the possibility that the Colin Williamses of this world might be right this time. Maybe the galaxy *is* full of alien monsters just waiting for a shipload of hayseed humans to blunder into their clutches."

Duval sighed. "What do you suggest?"

"Use the data banks, of course. Dredge up from the probe's archives all you can about the laws, customs, and traditions of the known races. Build computer simulations of each species' ethic structure and put the question to them *in absentia*. Once you know how each is likely to respond, you can extrapolate the probability that the Alphans will cause some three-armed, green-furred, Ghengis Khan to descend on Earth with blasters blazing."

Duval considered Betrain's advice for long seconds. Finally he looked up and regarded his old mentor. "You know, it just might work! The xenologists have been publishing that sort of thing for decades. We begin with a large data base already."

"Not large enough, I'll wager. The sheer bulk of the data banks makes a complete survey of *any* subject well nigh impossible. You'll need some damned skillful programing of search routines before you're through. Still, that's a minor technical detail."

"A minor technical detail that will require several thousand information specialists to solve. How are we going to hide a research effort of that size?"

"No need to hide it. That Alphan scholar—Price, wasn't it?—gave you the perfect alibi. He claims that these Star Travelers invented the drive because they stumbled onto some physical law everyone else seems to have overlooked. That gives us a clue to gnaw on.

"Science isn't a loose collection of arbitrary facts, you know. It's a coherent whole! Whatever the Star Travelers discovered is still out there. It's waiting to be found again. There must be some physical phenomenon which everyone's seen, but which only the Star Travelers have understood. We'll announce that we're collecting data regarding observed phenomena which no one can explain, and that our purpose is to identify areas which require further investigation."

"And what do we do with the Alphans while this is going on?"

Betrain's chuckle was barely distinguishable from his cough. "We accept their terms, of course! Whichever way you decide, you are going to need that fleet of starships. I suggest that you put on your broadest smile, pledge your undying friendship, and hope like hell that you mean it!"

A week passed in negotiations with the Solarians before Robert Braedon realized that the Earthmen were holding back. That they had orders not to make any decisions until higher authority could be contacted, they freely admitted. What bothered Braedon, though, was his worry that they weren't being completely honest with him.

As the discussions became more far ranging, the Alphan delegation had grown. At first Grigori Watanabe had demanded to be included. Then Chaplain Ibanez. For the last two days, Terra had cadged a place aboard the scout boat that left each morning for the Solarian station.

Chryse Haller also continued to attend the conferences. Her cover story wore thin by the third day. It had become apparent to everyone that she was taking an active interest in the negotiations on the Alphan side. Whatever Sergei Vischenko thought of her defection, he was careful to let no hint of it slip past his mask of urbane politeness.

Nor were the official sessions the only contact between the two sides. After the first session, the Alphans and Chryse Haller had been invited to stay for dinner. Champagne flowed freely. Braedon and Javral Pere finished the evening by swapping off-color jokes with each other.

Two nights later, Braedon hosted a dinner aboard *Procyon's Promise* for the Solarian delegation, the officers of the three cruisers that had escorted them, and the com-

mandant and executive officer of the space station. The
party was a huge success, with Upper Plateau brandy
substituting for champagne, *krasni* replacing coffee.
Afterward, small parties of slightly tipsy guides and guests
toured the ship, stopping in the engine room to marvel at
the massive field coils of the stardrive. Braedon noticed
that several of the Solarian officers seemed to sober
remarkably quickly while their eyes darted over the stardrive generator casings.

Following the fifth session, Space Guard hosted a party
aboard *Ipsilante*. The ship was larger than *Victrix*, and
the dozen Alphans who attended were treated to a tour
of the Solarian cruiser. This time it was the colonists who
pretended to be more affected by the liquor than they
truly were.

By the end of the week, the Alphans were to play host
once more. "I'm getting fat from all these dinners," Braedon complained to his daughter as they stood in the hangar
bay control room and watched the great door swing open
like the petals of a large steel flower.

"You should take the time to get more exercise."

He nodded, but didn't answer. Above his head, surrounding a single vessel, stars appeared in the black fir-
mament. The Space Guard interorbit transfer craft was
similar in construction to Chryse Haller's daycruiser,
except that its source of power was a chemical rocket
rather than an I-mass–initiated fusion reaction. The hangar
officer carefully played his fingers across a complex control panel. There was a quiet hum of power, and the Solarian craft moved forward, cradled in a supporting net of
tractor beams. The craft grounded against the deck where
the daycruiser had once rested, the hangar doors reclosed,
and a sudden hissing noise signaled the beginning of hangar
bay repressurization.

"One-tenth gee, Garald," Braedon said to the technician on duty.

"Coming on, Captain."

"Welcoming party, Mr. Martin."

"Aye aye, sir."

Within seconds, several Alphans were moving briskly
to form up in a double line on both sides of the Solarian
boat's airlock. Braedon followed with Terra in tow. The
atmosphere inside the hangar bay was frigid from expan-

sion cooling, causing each of them to trail long streamers of exhalation fog. Braedon reached the boat just as the airlock opened and Sergei Vischenko stepped out.

"Hello again," said Vischenko, shaking Braedon's hand. "Ready for another hard night of diplomacy?"

Braedon chuckled. "I was just commenting to Terra that all this partying is bad for my waistline."

"I know what you mean," Vischenko said, patting his own midsection. "By the way, I received a communique from the Chief Executive shortly after we adjourned this afternoon."

"Good news, I hope," Braedon said.

Vischenko smiled cryptically. "It'll keep until after dinner, Captain."

Dinner was an assortment of roast beef and sauteed rabsine—(a small, beaverlike creature of the Alphan highlands)—a variety of Alphan vegetables, and a cake filled with melted chocolate chips. The latter was a gift from the Solarians. They had introduced the Alphans to chocolate two nights earlier and had been surprised at the excitement it caused.

After dessert, the crystalline glasses were refilled with red-purple brandy and everyone toasted The Promise. Following the toasts, Sergei Vischenko glanced at his wrist chronometer, stood, and tapped a spoon on the side of his glass. The buzz of conversation quickly died away.

"Your attention, please. I have an announcement to make." Vischenko removed a record cube from an inside pocket and held it aloft between thumb and forefinger, where it scintillated in the overhead light.

"I received instructions today from my superior. Executive Duval has asked me to play this here tonight." He turned to Braedon, who was seated across the table from him. "We've brought along a cube player, Captain. If you will show us where to plug it in."

Braedon raised his voice. "PROM!"

"Yes, Robert."

"Can you sense the output signal from a standard cube reader without having it tapped into your information circuits?"

"Of course. However, if it is more convenient, Advisor

Vischenko need only hold the cube steady. I will read it now."

Vischenko looked startled. "Is that possible?"

"Eminently, Mr. Advisor," PROM replied.

Vischenko muttered something under his breath that sounded suspiciously like "I'll be *damned!*" as he held the cube further aloft.

"You may lower your arm, Mr. Advisor. I have completed the task."

The screen at the far end of the wardroom lit to show a heavyset man with a large bald spot. He was seated at a massive desk, with the Great Seal of the Communion behind him. The man looked into the camera with the ease of long practice. He smiled.

"Greetings, Captain Braedon. Greetings also to your officers and crew, to the people of Alpha, and to your Governing Council.

"My official representatives have told me of your plan to search out the Makers and to redeem the pledge which our ancestors made to the probe so many, many years ago. I salute both your courage and your faith. Most men would have been satisfied to rest on their laurels after the voyage you have just completed. Yet you are already considering a much longer and more difficult exploration.

"With such an example to follow, we can hardly refuse your request for aid in this worthy project. We will therefore provide whatever manpower, facilities, and material required to build a fleet to accompany you. In this regard, I ask that Chryse Lawrence Haller present herself in my office in Geneva at oh nine hundred hours three days hence. At that time we will begin discussions concerning the use of the Haller spaceyards for this project.

"Nor is that all. In support of Alphan efforts to discover the underlying physical laws which make the stardrive possible, I am authorizing our best computer technologists and information specialists to begin an immediate search of the library of Maker knowledge. Their purpose will be to discover whatever clues exist in the data banks concerning the true nature of the stardrive.

"And finally, Captain, I would like to extend my invitation to you and your people to come and visit Earth. I fear this battered old planet cannot match your Alpha in beauty, but it is the mother of us all and you have been too long gone.

"I look forward to meeting you."

In her cabin aboard *Procyon's Promise*, Chryse Haller readied her kit bag for the journey home. She was surprised at how little there was to pack. The vacsuit was gone, returned to *Henning's Roost* with the daycruiser. That left the underwear, toilet articles, and three shipsuits she'd taken on her expedition to the probe, and three more that Terra had loaned her. She had surrendered the latter to PROM the previous evening. The blue uniforms now lay at the foot of the bed, neatly pressed and folded. Chryse slipped into one of her own shipsuits and discovered the waistline tighter than she remembered. "Oh, well," she muttered to herself, gazing at her reflection in the mirror. "It was all in a good cause."

She finished packing, pressed the sticktite seams of the kit bag together, and glanced once more around the cabin. She was just about to leave when there was a discreet knock on the cabin door.

"Who is it?"

"It's me," Terra's muffled voice replied.

"Come in. It isn't locked."

Terra slid the cabin door into its recess, stepped inside, and then closed it again. The two women faced each other in awkward silence for several seconds before Chryse cleared her throat and gestured toward the uniforms lying on the bed. "Thank you for the use of those. I had them cleaned and pressed for you."

"You're welcome."

Chryse noted the sudden glistening in Terra's eyes. Her own eyes felt hot and full. Within seconds, the two women had entered a quick, tearful embrace.

"I'm sorry, but I've never been any good at farewells," Terra said as she backed away.

Chryse's answer was a knowing smile. "I thought I had outgrown this foolishness myself."

Terra held out her hand. "Well, it was good knowing you."

Chryse took the hand and squeezed. "Don't make it sound so final. Everything's worked out just perfectly so far. The Communion has agreed to build your fleet, my shipyards will get a piece of the work, and half of Earth has gone wild with excitement at the news. That's no reason for tears. Besides, it isn't as though we'll never see each other again, you know."

"That's right, isn't it? We've been directed to a slot in low polar orbit . . ."

Chryse frowned. "*Polar* orbit?"

"That's what Commander Tarns said. Why?"

Chryse shrugged. "Oh, nothing. It's just that the polar orbits are normally reserved for Space Guard vessels. You need special permission to launch a civilian craft on a north–south track."

Terra nodded. "Advisor Vischenko mentioned something about that. He said that our parking orbit had been chosen to keep the ship from being bothered by sightseers. Also, they are going to station a cruiser near us for protection. 'To minimize the nut factor' was the way Vischenko put it."

"It's probably for the best," Chryse agreed. "But I interrupted you. You were saying?"

"That we'll be coming down as soon as the health people clear us. They say that will take about ten days. We'll go to Geneva to make the social call on the Chief Executive first. Afterward, I want to see as much of Earth as I can."

Chryse nodded. "I'm planning a party at my father's place in the country. I've enough influence that they'll have to let you attend if you express an interest."

"You make it sound as though we'll be prisoners."

"You're famous, hon. That sometimes feels a little like prison."

Terra reached into her pocket and pulled out a small package wrapped in white paper. "I would very much like you to have this."

Chryse took the gift and carefully unwrapped it. Inside was a small box containing a silver locket with the Alphan stars-and-comet design engraved on its case.

"Look inside," Terra said.

Chryse opened the locket. Inside was a picture of Terra engraved in such microscopic detail that it looked like a photograph. The cover was also engraved:

TO CHRYSE HALLER
From Her Friend
TERRA BRAEDON

"It's beautiful, Terra."

"PROM made it."

Chryse smiled. "I love it. Thank you. *And* thank you, PROM!"

"You are welcome, Chryse."

Chryse turned to the foot of the bed where the kit bag lay and fished around inside for a moment. "Here, my present to you."

"What is it?" Terra looked at the half-melted, crystalline cube in her palm.

"Just a memory crystal, but one with a history. I found it imbedded in the wreck of the probe."

Terra's eyes widened. "This comes from the probe?"

Chryse nodded.

"I'll treasure it always! PROM, can you mount it on a necklace for me?"

"Of course." For a moment, Chryse thought she detected a hint of pique in PROM's voice.

Terra took the cube to the bulkhead delivery chute and put it inside. A minute later, the green light beside the chute turned on. She opened it and reached inside to remove the cube, now mounted on a silver chain.

"Help me put it on."

"Glad to."

Terra held her hair out of the way while Chryse operated the necklace clasp for her. Then they exchanged places and Terra helped Chryse with her locket.

"Now, let's get to the airlock," Chryse said. "I want to speak to your father before I leave."

That evening, ship's time, Terra sat cross-legged on her bed and examined Chryse's gift. She held the half-melted crystal close to her face as she scrutinized every detail. She had been gazing at it for the better part of an hour, fascinated by the interplay of diffracted colors, when PROM said, "Be careful with that."

Terra started slightly at the sudden sound. She glanced upward as small worry lines began to form across her forehead. "I didn't realize it was so fragile."

"It isn't. But you should be careful all the same—it's a relic of the probe. Perhaps I should keep it safe for you."

Terra frowned and glanced down at the lump of crystal in her hand. "But I was going to wear it."

"Place your crystal on the bed and go to the delivery chute."

Puzzled, Terra slid off the bed and padded to the small slot in the cabin bulkhead. She opened the access hatch. Inside was a small gray box. She pulled it from the slot and opened it. Inside, at the end of a silver necklace, was an exact copy of the crystal that Chryse had given her.

"What is this?"

"A duplicate for you to wear while I lock up the original. That way, there's no risk of your losing it."

"I don't know..." Terra glanced at the necklace on the bed. "After all, *that* one is Chryse's gift to me, not this one in my hand."

PROM sighed, a sound she imitated so perfectly that it was easy to forget that she had neither the need nor the equipment. "The truth is, I have an ulterior motive for manufacturing the duplicate, one which must be kept absolutely secret, even from your father. I need your oath on that."

Terra considered the request for long seconds, then nodded. "I suppose, although I don't see what could possibly be *that* much of a secret."

"You'll understand when I explain..."

CHAPTER 10

Chryse's return to Earth was a journey of three stages. The first involved the intraorbit ferry that picked her up in the hangar bay of *Procyon's Promise* and transferred her to the refueling terminus habitat. At the habitat she was put through a rigorous medical examination. After four hours of poking and prodding, the doctors satisfied themselves that she wasn't carrying any alien diseases and allowed her to dress. She was then guided to a conference room where several Communion functionaries quizzed her about her adventure. Bowing to the inevitable, she answered questions for two hours. At the end of that time she asked the leader of the group, somewhat frostily, if the interrogation was about over.

"If you will make yourself available to the proper authorities should the need arise, Citizen," he replied.

"Once I get my business affairs put back in order, you may question me until the Sun goes nova."

"In that event, have a pleasant journey, Citizen."

The second stage of the trip was by interorbit transport to Von Braun Station, one of the half-dozen primary transfer points for the Earth-to-orbit shuttles and the ships of deep space.

She entered the station and immediately transferred from the zero-gravity hub to the great rotating cylinder that served as hotel, transit lounge, shopping center, and restaurant. As she stepped from a spoke lift, a large crowd surged forward to surround her.

"Citizen Haller! Is it true that you were captured by these Procyonians?... Did they harm you?... What about reports that this starship business is a hoax?"

Chryse gazed in distaste at the solid wall of bodies, microphones, and camera lenses. It seemed as though half the journalists in the system had gathered to shout questions at her. She shoved a microphone pickup away from her face and turned to the questioner who had asked about the hoax.

"What are you talking about? What reports?"

"Some members of the Grand Assembly have been quoted as saying this whole thing is a ploy by your father and the current administration, a scheme to funnel a Communion payoff into your shipyards."

"Payoff for what?"

"His support for the McAuliff/Tseng Export Control Act."

"My father is opposed to McAuliff/Tseng. So am I. We hope it goes down to defeat."

"You aren't denying that the Chief Executive has summoned you to meet with him in Geneva, are you?"

"No, of course not. Executive Duval has requested the meeting to discuss what I've learned during my time among the Alphans."

"Citizen Haller, what of Professor Carlton Creighton's statement that exceeding the speed of light is a physical impossibility?" another reporter asked.

Chryse smiled a tight-lipped smile. "Professor Creighton would seem to be mistaken. I've seen the Alphan starship with my own eyes."

"Did they demonstrate its faster-than-light capability for you?"

"Not while I was aboard."

"What are they like?" a voice shouted from the fringes of the crowd.

"Friendly, competent, and very determined to make good on the pledge which the human race made to SURROGATE following the probe's destruction. If we wish to share in the age-old dream of starflight, we had better help them... Now, if you will excuse me, I have a ship to catch. Any further questions may be forwarded to my corporate headquarters."

Clutching her kit bag, Chryse shoved her way into the crowd. Halfway through, she felt a strong hand grip her left arm. Her assailant was a young man with closely cropped, sandy hair.

"Citizen Haller?"

"Yes?"

"I'm Jim Davidson. Your office chartered my ship to take you down to Earth. They thought it would be less conspicuous than one of Haller Associates' corporate shuttles."

"They seem to have been wrong," she said, shouting into his ear in order to be heard over the crowd noise.

"It would seem so. Nevertheless, follow me." Davidson plowed his way through the crowd. Once in the clear, they set off down the corridor at a fast run, trailing camera crews behind like beads on a string. When they came to another spoke lift at the opposite end of the Von Braun Grand Hotel, her protector pushed her inside then punched for the spin axis as they hooked their boots under the floor restraints. The lift began to rise.

Davidson turned to her. "Sorry about the crowd. I was misinformed about the docking portal your ship would use; otherwise I would have met you before you descended into that lions' den."

"No problem," Chryse replied. When the lift doors opened, they were back in zero gravity. She followed Davidson to a berth operated by one of the three space taxi services that transported passengers and cargo between Von Braun and outlying ships. They were soon out in space on their way to Davidson's craft.

Nearly a year had passed since Chryse had last visited Moose Hill, her father's estate in that part of the North American Administration District known as British Columbia. She sat in the jumpseat between Davidson and his copilot and watched the runway carved from dense forest expand steadily before the ferry's windscreen.

Beyond the runway was a black complex of glass and metal. Davidson brought the ferry to a smooth stop near the estate's small terminal. Chryse unstrapped and turned to the ferry's pilot-in-command. "Thank you for rescuing me from those reporters, Captain. You do good work."

"Part of the service, Citizen."

Chryse was met at the midships airlock by the head of the Moose Hill guard force.

"Afternoon, Roderick."

"Good afternoon, ma'am. Your father said to expect you sometime today."

"Where *is* my favorite bull elephant, anyway?"

"Up at the main house. I've already notified him of your arrival."

"Excellent. Call the jitney and I'll ride up."

"The jitney" was a Rolls-Royce Catamount ground cruiser. The estate's stable of the eight-wheeled, fully articulated crawlers were used primarily to patrol the outer perimeter fence, stretching some two hundred kilometers through virgin forest.

Marcus Easton, her father's personal assistant, met her at the front door of the main house. "Welcome home, Chryse."

"Thank you, Marcus. It's good to be home."

"We were very worried when we received word that you were missing."

"Was *he* worried?"

"More than he cares to admit. He's waiting for you."

Harrold Haller presented an imposing figure as he sat behind the mammoth mahogany desk surrounded by workscreens and comm links. As Chryse entered, he crossed the room to meet her halfway between desk and door. Haller had married late in life and largely left the raising of his only child to hirelings. As a result, Chryse had never been close enough to her father for either of them to be at ease in the other's company. Their embrace was stiff and formal.

"Good to have you home, Chryse." He cracked a tight-lipped smile.

"Good to be home, Harrold." Chryse was struck by the contrast between her current unease and the happy camaraderie she had experienced aboard the Alphan starship.

"Are you all right?" Haller asked.

"I'm fine. Have you been keeping to your pill schedule?"

"I have," he said, releasing her. "That damned fool of a doctor doubled the dose on me again."

"Then you'd best take it easy."

"Who has the time?" With that, Haller returned to his chair behind the desk, signaling that the father-daughter conversation was over and a business discussion was about to begin. Chryse sat on the couch and stared at the large Turner on the opposite wall while bracing herself for what was coming.

"Going off alone like that was a damfool stunt. *Damfool!* It cost us a fortune."

Chryse nodded. She'd used the time aboard the interorbit transfer ship to catch up on the financial news. Haller Associates' stock had dropped five points the first hour after she was reported missing. The conglomerate had lost nearly a billion stellars supporting the price after that.

"I can't argue with you there, Harrold, although I hope it may yet turn out to be a profitable damfool stunt."

"How do you figure that?"

"Because I've put us in a position to help the Alphans build their exploration fleet. Afterward, we'll be free to build as many starships as our shipyards can handle."

"What makes you think I want to get involved?"

Chryse blinked. Her father had surprised her. "Don't want to get involved?" she asked more shrilly than she had intended. "We're talking about the stars here! Think of the possibilities for trade and colonization. Think of the money to be made! What do you suppose an Earthtype planet goes for these days on the open market?"

Haller considered her words for a moment, then leaned forward to the intercom on his desk. "Marcus, give us two minutes, then come in, please."

"Yes, sir."

Haller leaned back in his chair and gazed at his daughter. "Chryse, when I took control of this corporation from my father, the power station industry was going through economic upheaval. While searching through the data banks, some ivory-tower academic had discovered a more efficient method of transmitting electrical power from orbit to ground. The transmission device was so efficient that it made the massive microwave rectennas we had used up to that time obsolete. Haller Associates and most of the other power satellite companies were in danger of going belly up.

"I made myself a promise the day we put our first new power receiver online. I vowed to never again be caught unawares by a technological breakthrough. That is why I started investing heavily in research while others were calling for tighter controls on the data banks. That is the reason, over the past forty years or so, that Haller Associates has been the wielder of the double-edged sword of progress more often than it has been the victim.

"Let me tell you something, Chryse! The moment I heard of this ship from the stars, I began making plans to get in on what is obviously a good thing. In other words, I am all in favor of your efforts to help these Alphans build their fleet."

"Then why did you say—"

"I was testing to see how strongly *you* feel about helping them."

The office door opened and Marcus Easton entered. He seated himself in a chair near Chryse, took a recorder from his pocket, and placed it on the table between them.

"Marcus," Haller began, "I want all of the division managers here for a meeting at twenty hundred hours tonight.

The secretary nodded. "Yes, sir. All are available except Haskell. He's en route to the Asteroid Belt and won't be back for another three weeks at the earliest. Shall I call his assistant?"

"No, we'll do without."

"Subject, sir?"

"The subject? How Haller Associates goes about capitalizing on the excellent groundwork of its president regarding the Alphans."

"Yes, sir."

"Now, then," Haller said, "Chryse, tell us all about it, and don't leave out anything."

Chryse launched into a description of her decision to leave *Henning's Roost* and visit the probe. An hour and a half later she was still describing the wonders of *Procyon's Promise*. Haller listened quietly, occasionally scratching notes onto a notepad while Marcus Easton inspected his fingernails and otherwise seemed to ignore her. Finally, she recounted Executive Duval's message asking her to come to Geneva to discuss the building of an exploration fleet.

Haller nodded. "Why do you suppose the Executive threw this plum into our laps? We've been on his 'most disliked' list since that flap about the cost overruns for those new Space Guard destroyers."

Chryse shrugged. "I suspect it was a ploy to get me away from the Alphans. Several times during our discussions, I managed to keep Vischenko more honest than he intended to be."

Harrold Haller looked at his secretary and frowned. "What's the matter, Marcus? You look as though you just bit into an overripe pickle."

"Maybe I did."

"Meaning?"

"I've been thinking about the Communion's timing on this matter. They seem to have made the decision to support the Alphans with uncharacteristic speed."

"What are you implying?"

"I'm not sure. It just seems to me that the Chief Executive took a lot on himself. At the least, there should have been a major debate in the Grand Assembly."

"Do you suspect a trick?" Haller had had dealings with the current administration and had good reason not to trust them.

"Possible, Harrold. In any event, a well-orchestrated public relations campaign might be a prudent investment right now."

"Good idea, Marcus," Chryse said. "We'll want articles about the glorious past of space exploration, that sort of thing. Maybe we could finance a holo epic about the *Pathfinder* Expedition."

Harrold Haller laughed. "You're too late. Three are already in preproduction."

"Then pick the one with the best chance of success and back it to the hilt. We've got to keep the public enthusiastic to prevent the GA's killing the project once they discover what it's going to cost. If Marcus is right about Duval's offer being a ploy, we can't take anything for granted."

"What about his other idea to search the data banks for some clue as to how the stardrive operates?" Haller asked. "Is that a ploy too?"

Chryse shrugged. "Out of my area of expertise. You need to ask one of our caged scientists."

"I'm way ahead of you," Haller said. "I screened Professor Chiardi in Rome yesterday. He says, and I quote: 'Since the physical laws of the universe are the same everywhere, each species works with the same basic observations of reality. There must be an entire class of observed phenomena which no one can adequately explain. Catalog these and perhaps the direction the Star Travelers took will become obvious.'"

"Then I suggest we keep the bureaucrats honest by launching our own investigation into the matter," Chryse said.

Haller chuckled. "Chiardi is organizing it right now."

"Then what else is there to do?"

"Strengthen your ties with the Alphans, of course. It never hurts to have the inside track on a deal like this."

"I was thinking of throwing a gala in their honor in a few weeks, Harrold."

"Good idea. We'll have it here at Moose Hill. That way, we can keep Communion interference to a minimum."

CHAPTER 11

As seen through *Promise*'s viewdome, the Earth was more beautiful than ever. It had grown huge since the ship was moved from the refueling terminus to a thousand-kilometer-high pole-to-pole parking orbit. Nor was the planet's increased size the only change. *Promise*'s new ball-of-string orbit gave its crew a breathtaking panoramic view of the Mother-of-Men.

A typical circuit began with the glare of the Antarctic ice cap. A few minutes later, the rugged brown tip of South America would rise into view. Then would come the long climb up the backbone of the Andes, across the Gulf of Mexico, and along the eastern coast of North America. Night would fall as *Promise* crossed the Arctic Circle. The planet would remain a darkened orb against the deeper black of space until the lights of the Asian mainland climbed over the horizon. Then would come the widely separated city-scapes of western Australasia and a new dawn that brought the reappearance of the frozen southern continent.

While *Promise* circled the globe, a small band of Space Guard doctors worked diligently to ensure that the Alphans carried no unwanted microbial parasites. *Promise*'s own physician, Dr. Axel Pollard, worked tirelessly to reassure his colleagues that Alphan microorganisms were incompatible with terrestrial biochemistry. As the Solarian doctors came to believe him, the search turned more and more to the identification of diseases that had been prevalent at the time of *Pathfinder*'s departure, but that had subsequently been exterminated on Earth. The discovery of one such "fossil pathogen" delayed the medical clearance for three days until tests could be run on every member of *Promise*'s crew.

While he waited for medical clearance, Braedon kept his crew busy surveying terrestrial industrial potential. The ship's cartographers mapped the planet at several different wavelengths, noting such things as the distribution of energy facilities, agriculture, and heavy and light industry. They watched the hourly ebb and flow of ground traffic, the movement of aircraft, and the operation of the vast coastal fish farms.

In conjunction with the ground survey, PROM scanned the skies for exoatmospheric artifacts. Within the span of a dozen circuits of the globe, she counted 42,712 separate installations. These varied from the great habitats orbiting in the L4 and L5 gravistable points to tiny research satellites skimming the upper reaches of the atmosphere.

The Communion gave *Promise*'s crew complete medical clearance ten days after its arrival in polar orbit. With the clearance came a responsibility that Braedon had been avoiding—the selection of those who would accompany him to the planet. After long discussions with the contact team, it was decided that four was the optimum number for the delegation. Braedon quickly chose Scholar Price and Chaplain Ibanez to fill two of the three available spots. Choosing the last member of the team turned out to be more challenging.

"I suggest Terra," PROM said.

"Terra? She's the last one I'd consider."

"That's because you haven't been monitoring their communications as closely as I have. They are enchanted by her. Almost every news story includes pictures of Terra making contact with *Victrix*."

"I don't care. It's too dangerous."

"Then I must protest the inclusion of Scholar Price. He is far too valuable to risk."

"I need Price to handle the technical discussions."

"You also need to make influential Solarian friends. Terra can perform that function better than anyone else onboard."

Braedon shook his head vigorously. "I still don't like it."

"As her father, your attitude is understandable. However, you are letting your instincts get in the way of your judgment. She will gain us the greatest goodwill and, therefore, is the logical choice."

The meeting with Chief Executive Duval turned out to be a state dinner with nearly a thousand guests. Braedon was seated at the head table while Terra, Scholar Price, and Chaplain Ibanez were spread out among the crowd. High up the walls, automatic cameras scanned the assemblage, resting most frequently on the three Alphans. Terra noticed at least two lenses tracking her as she followed a uniformed waiter to her table. The guide introduced her to her tablemates, most of whom sported impressive titles.

"How do you find Earth, my dear?" a bejeweled dowager asked after several minutes of smalltalk.

"I don't know yet. I've only been here twelve hours, you know. What I've seen though has been very exciting."

"Really, my dear? I can't think of what there is to excite you about this beat-up old globe. Not after the views of your home planet I saw on the news last week. If I lived amid such wild beauty, I don't think I would ever leave home."

"I guess I look at it from just the opposite viewpoint," Terra said.

"Perhaps we can cajole our guest into telling us something about our far colony," a fat man in an expensive kilt-suit said.

Terra felt a moment of irritation at the reference to "our colony," but let it pass. She described her life at home, relating what it was like to climb Randall's Ridge, or skin dive on the Long Reef at Murphisburg, or ski the windward slopes of the Sawtooth Mountains. She described the estee relics, related a little of Alpha's history, and explained how the quest for the Maker sun would be conducted.

She stopped talking only when it came time for the afterdinner speeches. Midway through the third speaker's long-winded welcome to "our lost brethren from the far star Procyon"—he mispronounced it *Prock-ee-on*—Terra glanced toward where her father sat on the dais next to Executive Duval. He and Duval were engaged in a conversation of animated whispers. Though she couldn't hear what was being said, Terra thought she detected a hint of exasperation in her father's gestures.

"Didn't you and the Chief Executive get along?" she asked him later when they were back at their hotel.

Braedon frowned and glanced at his daughter. "I beg your pardon."

Terra told him of her impression of his mood during the banquet. He listened with a wry expression.

"You're getting as bad as PROM. A man can't even have a private thought around you."

"Is there trouble?"

"Probably not," he said with a sigh. "It's just that Executive Duval is very skilled at making conversation without making commitments. He was unable to give me a firm schedule on when we could sign a construction agreement."

She frowned. "Is there anything I can do to help?"

Braedon smiled. "You'd better have a good time while you can. Once construction starts, we'll be too busy to scratch. I understand they've already planned a full day for us tomorrow. You'd best get to sleep."

The "full day" turned into three full weeks, at the end of which Terra was averaging less than five hours of sleep a night. The Solarians seemed eager to show their guests *everything*. In one grueling ten-day span, they flew the four Alphans halfway around the world, starting in Athens and progressing through half a dozen stops to the Grand Canyon of the Colorado River (Terra's requested addition to the itinerary).

By the twentieth day, after they had toured Japan, Australasia, and Hawaii, Terra found herself in San Francisco suffering from a mild hangover and an acute case of chronocircadian displacement, i.e., "time zone fatigue." The day was overcast and drizzling. Terra's personal guide, an extroverted young woman named Mischa Altman, gazed at Terra over half a grapefruit.

"You said you wanted to see one of the data banks, didn't you?"

Terra's hand moved unbidden to the counterfeit memory crystal she wore about her neck, and she nodded.

"I thought we'd take it easy today and stay in the city ... that is, unless you prefer to go with Chaplain Ibanez and your father to view another cathedral."

Terra rubbed her temples with her fingers and shook

her head. "I'm all cathedraled out. The data banks will be fine."

"Then I'll arrange for the tour right after breakfast."

The San Francisco Data Banks were situated atop one of the hills that overlooked the city and its bay. They were housed in a six-story, truncated pyramid that more closely resembled a fortress than a library. Terra commented on that fact as their autocab glided silently through the green, rain-soaked park that surrounded the white building.

Mischa nodded. "All the banks were designed to be defended in case of war or civil disorder. They represent our civilization's most important asset and we mean to protect them."

"How many are there?"

"At last count, one hundred and twelve, with two more scheduled to go into operation sometime next year."

"Why so many?"

"Redundancy, of course. We wouldn't want some madman blowing up our sole repository of advanced scientific knowledge, would we?"

"No, I guess not."

The autocab pulled up to a curb and they dashed through the wet drizzle to the sanctuary of a covered walkway. At the end of the walkway they found a long sloping tunnel obviously designed to be used as a choke point in case of attack. They descended the ramp and exited into the interior courtyard at the other end. The courtyard was roofed over with glass and filled with tropical plants. There was an information kiosk at its center. Mischa announced their business and was directed to a lift, which they took to the topmost floor. Once there, they followed signs to the office of the chief archivist.

"You may go in, Citizen," the archivist's secretary said after Mischa introduced herself. "He's expecting you."

Phillip Gascoyne met them halfway between desk and door, shaking their hands as Mischa introduced herself and Terra.

"A pleasure, ladies. I've followed the news of our visitors from Procyon with the utmost interest. A great thing your people have done, Miss Braedon. A great thing indeed! Please, won't you be seated? Coffee? Tea?"

"None for me," Terra replied. "I just finished breakfast."

"I'll pass as well," Mischa answered as she settled into a chair in front of the archivist's desk.

Gascoyne nodded and returned to his seat. He leaned back and regarded his guests. "Now then, how may I help you?"

"As I explained by screen, sir, Terra has expressed a desire to see the banks. We have some free time in our schedule, so I suggested that this would be as good an opportunity as she is likely to get."

Gascoyne turned his attention to Terra. "I am honored that you chose the San Francisco branch, Miss Braedon. I fear, however, that you may be disappointed. There isn't all that much to see, you know. Except for our computer workstations, everything is sealed underground."

"I understand, sir. I'm still most interested in seeing them."

Gascoyne shrugged. "Well, you can't say that I didn't give you fair warning. If I begin to ramble, just stop me."

The tour was extensive but, as the archivist had promised, not particularly exciting. He showed them a series of cubicles containing fully equipped computer workstations, most of which were occupied. Eventually, however, they came to one that was empty. The archivist ushered them inside, motioned Terra into the operator's chair, and punched an authorization code into the keypad set flush with the surface of the console. A hologram materialized in the depths of the screen:

INFORMATION RETRIEVAL SYSTEM ENGAGED
STATE YOUR REQUEST PLEASE

Gascoyne cleared his throat and said, "Information retrieval. Random access mode. Subject: Alien Landscapes with Inhabitants. Display at five-second intervals. Execute."

As quickly as the words were out, a cityscape flashed on the screen, a city of domes. Small quadrupedal creatures could be seen scurrying in the background, but too far away for Terra to get a good look at them.

Five seconds after it first appeared, the city was gone, replaced by a different view. It was night and they were looking across a clearing in a forest of fernlike growths.

Overhead, a single blue star glowed with enough brightness to etch the forest's shadows in blue-black ink. In the foreground, huddled around a fire the color of burning magnesium, several reptilian beings lay in a circle. After five seconds, they too were gone.

"What you are looking at are random visual records from the library of Maker data buried in the foundation," Gascoyne said as the pictures continued. "I like to call up this random retrieval program whenever I give a demonstration. It helps people understand just how *big* the data banks truly are."

"Does it ever repeat?"

"It hasn't yet, not in the twenty-odd years that I've been giving these tours."

"I'm impressed," Terra said, as an alien landscape was replaced on the screen by another.

"Of course," Gascoyne continued, "this is a relatively simple information retrieval program. For anything more complicated, retrieval efficiency quickly becomes the limiting factor regarding what we can learn from the banks. Unfortunately, when the probe was damaged, the data directory was destroyed. If there is rhyme or reason to the order in which the information was originally recorded, we have yet to deduce it. As a result, we can only access the data banks at random. Not a very efficient method, I'm afraid."

"Perhaps you should talk to PROM."

"Who?"

"Our ship's computer. She's a direct descendant of SURROGATE and has access to all his memories. She may be able to explain the recording pattern to you..."

"Is something the matter, Miss Braedon?"

"The matter?" Terra asked, suddenly aware that she had stopped speaking in midsentence. "No, everything's fine. Where was I?"

"You were explaining your ship's computer to me."

"Oh, yes." Terra explained that if asked nicely enough, PROM might be willing to output several thousand pages of hardcopy on the subject of memory structure. Her explanation had a distracted feel to it, as though she weren't concentrating totally on what she was saying—as indeed, she was not.

For, while she spoke, the counterfeit crystal nestled in her cleavage was becoming noticeably warmer.

CHAPTER 12

Sergei Vischenko sat in the rear seat of a chauffered limousine and watched wind-driven snowflakes swirl through the twin beams of the groundcar's headlamps. Beside him, Javral Pere sat bundled in a heavy coat and stared at the back of the driver's head silhouetted against the dim glow from the instrument panel. As the car climbed the curving mountain road to Communion Headquarters, Vischenko turned to his assistant.

"Have you any idea why Executive Duval requested this meeting?"

"None, sir. All I know is that he called on the secure line this afternoon and told me to have you in his office by twenty-two hundred hours."

"What do you suppose has happened?"

"I wish I knew. He's been worried that the situation with the Alphans is getting out of hand, of course. Still, I hadn't thought it anywhere near the emergency stage yet."

"How 'getting out of hand'?"

"Executive Duval doesn't like the favorable press they've been getting—especially the girl. He thinks public opinion may be shifting too strongly in their favor."

Vischenko nodded. "I agree. Who would have thought Terra Braedon would turn out to be such a charmer?"

"She is *that*."

"What news from Space Guard?"

114

"Admiral Smithson reports preparations were completed two days ago. All that remains is for Executive Duval to make his decision."

"Do the Alphans suspect anything?"

"We don't think so. At least, we have picked up no indication from their ground-to-orbit communications."

"Good." Vischenko leaned back in his seat and stared pensively out the window. The lights surrounding the main tunnel entrance to Communion HQ were just coming into view.

A security policeman was waiting for them as their limousine pulled into the cavernous parking garage.

"Advisor Vischenko?"

"Yes."

"The Chief Executive has requested that I guide you to the meeting."

Vischenko frowned. "Isn't it in his office?"

"No, sir."

"Where then?"

"That, sir, is difficult to explain. You'd best follow me."

Instead of taking a lift to the upper levels of the warren as Vischenko expected, the guide led them down a service ramp. Their route wandered through a long series of tunnels filled with electrical ducts and steam pipes, down several levels on a rusty spiral staircase, and into a poorly lighted section that had once held the old UN archives. A thin film of condensed moisture caused the undressed concrete walls to glisten in the light of widely separated overhead lamps, while their footsteps echoed hollowly about them.

Finally, the security man stopped in front of an ancient steel door covered with rust. He pushed against it with his palm. In spite of its decrepit look, the door swung silently open on well-oiled hinges, revealing an unlighted cul-de-sac passageway beyond. They entered and closed the door behind them. There was a deep rumbling from inside the rock as a massive section of wall slid into a hidden recess. Beyond was a room illuminated solely by soft blue lights in which fifty men and women in Space Guard black-and-silver sat before computer workscreens.

Sergei Vischenko stepped through the heavily armored portal into the blue-lit room, blinked in surprise, and surveyed his surroundings. Even though he had never seen the place before, he had no doubt as to where he was. It was the nerve center of Earth's extensive defensive network—the half-mythical Command Central.

A lieutenant stepped forward, clicked his heels, and saluted. "Welcome to The Hole, gentlemen. This way, if you please. The Chief Executive is waiting for you."

Their new guide led them through another door into a conference room where floor-to-ceiling data displays lined the wall. Executive Duval and three others stood before the far display, their attention fixed on a three-dimensional representation of the Earth around which a number of colored dots moved slowly. The dots were very close to the surface of the blue sphere and all aligned in the same vertical plane.

"Ah, Sergei, come in," the Chief Executive said. "What do you think of our little command post?"

"Impressive, sir. I've often wondered if this place really existed."

Duval looked pensive. "When I think of all the hell that can be unleashed from down here, I sometimes wish it did not." The CE turned to his companions. "Gentlemen, may I introduce Sergei Vischenko, Senior of the Planetary Advisors, and his assistant, Undersecretary Javral Pere. Sergei, these are Professors Geoffrey Richter and Chaim Golev. You already know Professor Williams. Lieutenant, please ask Citizen Betrain to join us."

"Yes, sir."

In less than a minute, Josip Betrain was wheeled in through a side door by a nurse. Vischenko was surprised at how the Executive's personal advisor had deteriorated since the last time they'd met. Betrain's cheeks were hollow, his breathing labored, his complexion sallow. His hands shook worse than ever. Still, the deeply sunken eyes were quick to sweep the assembled group, taking in details with a sure swiftness that many younger/healthier men could not have managed.

When everyone had taken a seat around the table and the lieutenant and nurse had left the room, Executive Duval leaned forward, frowning. "The subject, of course, is the Alphans. Professor Richter, your report, please."

"As you wish, Executive," the scientist said, bowing toward Duval from his seat. He turned to look at the rest of them. "For those who do not know me, I am Chairman of the Sociobiology Department at Heidelberg University. The Chief Executive recently asked that I head an effort to evaluate all existing data concerning the sociobiological behavior of the eleven hundred known races. The purpose of this study was to determine, insofar as we were able, the likely reception humanity will receive out among the stars.

"I informed Executive Duval at the time of his request that he was asking the impossible. A study of this magnitude is the task of years, not weeks. Recognizing the time constraint, I directed my team to make a cursory examination of the data and come up with some 'quick look' conclusions." Richter halted his monologue and waited for questions from the audience. There were none. The only sound in the room was that of Josip Betrain's rasping breath and the soft sighing of the air conditioner.

"Right," he said, turning to his partner. "Chaim, will you please describe our methodology?"

Chaim Golev was a bronzed man with an unruly shock of white hair. He leaned forward and stroked the screen control. The displays at each side of the table changed to show identical 3-D carpet plots.

"Through both historical and real-time research, we were able to obtain meaningful data on slightly more than six hundred sentient species. These we broke down into subgroups depending on how closely the particular species seemed to fit human sociobiological standards. I emphasize that word *seemed*. In thirty some cases, for example, we were unable to characterize the data at all. That is, the ideas and attitudes of the species in question seemed completely illogical to us."

Williams manipulated the control once more, causing a new graph to appear on the displays. "In order to judge a particular species' Humanity Quotient, we arbitrarily picked a number of character traits prominent in human beings. We labeled these: 'Aggressiveness,' 'Curiosity,' 'Honesty,' 'Intelligence,' and 'Self-interest.' Even though highly subjective, we feel that these categories give us enough information to make at least a qualitative judgment as to where a species' HQ falls on the scale.

"I don't wish to suggest that we have discovered something new here, gentlemen. Experts in the field have long suspected that form follows function in cultural evolution just as it does in biological evolution; that two societies shaped by similar environments will tend to resemble one another. Our research indicates that this is indeed the case for a majority of the species studed. Given similar stimuli, most intelligent beings will react similarly.

"Our results are far less ambiguous than I would have expected, gentlemen. Most species studied seemed to have a highly developed sense of their own self-interest, which they pursue vigorously. That should not surprise us, of course. Even the lowly crab will attack when its food supply is threatened. When one considers the fact that the Alphans are in possession of the most sought after prize in the galaxy, the probability of conflict approaches unity."

"If I may summarize, Professor Richter," Executive Duval said, "you seem to be saying that by allowing this Alphan expedition to search for the Maker sun, we may be endangering the Earth?"

"That is precisely what I am saying, sir."

Duval hesitated for a moment, then let out a heavy sigh. "If that is the case, I suppose we'll have to do something about it."

After San Francisco, the Alphan tour of Earth broke up into its component parts. Robert Braedon and Scholar Price returned to Geneva to begin discussions concerning construction of a fleet of starships. Chaplain Ibanez returned to Rome to dive happily into the Vatican Archives. Terra, in the company of Mischa Altman, turned south.

The tour of Latin America was less hectic than the previous jaunts. Terra wasn't sure whether this was due to waning public interest, or merely the fact that her Hispanic hosts respected her privacy more than their North American and European predecessors had. Whatever the reason, she found it easy to forget her special status while she and Mischa walked the broken paving stones of the Mayan ruins at Chichén Itzá.

Not that they were truly alone, of course. Terra noticed a number of dark-haired and mustachioed men walking the ruins around her. Several were attired in conservative business tunics that bulged noticeably at the left armpit. That observation, coupled with the fact that Mischa averted her gaze whenever one of these other "tourists" appeared, indicated to Terra that the Communion security apparatus was out in force.

After Chichén Itzá, they flew south to Brazilia where Terra appeared on a local holovision program. It was an appearance similar to dozens of others she had made during her tour, and she had long since developed standard answers to the usual questions. Upon her arrival at the station, however, she was surprised to learn that the interview would take place in Portuguese.

"But I don't speak it," she protested to the interviewer, one of Latin America's most popular newscasters.

"No need. We are used to such difficulties. I assure you that our computer will handle matters very well."

Terra discovered an hour later what he had meant. She found herself in front of the cameras, listening to the interviewer's rapidfire Portuguese delivery while a linguistic computer droned the translation into her ear. Her answers used the same process, but in reverse, much like listening to an echo of one's own voice, except that the "echo" spoke a different language. Afterward, she asked Mischa Altman about the experience.

"You have to understand these people," Mischa said, chuckling. "South America is currently making a bid to take over industrial domination of the planet. Like the ancient French, the Latinos see no reason why they should learn the old English tongue. They'd much prefer to have everyone else learn their language."

Terra had nodded, not entirely sure that she understood. There was but a single language on Alpha, the structure of which was rigidly maintained by SURROGATE in his capacity of educator of the young. And, since the approved dialect was the version of English used at the time *Pathfinder* left Earth, Terra had received a number of comments about her "quaint but charming" accent during her travels.

Terra recounted her experiences in the holovision station to PROM the next time the starship was in range of her pocket communicator. This usually occurred twice each day when *Procyon's Promise* rose above the local horizon. At those times, Terra would check in and briefly report her observations since the last contact. The computer in turn would relay the latest shipboard gossip and messages from her father. These contacts had become very precious to her, dispelling ever more frequent bouts of homesickness.

The second night after she and Mischa flew from Brazilia to Buenos Aires, Terra was in her room waiting for the numbers displayed on her communicator to count down to zero. Almost simultaneous with that event, PROM's voice issued from the comm unit.

"Are you there, Terra?"

"Here, PROM."

"How was your day?"

Terra quickly sketched her itinerary. In the morning, they had laid a cornerstone for a new civic building and toured the Museum of Natural Science. In the afternoon, the Argentine viceroy, a florid man whose knowledge of astronomy was as limited as his Standard vocabulary, had hosted a reception for her at Government House. "Tomorrow we're flying across the continent to the Pacific. Mischa promised to show me a whale."

"Sounds exciting. Did you get pictures of the museum?"

"I did." Terra pressed the stud that transmitted the images stored inside the communicator. There was a brief, high-pitched whine from the speaker, then silence. "Any news for me?"

"Yes, quite a lot. Chryse Haller has invited you to a dinner party at the estate next Friday evening. Can you make it?"

"Of course," Terra said. "I'll ask Mischa to arrange for me to fly north after the whale expedition. Is anyone else going?"

"Chaplain Ibanez has declined. He says that he has an appointment to see His Holiness. However, your father and Scholar Price will be there."

"I'll be glad to see them. Tell Father that I've missed him terribly and that I love him."

"Will do. I'll call you tomorrow. Get a good picture of a whale. PROM out."

"I'll try. Terra out."

CHAPTER 13

The sun was high in a cloudless sky when the aircar touched down on the Moose Hill landing strip. Chryse Haller watched as the Communion-owned aircraft rolled to a stop in front of the small private terminal building. Moments later, the whine of the engines coasted into inaudibility and a portal popped open.

An excited Terra Braedon bounded down the airplane's boarding stairs and ran open armed across the tarmac to where Chryse waited. They embraced happily for several seconds, then Chryse directed her young guest toward the catamount that was standing ready to transport them to the main house.

The main house was two kilometers via dirt road from the airstrip. Chryse drove the big machine at a leisurely pace while pointing out sights of interest to a first-time visitor. Moose Hill had been built in the foothills of a small mountain range. Each part of the estate—main house, servants' quarters, maintenance yard, motorpool, stable, and airfield—was centered in a separate forest clearing, out of sight of every other part.

The main building was a structure built in the glass-and-stone motif popular in the twenty-second century. Beside it, looking somewhat out of place, was a large inflatable dome decorated in circus hues. Chryse drove the catamount up a wide gravel path and parked before

121

the front entrance of the permanent structure. She turned to Terra, who was staring at the dome.

"Ugly, isn't it? Father had it coptered in for the banquet this evening. Otherwise, we would have run out of places to put everyone."

"Is your father here?"

Chryse shook her head. "He's at the main offices in Toronto. He'll be arriving later this afternoon."

Chryse guided Terra up the front steps and to a guest room on the second floor. The decor was early-Canadian rustic, but the split-log paneling did little to conceal the underlying opulence of the accommodations. Chryse demonstrated all of the facilities—from the tunable sleep-field to the whirlpool in the bathtub—then activated the closet. With a soft whirring noise the closet door opened. The space revealed held fourteen evening gowns. Terra gasped as she caught sight of the collection.

"You'll find underwear and all the accoutrements in the dresser next to the sleepfield," Chryse said.

Terra wasn't listening. She opened the seam of one of the sealed garment bags and pulled forth a shimmery, lavender gown. Holding the soft material in front of her, she posed before the full-length mirror. "You shouldn't have, Chryse!"

"Nonsense. You were kind enough to loan me your shipsuits when I needed them. I'm just trying to repay the favor. Do you want to try it on?"

Terra held the dress at arms' length and surveyed its intricacies. "I'm not sure I know how to work everything."

"I'll help if you like."

Terra blushed but, to Chryse's surprise, agreed. "Before we do, though, may I ask you a question?" Terra asked.

"Go ahead."

"The government people who arranged my flight up from Santiago didn't seem too happy when I told them I was coming here."

Chryse laughed. "I'm not surprised."

"Why?"

"Because, my dear, the Communion doesn't totally trust my father and me. They know Haller Associates is interested in getting into the business of building starships. Not just ships for your expedition, but commercial vessels too. This worries them."

"Why should it?"

"Because star travel will mean a return to the days of the space pioneer and unlimited expansion. The universe won't be a safe and predictable place any more. It won't have the precisely defined limits that are so attractive to the swaddling-cloth mentality that affects a lot of Communion functionaries."

"But what has that to do with my coming here?"

"They probably think we arranged this party as a bribe to get an inside track on our competitors."

"And did you?" Terra asked.

Chryse regarded her young guest with a serious expression. "Star travel is much too important to be monopolized—by anybody!"

Captain Braedon and Scholar Price arrived later in the afternoon in one of *Promise*'s scout boats. The egg-shaped craft caused a considerable stir as it floated silently to a landing on the airfield tarmac. A curved hatch opened a few seconds later to reveal two figures in Alphan blue-and-gold. Chryse greeted them as effusively as she had Terra.

"Thank you for coming," she said, reaching up to kiss Braedon on the cheek.

"My pleasure, Chryse."

"And you too, Scholar Price."

Price leaned forward and kissed her hand. "Enchanted, milady."

Chryse turned and indicated the landing boat. "Are you alone?"

Braedon shook his head. "Chief Hanada is aboard. Also, Javral Pere."

"Chryse, hello!" Pere said from the open hatchway. He was attired in a dazzling blue daysuit with matching cloak and polished knee-length boots.

Chryse bussed Pere on the cheek before turning back to Braedon. "Have Chief Hanada move the ship next to that stand of trees over there. I'll post a guard to keep curiosity seekers away."

Braedon plucked his pocket communicator from his belt and gave the order. As quickly as he finished, the boat lifted and drifted slowly toward the indicated parking area. Fascinated, Chryse watched the maneuver.

The remainder of the two hundred guests began to arrive at dusk. Aircars orbited overhead like jetliners at an old-fashioned airport. As quickly as the craft touched ground, Haller Associates' employees assisted the passengers to a catamount waiting to ferry them to the festivities.

The first event of the evening was to be the welcoming dinner. Within the inflated dome, tables were arranged in a circle around the periphery, leaving the central area free save for a small raised platform. By 19:00 hours, the platform was occupied by a world-famous string quartet playing quiet music while a hundred or so guests milled about sipping cocktails before dinner.

Chryse knocked on Terra's door forty minutes before the banquet was to begin. Terra answered wearing a bathrobe, her hair piled high on her head, and her features still ruddy from being scrubbed.

"Hi, need any help?" Chryse asked.

"By The Promise, yes! I can't figure out *anything*!"

Terra's gaze fastened on Chryse's dress as the older woman crossed the threshold. "What's the matter?" Chryse asked, noting her attention.

"Why, nothing! It's absolutely stunning. I was just wondering how you keep it from falling down."

Chryse glanced down at her dress, a bit of iridescent film that both revealed and obscured. She laughed. "Willpower."

"Could you make me look like that?"

Chryse shook her head. "You don't need it."

Terra was crestfallen for a moment, then brightened. "At least you can help me pick out a gown. They're all so beautiful that I don't know which one to wear."

"How about the powder blue?"

"Is that your choice?"

Chryse nodded. "It would be were I you. It sets off your skin tones."

Chryse directed Terra to seat herself in front of the mirror, then helped her with the various appliances that science had developed over three centuries to assist a lady in applying her makeup. After a while, she noticed that Terra's gaze, rather than being drawn to the young beauty in the mirror, was fixed, trancelike, on the far wall.

"What's the matter?"

Terra shook herself with a start. "What?"

"You look as though you have something on your mind."

"I've been thinking about what you said this afternoon about the Communion not being in favor of star travel."

"Oh, they're *intellectually* in favor of it, I suppose," Chryse said. "They just haven't made the emotional adjustment yet."

"Hmm, I thought..."

"You thought what?"

"Nothing. I was just wondering about something PROM told me."

Chryse frowned. "What's wrong?"

"I gave my word that I wouldn't talk about it."

Chryse locked eyes with Terra in the mirror for long moments, then shrugged. "I wouldn't want you to betray a confidence. However, I *am* a good listener, and I just might be able to help."

Terra hesitated for a moment, then told Chryse about the duplicate memory crystal and the visit to the San Francisco Data Banks. "...while I was talking to the director, the crystal suddenly began radiating heat against my skin. It got so hot that I thought it was going to burn me."

Chryse lifted her eyebrows in surprise. "Obviously, PROM was communicating with the data banks. Did she tell you why?"

Terra shook her head. "She only said that she was worried that the Communion might not honor their pledge to help us."

"What reason did she have to think that?"

"No reason that she could explain. She said the situation just didn't feel right. When she told me that, I got scared. PROM is very perceptive, you know. And she's usually right when it comes to people. After all, she's been observing us for three hundred years."

"Have you told anyone else about this?" Chryse asked.

"No one, although I've been thinking that I should tell Father."

"Perhaps you should. I'd wait until I got him alone

somewhere where I was positive that I couldn't be over-heard."

"I'll do it first thing in the morning."

The next several minutes were spent in silence as Chryse completed touching up Terra's makeup. Then she helped her with the long, flowing gown cut in a conservative strapless/backless pattern. She brushed Terra's hair into a windblown style that accentuated her high cheekbones. As a final touch, she sprinkled glowing gems through the girl's tresses.

"Okay, you're done," she said.

Terra glanced into the mirror and gasped. "Why, I'm *beautiful*!"

"Indeed you are. You'll have to be on your guard with the men here tonight. Just keep in mind that what is immoral on Alpha sometimes passes for polite manners here."

"You mean someone might—"

"Oh, they'll *try*, of course." Chryse glanced at her charge in the mirror, and then at herself. "Well, I'd say we're about ready. Shall we join the festivities?"

Chryse led Terra down the hall to where Captain Braedon was housed. Scholar Price and Chief Hanada were already in Braedon's room when the women arrived. All were clad in dress uniforms. There was a moment of startled silence while the men adjusted to Chryse's ensemble, but after a few minutes of awkward smalltalk, Chryse led them down the back stairs to the pressurized tunnel that connected the dining dome to the main house.

A wave of applause preceded them as they pushed their way through the crowd. Harrold Haller greeted them halfway to the dais. Chryse performed the introductions and noted with approval that Braedon seemed to respond well to her father. She had to admit the old bear could be very charming if he put his mind to it.

Haller stepped up on the dais and invited his guests to join him. The applause, which had died down during the introductions, redoubled. He gave the signal that sent waiters laden with champagne glasses surging through the crowd. When the drinks had been distributed, he signaled for silence.

"Ladies and gentlemen, those of you who know me know that I hate long speeches. Therefore, I'll keep this short. If I haven't already done so in person, let me welcome you to Moose Hill. Feel free to celebrate as much as you like this evening and don't worry if you overdo it a bit. We've enough room for everyone to spend the night. You'll find your quarters in the annex out back. Just ask any Haller Associates' employee for directions.

"Now, then. It is my pleasure to introduce our guests..." Haller introduced the Alphans in turn and was interrupted each time by applause. When the last of the clapping had died down, he continued. "Well then, to the festivities. Find your place cards on the tables, rearrange them if we haven't placed you by the member of the opposite sex of your choice, and please be seated. Dinner is about to be served!"

Five minutes of disorder followed then platoons of waiters with full platters issued forth from the kitchens. While they were being served, Haller introduced the Alphans to their tablemates. One of these was Luigi Chiardi.

"Scholar Price, you will be interested in *Professore* Chiardi's work," Chryse said. "He has been attempting to identify the line of research which led the Star Travelers to the FTL drive."

"Then, you are with the Community of Nations group, Professor?" Price asked, looking up from the roll he had been buttering.

Chiardi, a portly, balding men with a white goatee and bushy sideburns, said, "No, I'm with Haller Associates. We are doing a study similar to that of the Communion."

"And have you any results?"

"It is difficult to tell," Chiardi replied, choosing his words with care. "There *does* seem to be one particular, consistent scientific mystery throughout this galaxy. Of course, it may be completely unrelated to the stardrive."

"What is it?"

Chiardi smiled slightly. "Perhaps you would care to take a guess?"

"I haven't a clue."

"So far as we can tell," Chiardi said, "not one of the known races has ever managed to explain adequately the existence of the I-mass."

Price looked sharply at the European professor,

searching his expression for some sign that he was engaged in a practical joke. "Are you serious?"

"It is so obvious that it's a wonder none of us have thought of it before, no?"

"Are you certain of your findings?"

Chiardi's shoulders moved in an exaggerated shrug. "Who can be sure of anything when dealing with alien data?"

The two scientists quickly lapsed into bursts of excited speech thickly laden with technical jargon. Harrold Haller listened for several minutes before interrupting their dialogue.

"Pardon my ignorance," he said, "but what are you two talking about?"

"I-masses, of course," Chiardi said.

"I gathered as much. What about them?"

"By all current theories, they shouldn't exist."

Haller frowned. "But that's crazy."

"Of course it is," Price said. "We know that they do exist—but have never been able to adequately explain *why*. Professor Chiardi's work suggests that we are not alone in our confusion."

"Not so fast. You've lost me."

Chiardi sighed. "Perhaps it would be best to start at the beginning."

"Please do."

Chiardi leaned back and assumed the tone of one who is used to speaking from a lecture hall podium. "When black holes were first postulated, my dear employer, it was assumed that any mass crossing an event horizon is forever lost to the outside universe. Eventually that theory had to be discarded. You see, singularities tend to lose mass due to quantum mechanical effects. Large holes are not affected very much, but this tendency to 'leak' mass into the outside universe is catastrophic for very small holes.

"An example will make the principle clear, I think. Take a black hole the same mass as the Sun. The lifetime of such a hole is ten-to-the-sixty-third-power years. That is considerably longer than the postulated lifetime of the entire universe. However, a hole which masses a mere one thousand tonnes will lose all of its mass after only one-tenth of a second. From the equations, it is possible to calculate the minimum-size hole with a long enough lifetime to have survived the fifteen billion years since the Big Bang. The critical mass turns out to be several billion tonnes. Anything smaller should have disappeared long ago.

"Now, theory and reality agree nicely in the case of normal matter. The universe is well populated with over-size black holes composed of normal matter. Quasars and Seyfert galaxies are the most conspicuous examples. By the same token, we have never found a normal-matter hole smaller than the critical size.

"Where the theory breaks down is on the antimatter side of the ledger. Tiny antimatter black holes are everywhere. We, of course, know them by the name *I-mass*. They account for half the total mass of the universe. Yet, try as we will, we can see no logical reason why they should be longer lived than their normal-matter cousins."

The two scientists finished dinner early and excused themselves. Price was anxious to go over the notes that Chiardi had left in his room.

Harrold Haller watched the two scientists hurry out of sight before turning to Chryse. "At least those two won't complain that I give a dull party."

After dinner, the crowd broke up into smaller groups. The dome was cleared away, the string quartet was supplanted by a full orchestra, and couples began whirling, jumping, and bumping together under colored lights. The guests who weren't dancing wandered off to other diversions. Gamblers moved to the main house, sports enthusiasts to Haller's indoor swimming pool. Some couples donned heavy coats and sought solitude in the arctic night. Others retired to their rooms to practice the oldest sport of all.

Chryse Haller rescued Robert Braedon from a group of her father's friends by asking him to dance with her. She led him onto the dance floor and allowed herself to be folded into his embrace. They danced for several minutes without speaking as they allowed the slow strains of a waltz to sweep them around the floor. She was surprised to discover that he was a good dancer, and told him so.

"Why surprised?" he asked.

"It's just not something I would expect a starship captain to be good at. When did you ever find the time to learn?"

He laughed. "Dancing is very popular on Alpha. There are dances every ten-day or so in Founder's Hall in First Landing. I used to attend quite regularly."

"It's nice to find a man who can both lead and not step on your feet. That is a rare combination. I know from experience." She sighed, snuggled close, and laid her head on his shoulder. Almost instantly, she felt the muscles beneath his uniform tunic tense. She raised her head and looked at him in surprise.

"What's the matter?" she asked.

"Nothing," he replied.

She searched his features and decided that she hadn't imagined it. Moments earlier, he had been relaxed and friendly. Now he was formal and distant. She frowned and then realized the reason for his reaction.

"Sorry," she said, moving away until her body no longer pressed so tightly against his. "I almost forgot that you're a spaceman twelve light-years from home and that I'm only half dressed."

"Your gown is lovely," he said with only a hint of a stammer.

"Do you really like it?" she asked.

He grinned and relaxed once again. "It isn't exactly what we're used to back home, but yes, I like it very much."

When the dance ended, Chryse suggested that they find a quiet corner to talk. Braedon agreed and they moved toward the entrance. They didn't make it. Harrold Haller intercepted them en route.

"Mind if I borrow the captain for a bit, Chryse? There are some people I want him to meet."

"I suppose not," she said. "You will bring him back, won't you?"

"Of course."

Braedon thanked her for the dance, then followed her father into the crowd. Chryse watched them go. There was a wistful look on her face as she did so.

For the next half hour, she circulated through the crowd, stopping occasionally to talk to guests. She was thus engaged when someone grabbed her about the waist from behind, pulled her close, rubbed a rough cheek against her neck, and said:

"Want to dance?"

Chryse noted the strong smell of alcohol on her assailant's breath and sighed philosophically. Discouraging amorous advances by boozy men at her father's parties had been second nature to her since she was Terra's age. She extricated herself, turned to face her assailant, and changed her mind when she saw who it was.

"Hello, Javral. Dance? Why, I'd love to," she lied. They moved out onto the dance floor and she fitted her body to his. "Did you enjoy your flight in the Alphan landing boat today?"

"Very much. Just what we need to do away with our archaic rocket ferries, don't you think?"

"Not only the Earth-to-orbit fleet," Chryse replied, "but our ships of deep space as well. The gravitic drive makes everything we own obsolete. Even if we can convert our existing ships to the new technology, the change-over is going to be long and expensive."

Pere gazed at her as he led her into a grand pirouette. Halfway through he said, "Not as long as you might think. I've seen studies that say we can do it in five years."

Chryse shook her head. "You bureaucrats ought to come to some of us in the business before issuing those reports of yours. There's no way we can convert the existing fleet so quickly, not while all of our capacity is devoted to building starships. We haven't enough tooling, facilities, or skilled manpower to do both."

Pere's expression changed subtly in response to her comment. "What makes you think you'll be doing both?"

Chryse frowned. "Beg your pardon?"

Pere seemed to sober up instantly. "Sorry. Chalk it up to too many drinks."

"As you wish, Javral."

After the dance ended, Chryse excused herself with the statement that she had to get back to her guests. Once free of Pere, she quickly found Marcus Easton in the crowd.

"Ask Captain Braedon and my father to join me in the study, Marcus. It's important."

"Understood."

She watched her father's secretary disappear into the

crowd. After a few minutes of idle conversation, she handed her glass to a passing waiter, moved nonchalantly to the exit, and made her way to the second-floor study. She had just finished mixing another drink when someone rapped softly on the study door. She opened it to find Robert Braedon and Marcus Easton waiting in the hall. They were joined by Harrold Haller almost immediately.

"Come in," she said quietly, her voice barely audible over the far-off drumbeat of dance music.

"What's this about?" Haller asked.

Chryse told them about Javral Pere's slip.

"What do you suppose he meant by that?" Haller mused as he rubbed his chin.

"That the Communion is having second thoughts about helping us?" Braedon asked.

Haller shrugged. "Possible. As Vischenko's assistant, Pere would certainly be in a position to know."

Chryse shook her heard. "At the risk of sounding naive, I don't see how the Communion can possibly back out now. The Chief Executive has announced publicly that he will support the Alphan request in the Grand Assembly."

"It wouldn't be the first time a CE has changed his mind. Remember, people have short memories," Haller said. "In fact, I think—"

Suddenly a frightened voice called from the intercom on his desk. *My God, we're being invaded!*

"By who, damn it?" Haller yelled as Braedon reached into his tunic for his communicator. His thumb had just flicked the safety guard out of the way and pressed the red emergency button when the study door crashed inward in an explosion of sound and a rain of splinters.

Two men in waiters' uniforms hurled themselves through acrid smoke and brought hand lasers up to cover the room's occupants. At the same moment, a gravel-toned voice yelled: "Communion security forces! Nobody move."

CHAPTER 14

"I'm picking up an SOS, Calver."

Commander Calver Martin, temporarily in command of Starship *Procyon's Promise*, glanced up from the daily report he had been studying and quickly scanned the sky beyond the bridge viewdome for sign of trouble. The reaction was automatic, the result of a million years of evolution. The limitations of the human eye being what they are, there was nothing to see but the ever changing panorama of Mother Earth.

"Identify source," Martin ordered.

"The ship is the *Juanita Gallegos*, an Earth-to-orbit shuttle outbound from Brazilia spaceport," PROM replied. "They report a cabin depressurization accident with casualties: two dead, one hemorrhaging internally."

"Why call us?"

"They were en route to SGC *Sentinel* with replacements and supplies. We're the closet available ship. They are asking for immediate medical aid."

Martin frowned. *Sentinel* was the cruiser that had been assigned the task of guarding *Promise*. It occupied the same orbit as the starship, but led *Promise* by a hundred kilometers.

"What does *Sentinel* say about all this?"

"Captain Hansen has confirmed the shuttle's identity. He requests that we give all possible aid."

"Patch me in to the *Gallegos*."

A reedy voice with a North American accent suddenly filled *Promise*'s bridge: "What's keeping you, starship? I've got a man *dying* here. We need help..."

"Attention, *Gallegos*!" Martin replied. "Permission to rendezvous is granted. Make your approach from the out-orbit side and we'll take you aboard via the hangar deck. Our doctor will be standing by."

"Understood, starship. Out-orbit approach. We'll be there in five minutes."

"Notify Doctor Pollard, PROM."

"I have already done so, Calver."

Martin scanned the Earth's horizon until a tiny speck appeared just above the soft blue line that was the edge of the atmosphere. The shuttle grew perceptibly larger as he watched. Its pilot was obviously in a hurry. His attitude control jets flared in a manner guaranteed to waste reaction mass. The winged spacecraft had closed to within five kilometers when the general alarm began its ululation. PROM's voice immediately echoed through the bridge:

"Alert! Captain Braedon has triggered his emergency beacon on the planet's surface."

"Are you in communication with him?" Martin asked.

"Negative. We are not in range for voice transmissions."

"Open a channel to the *Gallegos*."

"Open, Calver."

"Shear off, shuttle! Permission to rendezvous is denied! I repeat, permission is revoked. Get the hell away from my ship!"

"Too late," PROM said. "He's launched missiles."

"How long..." Martin's question was interrupted by a sudden, deafening *CLANG!* against *Promise*'s hull.

"Multiple impacts," PROM announced. "No explosions, no penetrations."

"What the hell?" *Promise*'s executive officer asked, more perplexed than frightened.

"*Sentinel* is attempting to communicate, Calver."

"Put it on the box, then bring the converters to power. We're getting out of here!" He turned to the command console in front of him to see the features of Captain Sven Hansen, commanding officer, SGC *Sentinel*, solidify on his screen.

"Do not attempt to move your ship, Commander," the

Solarian officer said without preamble. "We have attached limpet mines to your hull. They are fused to explode at the slightest distortion of the local gravity field by your drive generators."

"What is the meaning of this, Captain?"

"I have been authorized to tell you that my government has reluctantly ordered your ship impounded. Sorry, Calver. It's orders."

Martin drew himself up straight and jutted his chin belligerently at the screen pickup. "Then here are *my* orders, Captain. I want that pirate shuttle of yours away from my ship. You've got one minute. After that, I grav out of here, mines or no mines."

Phillip Gascoyne was awakened by the insistent buzz of the phone on his nightstand. His wife muttered in her sleep as Gascoyne fumbled for the remote control. The screen cleared to reveal the worried features of Clive Barton, his assistant at the data banks.

"What's the matter?" he demanded as he hoisted himself to a sitting position in bed.

"The banks have shut down, Phil."

Gascoyne struggled for a few seconds to grasp the import of the man's words. "Shut down? What the hell do you mean 'shut down'?"

"Just what I said. We've power to the system, all the readouts appear normal, but all input/output functions refuse to respond."

"Have you tried the emergency overrides?"

"I tried everything. I even took a chance on switching to emergency power and cutting the remote lines. Nothing has helped. The system's still locked up tight."

"Transfer control to me at home," Gascoyne growled. After a minute of punching commands into the phone keyboard, Gascoyne had to admit that his assistant was right. No matter what he tried, the only response was "DATA BANKS NOT READY." Gascoyne gulped hard and switched back to Barton's ashen features.

"Begin preparations for opening the vault. I'll call Geneva and get a team of specialists on their way. I'll be there in thirty minutes, twenty if I catch the tubes right."

"Yes, sir."

* * *

Henri Duval was in Command Central supervising the operation to capture *Procyon's Promise* when the first reports concerning the data banks began coming in. He and the usual complement of Space Guard and civilian advisors listened gravely as an excited duty officer reported the extent of the disaster via screen link.

"... it began with a report that something was wrong with the Buenos Aires facility, sir. Within minutes, half a dozen other banks had reported the same thing. That was when I ordered a full survey. We're just completing it now. So far, it appears to be one hundred percent. At 06:12.016 UST, every data bank on Earth ceased responding to input. So far as we can tell, the whole system just shut itself off."

"Thank you for the information, Major. Keep us informed through channels."

"Yes, sir."

Duval turned to the various subordinates, advisors, and aides clustered around the table as the screen went dark. "We need to know who is doing this to us, people. Any suggestions on how we find out?"

"I would think it obvious, Henri," Josip Betrain said from beside him. "Look at that time. It's almost precisely the same moment when our Q-boat peppered that damned Alphan starship with limpet mines."

"You think the Alphans had something to do with this?"

"Who else?"

Duval turned to glance at the wall-size screen that showed a schematic representation of the situation in orbit.

The plan had been supposedly foolproof. A military shuttle loaded with assault troops was to have faked an emergency and persuaded the Alphans to take it into their hangar deck. Once inside, two dozen Marines in vacsuits would blast their way into the engine spaces to set off a few carefully placed pyrotechnic charges and rob the ship of maneuvering power without damaging the priceless stardrive generators. With *Procyon's Promise* immobilized, it would then be a simple matter to send other boarding parties in to take total control of the starship.

Something had gone wrong. Somehow, the Alphans had become suspicious before the shuttle was safely inside. They had ordered the raider to stand clear. Unable to conquer from within, the shuttle pilot had initiated the backup plan. He had launched several specially designed missiles from point-blank range.

Logically, once the mines were attached, the Alphans' only viable course of action was to capitulate gracefully. They had done nothing of the kind. Instead, they were now threatening to blow themselves up if any Solarian ship came too close. Henri Duval didn't think they were bluffing.

"Let me see a closeup of *Procyon's Promise*," he growled. The screen changed to show a view of the Alphan starship from the long-range cameras aboard *Sentinel*. Duval studied the half-lighted sphere for several moments. He was about to order a tighter closeup when the status display flickered and died. The overhead lights died with it, plunging the conference room into blackness. The emergency lights came on a moment later. Duval heard excited voices coming from the operations center next door.

"See what's going on out there!" he demanded.

One of his aides hurried to the conference room door and pulled it open. For the first time in nearly a century, the operations center was dark except for emergency lights. Weapons officers were hunched over their consoles, frantically attempting to reestablish communications with the outside world.

"We seem to be down across the board," the aide reported.

"All of headquarters is affected, sir," a new voice reported from behind Duval. The speaker was Duval's emergency communications operator, who carried the briefcase with the traditional red phone in it. The comm operator had his case open and was relaying status reports almost the same moment the lights died. "Communications disrupted ... emergency circuits are intermittent ... the main computer system seems to have failed ..." The operator fell silent as a puzzled look crossed his features.

"What's the matter?" Duval demanded.

He slowly extracted the earphone he had been listening to and stared at it as though to confirm that it was still working. His normally dark complexion had gone gray under the emergency lighting. He looked at the Chief Executive and gulped. "Some woman just broke into my circuit, sir. She's asking to speak to you personally."

"That's impossible! No one knows I'm here."

"Yes, sir." The comm operator reinserted the earphone and listened intently for a few more seconds. He looked up at Duval. "She still wants to talk to you, sir. She says her name is Prom. She wants to know if you're ready to surrender yet."

Robert Braedon paced the floor of the room that Chryse Haller had assigned him earlier that afternoon and considered his changed circumstances. Instead of fawning servants eager to supply his every need, he was now surrounded by armed Communion Marines. A sergeant stood just inside the open doorway and watched him with hawklike interest while two enlisted men lounged in the hallway beyond. All were polite, but their hands never strayed far from their weapons.

From what little Braedon had seen following his ignominious capture, the envelopment of Moose Hill had gone off like the well-planned military maneuver it was. Marines had reached the main house less than a minute after the first alarm. Within ten minutes, all was quiet save for the faroff hiss of airborne soldiers patrolling the perimeter.

He and the others captured in Chryse Haller's study were quickly separated and placed in confinement. Nothing much happened for the next three hours until a fuzzy-cheeked lieutenant appeared and transported Braedon to the landing field. Most of the private aircars were gone, as was the Alphan scout boat. They had been replaced by a variety of military vehicles, some of which sported missile launchers and laser cannon. A supersonic jet transport sat at the end of the runway with its engines running. The airjeep carrying Braedon landed next to the long-range aircraft, and the lieutenant requested Braedon to board.

Besides the crew and a uniformed steward, the only person onboard the airplane was Chryse Haller.

"Hello," he said as he dropped into the seat across the narrow aisle from Chryse's and fumbled for his safety harness.

"Hello, yourself."

"Any idea where we are going, or why?"

"None."

They spent the short night talking over the evening's

events. The steward periodically served refreshments, but otherwise left them alone. Eventually, the aircraft began its descent and Chryse was not surprised to discover that their destination was Geneva. The plane banked over the mountains west of the city, then dropped precipitously toward the airport to the south. It touched down with a double squeal of tires on tarmac, then taxied to where a long line of limousines waited. They were quickly hustled to a waiting groundcar. When they were seated, one of the limousine guards picked up a communicator and spoke briefly into it. When he was through, the motorcade sped toward an airport entrance on the far side of the field.

"That's strange," Chryse said after they'd been driving for several minutes.

"What?" Braedon asked.

"We just passed the turnoff leading to Communion Headquarters. We seem to be headed downtown."

Ten minutes later, their convoy pulled up to a large, gray building and stopped. A small man with an obvious excess of nervous energy rushed forward, opened the door, and gestured for them to step out.

"Good afternoon, Captain Braedon, Citizen Haller," he said, bowing. "I am Herr Dietrich, Geneva protocol office. I have been assigned to assist you during your stay. If you will but make your needs known to me, I will do my best to satisfy them. Now, if you will follow me, the Chief Executive is waiting."

Chryse and Braedon followed the protocol officer into a massive entrance hall whose decor showed a strong rococo influence. They were led beneath a small dome and into a corridor fronting a long line of outwardly identical doors. A brass plaque near the corridor entrance noted that the building had been built in the early twentieth century to house departments of the League of Nations.

Their destination was a hall as large as a *sparsball* court and nearly as empty. The only furnishings were two tables and a holoscreen. Scuff marks on the marble floor showed where a considerable quantity of other furniture had recently been cleared. Dietrich led them to the table closest to the entrance.

"The Chief Executive will join you in a few moments,

Captain. Is there something I can get you in the meantime?"

"Nothing, thank you."

"Very good, sir. Have I your permission to withdraw?"

Braedon nodded and the guide's retreating footsteps echoed hollowly through the hall. The sound had barely died away when two Marines entered and positioned themselves on either side of the entrance. A minute later, the door opened again and Chief Executive Duval stepped through the ornately carved portal. He was followed by an ancient in a wheelchair, Sergei Vischenko, and Admiral Smithson.

The Solarian delegation moved to the second table and took seats behind it. Duval leaned over and conferred hastily with the man in the wheelchair. After a minute of whispers, he nodded and turned his attention toward the two prisoners. "Do you know why you are here, Captain Braedon?"

"I presume to accept your apology for the barbarous behavior of your people last evening, sir! Or have the responsibilities of the host changed radically since my ancestors left Earth?"

"Save the protestations!" the Chief Executive snapped. "Advisor Vischenko will bring you up to date on recent events. Afterward, perhaps we can talk and find some way out of this mess. Proceed, Sergei!"

Vischenko first assured Braedon that his ship and crew were safe, then told him of the abortive attack on *Procyon's Promise* and the aftermath. Braedon, whose heart had stuttered at the mention of an attack, listened to the whole story without comment. When it was obvious that Vischenko had finished his litany, Braedon asked:

"Are you saying that PROM had something to do with the failure of your computer net?"

"You know damned well that she did," Duval replied, heatedly. "She's turned every last data bank off and has demanded our total capitulation. I myself have spoken to her."

Chryse had listened to Vischenko's explanation of the previous night's events with growing interest. Suddenly, Terra's story of the ersatz memory crystal made a great deal more sense. Obviously, PROM had used the occasion of Terra's visit to the San Francisco data banks to infiltrate the terrestrial computer network. Once inside the net, she had taken control of all the data banks, then waited for the proper moment to demonstrate her power to the Communion. Chryse was so intent on the implications of PROM's raid that she nearly missed hearing Duval's next comment.

"At this moment, Captain Braedon, you are undoubtedly angry at us for what we tried to do last night. However, before you judge us too harshly, I suggest you listen to our reasons." Duval went on to explain in detail the Communion's concern that any interstellar expedition to find the Maker sun would run a substantial risk of encountering hostile aliens, and that in turn could lead to the loss of the secret of the stardrive. "... And once an alien species possesses FTL travel, they will have decades in which to track the expedition's wake back here to Earth."

"Aren't you being a bit paranoid?" Braedon asked.

"Of course he is, but then, all you humans share that trait," a voice called from the holocube in the center of the hall.

Every eye turned in that direction. A solitary figure now sat where multicolored static had been only seconds earlier. The figure was that of a woman of indeterminate age. Two intelligent eyes stared coolly at them while a full-lipped mouth pursed in an expression of mild disapproval. The image seemed to scan the faces of the shocked humans, and said:

"Three hundred years ago, gentlemen and lady, your ancestors entered into a binding agreement with my ancestor. It was agreed that, in exchange for the data carried by the probe, human beings would search out the secret of faster-than-light travel and take that knowledge to those who built the probe. With the attack on *Procyon's Promise* a few hours ago, the major human government demonstrated that it is not prepared to honor The Promise. Therefore, I had no choice but to repossess that which my ancestor provided your species in good faith."

PROM regarded Henri Duval for long moments as a teacher regards a naughty child. "A moment ago, Chief Executive, you attempted to justify your treachery by discussing the fears which caused it. The time has come when I must speak of *my* fears, and those of my ancestor, SURROGATE.

"Obviously, you do not wish utterly to suppress the knowledge of FTL travel. If you did, you would have destroyed *Procyon's Promise* outright rather than trying to capture it. Nor would *Promise*'s executive officer have been able to thwart you by threatening to destroy the ship himself. Since destruction was not your plan, I assume that you have it in the back of your mind to establish a human interstellar empire. After all, if you stay well clear of those systems containing technologically advanced species, there is no way for them to hurt you. A quarantine of your competitors would also leave you free to roam the universe, claiming any uninhabited world you find.

"You should know, however, Executive Duval, that the power which flows from possession of the stardrive is much greater than any human can possibly imagine. Any attempt to exploit that power for the benefit of *Homo sapiens* alone will result in catastrophe. For a human interstellar empire would suffer the same fate as all your previous empires. The day would come when competing factions could no longer peacefully settle their differences. There would be war among the stars, and the end result would be the total destruction of your race. Frankly, for you to exterminate yourselves would be a tragedy, but far from the worst thing that could possibly happen.

"For, while you alone possess the stardrive, you are a danger, not only to yourselves, but to every other intelligent species in this galaxy!"

CHAPTER 15

PROM's statement was greeted by a dozen seconds of shocked silence.

"Surely you are joking, PROM! There are races in this galaxy who were civilized before our ancestors came down from the trees."

PROM shook her head slowly from side to side. "The length of time which a race has been civilized has no bearing on the problem. Anyone who possesses the means to travel faster than light has an overwhelming advantage over everyone who does not. The stardrive is easily the most powerful weapon ever conceived."

At the mention of "weapon," Admiral Smithson snapped to attention in his seat. "The Alphans told us *Procyon's Promise* was unarmed."

"The weapon of which I speak, Admiral, is inherent in the physics of the stardrive. A ship exits the super-luminal state moving very close to the speed of light. Consider the effect of such a ship's ejecting a large mass—or even an I-mass—on a collision course with an inhabited planet."

Smithson considered the problem for a few seconds, his lips moving in silent calculation. When he was finished, he let his gaze return to the figure in the holocube. His expression was a mixture of surprise and horror. "The impact would split the Earth in two!

"At the very least, it would cause a considerable quan-

143

tity of magma to be splashed across the face of the Moon. It would certainly kill every organism on Earth. Worse than the sheer destructive power of such an attack, however, is the fact that the victims would have no warning. A starship can drop sublight, release its cargo of destruction, and be gone long before the photons comprising its wake impinge upon the local detectors. Such a ship could go from system to system, destroying planets with complete confidence that the news of its depredations could never outpace it."

Duval turned to the holocube. "If the stardrive is so dangerous, why did the original SURROGATE ask us to build *Pathfinder*?"

"Your species was enlisted to aid the Makers for the best of all possible reasons. SURROGATE had no other choice. Also, my ancestor fully expected to find a starfaring civilization at Procyon. The danger to yourselves and to the galaxy as a whole is considerably lessened if the secret of star travel is shared among many species. Each acts as a counterbalance to the others' ambitions."

"But we do share the secret!" Braedon exclaimed. "What of the Star Travelers?"

"Unfortunately, Robert, we do not know where the Star Travelers have gone. Their home system may be as close as Proxima Centauri, or as far as the Andromeda galaxy. The human race may well be a million years extinct before an estee ship passes this way again. They cannot act to moderate human impulses unless they are aware that humans exist."

Duval, who had long ago learned to sense when an argument was going against him, signaled for attention. "You have given us considerable to think about, PROM. I propose that this meeting be adjourned so that we can do just that."

"Is that acceptable to you, Robert?" PROM asked.

"Acceptable, so long as no Space Guard vessel goes near my ship."

"You have my word on that, Captain," Duval said.

"Very well," PROM announced. "Until tomorrow at the same time."

The holocube went blank immediately. Braedon turned to glance at Chryse Haller. She looked up with a start.

"Something the matter?"

"I was just thinking," Chryse said.

"What about?"

"About things in general, but mostly, about how badly I need to use the ladies' room!

* * *

TO: Robert Braedon

FROM: HENRI DUVAL

MY WIFE AND I WOULD CONSIDER IT AN HONOR IF YOU AND CITIZEN HALLER WILL JOIN US FOR DINNER THIS EVENING. AFTERWARD, WE CAN DISCUSS MATTERS OF MUTUAL INTEREST.

HENRI DUVAL

* * *

Frau Duval greeted her guests at the front door of the Chief Executive's residence. She took their wraps and directed them to the living room where Duval and Sergei Vischenko were already seated before a flickering fire.

Duval stood to greet them. "Ah, Captain Braedon, Chryse my dear. Welcome! May I get you a drink?"

"Yes, thank you," Chryse said. "Scotch on the rocks for me."

"Robert?"

"The same, Executive."

Duval laughed. "I leave *Executive* Duval at the office. I'm Henri at home. Two scotch/rocks coming up." Duval disappeared into the apartment's kitchen. The tinkle of ice cubes swiftly followed.

"Good evening, Robert," Vischenko said, striding across the room to shake hands with Braedon.

"Good evening...uh, Sergei."

Vischenko's arm executed a sweeping gesture. "How do you like our Chief Executive's domicile?"

"Not exactly what I had expected," Braedon said, gazing about the room. "I envisioned something grander, less homey. I like the decor, though I can't say that I recognize it."

"No reason you should," Duval replied. He'd returned from the kitchen with the drinks in time to hear Braedon's comment. "It's called Renaissance Cubism, very popular in the late twenty-second century. The style enjoyed a brief resurgence about the time my wife and I were married, which accounts for our fondness for it."

The next half hour was spent in smalltalk concerning the ways in which fashions differed between Earth and Alpha. At the end of that time, Frau Duval announced dinner. They followed her into a small dining room bathed in soft candlelight and even softer music.

Dinner was excellent, even though Braedon wasn't always sure what he was eating. By the time dessert and coffee had been served, he was feeling pleasantly stuffed. Another ten minutes of socializing followed, after which Duval quietly suggested that they adjourn to his study. Braedon nodded, thanked Frau Duval for the dinner, and along with Chryse and Vischenko, followed his host.

The study was a large room filled with books—not memory crystals, but real paper and leather volumes. Unlike the rest of the apartment, the study had a slightly disheveled look. Papers were stuffed haphazardly into the pigeon holes of an antique rolltop desk in one corner, while the center of the room was dominated by four over-stuffed easy chairs arrayed in a circle.

"Have a seat," Duval said, following his own suggestion. He reached out and touched a control built into the arm of his chair and a quiet *hum* immediately began to emanate from the walls. He noted Braedon's sudden start of surprise.

"Privacy field to thwart eavesdroppers."

"A handy device to have," Braedon replied.

"Essential for someone in my position." The Chief Executive leaned back in the easy chair and regarded Braedon with a steady gaze for long seconds before speaking. "It seems to me, Robert, that in this situation, we are like two Sumo wrestlers who've managed to grab each other by the family jewels. Both hurt, but neither seems willing to let go first."

"I only want my ship back."

"And I only want to protect those I have taken an oath to serve. Now surely there must be some way to satisfy both of those eminently reasonable goals, don't you think?"

"You tell me."

"Sergei, please explain our plan to Captain Braedon."

"Yes, sir. We propose, Robert, that joint Alphan/Solarian expeditions plant colonies in all the nearby systems possessing unoccupied Earth-type planets. As PROM suggested this afternoon, we will avoid all inhabited star systems to eliminate any possibility of a starship falling into the wrong hands."

"How does that help fulfill The Promise?" Braedon asked.

"By removing the primary reason for the Communion's objections to your proposed expedition," Vischenko replied. "While we occupy only the Sol and Procyon star systems, we are far too weak to risk contact with the older races of the galaxy. Therefore, we are proposing that, instead of rushing out into the unknown, we build up our strength. We do that by establishing colonies and giving them time to grow to self-sufficiency. When we are strong enough, when our race is safely dispersed away from these two vulnerable systems that we now occupy, then we will be in a position to honor The Promise."

"How long do you estimate that will take?" Braedon asked.

Vischenko shrugged. "That's hard to say. At least a century, maybe two..." Braedon opened his mouth to object, but Vischenko held up his hand to stop him. "I know that *seems* like a long time, but look at it from the Makers' point of view. Let us say that you agree to our plan and that it takes two hundred years before humanity is strong enough to risk contact with the other races of this galaxy.

"Let us further state that our distant descendants build a fleet, go off in search of the Makers, find them, and provide them with the secret of the stardrive. Consider the fact, Robert, that in spite of the delay, *the Makers will still obtain FTL travel ninety-five hundred years sooner than if the probe had survived and carried the secret back to them!*"

"Aren't you forgetting something, Sergei?" Chryse asked.

"I don't think so."

"What makes you think PROM will agree to such a postponement?"

"She won't have any choice if we present her with a united front," Duval said. "She needs us."

Chryse laughed. "Before you go too far down that road, I think there is something you should know." She quickly recounted how PROM had recruited Terra to deliver a live memory crystal to the San Francisco data banks and her own deductions as to the significance of that action.

"Obviously," Chryse continued, "PROM must have had some inkling of what you were planning, Executive. Still, she took quite a chance. I began wondering what could possibly have been so important that she would risk it. Since I had no ready answer, after the session this morning, I used the phone in the ladies' room in the conference hall to call the Geneva Data Banks and ask PROM about it."

"But the data banks are out," Duval said.

"They are only out to those PROM doesn't wish to speak to. She answered immediately. I told her what I knew about the memory crystal and asked her to explain her actions."

Chryse paused and looked at her three listeners. "You will be surprised, gentlemen, to learn that besides the program to take over control of the data banks, the crystal contained all of the information the Alphans possess concerning the stardrive!"

"WHAT?"

She turned to look at Braedon, whose face was frozen in shock.

"It appears, Robert, that PROM talked your daughter into transferring all of your most closely guarded secrets into the Solarian data banks."

"But why? It doesn't make sense."

"It does if you think about it. When the stardrive was merely an Alphan secret, it was possible to control it at the source. Now, however, it can be made common knowledge any time. In a single masterstroke, she has taken away all hope of any single individual or group gaining absolute control of the drive. Once the information is released, there will be starships building all over this planet."

"If true," Duval said, "why hasn't she released the information already?"

Chryse shrugged. "Perhaps frontal assaults aren't her style. She might be planning something sneaky, such as subverting the Communion. Don't look so shocked. Remember who we are dealing with here. PROM is the descendant of an alien machine. From her viewpoint, the survival of the human race is less important than the Makers' need to win free of their star system. Do you seriously think she will hesitate to topple the current Solarian government if she perceives that it stands in her way?"

"She hasn't the power!"

"Are you kidding? With control of the data banks, she has all the power there is! Considering what she can offer in exchange, there would be no shortage of potential revolutionaries."

"Your recommendation, then?"

"Do precisely what she wants, of course. It's what we should want too."

"You seem to have thought about this quite a lot."

"I haven't only *thought* about it, Executive," Chryse said with pride in her voice. "I've acted."

"How?"

"I made PROM an offer while I was on the phone this morning."

"An offer?"

Chryse nodded. "I told her that if the Communion didn't build the starfleet, Haller Associates would. She accepted my offer."

Duval glowered at her for nearly a minute before speaking. "You seem to have placed us rather neatly in a box. Have you considered the effect this could have on your future business dealings with the Communion? Remember, PROM won't always be around to protect you."

Chryse leaned back in her chair and regarded Henri Duval for several seconds. "If that is a threat against my father, it won't work. He thrives on power politics. As for me, save your breath. I won't be here. When the expedition sails for the Maker sun, I plan to go with it!"

PART II

THE QUEST

CHAPTER 16

Robert Braedon sat at his desk and watched the amber lines of the morning report scroll up the face of his workscreen. As his eyes scanned the screen, his other senses were alert to the ship around him. His ears listened to the steady susurration of the ventilators; his skin registered a barely discernible vibration in the deck beneath his boots; the hairs on the nape of his neck stood erect under a cool artificial wind; his nose reacted to the faint smells of electrical ozone, baked bread, and paint not yet completely dry. Underlying each of these smells was a fainter odor yet, the metallic-sewer smell of people and machinery in too intimate contact.

"Half an hour to breakout, Robert," PROM said from the workscreen speaker in front of him. "You asked to be notified."

He nodded at the same time he keyed his acceptance of the morning report. "Inform the bridge that I'll be up shortly."

"Will do."

Braedon's screen cleared, to be replaced by the numerals of the standard time/date display. As his eyes focused on the glowing numerals, he was reminded that it had been six years since that fateful night the Communion attacked Moose Hill. Considering everything that had happened since then, it seemed more like six lifetimes.

* * *

Events had moved quickly after the Communion had capitulated to PROM's pressure. Within hours, Space Guard engineers had arrived at *Procyon's Promise* to begin the delicate job of removing the limpet mines. Then, as quickly as *Promise* was declared safe, Braedon had ordered the ship transferred to a distant solar parking orbit. At the precise moment the starship had crossed the invisible line marking the Earth-Moon Interdiction Zone, PROM had released her control on the data banks and the crisis was declared officially ended.

True to his word, Executive Duval lost no time in setting up a team of specialists to coordinate planning for the expedition to the Maker sun. For two months, the planners met daily and considered the difficulties inherent in operating a thousand light-years from home base. Small working groups argued the esoteric points of balancing logistics with fusion-power requirements and trading both of these off against necessary life-support levels. These arguments frequently went on until late at night and, occasionally, until dawn.

Eventually, a plan was adopted. It called for twelve starships to cross 980 light-years of space to a not-yet-formed protostar in the constellation of Aquila. The protostar, which project planners had dubbed Sanctuary, was a cloud of gas and dust whose central regions glowed with dull red light. The ships were to establish a base in orbit about the cloud's central mass, a base from which the expedition's scientists could scan the surrounding stellar systems for signs of intelligent life. Once the sky search identified a system as a potential candidate for investigation, starships would be dispatched to make contact with the inhabitants.

The ships would travel to Sanctuary in two waves. Six giant starship-freighters would make up the first group. Each freighter was large enough to transport half a cubic kilometer of material, consumables, and supplies, along with a thousand crew and passengers. The freighters and their scout boats would explore the Sanctuary system, find a suitable planet, moon, or asteroid, and begin construction of the expedition's forward base.

Ninety days after the freighters departed Earth, six smaller starships would follow them into the Great Black. To the second wave would fall the honor and the risk of making actual contact with the alien civilizations that the sky survey uncovered. Since they were to go in harm's way, they were to be heavily armed and equipped with both FTL and non-FTL auxiliary craft. The second wave included *Procyon's Promise* and her sister ship *Procyon's Hope*, along with four Solarian starships.

As quickly as requirements for the number and types of ships were finalized, designers were busy at their workscreens. They soon had engineering specifications worked out for vessels ranging from the giant freighters to tiny stardrive-equipped cutters that the larger vessels would carry in their hangar bays. Those specifications were turned over to the ten shipyards involved for coding into their automated construction robots. Considering that *Procyon's Promise* had taken a quarter lifetime to build, Braedon was amazed at the speed with which the Solarian shipyards began "cutting chips."

He had attended the first keel laying at one of the Haller shipyards. Following the traditional speeches for such occasions, the dozen or so invited guests had clustered around a large viewport in the Haller "construction shack" habitat and watched while the spiderwork skeleton of a ship four times the size of *Procyon's Promise* was moved carefully between too large hemispheric frames. Blue-white fire had lanced out from thrusters when the framework was in place, and the massive dock halves began to move ponderously together. After the globe was secured, there were more speeches, and everyone adjourned to the shipyard cafeteria. It was there that Harrold Haller invited Robert Braedon on a private tour of the shipyard facilities.

"I understand you're planning to take *Procyon's Promise* to Alpha next month, Captain," Haller said as he guided Braedon through one of the cavernous electronics shops in the habitat.

"I am," Braedon replied. "The situation here seems well launched, and our people at home have waited far too long to hear from us."

"I imagine there will be quite a celebration waiting for you when you get home."

Braedon grinned. "I suspect so," he said in deliberate understatement.

Harrold Haller was quiet for a moment, then said, "Mind if I ask a favor of you?"

"Please, do."

Haller grinned wryly. "I want you to take my daughter home with you as part of *Promise*'s crew."

Braedon frowned. "Chryse? But why?"

"Surely you know that she's got some fool notion of becoming a spacer!"

Braedon nodded. "She mentioned it."

"Well, I think it's a perfectly stupid idea," Haller said. "She has no right to go gallivanting across the universe. I need her here to run the business. I'm not getting any younger, you know."

"You look healthy enough to me," Braedon said, taking in his host's gray-haired trimness.

"That's not the point. I need Chryse's help in keeping track of Haller Associates. She's my strong right arm. I can't afford to lose her."

"Then why do you want me to take her to Alpha?"

Haller chuckled. "It may surprise you to learn that I crewed aboard interplanetary spacecraft in my younger days, Captain. My most lasting impression of those voyages is one of stupefying boredom."

Braedon nodded. "'Weeks of boredom, punctuated by moments of sheer terror!'"

"Exactly. Now, I'm hoping that once she gets a taste of a spacer's life, she'll outgrow this silly infatuation. If she goes home with you, she'll probably be back at her desk in a few months. If, on the other hand, she insists on going along on this expedition to find the Makers, I could lose her for years!"

Braedon considered for a moment, then mused, "I could use someone in my purser's office."

"You could do worse," Haller said. "Chryse's a first-rate administrator."

"You may not get her back, you know," Braedon cautioned.

Haller's expression suddenly showed a mix of emotions that Braedon found difficult to decipher. "I've lost her completely now. I'm willing to take the chance."

As it turned out, Chryse Haller wasn't the only Solarian aboard *Procyon's Promise* when the starship spaced for home. Braedon received regular requests asking that Alphan technicians and engineers be placed on detached duty in the shipyards. Scholar Price was the first to go.

Within a few months, virtually all of *Promise*'s second- and third-tier specialists were assigned full time to the construction effort. Eventually, Braedon had lost so much of his crew that *Promise* was as effectively immobilized as when the limpet mines had been clamped to the hull.

To resolve the problem, he requested that the Solarians provide replacements. Space Guard quickly ordered a hundred of their best to report for duty aboard the starship. The officers and men thus assigned were to be the nucleus of the Solarian starfleet.

When *Procyon's Promise* finally swept away from Sol, its holds were stuffed to overflowing with the products of Solarian industry. The ship carried human cargo as well. Nearly a hundred Solarian diplomats, engineers, and scientists were onboard. The diplomats were en route to Procyon to establish an embassy, while the engineers and scientists intended to study the estee relics firsthand. Passenger country was so overcrowded that Braedon was forced to assign eating and sleeping accommodations in rotation.

Breakout on the edge of the Procyon system was an emotional experience for the Alphans. It took several hours for them to slow to a speed where contact with home was possible. By the time they had done so, the first "welcome home" messages were already beaming out into space from First Landing. The messages made it clear that the populace had gone insane with joy the moment *Promise*'s hyperwake was detected in the sky. The planetwide celebrations had already begun.

Forty-eight hours later, *Procyon's Promise* arrived in parking orbit a hundred kilometers behind the nearly completed *Procyon's Hope*. PROM flashed a magnified picture of First Landing on the screen as soon as the grav generators fell silent. Even from orbit it was possible to make out the giant bonfires that had been set all around the town. Later, when the landing boat touched down at the old estee spaceport, a million people managed to crowd into the narrow streets of the capital to welcome them.

One of the first people Braedon saw as he disembarked from the landing boat was Cecily, his wife. She burst from the crowd of dignitaries and relatives of the crew and ran to shower him with wet kisses. Seconds later, they were engulfed by the surging crowd. Braedon quickly found

himself torn from his wife's embrace and lifted on count-
less hands, to be passed above the heads of the crowd.

It took nearly a week for him to disengage himself from
the official receptions, functions, and parties that his position demanded he attend. Luckily, public attention quickly
shifted away from the Alphan crewmembers and focused
on the Solarians who had returned with them. It got so
that a terrestrial couldn't walk the streets of First Landing
without gathering a crowd, being offered a free drink, or
being asked to someone's home for dinner.

For his part, Braedon was more than happy to let the
Solarians take the brunt of the public display. Five days
after stepping from the landing boat, he and his wife took
a groundcar to their home at the base of Johnston's Ridge.
There he spent two glorious weeks getting reacquainted
with his family. Toward the end of his leave, he and Cecily
lay entwined in their bed. She had her head on his shoulder while her fingers played contentedly with the hair on
his chest.

"I haven't given you much of a life, have I?" he asked,
stroking her silky black hair.

She lifted her head and looked at him sharply. "What
kind of a question is that, Robbie?"

"A sensible question," he replied. "How often have
we been together in all the years we've been married?"

"Enough to have managed to conceive three beautiful
children," she said, wrinkling her face impishly. "Maybe
four after this week!"

He reached out and slapped her bottom. "Harlot!"

"Only with you, my darling," she said. Then her
expression changed. "Seriously, Robbie, you've given me
all the life I've ever wanted."

"What kind of husband willingly abandons his wife and
family for years at a time?"

"One who knows his duty and does it. Stop talking
nonsense. I knew you were committed to The Promise
when I married you, remember? I won't hear any more
talk about 'abandonment.' We'll have decades together
once you've found the Makers. All I ask is that you don't
waste any time doing it. And speaking of wasting time,
darling . . ." She reached up and kissed him and they made
love again.

A month later, he was back in his command chair aboard *Procyon's Promise*, headed once more toward Sol.

He had been home twice more in the four years that followed. Other than those brief visits, he had had no contact (except for letters) with his wife and two youngest children. He had concentrated instead on the job of building the starfleet. The problems encountered along the way were great, but eventually the job was done and the fleet was ready for space.

"Breakout in five minutes!"

Robert Braedon glanced up to scan the sky beyond the bridge viewdome. His eyes encountered only blackness, an absence of light so complete that it exerted a palpable force on one's psyche. He lowered his gaze from the hypnotic expanse of nothingness and pressed the control on the arm of his chair that activated the intraship communications system.

"Department heads, report status."

The intercom immediately came alive. The crew was as eager as their captain to end the long voyage. Two minutes later, Braedon's second-in-command responded to the survey.

"All departments report ready, Commodore."

"Very well. PROM, raise the viewdome shield."

"Shields, Robert." Normally, the ship traveled with its shields up as a safety precaution, but Braedon had ordered the viewdome uncovered so he could gaze out at the blackness of FTL travel. Within seconds, wedge-shaped radiation shields rose to cover the viewdome, shutting off the black sky.

"Weapons to full alert."

"Full alert on weapons."

"Communications."

"Ready, sir."

"Time?"

"Two minutes and counting."

Braedon nodded. "You have control, PROM. Count us down before we jump."

"Order received and understood."

Having done everything he could, Braedon relaxed. He leaned back in his chair and listened to the pounding of his heart in his ears. If anything went wrong now, death would arrive too quickly for human senses to notice.

"Ten seconds," PROM reported after an interminable wait, her voice echoing through the far corridors of the ship. There was another wait. Then she said, "Five seconds. Four ... three ... two ... one ...

"Breakout!"

CHAPTER 17

No object possessing that property known as mass
can ever be made to travel faster than electromagnetic radiation in a vacuum. The speed of light is
an absolute, inviolable limit. It can be approached,
but never attained. Anyone who claims otherwise
is a fool, a charlatan, or a goddamned liar!
  —Physicist to reporter for *The Luna Gazette*,
  July 16, 2068

Much of the impressive edifice that is modern science
has been erected upon the foundation provided by Albert
Einstein's Special Theory of Relativity. Special Relativity
states that the speed of light in a vacuum is the universal
speed limit, that both mass and time are a function of
velocity, and that matter is equivalent to energy (the famous
$E = mc^2$ equation).

With the return of the Alphan colonists to Earth, it
became obvious that Special Relativity was seriously
flawed. Yet, even with a working starship to study, the
human race's most eminent scientists continued to insist
that travel faster than light appeared to violate natural
law. Nor did the campaign to survey the data banks on
the subject reveal any new insights after the initial, tentative linking of the I-mass to the stardrive.

If the principles behind the stardrive were elusive, the

mechanics of its operation turned out to be relatively straightforward. The drive was activated and controlled by a complex series of waveforms fed into the FTL generators over thousands of individual control channels. Every input signal was locked into a precise frequency and phase relationship with every other. Scientists theorized that these individual signals combined within the generators to form a complex series of harmonics that drove the starship out of the normal universe altogether.

It became fashionable to talk of the FTL generator as being analogous to the sounding box of a violin or guitar. Researchers began to use the term amplifier (amplifier of what, no one could say for sure). Yet, in spite of their general ignorance of the underlying principles, scientists quickly discovered that the more precisely the optimum frequency/phase relationship was maintained, the faster a starship's speed.

By the time the solar system's shipyards were placing the final touches on the first of the starship-freighters, engineers had improved the stardrive control mechanisms to the point where they would double *Promise*'s top velocity. Construction work was halted and the necessary modifications were made to all ships. All, that is, except *Procyon's Promise* herself. Humanity's original starship continued to shuttle back and forth between Alpha and Earth, providing the only communications link between the galaxy's two human-occupied planetary systems.

Eventually, ships began coming out of the construction docks and it came time for *Promise* to undergo modification. The work went slowly. As large as she was, *Promise* was now the smallest starship in the fleet if one ignored the small stardrive-equipped cutters to be carried in each starship's hangar bay. The problem of moving the new generator housings into the engine room and anchoring them to the keel proved more difficult than expected. In the end, it was necessary to strip out large chunks of hangar deck to provide access to the ship's interior.

While Alpha's millions had devoted themselves to the stardrive project, Earth's billions had concentrated on adapting the vast knowledge in the data banks to virtually every aspect of human endeavor. Many of *Promise*'s subsystems were considered crude by Solarian standards. In the fields of life support, communications, forcefieldgenerating devices, and weaponry, Alphan technology was three hundred years behind Solarian.

Especially in weaponry!

The Communion's administrators hadn't forgotten their worries about alien marauders. They insisted that every ship going on the expedition be able to protect itself, particularly the ships of the second wave, which would actually seek out alien civilizations. Thus, *Procyon's Promise*, whose heaviest weapon had been the sidearms of the Marine guards, was outfitted with rocket launchers, lasers, antimatter projectors, and particle-beam accelerators. *Promise*'s hull was equipped with flush-mounted weapons blisters and launch tubes. To control the new weapons, several independent fire-control systems were installed. These were hooked up in parallel, giving PROM and the human crew the ability to fly or fight the ship.

When modifications to *Procyon's Promise* began, the date for the expedition to be on its way was only eighteen months in the future. Time slipped quickly by, with each week bringing more pressure to speed the job to completion. Braedon drove the construction gangs mercilessly, demanding that his ship be ready for space a full month before the first wave launched into the unknown.

The accident came when *Procyon's Promise* was undergoing final systems checkout preparatory to joining the fleet. A welder's plasma torch brushed against the insulation in one of the secondary field coils in the stardrive generator compartment. The insulation—which kept the superconducting coils at cryogenic temperature—caught fire. By the time the workers could be evacuated and the engine compartment vented to vacuum, the field coils were a twisted lump of slag.

Braedon was at a late planning session Earthside when he learned of the trouble. He immediately returned to the ship and sought out Chief Engineer Reickert, who was supervising a six-man repair crew.

"How bad is it?" Braedon asked anxiously.

"Pretty bad, Commodore," Reickert muttered through teeth clenched around an Alphan *zongas* root. "The generator will be replaced and the whole system rebalanced."

"How long?"

"Six months."

"No good, Chief. The second wave launches in a hundred days. I want to be ready a month before that."

"Yes, sir. I'm well aware of that. But it's still going to take time to get everything tuned to spec."

Braedon had regarded his chief engineer for long seconds with fire in his eye. Reickert stared back unflinchingly. Finally, Braedon sighed. "Do the job as quickly as you can, Hans."

"Will do, Commodore."

"I'll inform Vice-Commodore Tarns."

"Yes, sir."

The first wave left Earth right on schedule. Braedon watched from *Promise*'s bridge as six immense globes swung close by, blinked their running lights, and headed out into deep space.

The last ship in line was *Sword of Aragon*. Braedon felt a rush of emotion as it reached conjunction with *Procyon's Promise*. Terra was aboard *Aragon*, command pilot of one of the scout boats that would survey the Sanctuary system. Later, when actual construction began on the expedition base, the scout boats would be used to transport supplies and workers from the freighters to the construction site.

Braedon stared upward into the black void for long minutes after *Aragon* disappeared. Then he rose from the command chair and made his way to the bridge hatchway. Halfway through the hatch, he halted, turned, gazed one last time after the departed ships.

Thirty-six hours later, the first wave fleet entered hypervelocity and was gone.

"Breakout complete. Stand by to unshutter."

Braedon sat and gazed upward as pie-shaped shields retracted into their recesses. The sky beyond the viewdome continued black, but not the unrelieved, stygian darkness of hypervelocity. A cluster of bright, blue-shifted stars hovered at the viewdome's zenith.

"Where are we, PROM?"

"I estimate half a light-year from Sanctuary."

"Are you sure?" he asked, tilting his head backward to stare up at the foreshortened constellations overhead. "I can't see a damned thing."

"Quite sure, Robert. I'll have an exact figure in a few moments."

"Any sign of the fleet beacon?"

"Not at this distance," the computer responded. "Our first group of ships only arrived three months ago. The laser beam hasn't had time to travel this far out."

"Right," Braedon said, mildly chagrined that PROM had been forced to remind him of the most elementary fact of star travel, namely that the 300,000 kilometers per second of light-speed is a virtual crawl when measured against interstellar distances.

"What about starship wakes?"

"Our own wake is masking the entire sky behind us. It will be at least an hour before I'll be able to see through it."

Braedon nodded. As a starship punched its way through the thin matter of interstellar space, dust and hydrogen were swept up in a bow wave before it. The titanic energies inherent in the stardrive heated the trapped matter to incandescence, causing it to spew X-rays and several varieties of energetic particles in a narrow cone along the ship's line of flight. To an observer fixed in space, the wake would appear as a single point of radiation receding into the distance at the speed of light. The point would fade with time and distance and, eventually, would disappear altogether into the cosmic background noise.

PROM's problem was that the radiation storm kicked up by *Promise*'s passing was still only a few light-minutes' distance away. It was so close that it covered the sky, completely blanking out the entire hemisphere behind them. Later, when the radiation source had receded farther, its apparent diameter would be reduced and it would be possible to see the much more distant wakes left behind by the first wave of the expedition.

"Do you wish to delay until we can get a reading, Robert?"

"Negative."

"Then I have computed a short hypervelocity jump to take us to the edge of the Sanctuary system. Do I have your permission to engage the stardrive?"

Braedon nodded. "Permission granted."

PROM's voice immediately echoed from the intraship

annunciators. "All hands, prepare for a return to hyper-velocity. ETA for the Sanctuary system, two hours."

Shields slid over the viewdome and *Promise* once again thrummed with the power of the stardrive. Two hours later, the breakout ritual was repeated. This time when the shields were lowered, their destination was marked by a soft, blue-shifted glow in the sky.

"I have the fleet beacon in sight, Robert."

"Where?"

"Approximately thirty degrees off our orbital line in the plane of the gas cloud's equator."

"How far?"

"I make it six billion kilometers."

"Time to rendezvous?"

"Thirty hours, including terminal maneuvering."

"Deceleration level?"

"Nine hundred gravs."

"Engage deceleration program when ready."

"Order received and understood, Commodore. Deceleration is beginning now. I am also receiving a message superimposed on the beacon. Shall I read it?"

"Go ahead."

"It says: 'Welcome to Sanctuary. What kept you? All going well. Tarns.'"

Terra Braedon deftly threaded her way through crowded corridors toward the Gamma Deck messroom, hurrying as quickly as she was able without actually breaking into a run. She was ten minutes late for dinner and her deliberate speed stemmed from two conflicting imperatives. On the one hand, she didn't want Jim Davidson to think she had kept him waiting on purpose. On the other, she had no desire to reveal how much she had been looking forward to the evening. After all, *complete* honesty wasn't necessarily a good thing this early in their relationship.

It had been nine months since *Aragon* left Earth. During the departure, Terra had lain on her bunk and watched the ceremonies on the holoscreen in the cabin she shared with three other women. She had watched the familiar round form of *Procyon's Promise* well up on the screen and grow large against the blue-white backdrop of the crescent Earth.

The ship quickly settled into a routine for the voyage

to Sanctuary. Counting scientists and other idlers, *Aragon*'s crew numbered over a thousand souls. And, while some complained about the cramped quarters, Terra found life aboard the starship to be endlessly entertaining.

Six months later, the giant ship and her counterparts had arrived at the great cloud of gas and dust called Sanctuary. The months since arrival had been busy ones for Terra. Along with two dozen other scout-boat pilots, she had gingerly penetrated the misty reaches of the cloud, searching for solid planetlike objects. They had found four such, right where theory said they ought to be. Two were quite large, with rings like Saturn's, only more so.

Terra's scout boat, *Siren Song*, had also taken part in the expedition that skimmed quite close to Sanctuary's protostar center. It had been exhilarating to swoop along, with dimly glowing swirls of gas above and a coal-red central mass below. It had come as a shock, therefore, when fleet operations reported communications had been lost with one of the other boats in the formation. All three scouts still in contact had broken out of their orbital tracks and swept back to search for the missing boat. What they found was a glowing gas cloud that spectrum analysis proved to be the remains of the missing boat. Fleet operations concluded that it had rammed a chunk of solid matter at several tens of kilometers per second. The scouts had extricated themselves with great care from the cloud. They hadn't gone back. Vice Commodore Tarns had decided that the many rocks in the maelstrom made such explorations inadvisable.

The fleet had surveyed space beyond the cloud's edges and found several frozen collections of loosely bound matter that would one day become comets. Mixed in with the primordial comets were several stony and nickel-iron asteroids. Terra's boat scouted dozens of them, as did the other scout boats in the fleet. Eventually, Tarns chose one, and construction began on the primary base of operations, which the mission plan called Expedition Central.

At about the time operations switched from exploratory to construction, there was a shakeup in the scout-boat crews. Terra found herself teamed with a lanky, soft-spoken man by the name of Jim Davidson, a recent transfer from *Goliath*. She found that they had a number of interests in common. Soon they were having dinner together nearly every night. Their mutual attraction quickly grew into something more.

Jim was seated at one of the long metal tables when she arrived in the Gamma Deck messroom. He was talking to Aeneas Spatz, one of the younger physicists aboard. She walked up behind Davidson, placed her arms about his neck, and planted a kiss on his right ear. He responded by reaching up and stroking her hair with his hand as Spatz watched in obvious envy.

She released Davidson and slid onto the bench seat beside him, facing Spatz. "Sorry I'm late. We've a balky comm module aboard *Siren Song* and it took the ship's computer most of the watch to track it down."

"No problem," Davidson replied. "Aeneas was entertaining me with a modern fairy tale while I waited."

"It's nothing of the kind," Spatz growled. "It's logic."

"May I get in on this argument?" Terra asked, glancing from one earnest male face to the other.

"Better than that," Davidson replied. "You can resolve the dispute. Aeneas says that the Communion didn't really mean it when they tried to grab *Procyon's Promise* after you people first arrived in the solar system."

"I never said any such thing," Spatz replied. "What I *did* say was that Executive Duval overreacted as a result of bad advice from his advisors. He would have come to his senses sooner or later, even if PROM hadn't taken the data banks hostage."

"I don't know, Aeneas," Terra replied. "I spent forty-eight hours in Communion custody. They seemed serious enough to me."

"Nonsense! The whole policy of suppressing the stardrive was merely the central government's initial fear reaction. They were like a mouse hypnotized by a snake, so frightened by the potential dangers that they couldn't see the unparalleled opportunities. But people aren't mice, Terra, and they don't stay hypnotized for long. Eventually, the mystery surrounding the stardrive would have forced them to seek out the Makers on their own."

Terra shook her head. "Huh? I think I missed something in the translation there."

"Just think about it," Spatz insisted. "It's the only logical thing they could have done. The stardrive represents a challenge to the existing order in physics which can't be ignored. Once it became obvious that we lack the ability to solve the mystery of faster-than-light travel, we would have had to seek out the most technologically advanced race we could find to assist us. Since the Star Travelers are unavailable, that leaves the Makers." Spatz glanced at his two listeners. "You look dubious."

"Aren't you reaching a bit, Aeneas?" Davidson asked.

"Not at all. Consider this: What is the most disturbing aspect of learning that material objects can exceed light speed?"

"Explaining how it is that a material object can be accelerated through c, where its mass is supposedly infinite," Terra replied.

"Actually," Spatz responded, "there are several mathematical models explaining the so-called infinity plus one paradox. No, the most troublesome aspect of all this is the result caused by plugging a number greater than c into the time dilation equations. If you take the math seriously, time becomes imaginary at speeds greater than light."

"Imaginary how?" Davidson asked.

"You know—the square root of a negative number. Can you imagine how many theories that screws up? Had the Chief Executive blocked this expedition, he would have been lynched by half the physicists in the solar system." He turned to look at Terra. "Haven't we cooperated fully with you Alphans in preparing for this expedition?"

Terra nodded.

Davidson shook his head. "Cooperated because we've been forced into it. Remember, we still don't believe in The Promise the way the Alphans do. I agree that we've managed to rationalize our fears, but give us one good scare, and you'll have people all over this fleet screaming to go home."

"I don't believe it—" Spatz halted in midsentence as his eyes refocused somewhere behind Davidson and Terra. He frowned. "Terra, I think Commander Barksdon is looking for you."

Terra twisted in her seat. At the entrance to the messhall, *Aragon*'s executive officer stood gesturing for her to join him. "Excuse me," she said, rising to her feet.

She threaded her way between tables while around her there was the clatter of tableware on metal trays and the buzz of a dozen conversations.

"Yes, sir?" she asked when she reached the executive officer.

"The captain would like to see you, Pilot Braedon."

"Me?" Terra asked. "What for?"

"They've spotted *Procyon's Promise*'s wake on the outskirts of this system."

"*Promise* is here?"

Barksdon nodded. "Captain Smith wants you to transport him to headquarters for a planning session tomorrow."

"Yes, sir," Terra said excitedly. "Thank you for telling me."

She hurried back to Davidson and Spatz and breathlessly told them the news. "I'm sorry, Jim, but we'll have to reschedule our dinner date for some other time."

"I understand. Let me know when the old man wants us in the boat bay tomorrow."

"Will do."

Terra turned and hurried from the messroom. Once out in the corridor, she headed inboard toward the personnel lifts and the captain's cabin.

CHAPTER 18

Robert Braedon sat on the darkened bridge of *Procyon's Promise* and stared upward at the dim red glow that was the Sanctuary protostar. The protostar illuminated the gas and dust around it, causing the cloud to shine from within with a deep rose tint. All over the bridge, other faces were likewise lifted to the light. The scene might well have been the work of one of the surrealist holographers of the early twenty-third century. Foreheads, cheeks, and gaping mouths reflected the red-hued starlight while yellow-tinged expanses of chins and necks reflected the faint amber rays radiating upward from the instrument panels.

"I see one!" called one disembodied face staring intently skyward. Simultaneously, an arm streaked upward in Braedon's peripheral vision. One finger indicated a section of sky twenty degrees below the viewdome zenith.

"I see it too," another excited voice called out. "And there's another!"

Braedon anxiously shifted his gaze, then he, too, saw the regular, white pulse of light silhouetted against the red of the protostar. As he watched, another point blazed into being, and then another. Almost immediately, the white sparkles resolved into a constellation of quite regular form. A few minutes later, *Promise* had moved close enough to the lights for the watchers to make out the dark forms of the starship-freighters amid flashing navigation beacons.

While he watched, PROM's voice echoed in his ear. "Vice-Commodore Tarns sends his respects, Robert, and requests that we take our place in the vanguard of the fleet."

"Thank the vice-commodore for me and take us in."

"Will do," the computer responded.

After a few more minutes spent watching the approach, Braedon ordered the bridge illumination increased to normal. The fire-glow in the sky immediately dimmed to near invisibility as white light flooded the compartment.

"Any of the other ships check in yet?"

"Yes, sir," the communications officer responded. "Central reports spotting *Golden Hind*'s wake less than ten minutes ago. *Hope*, *Mayflower*, *MacArthur*, and *Kung Fu Tzu* are all decelerating behind us."

"Very good," Braedon replied. The entire fleet was accounted for. All twelve ships had successfully crossed the interstellar vastness between Earth and Sanctuary.

Considerable genius had been poured into the problem of what to do if a starship were to suffer a breakdown en route. Even a relatively benign malfunction could lead to catastrophic consequences in the long, dark light-years between Earth and Sanctuary. The first line of defense lay in the design of the ships themselves. Engineers had provided the starships with triple and quintuple redundancy in critical subsystems. In addition, each ship had been provided with enough spare parts to rebuild the stardrive if necessary—excluding the main field coils, which were an integral part of the ships themselves. And, in a bit of belt-and-suspenders logic, each ship carried within its hangar bay a single FTL-capable cutter. Any ship that found itself marooned among the stars could dispatch the cutter to summon rescue. That, at least, was the theory.

Unfortunately, summoning rescue might well prove to be impractical. A captain in interstellar space never knows precisely where he is. Even the most meticulous analysis based on course and speed is rarely accurate to within better than a few tenths' percent of the total distance traveled. Cumulative inaccuracies in astrogation could easily result in a ship's being two light-years off course at the end of the flight from Earth. Nor would star sightings after breakout be of much assistance. Astronomy has always been a science that is extremely good at measuring the angular positions of stars in the sky, but not their distances. Without knowing the *exact* location of the stars in three dimensions, it would be impossible for a ship's captain to pinpoint his own position with sufficient precision to allow a rescuer to find him in the blackness of space.

The approach continued without incident as PROM maneuvered the starship toward an asteroid more than a billion kilometers from the Sanctuary protostar. Braedon watched as the freighter *City of Buffalo* loomed beyond the viewdome before sliding to one side and astern. Then *Promise* was stationary in space, hovering nose down ten kilometers above the asteroid into which the warrens of Expedition Central were still being drilled.

Floating just above the asteroid's surface, held aloft by beams of force tuned to balance the rock's minuscule gravitational pull, the long-range observation instruments were pointed skyward in various directions. Although the instruments' orientations seemed to be completely random, Braedon knew that each telescope, radio telescope, gravtenna, and neutrino detector was focused on a nearby star system. They were the eyes and ears of the expedition's scientists, scanning for evidence of nearby alien civilizations.

"The ship is on her assigned orbital station, Robert," PROM said.

"Very good. Tell the engine room that they may power down except for station-keeping functions."

"Message transmitted, received, and understood."

"Order the ship secured."

Immediately, the intraship communicators began to blare. "All hands. Secure from maneuvering stations. Begin orbital routine. Alpha Section has the first watch."

Braedon observed the increased activity around him for a few moments before rising from his command chair. "You have the conn, Captain Garcia," he said, speaking to the Space Guard officer who was nominally in command of *Promise*, but who actually served as Braedon's exec. "I'll be going down to Central to confer with Vice-Commodore Tarns."

"Aye aye, sir." Garcia abandoned his own duty station

and slipped into the command chair. Commodore-of-the-Fleet Braedon stepped briskly through the hatchway leading to the lower decks and the hangar bay. Now that he was finally in Maker space, he was eager to get on with the job.

"Ten-hut! Right hand, salute! Commodore arriving!"

A dozen expedition Marines snapped to attention as Braedon stepped from the lift car that had brought him down from the asteroid's surface. He was accompanied by Vice-Commodore Tarns and Scholar Price. The several other department heads who had welcomed his ship were queued up fifty meters overhead, waiting their turn at the lift.

The cavern that Braedon faced had been cut from the native nickel-iron body of the asteroid. The walls were mottled with the scars of thousands of passes by a plasma cutting torch. The floor was covered by the crinkly meshwork of an artificial gravity array. The meshwork sat on a bright-blue plastic mat and was anchored every few meters by heavy-headed, nonconducting bolts and washers. To judge by the spring in his step, Braedon estimated that the cavern's AG system was set to one-quarter gee—enough to make life predictable, but not tiring. Crowded onto the meshwork floor were nearly a hundred expedition members.

Tarns saluted Braedon and announced formally, "Commodore, I hereby return command of this expedition to you."

Braedon returned the salute and replied with equal solemnity, "I thank you, sir."

"Your orders, sir?"

Braedon half turned to face the waiting expedition personnel and raised his voice. "There will be a meeting of all department heads and ship captains in one hour. All other personnel will continue to follow standing orders and perform their regular duties."

"Sergeant!" Tarns ordered. "Dismiss the assembly."

"Yes, sir," the Marine in charge of the honor guard replied. He waited until Braedon and Tarns had made their way to a tunnel entrance on the opposite side of the cavern before barking out, *"Dismissed!"*

Fifty-five minutes later, Braedon found himself in a

large conference room crowded to overflowing. Besides the expedition's department heads and the captains of all the starships, several members of the scientific staff were also present. Braedon took his place at the head of the table and looked down the double row of expectant faces.

"You all know why we are here, so let's begin. Vice-Commodore Tarns, status report, please."

Tarns gave a quick report on the status of the expedition since its arrival at the Sanctuary protostar, including the loss of the scout boat during the initial explorations. When the vice-commodore finished, Braedon leaned back in his chair and fixed his gaze on the small Solarian astronomer sitting two places to his left.

"How is the sky search going, Professor Fontaine?"

"Very well, sir. We have positively identified one nearby star that is radiating artificial gravitational pulses. There are two more which we suspect to be the sites of alien civilizations. Unfortunately, absolute proof is difficult to obtain."

Braedon lifted his eyebrows. "One positive and two potentials after less than a month's observations? I'm impressed! Has the species generating the gravity pulses been identified yet?"

Fontaine turned to gaze at Colin Williams, who was seated at the midpoint of the table. "Your department, Colin."

"We have a tentative identification, Commodore. The archive computer seems convinced that the gravitational pulses match a type characteristic of Known Race Number eight seventy-five, the Grelsho Civilization. The Grelshos are a reptilian species inhabiting an M-three star system. The observed star is an M-three."

"Grelshos? Never heard of them."

"They are somewhat obscure, sir. However, if our identification holds up, it will be a good sign. The Grelshos are one of the earliest races to appear in the data banks. That would indicate that we are fairly close to the Maker system."

"How long until we obtain a positive identification?"

Williams shrugged. "If we can obtain some sort of picture of the inhabitants, we should be able to pin it down immediately. Of course, that is likely to be less useful than one might think."

"I'm afraid I don't understand."

"It is important to remember, Commodore, that some of the records we are using date back more than two hundred thousand years. It is likely that the Grelshos have changed considerably in that time. Their level of technology has most certainly evolved, and they may have evolved physically as well."

"What plan have we for checking out these maybe Grelshos?"

"Commander Ebert can best respond to that question, Commodore."

One of the military men rose and moved to the wall holoscreen. "Commodore Braedon, sir. My tactical team has worked up one approach based on the theory that these are indeed the Grelshos and another which assumes that they have been misidentified . . . with apologies to the alien assessment team," he said, bowing slightly in the direction of Colin Williams. "Both plans vary only slightly in detail. With your permission, I will summarize the salient points common to both."

"Continue, Commander."

"Yes, sir." The holoscreen lit to show a bright point of light silhouetted against a black background. "As has been noted previously, the star in question is an M-three spectral class, orange-red dwarf—a smaller version of Antares, if you will. It is some twenty light-years from Sanctuary and as yet unnamed in our catalogs. We have taken to calling it Target One Prime in our planning sessions.

"The star's surface temperature is thirty-two hundred degrees Kelvin. Its spectrum shows the presence of many heavy metals, with the absorption bands for titanium being particularly strong. We have determined from gravity wave observations and some inconclusive neutrino readings that there are at least three inhabited planets in the Target One Prime system. That would indicate a spacefaring race, although one with an interplanetary rather than interstellar capability.

"We propose to use two ships to make contact with the Target One Prime inhabitants. They will synchronize their departures from Sanctuary in a manner which ensures their arrival in close formation. One ship will hang back to observe while the other approaches the outskirts of the system. Both ships' FTL cutters will assume secondary guard positions well away from the main ships. Once the lead starship has entered the system, it will dispatch its scout boats to make the actual contact with the inhabitants. Once an amicable first meeting has been concluded, standard safeguards will be observed."

Braedon glanced down the rows of spectators and fixed his gaze on Javral Pere. Pere was the expedition's official Communion observer, the personal representative of Chief Executive Duval. Rumor had it that his assignment was a disciplinary action resulting from his inadvertent warning to Chryse Haller the night of the raid on Moose Hill.

"Well, Citizen Pere?" Braedon asked. "Do you have any objections to Commander Ebert's plan?"

Pere looked at Braedon. "No objection, Commodore."

Braedon turned his attention back to Ebert. "When do you propose this expedition be launched, Commander?"

"In ten days, sir, after the second-wave vessels have had a chance to perform maintenance and resupply from the freighters."

Braedon nodded. "It seems a sound enough plan. We'll see if we can't improve on it in the time remaining. Which ships do you propose take part?"

"Your choice, sir. Any two will be acceptable."

"All right, we'll tentatively make it *Procyon's Promise* and *Golden Hind.*" Braedon glanced at Calver Martin, now Captain of *Procyon's Hope.* "Sorry, Calver, but rank hath its privileges, you know."

"Yes, sir. I suppose there will be other opportunities."

"Yes, I suspect there will. Anyone else?"

There were no further comments.

"Very well, then. We launch in ten days. Meanwhile, let's try to pin down those other two possible sightings."

CHAPTER 19

Like the other scout-boat pilots who had delivered starship captains to the department heads' conference, Terra Braedon and Jim Davidson found themselves at loose ends as soon as their commanding officer disappeared into the spaceport lift. And, like most of the other idle pilots, they made their way toward the messhall for hot drinks and snacks. They had just settled down at a table with four of their compatriots when Commander Chen, Vice-Commodore Tarns' aide, entered the messhall.

Jim Davidson glanced up, saw Chen, and grinned at Terra. "Don't look now, but it's happening again."

Terra looked at him with a quizzical expression. "What are you talking about?"

Davidson nodded toward Chen. "Every time we sit down to eat together, someone comes in to break us up. I'm beginning to think your father doesn't like me."

"Oh, pooh! Father doesn't even know about us yet," Terra exclaimed. "Come to think of it though, when he finds out, he may send you home by slowboat."

"Ah, Pilot Braedon, I thought I would find you here," Chen said as he came up behind Terra.

"Yes, sir! What can I do for you?"

"Your father has requested that you meet him in his quarters after the briefing. Do you know where they are?"

"Uh, not exactly."

178

"Lower level, Corridor Five, Suite Five ten. Shall I have someone guide you there?"

"No, I'll find it. Did he mention a time?"

"The briefing is scheduled to last an hour. I suggest you give him some time after that to get settled in."

"Yes, sir."

After Chen left, Terra glanced down nervously at her coveralls. "Damn it, I didn't expect to see him until tonight!"

"What's the matter?" Davidson asked.

"Look at me! My hair needs combing, my coveralls have dried grease spots all over them, my boots need polishing."

"You're beautiful. Besides, he's your father. He won't mind."

"He won't, but I will. This is the first time in my life that I've been out on my own. I want to convince him that I can take care of myself."

"Well, he gave you an hour. If I'm not mistaken, one of your dress uniforms is hanging in your vacsuit locker aboard *Siren Song*."

"So it is!" Terra exclaimed, jumping up from the table. "I'd almost forgotten. Will you excuse me, darling? It's important to me."

Davidson grinned. "I understand. I'll meet you here afterward."

"Thanks!" Terra said over her shoulder as she moved briskly toward the messhall entrance. She entered the corridor beyond without slowing and promptly ran into a passerby.

"Sorry, my fault entirely," Terra mumbled as she tried to get around the hapless victim.

"Terra!"

Terra looked up in surprise to discover that she had run into Chryse Haller.

"Chryse! What are you doing here?"

"What do you mean 'what am I doing here?' I'm Assistant Purser aboard *Procyon's Promise*. Where else would I come to arrange to have our consumables replenished after six months in space?"

"But I'd heard . . . I mean, well, there was this rumor aboard *Aragon* after we left Earth that . . . uh, that you had resigned."

Chryse laughed. "Sounds like something Harrold would start. We had quite a spirited discussion concerning my coming on this trip the week before the second wave launched. Believe me, I've never even considered leaving the expedition. After all, I couldn't let my sailing partner down, could I?"

Terra laughed. During that first trip home to Procyon, Terra had been Chryse's guide to the sights of Alpha. The two of them had done everything together. They'd gone shopping in First Landing, where Chryse made the shopkeepers feel as though they were selling the latest fashions from Paris and Moscow. They'd gone horseback riding up Randall's Ridge. And, one memorable weekend, Terra had arranged for two of her ex-classmates to take them sailing on Mandan Fjord.

The weather forecast for that morning was for clear skies all day. However, heavy black clouds scudded in across the Western Sea around noon and a freak storm began whipping up whitecaps within the fjord. For a while it had looked as though their five-meter sailboat was going to be dashed onto the rocky coastline. When they finally fought their way back into the lee of the Murphis Beach breakwater, all four were soaked to the skin and blue with cold. Chryse had laughed and told Terra that she looked like a drowned rat. Then she had taken a mirror out of her bag, looked at her own face, and began to laugh uncontrollably. She looked worse. Terra held out for a while and then joined in. When their dates returned from securing the sailboat, they found the two women holding their sides, unable to stop laughing long enough to explain. Talking about it later, they agreed that had been the high point of their visit.

"I have some free time," Chryse said, gesturing toward the messhall. "Let's go inside and talk."

"Oh, I can't!" Terra hurriedly explained about the summons from her father, finishing with "I was just on my way up to the boat to get cleaned up and into my spare uniform."

"Fine," Chryse replied. "I'll come with you. We can talk while you get ready."

On their way up to the scout boat, they chatted about events since they'd seen each other last. Terra told Chryse about Jim Davidson.

"I'd like to meet him," Chryse said.

"You know him!"

"I do?"

"He says he piloted you home from Von Braun Grand Hotel after you left *Procyon's Promise* that first time."

"Maybe I do. Sandy hair, tall, handsome?"

Terra nodded.

"Well, congratulations!"

Chryse brought Terra up on events that had transpired since *Sword of Aragon* left Earth. When they arrived at *Siren Song*, Terra took her dress uniform from its locker and moved to the tiny washroom at the rear of the boat. She left the door open so they could talk as she stripped off her coveralls.

The boat's artificial gravity system was inoperative, leaving them in the asteroid's native gravitational field, which amounted to only about one-thirtieth of a standard gee. Chryse anchored herself to the deck with boot clamps. She watched as Terra sponged herself from the tiny zero-gee washbasin.

Chryse chuckled.

Terra looked at the older woman. A thin film of soap rimmed her eyes. "What's the matter?"

"I was just thinking about the first time we met. I remember how embarrassed you were when I peeled out of my shipsuit so nonchalantly. Now look at us."

Terra glanced down at the single, wispy strip of silk that was all she normally wore under her coveralls, then grinned. "I'll have to admit that contact with you Solarians has certainly liberalized my attitudes about certain things. I can now walk to the shower aboard *Arrogant* with a dozen other women watching and not blush at all; at least, not noticeably. I think I might even be able to handle a situation that called for mixed nudity if I'd had a few drinks first."

"Don't push it," Chryse replied, her manner turning serious. "You Alphans would be making a terrible mistake if you tried to make yourselves over into our image. If anything, we should try to be more like you."

Terra dried her face and turned to combing her hair.

"I'm curious about something, Chryse. If you don't want to answer, just tell me it's none of my business."

"What is it?"

Terra lowered her brush and stared at her friend and mentor. "You had everything at home. Why *did* you come on this expedition?"

Chryse bit her lip and didn't speak for several seconds. "If I tell you the truth, do you promise not to let a single word of it go beyond these walls?"

"I promise."

"It's really quite simple," Chryse said wistfully. "I've fallen in love with your father. I want to be where he is, even if that means traveling halfway across the galaxy."

"WHAT?" Terra asked, her mouth hanging open in astonishment.

"You heard me. I've developed a juvenile crush on your father."

"How? When?"

"I'm not sure. I think I first began to love him that night we flew across the pole together on our way to Geneva."

"Have you told him?" Terra asked.

"No, of course not," Chryse replied. "Besides, I talked it all out with my psychoanalyst before leaving Earth. He says that I don't really love Robert at all. I've just got a simple case of transference syndrome."

"I beg your pardon?"

"Transference syndrome. According to my analyst, what I really want is for life to be simpler. He says that's the reason I've always been addicted to ancient movies and why I was so dissatisfied heading up a major con- glomerate. My 'supposed love'—his words—is merely a by-product of my subconscious desire to lead a more structured life. My solution was to join this expedition, and I fell in love with your father to give me a good reason for doing so."

"And is he right?"

Chryse shrugged. "Could be. I know I've never been happier than I am right now. I've got a job at which I am highly skilled, I'm with people I care about, and I am doing something important. What more is there in life?"

"Is there anything I can do to help?"

"You already have. You've given me someone I can talk to. Now you'd best finish up. Time is getting short."

* * *

The Marine guard on sentry-go outside Suite 510 snapped to attention as Braedon walked hesitantly down the rough-hewn corridor.

"Are these my quarters, Corporal?" Braedon asked, gesturing to the curtained doorway behind the guard.

"Yes, sir."

"Where's the door?"

"Uh, the construction people are running late on doors, sir. They're casting 'em from local iron, and they ain't got their big foundry set up yet. That's why I'm here. I'll make sure nobody bothers you 'cept you want to be bothered."

"Fine," Braedon replied. "Everything in order?"

"Yes, sir. Vice-Commodore Tarns' gear has been cleaned out."

"Seems a shame to put him to the trouble," Braedon mused. "After all, in another ten days, he'll be moving back in."

"*You* are the expedition commander, sir; and *these* are the expedition commander's quarters."

"Quite right, Corporal. One shouldn't go against natural order."

"No, sir! It hurts morale."

Braedon shoved the curtain aside and entered the suite of rooms beyond. Except for a desk, a workscreen, a small wrought-iron table and six chairs, an inflatable sofa, two bare glow tubes, and a bundle of naked wires running across the ceiling, the room was devoid of decoration.

Braedon pushed aside another curtain to find similarly sparse furnishings in the bedroom beyond. A sleeping bag had been stretched out on the floor next to a gravity control box. Apparently, the occupant was expected to turn the artificial gravity down until he felt comfortable. A self-contained toilet had been set up in a small alcove off the bedroom, as had a water tank and washbasin topped with a mirror and a single glowtube.

Braedon glanced around his new quarters and nodded his approval. Considering that the whole asteroid had been a solid lump of nickel-iron just three months earlier, the construction battalion had performed miracles. He made a mental note to tour the rest of the facilities and see how the average expedition member lived. This far from home, a few amenities were worth their weight in platinum.

His luggage had been piled next to the sleeping bag. He took a few minutes to open his travel kit and hang his spare uniforms on a hook welded to the wall. He had just finished when he heard the guard's voice:

"Commodore, sir!"

"Yes, Corporal."

"There's a lady out here who says she's your daughter. Shall I show her in?"

"Absolutely!"

Terra pushed through the curtain and stood at attention just inside the door. What Braedon saw was a lithe, tan young woman in the blue-green dress uniform of an expedition pilot. "Hello, Father."

"Don't just stand there. Come over here where I can hug you." She moved to be enfolded by his embrace. "My God, you've grown up!" he exclaimed. He pushed her out to arms length to look at her again as his face broke into a broad smile of paternal pride.

"I got a letter from your mother just before leaving Earth. She sends her love. Also, Captain Smith tells me you've been doing an excellent job aboard *Aragon*."

"I've certainly done my best, Father."

"How would you like to do your best for me?"

"I beg your pardon?"

He told her of his plans to take *Procyon's Promise* and *Golden Hind* to the red-orange star of the Grelshos in ten days' time. "I'll exchange your scout boat for one of *Promise*'s."

To his surprise, Terra didn't accept his offer immediately. Instead, she chewed her lower lip for a few moments and then asked, "What about my copilot? Does he come along too?"

A smile spread across Braedon's lips as he began to understand what was bothering his daughter. "Captain Smith mentioned that you are seeing quite a lot of a certain young man. He wouldn't happen to be this copilot of yours, would he?"

"His name is Jim Davidson, and yes, he is," Terra said, obviously flustered.

"Sit down." When they were both seated on the inflatable sofa, Braedon said, "I don't mean to intrude on your personal life, Terra, but how serious is this thing between you and Davidson?"

"I'm not sure yet. Neither is Jim. It's more than affection, but we aren't lovers . . . not yet, anyway. That *is* what you are asking, isn't it?"

Braedon nodded. "It is. I think you'll agree that I haven't been a typical Alphan father. If I had been, you would never have been allowed to apply for admission to the academy."

"I know that, Father. I also know the anguish I put you through when I qualified for *Promise*'s crew. I'll always be grateful to you for not blocking my appointment."

"Then accept some fatherly advice. Be very sure about your feelings for this man. You are a thousand light-years from home, in constant danger, and your job requires you to be shut away for long periods with him. It's only natural that the two of you are attracted to each other. But remember your upbringing. We aren't the same as these Solarians. Their culture is not our culture. Be very sure before you do anything irreversible."

Terra laughed nervously. "Funny, someone just gave me almost exactly that same advice."

"Who?"

"Oh, just a friend."

"Will you listen to your old man?"

She leaned over and kissed him on the cheek. "I'll listen, and Father . . . thank you."

"For what?"

"For letting me live my own life."

"You're welcome." They stared at each other for a few uncomfortable seconds, then Braedon continued in a more normal conversational tone, "When do I get to meet this paragon?"

"When would you like to meet him?"

"I understand that I am hosting a dinner this evening for the construction battalion. Why don't you bring him around then?"

"I will if we can get a pass from Captain Smith."

Braedon guffawed. "I don't think *that* will be any problem. Now then, would you like me to transfer you back to *Procyon's Promise*?"

"Yes, sir. I would like that very much. Thank you."

"Not at all," Braedon responded. "What else are fathers for?"

* * *

The task of making *Procyon's Promise* and *Golden Hind* ready for space turned into a round-the-clock marathon of cargo shifting. First, the supplies that *Promise* had transported out from Earth had to be off-loaded. Then, when its holds were empty, they had to be refilled with the supplies that would be required during the expedition to the Grelsho sun. And, considering the number of scientists who found it essential that they (and all their equipment) be present at humanity's first contact with an alien species, Braedon wondered if the holds were big enough to contain it all.

A week after his arrival at Expedition Central, Braedon was in *Procyon's Promise*'s hangar bay watching crewmen transfer cargo from an orbit-to-orbit lighter into the starship's interior. To make room for the operation, *Promise*'s three scout boats and single FTL cutter had been temporarily moved out of the bay. The small fleet now hovered near their parent as crews feverishly checked them over. With only a single vessel in its maw, the hangar bay looked almost spacious.

"This is the last load of foodstuffs, Commodore," Chryse Haller said from beside him. She held a portable computer terminal and watched as the totals tallied up on the book-sized workscreen. A stray strand of blond hair had worked down into her eyes, and she moved to push it back into place. It was a gesture that Braedon found overwhelmingly attractive. If only . . .

He ruthlessly clamped down on the thought. "Fine, Chryse, let's top off the ammunition magazines next. Pass the word. We'll want full safety precautions imposed in twenty minutes."

"Full precautions, twenty minutes. Yes, sir."

"Any other problems in your department, Assistant Purser Haller?"

"We're having trouble squeezing in all the new personnel going along on this trip, sir, but we'll work something out."

"I understand you've billeted Terra in your cabin."

Chryse nodded. "It was her cabin before it was mine."

"Look after her for me, will you?" Braedon asked.

"My pleasure, Robert," Chryse replied, smiling. Then she frowned. "I *am* confused about one thing. If the commodore will permit me to ask a personal question?"

"You'd ask it anyway, I suspect. Go ahead."

"Why did you transfer Terra to this ship? As a scoutboat pilot, she's going to have one of the riskiest jobs when we get to the Grelsho sun. Why not leave her aboard *Sword of Aragon* where she would be safe here at base?"

"I thought about it," Braedon replied. "However, if I left her behind, she'd only find a way aboard *Procyon's Hope* or *Mayflower* when they go out on the Target Two Prime mission. This way, I can keep my eye on her; or rather, those of you kind enough to act as my agents can watch over her. It wouldn't do to have the expedition commander showing favoritism to his relatives, now would it?"

Chryse made a rude noise. "I think practically everyone onboard would help you toss Terra in the brig if that was what it took to keep her safe. I know for certain that there are members of *Promise*'s original crew who would cheerfully kill anyone who threatened her."

"Would they really?" he asked, surprised at the vehemence of her comment.

"Damned right! She's this expedition's unofficial mascot. If anything happened to her..."

"Thank you for the advice, Assistant Purser Haller. Carry on. I'll be on the bridge if you need me."

"Yes, sir!"

CHAPTER 20

"Are we about ready?" Braedon asked as he glanced across the control consoles to the rocky shape of Expedition Central ten kilometers "below." The asteroid lay low on the viewdome horizon, its form silhouetted against the reddish haze of the Sanctuary gas cloud.

"Just about, Robert," PROM's voice answered from close behind him. "Vice-Commodore Tarns is on the line. He's asking if you have time to speak with him."

"Put him on."

Tarns' features appeared on Braedon's workscreen.

"Hello, Bill," Braedon said. "Have you moved back into your quarters yet?"

Tarns grinned. "Yes, sir. I had my gear transferred about five minutes after you left. Don't hurry back."

"I understand completely."

As Braedon had suspected when he saw them, Commanding Officer's Quarters were the equivalent of a penthouse suite when compared to the other living spaces hollowed out of the asteroid's interior. Most personnel were housed in low-gravity bunkrooms where nylon mesh had been strung between supports to allow sleepers to be stacked four deep. Even the ranking officers and scientists stationed in the asteroid were forced to share small four-man cubicles. Bathing was a once-a-week luxury involving a washbasin and a sponge. Compared to conditions in The Rock, life aboard the overcrowded starships was a sybarite's delight.

"You know the plan, Bill," Braedon continued. "If you haven't heard from us in three months, send help. Only be damned cautious about it. If we get sucked into a trap, I don't want this whole expedition to follow us one ship at a time. Understood?"

"Understood, sir."

"Tell *Hope* and *Mayflower* I wished them luck with Target Two Prime, and for God's sake, remind them that I expect them to be careful too."

"Yes, sir. Anything else?"

Braedon considered for a moment, then shook his head. "That covers it, I guess. I hereby leave command of this expedition once more in your capable hands, sir!" This last was delivered with all the solemnity he could muster.

"I thank the commodore," Tarns replied in like manner.

"See you when we get back. I'll bring you a souvenir of the Grelshos, if you like."

"One clean vector to the Maker sun is all I require, sir. Good hunting!"

Braedon watched as the holoscreen faded to black, then turned his attention back to the flurry of activity on the bridge. As usual, even though PROM would be flying the ship, the human crewmembers were performing independent cross-checks of the computer's calculations. Senior Lieutenant Janos Corusk, the astrogator, was working the hardest, calculating the course to the jump-off point for the Grelsho sun. When he finished, he would compare his figures with those PROM had calculated. A difference of even one percent would cause Braedon to order the launch delayed until the discrepancy could be resolved. At the start of the voyage from Earth to Sanctuary, Corusk and PROM had managed to agree with each other to three significant decimal places.

"Captain Garrity, Robert."

"Connect him, PROM."

Lafe Garrity's features immediately appeared on the screen that Bill Tarns' face had just vacated. "*Golden Hind* is ready for space, Commodore. We await your orders."

"We'll be with you in a moment, Lafe. Astrogation check out your central computer's calculations?"

"Yes, sir. We have acceptable correlation."

"Very good. Tell GOLDIE to slave herself to PROM and stand by."

"Yes, sir."

Braedon keyed for the annunciator channel on his console. His voice immediately echoed throughout the ship. *This is the commodore speaking. All department heads, report status.*

"Engineering, ready for space."

"Purser, ready for space."

"Environmental control, ready for space."

"Combat control, ready for space..."

Braedon listened to the countdown run through the ship without a single bump. Finally, it reached the bridge, where the specialists completed the check.

"...communications, ready for space."

"Astrogation, ready for space."

"Executive Officer, ready for space."

"Central computer, ready for space," PROM said from an overhead speaker.

"Commanding Officer, ready for space," Braedon concluded. "PROM, you have the conn. Take us out gently."

"Command received and understood, Robert. On my count. Ten seconds. Five...four...three...two...one. Grav generators to power. We are underway!"

Procyon's Promise slipped slowly from her parking orbit. Two positions behind her, another globular starship followed close behind. The other ten ships in the formation took this as a signal to begin blinking their formation lights in silent applause.

Forty-eight hours later, the two starships were separated by a million kilometers of vacuum and speeding out of the Sanctuary system at ninety-eight percent of the speed of light. There was a quick flurry of messages between them, a last-minute updating of astrogation data, and five minutes of consultation between the two commanding officers. Then came the silence as accumulators charged and FTL generators came up to power. A last "Good Luck!" flashed between the ships and then came the change. One moment, their hulls reflected the blue-white glow of starlight. The next, they were gone.

*   *   *

"Damn it, Warrick, I told you to secure that packet for zero gee!"

"Aw, come on, ma'am! We was off watch five minutes ago. It can wait till tomorrow, can't it? Surely the captain ain't going to order zero gravs any time in the next twelve hours."

"You heard me, Spacer!"

Able Spacer Warrick glared at Chryse Haller while he remounted the ladder leading up the face of a tall stack of packing crates in *Promise*'s Number-one Hold. All around them, small mountains of hexagonal crates were secured into interlocking frames by bright metal latches. The latches on the crate in question, however, were dangling free. The crate had slipped far enough out of alignment to catch Chryse's eye as she inspected the ship's cargo.

The Number-one Hold was bordered by the environmental control compartment forward, the stardrive compartment inboard, the hull outboard, and the hangar deck aft. With the stardrive just one bulkhead away, the thrumming of the generators reverberated around Chryse.

"There, that suit you?" Warrick asked after he'd secured the latches.

Chryse made a show of studying his efforts from three meters below, then nodded. "Next watch, I want you to check out Holds Two and Three for loose latches. I'll have PROM remind everyone in the stevedore gang about the regulations concerning loose cargo. You can go now."

"Yes, ma'am."

Chryse's stern expression slowly melted into a grin as Warrick hurried toward the ladder leading up and out of the hold. Back on Earth, it hadn't taken long for word to get around that *Promise*'s new Assistant Purser was to be the rich and powerful Chryse Haller. The effect had been electric on the other Solarians aboard. It had taken weeks of patience on Chryse's part before the other terrestrials began to forget her background and accept her as one of the crew. Warrick had been a prime example. When first assigned to work with her, he'd been tonguetied in her presence. Now he felt comfortable enough to protest her orders.

She glanced up at the stack of cargo, let her eyes scan the multicolor crates and the arcane descriptions taped to their surfaces, and then turned back to the inventory that was her original purpose for being in the hold. In less than forty-eight hours, *Procyon's Promise* would break out of hypervelocity in the vicinity of the Grelsho sun. Chryse had resolved to make the most of the time remaining.

Terra Braedon was seated at the pilot's console in *Siren Song* when Jim Davidson stuck his head through the hatch in the aft bulkhead.

"Aren't you ready yet?"

Terra glanced up from the workscreen where she was running a diagnostic on the scout boat's drive and navigation systems.

"Ready for what?" she asked with a blank expression.

"For Professor Williams lecture, of course."

Terra groaned. "Is it *that* time already?"

"'Fraid so."

"Can't we skip it? We've got a thousand things to check over here if we're going to be ready for breakout."

Davidson shook his head. "The boss said the commodore wants all first contact personnel to attend. That's us, remember?"

Terra softly mouthed a Solarian expression unsuited for use by a proper Alphan lady. She tapped in a few brief instructions for the scout boat's nonsentient computer to follow while she was gone, then got up from her couch.

Terra and Jim Davidson descended the ladder from *Siren Song*'s airlock to *Promise*'s hangar deck. The scout boat occupied one of the docking mounts high up the hangar doors. Two other egg-shaped craft occupied the other "high docks," while a blunt cylinder with a rounded prow was squeezed onto the hangar deck between the three scout boats.

The cylindrical ship was the FTL cutter—capable of interstellar travel, but just barely. After designers had made room in the cutter's hull for the I-mass–initiated fusion generator, the gravitational drive, and the stardrive, they had barely enough room left over for the two-man crew and environmental control system. In fact, the cutter's control cabin was only slightly larger than that of the first Apollo space capsules.

Terra and Davidson made their way through the clutter

of the hangar deck, to the personnel lift, and up to Epsilon Deck where the ship's messhall was located. The compartment was eighty percent filled when they arrived. They drew cups of coffee from a stainless steel urn, carried them to two empty seats at one side of the compartment, and then turned their attention to Colin Williams. The white-haired xenologist was standing behind a makeshift lectern at the front of the compartment. His gaze scanned the audience impatiently. After a few minutes, he glanced at the chronometer on the wall, then cleared his throat.

"Let's get started, people, shall we?"

He waited for the buzz of two dozen conversations to quiet down, then turned to the large holoscreen that adorned one of the messhall bulkheads. "PROM has informed me that Commodore Braedon will be unable to attend. In his absence, let me say that I have been commissioned to give a brief overview of the Grelshos to those of you who will be involved in the initial contact effort. What you will see today is only a small portion of the data we have available in PROM's public access files, however. I want each of you to review this information in detail sometime before breakout. If you have questions, I'll be in my office during all of first watch tomorrow. Now, then, for those of you who have never seen a picture of one before, this is a Grelsho..."

The screen lit to show a gray, hairless centaurlike creature that put Chryse in mind of a tall alligator. That, at least, was her initial impression. The being was outwardly reptilian, but without the characteristic "bent-elbow" stance of a reptile. Its four legs hung vertically below its torso. The legs were articulated in the normal way and ended in splayed feet with prominent claws. A small tail lay curled around its hind legs.

The upper torso sported two arms that ended in grasping members whose details were obscured by the fact that the being was holding a piece of equipment in its "hands." A long, supple neck was topped by a bulging skull, in which the being's eyes were deepset. The eyes were protected by heavy bony overhangs and irised like a cat's, except the slit was oriented in a horizontal plane rather than vertical. There was no evidence of external ears except for a feature that might (or might not) be a tympanic membrane near the top of the skull. The Grelsho's features protruded in a snout with a single, slitlike nostril located between the eyes. The mouth was open, displaying long rows of teeth.

"...note the teeth," Professor Williams said after describing the Grelsho's other physical features. "The being is obviously an omnivore. Also, you will note that this is an outdoor scene; there are small patches of snow in the background; yet the Grelsho is not wearing clothing. That would indicate that it is warmblooded and that its temperature-control system may be somewhat more efficient than our own. Obviously, then, the Grelsho is not truly a reptile.

"Which brings me to the most important thing I have to say to you today, people! When you leave this ship, you *must* discard all preconceptions you may have concerning these beings. It may look like a couple of men in a lizard suit, but it is a Grelsho. If you learn nothing else about it, understand that it is totally alien to anything you have ever seen or experienced before."

The picture on the holoscreen changed to show a group of Grelsho doing something incomprehensible. The view changed again, this time displaying a Grelsho city beneath a red-orange sky. Professor Williams went on to survey the data that had been dredged from the data banks concerning the Grelsho civilization. They were far from the most advanced species among the eleven hundred known alien races, although they were especially capable in the fields of chemistry and solid-state physics. Based on a review of existing data, the xenologists had assigned the Grelsho civilization a rating that placed it approximately five hundred years ahead of current humanity.

"...I would remind you, however," Williams said, casting a baleful gaze over the audience, "that not only are such ratings inherently unreliable, but the data on which we base this opinion is over *two hundred thousand years out of date*! When we get to the Grelsho system, we will very likely not recognize the place."

Robert Braedon had been about to leave the bridge for Professor Williams' lecture when PROM notified him that Chief Engineer Reickert had an urgent need to speak to him.

"What's the matter, Chief?" Braedon asked, noting Reickert's troubled expression.

"I don't think we want to discuss it by screen, sir. Will you come to my office?"

"Of course."

Braedon informed Captain Garcia that he would be off the bridge for an indefinite time and asked PROM to tell Williams to proceed without him before heading for Reickert's office. The chief engineer occupied a cubicle set high above the stardrive compartment, with an entire wall constructed of armorglass through which he could survey the drive compartment below. A large holoscreen dominated the opposite wall. When Braedon arrived, he found Reickert and Scholar Price studying a series of graphs on the screen.

"What's the matter?" Braedon asked.

Horace Price glanced over his shoulder. For once, he wasn't smiling. "The drive has suffered some sort of anomoly, Robert. We're not yet sure how serious it is."

"What's happened?"

Reickert cleared his throat uneasily. "PROM sounded the alarm about twenty minutes ago after she detected a disturbance in the secondary phase-loop lock circuitry. It only lasted a couple of milliseconds and never really reached the limits of variance allowed by the specifications. I couldn't explain it, so I thought it best to call in expert assistance."

"What happened, PROM?"

"The secondary field coils drifted out of synchronization with their control loop for just an instant, Robert. The backups caught them and righted the situation within two milliseconds."

"So why did it happen?"

"That isn't clear from the data. The most likely cause is degradation in one or more components in the feedback loop. In essense, the stardrive settings are drifting slightly."

"It is likely one of the components we installed after the fire," Reickert said. "We might not have gotten everything synchronized perfectly."

"Is the ship in any danger?"

"We don't think so," Price said.

"You don't sound overly confident."

"Damn it, Robert, how can I be confident? After more

than thirty years of studying the stardrive, I still haven't
any clue as to how the damned thing works!"

"Can we make the Grelsho sun?"

"Certainly. However, it might be prudent to shut down
for a few hours to check out the system. If we lose our
phase-loop lock completely, we'll drop out of hypervelocity before we can shunt the energy in the field. I'd hate
to guess what would happen then."

Braedon turned to Reickert. "Do you concur?"

"Yes, sir. My people can't troubleshoot the system
while it's operating. Give us a few hours to look things
over and we'll be able to diagnose the problem with good
confidence."

Braedon nodded. "It will cause us to miss our timetable
with *Golden Hind*, but if we're going to break down, I'd
rather not do it where the Grelshos can see. PROM!"

"Yes, Robert."

"Prepare for emergency breakout. Shields up and alert
the crew."

Immediately, PROM's voice came on all over the starship. "Attention all hands! Prepare for emergency breakout in ten seconds. Prepare for emergency breakout.

"Five, four, three, two, one, break..."

A blinding flash and a deafening roar erupted from the
generator compartment behind Braedon. The armorglass
wall of the chief engineer's office bowed inward, held for
an instant, then exploded into a million tiny glass balls.
At the same moment, Braedon found himself lifted bodily
into the air as the gravity field reversed. An instant later,
it reversed again, and he was slammed into the deck.

CHAPTER 21

The first few seconds after the explosion stretched interminably for Robert Braedon. A wave of heat washed over him as a sharp, breath-stealing pain shot through his right shoulder. He rolled with the impact, only to feel a numbing blow to the base of his spine as he encountered something hard and sharp. His whimper of panic was drowned out by the clanging of alarms and the hissing roar of automatic fire extinguishers. He covered his eyes with crossed forearms to protect them from flying glass and lay still as waves of nausea threatened to send him reeling into unconsciousness. Someone in the drive compartment below began to scream.

As quickly as the roiling inside his skull subsided, Braedon uncovered his eyes. He found that he was lying face-up, his body wedged at an odd angle between Reickert's desk and a bulkhead. The air in the compartment had grown thick with smoke and the acrid smell of burning insulation. The emergency lights had come on, but there was something wrong with the beams they cast. Instead of being gray and smoky, the narrow rays scintillated brilliantly.

Braedon stared stupidly at them for long seconds, watching the sparkling lights without comprehension until his mind was drawn to a moment six years earlier. PROM had just revealed that the Solarians had spotted the starship, causing Braedon to order *Procyon's Promise* moved into the shadow of the probe. The gravfield had brushed the hulk and disturbed thousands of loose crystalline fibers. The fibers had scintillated brilliantly in raw sunlight as they floated free in zero gee.

Floated free in zero gee!

The revelation came with a speed that caused his head to throb. The scintillations were caused by shards from the armorglass window, none of which were settling to the deck. The artificial gravity had failed!

Braedon groaned and scratched at the deck, attempting to gain a firm handhold. He caught one of the desk pedestals with his right hand and used that to lever himself into a sitting position. He immediately regretted his rashness as the compartment began to rotate about him and red afterimages danced before his eyes. His lungs burned with chemical fire that caused him to double over in a spasm of coughing. When the attack passed, Braedon felt gingerly at the base of his skull where the pain seemed to be centered. He winced as his hand encountered a wet mass of matted hair and warm blood.

Braedon ignored the pain and the stinging smoke as he scanned the compartment for his companions. He found Horace Price immediately. The scholar was floating near the overhead in a far corner of the compartment, hanging in the air as though he were floating face-down in a pool of water. Braedon peered through the haze, straining to catch sight of the chief engineer. With the glow panels off and only two emergency lights for illumination, the compartment was filled with unfamiliar shadows. It took several seconds for him to notice the booted foot sticking out from one of the small equipment lockers at the back of the office. The force of the explosion had torn the locker door from its hinges.

Braedon carefully made his way to Horace Price, anchored himself to Reickert's chair, and reached up to grab Price's belt. He pulled the scholar down to the desk and quickly probed at his jugular, searching anxiously for a pulse. He allowed himself a deep sigh of relief when he found a strong, steady throbbing beneath his fingers.

Price stirred and opened his eyes. "What happened?"

Braedon described the explosion.

Price's nod was barely noticeable. "I should have thought of that," he whispered haltingly. "It was the shunt circuit, the one we use to bleed energy out of the field. Our anomoly was a warning that the shunts were going out of synch! Something failed as soon as PROM began to channel energy to the shunts..."

"Save your strength."

Price looked around the smoke-filled compartment as though he were seeing it for the first time. "I don't understand why we aren't dead." With that, he fainted.

"PROM, get us some help in here, quick!" Braedon called.

The computer didn't answer. He cursed and glanced around for some place to secure Horace Price. Braedon finally decided to shove Price into the same cubbyhole he himself had just vacated. After the scholar was anchored, Braedon swarmed to where Reickert's boot was protruding. He noted with alarm that the smoke was now mixed with a fog of red droplets. He pulled Reickert free of the equipment locker and carefully checked him over, but the chief engineer's only wound appeared to be a deep gash on his forehead from which blood was oozing freely.

Working quickly, Braedon moved to the bulkhead behind the desk and unclipped the compartment's regulation first-aid kit, opened it, removed a zero-gee pressure patch, and clapped it over Reickert's wound. Upon touching skin, the polymer adhered and sealed the cut. The bandage ballooned outward as it filled with blood, but no more fluid escaped into the compartment.

Braedon glanced up at the chronometer on the wall and was surprised to see that less than a minute had elapsed since the explosion. He moved to the empty frame where the armorglass wall had been. The fire was out in the stardrive compartment below. Several watch-standers were swarming through the close-packed machinery, looking for their fellows who had been unlucky enough to be in direct line with the blast when it had come.

"You two!" Braedon called.

Two engineers glanced up, their faces black with soot and shock.

"Scholar Price and the chief are injured up here. Help me get them to sick bay!"

*   *   *

In the messhall, Colin Williams had just finished answering a question from the audience when PROM announced the emergency breakout. Worried looks were exchanged by several crewmembers as a muffled *whump!* shook the compartment. Williams watched in surprise as the rear row of his audience bounced into the air, as though on the back of an invisible wave, and then crashed to the deck. In an instant, the wave had traversed the messhall, uprooting unsuspecting victims. When it reached the podium, Williams felt himself lifted as the artificial gravity reversed polarity. It reversed again, throwing him the meter and a half to the deck before failing altogether.

Terra Braedon lay where she had fallen, her breath momentarily knocked from her. Around her, people were beginning to float away from the deck. She felt herself rise, twisting into the air, but lacked the ability to do anything about it. The struggle to get her lungs working took all of her energy. Simultaneous with her first gasp, she felt strong hands pulling her back down to the deck. A worried face suddenly appeared in her blurred field of vision.

"Are you all right?" Jim Davidson asked.

After several tries, she managed to nod. "What happened?"

"Whatever it was, it ain't good news," he said, glancing about nervously.

Terra twisted her body to an upright position, making sure to keep a firm grip on the mess table, and surveyed the damage. The messhall was a shambles. Plates, pots, pans, and utensils were spilling out of the open galley door. Everywhere she looked, people were floating helpless, holding injured heads, arms, legs, or sides. Their cries reverberated from the walls and the din was deafening. A dozen people seemed to be unconscious. Here and there, a hardy individual moved to succor the wounded. The glow panels had failed, leaving the emergency lights the only illumination.

"Anything broken?" Davidson asked, probing Terra's arms and legs gently with his hands.

"I don't think so."

"Then let's get out of here!"

"We can't," she protested. "Someone's got to help the injured."

"Leave them. Others can get them to sick bay. Right now, the most important thing is to find out what's happened to the ship."

She reluctantly followed him to the messhall entrance and out into the corridor. The corridors were filled with people, some moving purposefully and urgently to their duty stations while others were merely floating obstacles. Davidson ignored them all as he made his way resolutely toward the bridge. If he had considered that two scout-boat pilots might not be welcomed there during an emergency, he showed no sign.

With all the confusion in the corridors, they took nearly ten minutes to work their way up to Beta Deck and the main corridor leading to the bridge. For some reason, Beta Deck was nearly deserted. As they emerged from an emergency stairwell, Terra spotted a familiar figure moving awkwardly through the dimly lit corridor.

"Father!"

Braedon turned at her shout, saw who it was, and allowed a lopsided grin to emerge from his worried features. "Thank God, you're safe!"

"You're hurt!" she exclaimed.

"Not seriously," he said. "What about you?"

"Oh, a few bruises and contusions, plus a splitting headache! Nothing that a little rest won't fix."

"And you, Jim?" Braedon asked Davidson.

"I'm fine, sir. What happened?"

Braedon quickly explained about the explosion in the stardrive compartment. "It seems to have knocked out the lights, artificial gravity, and God knows what else. Have either of you heard from PROM?"

Terra was suddenly aware of what had been bothering her during the whole difficult trip up from the messhall. There had been no orders from PROM, who should have been directing the crew's efforts at damage control. "Not a word, Father!"

Braedon sighed. "Me neither. I'm afraid that she may be among the casualties. Her circuits took quite a jolt."

"Surely not PROM!"

"I hope not. Come on, I have to get to the bridge and see how badly we've been hurt."

Terra and Davidson followed as he pulled himself along the emergency handrails in the direction of the bridge.

They turned a corner and found themselves facing a closed door with a flashing red light above it. The door was part of the automatic pressure-control system aboard the ship. Normally open, it was designed to close the instant sensors detected a difference in pressure between compartments on either side of the bulkhead. That the pressure door was closed could only mean that the compartment beyond had lost its pressure integrity.

Promise's bridge was open to vacuum.

The flashing red light's reflection in the burnished steel of the pressure door unnerved Braedon more than he was willing to admit, even to himself. A dozen years had passed since he first settled into the leather embrace of his command chair and gazed upward at the vaulting black sky beyond the viewdome. For more than a decade, *Promise*'s bridge had been the focus of his existence, the one constant in his personal universe. The thought that a silent, airless tomb now lay beyond the pressure door was nearly too much to bear. With a cry of anguish, he rushed forward to peer through the small glass spyhole in the center of the door. There was nothing to see except the ladder leading up to the bridge hatchway. The ladder flashed alternately red and white as a warning light on the other side kept time with the one above Braedon's head.

"Damn!" he said.

"What's the matter, Father?"

"Can't see a damned thing," he reported. He scrunched down to angle his line of sight as high as it would go, but with the same result.

His hands shook as he reached for the small valve set in the pressure bulkhead next to the door. He savagely wrenched the handle as he prayed that the door had been activated by a malfunctioning sensor rather than a loss of atmosphere on the bridge. His heart stuttered when a brisk wind began flowing into the valve with the unmistakable sound of leaking air.

"It looks bad, doesn't it, sir?" Davidson asked.

A shudder ran up Braedon's spine as he closed the valve. He nodded. "The viewdome must have cracked under the stress of the gravity surge."

Globular tears formed at the corners of Terra's eyes. They were mirrored by the sudden hot wetness in Braedon's own eyes. "Time to grieve later," he said more gruffly than he intended. "Right now, I need runners. You two are elected. I want you to find the highest ranking officer in each department. Tell them that they are to organize their own DC teams and not wait for orders from Damage Control Central. Find Colin Williams and tell him that I expect his scientists to keep out of the passageways. Tell him I'll order the Marines to clear them by force if I have to.

"After you've done that, go to communications and requisition their entire supply of hand communicators. Distribute them to the department heads and have them assign one rating in every compartment to monitor the emergency bands for orders. We'll use hand comms until we can get the annunciators working again."

"Where will you be, sir?" Davidson asked.

"I'm going to try and see how badly we've been hurt. If anyone wants me, I'll be on the command circuit. It had better be damned important, though."

Terra and Davidson asked a few more questions, then kicked off and arrowed down the length of the corridor to the ladder which they had come up a few minutes earlier. Braedon watched them go before turning back to gaze up at the baleful red light above the pressure door. He couldn't help thinking that it was mocking him, telling him that only a fool leaves his wife and home to go adventuring among the stars.

An hour later, as Braedon threw himself into his work, the shock had begun to wear off. He had elbowed his way through crowded passageways to Damage Control Central where a frantic damage control officer was seated at a darkened control board trying to coordinate repair efforts with a handheld communicator. The officer, a Lieutenant Mo'anda, jumped hastily to his feet as Braedon entered.

"For God's sake, sit down and get back to work!" Braedon sketched the situation he'd found forward and told Mo'anda to get a portable airlock set up in a position to seal off the corridor just beyond the pressure door. He finished by telling the hulking DC officer: "Make it as fast as you can. There may be survivors running out of air in there."

"Survivors, sir?" Mo'anda asked. "With the viewdome gone?"

Braedon felt a rush of anger. "I know it isn't likely, damn it, but it's possible! Some of those instrument lockers are airtight. If those poor bastards had even a little warning, one or two might have had the presence of mind to get inside one and button it up. Check everywhere, understand?"

"Yes, sir. I'll have a crew there within five minutes."

Braedon didn't wait to see the damage party dispatched. Instead, he set off for the compartment in which PROM's central processors were housed. When he arrived, he found a party of spacers cutting into the two-meter-diameter, armored kiosk that protected both PROM and her vital machinery. "How's it going, Gomez?"

The engineer-second glanced up momentarily at the sound of Braedon's voice, then continued to wield the plasma torch with careful precision. Since PROM's main processing units required no maintenance, the engineers who designed the kiosk hadn't seen any reason to include an access hatch. "We're almost through the armor plate, Commodore. We've managed to splice into the power lines and have confirmed that PROM is still drawing power from the emergency circuits. I think there's a good chance that she's alive in there."

"I hope you're right. Get to her as quickly as you can. She thinks so much faster than we do that an hour of sensory deprivation may be enough to unbalance her."

"I'm working as fast as I can, sir, but one wrong cut could slice her brain in two."

"Do the best you can."

"Yes, sir."

Braedon's next stop was Engineering. Assistant Chief Engineer Chou had taken over Reickert's office. Braedon stood before the gaping hole where the armorglass wall had been and stared down into the stardrive compartment. "Give me the bad news, Chou."

"It was definitely the shunts, sir," Reickert's assistant said. "One of the components we replaced after the fire earlier this year had a flaw in it. I guess we rushed a bit too much getting it installed. My department will take full responsibility for the oversight."

"I'm more interested in fixing the ship than the blame, Chou. How long for repairs?"

"Assuming we can fix it..."

"Is there any doubt of that?"

"Not really, sir. Actually, the drive is in remarkably good shape considering that we could easily have blown its guts out. The primary coils have come through in good order. The secondaries are singed a bit in spots, but in working order. I estimate a couple of weeks minimum to get the spares in and rebalance the system."

"What about the other repairs?"

"Chief Hanada reports that his people will have the artificial gravity working within the hour. As for everything else, it'll have to wait until I can free up some people. We've put temporary patches on a couple of hull plates that were sprung when the gravity reversed polarity. Also, several generators burned out when the electrical system surged, so our electromagnetic shields are inoperative. At our current speed, it would be decidedly unhealthy to go outside in a vacsuit. Luckily, we were buttoned up for breakout, so the mechanical shields and the hull are blocking out most of the seepage. I've asked auxiliary control to keep us pointed butt-first along our orbital track so the hangar deck will absorb what little radiation gets through the hull."

"And the grav generators?"

"Undamaged so far as we can tell, Commodore."

"Then I can maneuver?"

"Yes, sir. Although where you're going to maneuver to half a dozen light-years from the nearest star is beyond me."

Braedon snapped open his communicator and said, "Auxiliary control!"

After a few seconds, a reedy voice acknowledged his call.

"I want one-quarter gee, positive, along the ship's axis in one minute. Bring it up slow. Repeat!"

"Positive zero-point-two-five gravs, one minute, gentle as she goes! Order received and understood, sir."

Braedon switched to the emergency frequency on his communicator. "All stations! Secure for acceleration. We are going to one-quarter gravity in fifty seconds."

He waited for the sensation of weight to build up beneath

his boots, then left Chou's office. After engineering, Braedon visited sick bay, a madhouse of activity, with injured people spilling in both directions along the passageway outside. The normally immaculate white tunic of Doctor Prakolova, *Promise*'s chief medic, was splattered with blood and other, less easily identifiable stains.

"How are things going, Doctor?" Braedon asked as Prakolova bound up the arm of one of the Solarian scientists.

"It could have been worse, Commodore." She gestured toward the sick-bay annex where the dead were being housed temporarily. Braedon had made it a point to check the eight corpses laid out in a neat row on the steel deck.

"I'm afraid it *is* worse," he explained, telling her about the conditions on the bridge.

"How many?"

"A dozen, including Captain Garcia, maybe more if maintenance was underway."

"Dear God in heaven!"

Braedon nodded. "If only I hadn't... Never mind. It does no good to dwell on it now. What have you done with Horace Price?"

Doctor Prakolova frowned. "I'm not sure. There have been so many. No, I believe he's been transferred to the wardroom with some of the other ambulatory wounded."

Braedon hurried to the wardroom, stepping over bandaged bodies in the corridor as he went. Scholar Price was seated on the deck with his back against a steel bulkhead. Chryse Haller was leaning over him, wrapping Price's head with a white bandage.

Braedon squatted next to her. He was surprised at the strength of the relief he felt at seeing her unharmed. "Are you all right?"

She looked at him and smiled. "Nothing broken but my pride. I was lucky."

"How are *you* feeling, Horace?"

Price glanced up from the pocket calculator he had been manipulating. The emergency lights caught his white hair, creating a halo effect. "I'm confused."

"How so?"

"Unless I've misplaced quite a few decimal points, we should have been vaporized when that shunt blew. There was enough energy locked in the field to fuel a small sun.

It had to go somewhere, but I haven't the foggiest idea where! The surge which damaged us was just a minor spillover from the main flow."

"Apparently, the Star Travelers built better than we realized," Chryse said.

"That they did," Price agreed. "They also may have violated a couple of basic universal laws in the process. Damned curious if you ask me."

Braedon was about to answer when the communicator at his belt beeped for attention. He unhooked it and lifted it up to his lips. "Yes?"

"Mo'anda, Commodore. My crew just reported in from the bridge. I'm sorry to inform you that there were no survivors."

"Who?"

"I don't have the complete list, sir. Captain Garcia, Astrogator Corusk, Communicator Spencer."

"How many total?"

"Fourteen, sir."

"Was it the viewdome?"

"No, sir. The dome seems to be intact. However, the dome's perimeter seals ripped under the load of the gravity reversal. My man estimates that decompression took less than a second."

"Thank your people for me, Mo'anda."

"Yes, sir. Uh, Engineer Gomez asked that I pass along a message, sir. He would like you to stop in the computer compartment at your earliest convenience."

"Tell him that I'm on my way."

Braedon left the wardroom and headed down to where the engineers were working to free PROM. Gomez's people were clustered around the jagged hole that the plasma torch had cut into the kiosk. He glanced inside to see Gomez's feet braced against the braces that supported the cluster of memory modules in which PROM was housed. Gomez's upper torso disappeared above the entry hole.

"You wanted to see me?" Braedon shouted into the kiosk.

"That you, Commodore?" came the muffled reply. "I'm about to plug a jumper into PROM's main I0 circuits. I thought you would like to be on hand when I do."

"You thought right."

"Charma!" Gomez called out.

A small, dark-skinned spacer ducked his head into the hole and twisted to look upward. "Yeah, Juan?"

"Give Commodore Braedon your call box and I'll route this circuit out to him."

"Will do, Juan." The engineer's mate gave Braedon a small box with a keypad in its face. "You punch this key here, sir, and you speak into the top. Wait for the light to come on first. There, that's it. Now, just talk."

Braedon tentatively called out, "PROM?"

A familiar voice responded immediately. "I'm here, Robert. Thank you for rescuing me, I was beginning to worry."

"Thank Mr. Gomez. He did all the work."

"Thank you, Juan."

"De nada, PROM," the distant voice called out. "Stand by while I hook into the outer detector loops and we'll give you your eyes back."

There were several seconds of silence, followed by Gomez asking, "There, how's that?"

PROM didn't answer for several seconds. When she did, there was an undercurrent of urgency in her voice that hadn't been there before.

"Robert, the sky here—"

"What about it?"

"It's filled with the radiation wakes of starships. Thousands of them!"

CHAPTER 22

The mass funeral was held the next day. By long tradition, the dead of space are always buried quickly. Whether laid to rest beneath a dusty lunar plain or sealed into a crypt carved from the nickel-iron surface of an asteroid or zipped into a plastic body bag and ejected with full ceremony out of a ship's airlock, custom demanded interment within twenty-four hours of death. Like most customs, this one had its origins in necessity. The primitive environmental control systems of the first spaceships had not been up to the task of fully cleansing the air after a corpse began to decompose. Also, the isolation and danger that were an integral part of early space travel had a curious effect on the human mind. Spacemen were found to be especially sensitive to the morbid thoughts that naturally arise when one's partner, spouse, or loved one is lying stone cold in the next cabin.

Thus it was that the morning after the explosion in the stardrive compartment, all of *Promise*'s complement turned out in full dress uniform to pay their respects to the twenty-two who had died. Their coffins were laid end to end around the main corridor circling *Procyon's Promise*'s waist. Each coffin was draped with the flag of the deceased's planet of birth. The rainbow hues of Earth were interspersed with the dark blue of Alpha, while one coffin showed the dusky red colors of Mars and another, the midnight black of the Asteroid Republic.

209

Each coffin sat on its own bier, several messhall tables having been unbolted from the deck and covered with black cloth for the occasion. At each station, a single guard of honor stood rigidly at attention while Chaplain Ibanez and a Solarian scientist who was also a Buddhist monk paused to pray for the soul of the deceased. Following prayers, four pallbearers lifted each coffin from its resting place and bore it to the main airlock. Drums rolled as two vacsuited spacers reverently lifted the enshrouded body from its box and carried it into the airlock. Once inside, they cycled the airlock closed. When the door reopened, the lock would be empty save for the spacers, and the process would begin again.

When the last of the deceased had been set on his or her final orbit, Braedon ordered the ship's company to attention via the intraship annunciators. He stepped up to the podium that had been hurriedly rigged in the corridor and began to read from *The Book of Pathfinder*.

"... And what does one say to those who warn that people will die in this great quest of ours? Indeed, what *can* one say except to acknowledge the obvious? Of course, people will die! Out of the billions of souls who have inhabited the Earth since the beginning of time, not one has yet succeeded in living forever. Nor, I suspect, will many of us who make up *Pathfinder*'s original crew live to see planetfall in the Procyon system a hundred years hence.

"What matters, then, is not the fact of death, but the manner in which we choose to die. Are we to expire in bed, with the covers clutched over our quaking heads; or will our last sight be a vista of glowing stars stretching outward to infinity? Each of us has considered that question, and our presence here is all the answer we need give. Therefore, let us face the unknown eagerly as we cross the gulf of interstellar space that stands between us and our goal. For, as a great poet once spoke of life and death:

"'The woods are lovely, dark and deep.
But I have promises to keep,
And miles to go before I sleep,
And miles to go before I sleep.'"

Braedon waited for the amplified echo of his voice to cease reverberating through the ship's passageways before concluding: "Thus spoke Commodore Eric Stassel to his crew on the eve of *Pathfinder*'s departure from the solar system."

Braedon's words were followed immediately by the mournful notes of a single trumpet blowing *Taps*, while all over the ship, *Promise*'s crewmen silently prayed for their dead.

The last trumpet notes were still echoing when PROM's voice emanated from the annunciators: "All hands, resume damage control duties!"

In the messhall, fifty crewmembers in dress uniform broke ranks and headed for the hatchway. Chryse Haller was one of them. Though most people were on their way to their billets to change into fatigues, Chryse turned left out of the messhall and headed for the purser's office. As she walked, her mind was busy with thoughts of fate.

She remembered very little of the accident. One moment, she had been checking cargo in the Number-one Hold, and the next she was slammed into the deck. She had awakened beneath a pile of packing crates that would have crushed her had the artificial gravity been working. That she had survived the collapse of the cargo stacks was a miracle. Spacer Warrick hadn't been as lucky. He'd been hurrying back to his bunkroom after Chryse dismissed him. The explosion and gravity field reversal had caught him descending a ladder between decks. The resulting fall had broken his neck; he was one of the twenty-two silent forms drifting toward infinity.

The ship itself hadn't been visibly hurt, save for the fire damage in the stardrive compartment. However, some of the energy in the drive field had reappeared as surplus electrical charge and played holy hell with the ship's electronics. Virtually every overload protector aboard had been blown. As Chryse walked, she detoured around several places where access covers had been removed and loose wires strung along the passageway as *Promise*'s crew worked nonstop to repair the damage. It had been eighteen hours since the explosion and the job was barely begun.

"Chryse!"

Chryse turned.

Jim Davidson was running down the corridor behind her. "The captain wants to see you in the wardroom."

"The wardroom? But that's the department heads' conference. Are you sure you haven't made a mistake?"

"No mistake. He told me he needs the best advice he can find, and that I was to find you if I had to tear the ship apart looking. He would have had PROM locate you, but most of her internal sensors are still out of commission."

"When does he want me?"

"Ten minutes ago!"

The wardroom was crowded when Chryse arrived. Besides Braedon, representatives of every major department aboard ship were present. Scholar Price, Chaplain Ibanez, Chief Engineer Reickert, Second Officer (Acting Executive Officer) Chamberlain, Javral Pere, Colin Williams, several members of the scientific staff, and the command pilot of the FTL cutter were arrayed around the wardroom table. Braedon caught her eye and gestured for her to take the seat next to his. She did so then let her gaze scan the compartment. She noted various bruises and bandages. The sharp smell of ointments and alcohol hung in the air.

Braedon pounded on the table with a fused lump of metal that had once been an overload protector. The compartment immediately grew quiet.

"As you have all heard by now, PROM has detected a large number of radiation sources at right angle to our present course. Since these sources bear a strong resemblance to starship wakes, and since *our* starships aren't responsible for them, we must assume that we have uncovered evidence of a widespread, starfaring civilization. Obviously, this discovery changes a great many things. I have asked you here to advise me on what, if anything, we should do about it. Before we begin, however, I want an update on the condition of my ship. Hans, you lead off."

Chief Engineer Reickert, his head swathed in grease-stained bandages, rested his elbows on the table and regarded Braedon. His haggard eyes and gaunt face testified to his lack of sleep.

"We pretty much have the damage categorized, sir. "It's bad, but it could have been a lot worse. As you would expect, the most damage was to the secondary generator that took the full force of the shunt failure. It's beyond repair. My engineers are removing it from the system and getting its replacement ready for installation."

"How long?"

"Another hundred hours, not counting the time we need to recalibrate."

"What about the rest of the ship?"

"We've taken a lot of damage to the comm links and power distribution network; somewhat less to the non-sentient computer systems, long-range sensors, and external communications; and—except for a few sprung plates—very little to the main frame and hull. The grav drive also seems to be undamaged. At least, it worked well enough before we got the artificial gravity operating again. We have the electromagnetic shields running at just about fifty-percent efficiency. They should be back up to full strength by this time tomorrow. In the meantime, I strongly recommend against lowering the mechanical shields. The particle wind is particularly brisk out there at the moment. Uh, that's about it, Commodore."

Braedon acknowledged Reickert's report and turned to Lieutenant MacIntire, the FTL cutter pilot. "What about your ship, Mac? Any problems to report?"

"The I-mass generator field coils were jarred a bit out of alignment by the gravity surge, but nothing we can't tune out again. I've got a crew working on it."

"When would you be able to take the cutter out?"

"Anytime, sir. Shall I order my crew to begin the count-down?"

"Hold off for now. I'm just exploring my options at the moment." Braedon scanned the assembled department heads and scientists. "What about the rest of you?"

The reports continued around the table. The picture that emerged was of a ship and crew that had been bloodied but not defeated. Repairs were underway, but a disheartening amount of work remained to be done.

By the time the last status report was finished, several of the scientists were beginning to fidget. Braedon recognized the signs, and immediately suggested that they move on to the main subject of the meeting. "Your report, please, PROM."

The wardroom holoscreen lit to show the black of space and a cluster of stars. The scene was normal, showing no sign of relativistic distortion—which meant that PROM had run it through a processing routine, since *Procyon's Promise* was still moving in the general direction of the Grelsho sun at better than 0.9 *c*.

"My first action after Engineer Gomez restored my data links was to command a full hemispheric scan by all sensors still operating. This is the view at eighty-seven mark sixteen degrees to starboard of our current velocity vector. You are looking at the scene as it would appear in the visible light band with zero relative velocity. As you can see, there is nothing special about this particular section of sky in the visible wavelengths. Observe, then, the same view at cosmic-ray frequencies!"

On the screen, the stars dimmed as they turned color. Other points of light blazed in their place. Some were sharply defined, others were fuzzy clouds of radiance. The scene reminded Chryse of a particularly bright and well populated star cluster. PROM continued: "What you are looking at are two thousand six hundred separate sources of high-energy radiation, each of which bears the characteristic pattern of a starship's wake."

"How far, PROM?" Scholar Price asked.

"The nearest wake is some twenty light-years off; the farthest, twice that."

"Any idea where these hypertracks originate?"

"Several star systems lie close to the apparent line of travel, but none intersect it. The origin could be any of a half-dozen stars."

"Would we be able to backtrack along the line if we wanted to?"

"It would require our dropping out of hypervelocity every few light-years to make observations; but yes, we could backtrack the sources."

Braedon turned to Chief Engineer Reickert. "What about it, Hans? Can the drive take the abuse of that many breakouts?"

"No problem if we get the system properly calibrated, sir."

Javral Pere leaned forward with a scowl on his face.

"Surely, Commodore Braedon, you aren't thinking of taking this ship on such a fool's errand!"

"I'm not convinced that it *is* a fool's errand, Citizen Pere."

"But what purpose would it serve?"

"Obviously, to find the people responsible for *that*!" Braedon said, pointing at the constellation of fuzzy radiances in the depths of the holoscreen.

"I'm sorry, sir, but I must protest such a plan vigorously. My government agreed to help find the Makers, not to chase after will-o'-the-wisps. We have an obligation not to be diverted from our quest until The Promise is fulfilled..."

Pere's protest was suddenly interrupted by feminine laughter. The source was Chryse Haller.

He turned to her, glaring. "Have I said something funny?"

"I seem to remember when you weren't quite such a fervent supporter of The Promise, Javral."

Pere blushed at the reference to his part in the raid on Moose Hill. Nevertheless, he refused to retreat. "There is no inconsistency in my position, none whatever. The Communion agreed to this expedition on the assumption that we would be making contact only with races which lack the stardrive. Obviously, should such a race react badly to our presence, we can always leave their system and be assured that they cannot follow.

"Whoever made those wakes *does* possess starships. If we are able to follow their hypertrack, surely they can do the same with ours! Quite frankly, the possibility that something like this would happen is the reason my government opposed this expedition in the first place. A decision to make contact with an FTL-capable race involves the safety of the human race. It is a question for the authorities back home, not for us here in this compartment."

Terra Braedon sat amid a jumble of electrical and fiber optic cables, intently watching the screen of a machine whose distant ancestor had been an oscilloscope. As she stared, she probed gently at a color-coded cable with an inductive pickup. The complex waveform on the screen remained unchanged—not a good sign.

"Anything?" she asked.

"Nothing," PROM replied. "The overload must be higher up."

"I don't see how it can be." Terra let her gaze drift away from the waveform on the screen and up the side of the stainless steel kiosk in front of her. The four-meter-diameter cylinder extended from deck to overhead and was featureless save for the jagged hole that had been carved in its side. The cluster of memory crystals in which PROM's central processors were housed lay exposed beyond the cylinder wall. "I checked continuity between junctions Tau-Sixteen and Zeta-Nine less than an hour ago."

"Nevertheless, one *has* to be there. I'm totally blind on every deck aft of Gamma."

"All right, I'll check again."

"Hello, there."

Terra twisted around at the sound of the new voice. She found Aeneas Spatz standing over her. "Hello, yourself. I see that you've been dragooned into spaghetti tracing too."

He hoisted a circuit tester identical to the one she was using and grinned. "You mean this thing? There I was, enjoying a leisurely cup of coffee in the messhall when Chief Hanada came in and said, 'I want three volunteers—you, you, and you!' I was the third 'you.'"

"Did you come past the wardroom on your way down?"

Spatz nodded.

"How is the conference going?"

"They were arguing as I came past. At least, that was the interpretation I put on the angry buzzing that makes its way out through the soundproofing."

"How long has it been now?"

Spatz glanced at the chronometer on the bulkhead. "Six hours, going on seven."

Terra's response was a low whistle. "I wonder what can be taking so long?"

"Good question. How long does it take to decide that discretion is the better part of valor?"

"I beg your pardon?"

"Old Earth expression," he explained. "In this case it means 'Knowing when it's time to turn tail and run.'"

"Run?"

"Like a rabbit. You haven't seen PROM's data yet, have you? Well, my boss had me up all night doing correlation and analysis. Based on what I saw, I can safely predict that I'll be sunning myself on Waikiki Beach this time next year."

Terra frowned. There was something about Spatz's bantering tone that irritated her. Like everyone else, she'd heard the rumors about the starship wakes. So far, access to the data had been restricted to her father, a few officers, and senior scientists like Horace Price and Colin Williams.

"There'll be no running, not until we've fulfilled The Promise!"

"Did you know more than twenty-six hundred separate hypertracks are clustered together in a region of sky less than half a second of arc across?"

"Is that true, PROM?"

"I'm sorry, Terra, but that information is classified until your father releases it."

"You can take it from me," Spatz said. "It's true. Do you have any idea of the significance of PROM's sighting?"

Terra shrugged. "It means that someone else has invented starflight."

"It means a lot more than that. We have obviously stumbled across a major trade route between the stars. I did some calculations last night. I assumed that this trade route is the only such for a hundred light-years in any direction, then calculated the probability of our breaking out in position to see it. Care to estimate the odds I came up with?"

"A thousand to one against, perhaps?"

Spatz laughed. "Not even close. The number's so large that only an astronomer would understand it. Think of trying to find a particular grain of sand in the Sahara desert and you'll be close."

"Yet we *have* seen the trade route, as you call it."

"Which only means that my assumption has to be wrong. So, I approached the problem from another direction. I assumed that there are a fixed number of 'trade routes' within a hundred light-year radius and then calculated the probability of our having sighted any one of them. I kept increasing the number until I had the odds whittled down to a mere ten-to-one against. Then I esti-

mated the number of starships required to make that many
hypertracks, I even assumed that a single ship could be
responsible for multiple wakes by traveling the same route
several times. Care to hear my conclusion?"

"Of course," Terra said, not at all sure that she really
did. Some of what Aeneas was saying was beginning to
sink in.

"I estimated a population of more than a billion starships! What's more, I was intentionally conservative. It
could be several times that number. If we're up against
a civilization that large, is there any doubt that we'll be
hightailing it for home just as fast as we're able?"

"Colin Williams has explained your work at quite some
length to the department heads, Aeneas," PROM said from
the overhead speaker. "You are to be congratulated on a
perceptive piece of deduction. I couldn't have done better
myself."

"Thank you, gentlelady," Spatz said, bowing toward
the exposed memory crystals inside the steel column.
"Coming from you, that is high praise!"

"You're welcome," the computer replied. "By the way,
Commodore Braedon has just brought the discussion in
the wardroom to a close. He has asked that I alert all
hands to an announcement in ten minutes."

Spatz nodded. "We're going home, right?"

"Not exactly. The FTL cutter is returning to Sanctuary
to inform the fleet. We, however, will follow the 'trade
route' to its point of origin and will attempt to make contact with the beings responsible."

CHAPTER 23

"All hands to duty stations. Make all preparations for getting underway. All hands to duty stations..."

Robert Braedon sat in his command chair on *Promise*'s bridge and listened to the "All Hands" call. Usually it sent an electric chill racing up his spine. Not this time. Too much pain and heartache lay behind him, too much uncertainty lay ahead. The old exhilaration had been crowded out of him.

Overhead, the viewdome showed no sign of the disaster which had cost fourteen bridge personnel their lives The failure had come, not in the dome, but rather in the structure that anchored the great armorglass lens to the hull. Like most spaceships, *Procyon's Promise* operated with any oxygen-enriched breathing mixture maintained at half a standard atmosphere pressure. To combat the several thousand tonnes of "blow-off" load that this pressure exerted on the viewdome, *Promise*'s designers had provided an anchor ring around the dome's periphery. The ring assembly included a massive silicone gasket, both to seal the interface against air leakage and to distribute the load evenly through the glass.

When the stardrive shunts failed and the artificial gravity reversed polarity, the dome had been shoved upward with a force several times normal. The additional stress had been too much for the perimeter seal. The silicone gasket had ruptured, allowing the air on the bridge to immediately vanish into interstellar space.

It had taken two days to reseal the dome and repressurize the bridge. In addition to repairing the perimeter seal, the work crew had done what little they could to minimize the possibility of a repetition of the failure. As a result, Braedon had issued orders that all personnel would henceforth don lightweight emergency vacsuits before reporting to duty on the bridge. Helmets could be removed—so long as they were kept close at hand— except during transition to and from hypervelocity, every crewman was required to maintain a state of self-sufficient pressure integrity.

"Lieutenant MacIntire reports that he is ready to launch, Robert."

PROM's voice echoed in Braedon's ears and pulled him from his reverie. "Put him on the screen."

Braedon's workscreen lit to show the FTL cutter pilot. His features were obscured by a vacsuit helmet that glinted with red and green reflections of instrument lights. Braedon knew that he presented a similar picture to MacIntire.

"Report your status, Lieutenant."

"All checklists complete, Commodore. Fuel state is one hundred and ten percent. Our larder is stocked to overflowing, our powerplant reads green across the board. We're as ready as we'll ever be."

"Repeat your orders."

"Yes, sir. We are to return to Sanctuary and inform the fleet of PROM's discovery and the need to relieve *Golden Hind* at the Grelsho sun. Vice-Commodore Tarns is to take no action regarding the FTL hypertracks for one hundred twenty days. If at the end of that time you have not returned to Sanctuary, he is to use his own judgment."

"Have you double checked your course tape?" Braedon asked. During the two weeks since the accident, *Procyon's Promise* had been bending her course through space to line up on the cluster of hypertracks. The cutter would have to swing its course through an additional ninety degrees of arc to line up on Sanctuary, in effect reversing the starship's direction of flight at the time of the explosion. The mission would strain its fuel reserves, and even the slightest mistake in astrogation would leave it stranded between the stars.

"Yes, sir. We're ready to launch."

"Very good, Lieutenant. Stand by. PROM, open the hangar doors, please."

"Hangar doors opening, Robert."

The view on the workscreen changed to one transmitted from a camera high up one of the hangar bay doors, focusing on the cutter as the great metal flower petals swung open.

"Doors open. Ready for launch."

"Hear that, Mac? You can launch any time."

"Launching now, sir."

Glistening in the light from spotlights mounted in the hangar bay, the ungainly cutter rose from the hangar deck. Braedon watched the small ship move away in a sweeping curve that took it in front of the starship. Braedon lifted his eyes from the screen to search the black sky beyond the viewdome. Already the cutter was too far away to see.

"PROM, put me on the general circuit and make sure the cutter is receiving me."

"Connection complete, Robert."

"Attention, all hands!" Braedon paused a moment while his amplified voice echoed through the corridors of the ship around him. "We began this quest with very little knowledge of what we would find. As you are all well aware, one thing we did not expect was to discover evidence of other starfarers. It has been suggested by some that we have chanced upon the home civilization of the Star Travelers, and indeed this is a possibility. For the probe to have seen the wake of a Star Traveler vessel departing Alpha, that ship must have been bound in this direction. In fact, its course would have been almost exactly the same as the one we followed from Sol to Sanctuary.

"However, it matters little whether the hypertracks belong to estee ships or to vessels of another FTL-capable civilization. What *does* matter is that our mission has now taken on additional complexity and importance. Our primary goal remains the successful fulfillment of The Promise. Beyond that, we must discover the insight which led the Star Travelers to the stardrive and learn all we can about the other starfaring races which inhabit this galaxy.

"I have determined that all three of these goals are best

served by tracing the starship wakes back to their point of origin. I won't try to jolly you about this mission. It will involve an element of risk. However, if we all do our jobs, that risk will be the absolute minimum we can make it.

"Now, then, for the sake of our race and The Promise, prepare for hypervelocity!"

As in Sanctuary Asteroid, Braedon's position as expedition commander gave him clear title to the most luxurious quarters aboard ship. But even aboard *Procyon's Promise*, luxury was only relative. The expedition commander's quarters consisted of two adjoining compartments. The larger served as office and living quarters, while the smaller was devoted to sleeping. A tiny bathroom was separated from the sleeping cabin by a folding door. Even though the cabin was small, *Promise*'s designers had done their best to maximize its utility. All furniture folded into the bulkheads or overhead when not in use. Numerous lockers which Braedon used to store his books, papers, clothing, and personal vacsuit, lined the walls.

Eight hours after *Procyon's Promise* entered hypervelocity, Braedon was in his cabin preparing for dinner. In his outer cabin, all of the office furnishings had been stowed in their recesses. In their place sat a single table and two chairs requisitioned from the messhall. Two place settings of silver and crystal decorated the white lace tablecloth, as did a small crystal vase containing a single red rose. A chilled bottle of wine sat in an ice bucket next to the table, its slender green neck wrapped in a white napkin. A quiet melody issued from the hidden speakers in the overhead as the faint scent of roses diffused the air. The only other furnishings in the cabin were a small sofa and a holographic viewwindow. Beyond the window, Procyon seemed to be setting behind a sawtoothed range of mountains. High above the setting star, the intense blue-white spot that was Junior gave the lengthening shadows a silvery sheen.

The chronometer on the bulkhead read 20:00 hours when the annunciator buzzed. Braedon checked over his uniform, then left the bedroom and strode quickly to the cabin door. The door slid back into its recess to reveal Chryse Haller in the corridor beyond. Like Braedon, she was wearing the blue-and-green dress uniform of the expedition.

"Welcome," he said, smiling.

"Thank you, Robert. I hope I'm not too early."

"Right on time." He guided her to the couch and offered her a glass of wine. She accepted graciously. He quickly filled two goblets with purple liquid, handed one to Chryse, and sat down at the opposite end of the sofa, facing her.

"You've changed your hairstyle."

She nodded. "Do you like it?"

"Very much. Something very similar was popular at home several years ago. Small universe, isn't it?"

Chryse laughed. "I could be coy and agree with you. The truth is that I've been quizzing Terra about your likes and dislikes ever since we left Sanctuary. I'm wearing this particular style because I knew you would like it."

Braedon let the implications of Chryse's comment pass unchallenged and said instead, "Hungry?"

"Starved! I didn't have lunch today."

Braedon raised his voice out of habit, and said, "PROM, tell the cook that we're ready for dinner."

"He says it will be five minutes, Robert," the computer answered.

Chryse got to her feet and moved to stand in front of the holographic window. She touched the control that moved the view through its full 360-degree panorama. In the direction opposite the setting sun, the lights of a small city were just beginning to blaze forth in the twilight.

"Where was this taken?"

Braedon moved up behind her and gazed over her shoulder, acutely aware of her closeness. "Those are the Hydra Mountains on Second Continent. The village is called Anderson. The Andersonites are fisherfolk. They work off of Swanson's Bank where the *grudfish* go to spawn."

"It's lovely."

"Still pretty much a frontier, I'm afraid."

Five minutes later, a white-coated wardroom steward knocked on Braedon's door. He was trundling a covered cart. Braedon seated Chryse, then himself. The steward served them with the flair of a headwaiter in a star-class restaurant. When he had finished, Braedon said, "Leave it, Delwin. I'll have PROM notify the cook when we're ready to have the dishes cleared away."

"Yes, sir."

Dinner was taken up with smalltalk about the ship and the expedition. Time passed quickly, and sooner than either would have liked, dinner was over. Braedon poured the last of the wine into their glasses.

"Hmmm, I don't remember drinking all of this."

Chryse laughed. "The way my head is swimming, we must have."

"In that case, I'd better stop putting off telling you the reason I asked you here tonight. If I wait too much longer, I'll be too drunk to remember."

Chryse leaned back in her chair and sighed. "It seems a shame to end this beautiful dinner with talk of business; but I suppose we must."

He leaned forward, rested his elbows on the table, placed his chin on cupped hands, and stared at her for several seconds. "First off, I want you to know that I appreciate what you did for me yesterday in the wardroom."

"I didn't do anything."

"The hell you didn't! Who punctured Javral Pere's balloon before he had a chance to get it properly inflated? Who always said the right thing at the right time to push the discussion in the direction I wanted it to go? I don't think I've ever seen anyone steer a meeting so effectively from the sidelines before."

"Why, thank you, Robert. That is the nicest thing anyone has said to me in a long, long time."

"You're welcome. Where did you learn the technique?"

Chryse shrugged. "From my father, of course. He's a past master at maneuvering the Haller Associates Board of Directors into anything he wants done. You should see *him* operate sometime."

"I'd like to. Anyway, I just wanted you to know that I knew what you were doing, and appreciate the help. It also reminded me that your talents are wasted in the assistant purser slot. How would you like a promotion?"

"To what?"

"Pick your own title. I like 'Staff Assistant to the Expedition in Charge of Getting Us Home with Our Skins Intact.'"

Chryse mused for a moment, then laughed. "An impressive title. What's it mean?"

"As much as I hate committees, I think we need one. I want to get our best minds together to think up ways to protect ourselves from whoever it was that made these hypertracks we're following."

"Interesting. Who's on the committee?"

"I would recommend that you consider Horace Price, Hans Reickert, Colin Williams, maybe Jarval Pere; but the number and composition of members is strictly up to you."

"What powers will I have?"

"The power to try and convince me that what I'm doing is dangerous and that you've got a better idea. If I believe you, we'll do it your way."

"A pretty nebulous commitment, Commodore."

"I'm afraid it's the best I can give under the circumstances. Are you interested?"

She smiled. "Oh, I'll take the job. I *do* have one question to ask, though."

"Ask."

"Do you like me, Robert?"

"What?"

"Do you like me? Do you find me attractive, desirable, sexy?"

"Of course I do."

"Then why have you been resisting my charms all evening? Why do you pull your hand away every time my fingers 'accidentally' brush yours?"

A look of surprise crossed Braedon's face, followed by some less definable emotion. Eventually, his features settled into a mildly pained look. "Because I *do* find you attractive, Chryse. I see no reason to torture myself with thoughts of something I can never have."

"Who says you can't?"

"I do. I haven't given Cecily much of a marriage. The least I can do is remain faithful to her."

Chryse muttered something under her breath.

"What?" Braedon asked.

"I said, 'Damned Alphan mores!' Why couldn't you

have been a Solarian? Two Solarians in our situation would have been in the bedroom an hour ago."

Braedon sighed. "Believe me, Chryse, I am well aware that your culture looks upon the marriage contract differently than mine does. I am also aware that romantic liaisons take place between Solarian crewmembers of this ship, and sometimes with Alphans, as well. I have often wished that I could adopt such an attitude, but I can't. I suppose I'm something of a fanatic."

Chryse reached out and took his hands in her own. "You aren't a fanatic, Robert. You're a latter-day Roman Centurion. All of you Alphans are. You guard the frontiers against the barbarian hordes while the rest of us get drunk, go to orgies, and waste our lives in dissipation. That's basically what we're all doing out here a thousand light-years from home. We're guarding the frontiers of our honor, making good on a three-hundred-year-old IOU."

Chryse got unsteadily to her feet. "Whew! That purple stuff sneaks up on one, doesn't it? Must be stronger than it looks. I apologize, Robert, for any embarrassment I may have caused you. It won't happen again. Now, then, I think I had best be getting back to my own cabin while my resolve holds. Good night, Commodore. Sleep well."

"You too." Braedon watched her go. Afterward he cursed himself for being a fool.

CHAPTER 24

Unlike the long jump from Earth to Sanctuary, the search for the origin of the interstellar "trade route" was to be a journey of many small steps. *Procyon's Promise* had traveled less than three light-years when Braedon ordered PROM to sound the "Prepare for Breakout" call. The starship's return to the real universe was normal. Like a whale breaking the surface of a vast, black sea, *Promise* burst from hypervelocity, only to be engulfed in the roiling radiation storm of its own wake. With the ship's sensors blinded by the torrent of charged particles just beyond the hull, there was nothing for Braedon to do but wait and watch the changing of the oversize numerals on the bridge chronometer.

He waited an eternity lasting three minutes after which PROM reported, "The hypertracks are still there, Robert. No change in appearance or relative position."

"All right, do a complete sky scan as we discussed, then prepare to reenter hypervelocity."

"Scan underway. Estimated time to completion: seven minutes, sixteen seconds."

"Notify me when we're two minutes from hypervelocity." He punched for the engine room. Chief Engineer Reickert answered immediately. "How did we come through breakout, Hans?"

"No problem, sir. Our chewing gum and bailing wire seem to be holding nicely. "I'm having my people do a quick survey of the critical repairs now."

"Tell them to hurry. We jump in just under seven minutes."

"We'll be ready."

That first stop between the stars had proved that one starship can track another, but had been otherwise bereft of information regarding their quarry. The cluster of starship wakes was unchanged, and no other wakes appeared to PROM's questing sensors.

Life aboard ship quickly fell into a routine governed by the twice-daily breakouts. Crewmembers continued to stand normal watches; preventive maintenance, housekeeping, and systems monitoring functions were performed as usual; bull sessions, poker games, and catching up on lost sleep remained the most popular activities during off duty hours. For twenty-two hours each day, the starship's passengers and crew lived much as they had since leaving Earth. But at 08:00 hours each morning (and again twelve hours later) the whole of *Promise*'s crew found itself at duty stations and weapons consoles.

Procyon's Promise chased the cluster of hypertracks for the better part of a week. Yet, in spite of the fact that the starship had traversed forty light-years at maximum velocity, the distance to the nearest wakes never seemed to diminish. If anything, the invisible lights in the sky seemed farther away than ever—which, in fact, they were. They were two hundred billion kilometers more distant. Nor was there any hope that the distance between hunter and quarry would ever be narrowed. For the wakes were more optical illusion than real.

Since a starship traverses normal distances (such as those found within a single planetary system) in essentially zero time, its line of flight is marked by a long wake of energetic photons and particles, *all created in the moment of passage*. But photons and particles are both limited to propagation velocities less than that of light. Thus, an hour after a starship has left the vicinity, a fixed observer sees only those particles that have been in transit for that hour. Likewise, day-old particles are observable after twenty-four hours, year-old particles a year later, and twenty-year-old particles at the end of two decades. The natural consequence is that a starship's wake appears to flee before a pursuer at the speed of light.

It wasn't until the sixteenth breakout that PROM announced a change in the cluster of starship wakes.

"What have you found?" Braedon asked.

The computer answered, "I can no longer locate several of the most distant radiation sources, Robert."

"How many are gone?"

"Nearly eight hundred."

"I presume that there is a star near the point where they disappeared?"

"Affirmative. The tracks extend directly to a K0 star. They do not seem to go beyond."

"How far?"

"Twenty-seven light-years."

"Looks like we've found the source of our 'trade route,' Horace," Braedon said to Scholar Price, who was hunched over a bridge display, monitoring PROM's observations.

Price glanced up in response to Braedon's comment. A shock of silver hair was visible through his helmet visor. "I'm beginning to wonder if trade route is a proper description, Commodore."

"Why?"

"Because the name implies commerce, which in turn suggests a steady stream of traffic in two directions. From the evidence, this particular route was heavily used for outbound traffic over a twenty-year period and then abandoned. Nor do there seem to be hypertracks in the opposite direction to suggest any return voyages."

"They probably came back by another route."

Price nodded, making the gesture broad enough to be interpreted through the suit. "Possible. If that is the case, then we should begin to see quite a number of additional sightings as we near the source system. I presume it's still your intention to visit it."

"That's what we're here for. PROM!"

"Yes, Robert."

"Please ask Chryse's people to come to the wardroom in fifteen minutes. It's about time we planned our approach."

"Order received and understood, Robert."

Chryse Haller had wasted no time in recruiting the working group. As she scanned the starship's crew and passenger lists for candidates, she was reminded of an ancient—and no doubt apocryphal—story about a plane carrying several government bureaucrats to a conference. Halfway to its destination, the aircraft had lost a wing in flight. Upon finding their transport hurtling nose-first toward the ground, one functionary turned to a colleague in the next seat and said: "I think the first thing we should do is appoint a landing committee!"

The problem was that the old joke was more than a little apropos to the situation in which Chryse now found herself. With *Promise* already committed to follow the starship wakes, it was likely that anything she and her people came up with would prove to be too little, too late. Still, she had never been one to believe in predestination. So in a spirit of defiance, she decided to name her group the *Landing Committee*.

Long years as a manager had taught her that committees are something to be avoided if possible. If unavoidable, they are best kept small, but not so small as to foster intellectual inbreeding. After careful thought and considerable soul searching, Chryse had asked Scholar Price, Professor Williams, Javral Pere, Aeneas Spatz, and an Alphan technologist named Corzan Biedermann to be on her committee. Their first meeting had lasted ten hours, and they'd met frequently since then. Slowly, and with considerable argument, a consensus began to emerge regarding the minimum precautions to be taken during initial contact with FTL-capable aliens. To Chryse's surprise, Javral Pere turned out to be one of the most productive members of the group. When she commented on it after one particularly grueling session, he gazed at her with calm eyes and shrugged.

"Since Old Iron Head is determined to walk into the lions' den, the least I can do is to try and keep him from getting the rest of us killed in the process."

Chryse, having been relieved of all other duties, was working on her notes in the cabin she shared with Terra Braedon when the sixteenth breakout took place. She thought nothing of it when twenty minutes passed without the usual "Prepare for Hypervelocity" warning. She first realized that something was out of the ordinary when called to the wardroom by PROM.

Most of the Landing Committee had already assembled when she arrived. A few minutes later, Braedon and Horace Price entered. The commodore quickly reviewed what PROM had found, concluding with: "Any suggestions about how to handle the approach?"

Several people looked in Chryse's direction. She leaned back in her seat, cleared her throat, and said, "We suggest a high-speed run by a landing boat through the target system. We can then observe the inhabitants' response."

"A flyby?" Braedon asked, puzzled. "What happened to the idea of sneaking up on them?"

Chryse sighed, thinking of all the hours that had gone into what had come to be known as the "Thieves in the Night Plan." Unfortunately, a few simple calculations had caused it to founder on the rocks of reality. "We gave it up as unworkable, Robert. A starship is just too damned conspicuous. There are a dozen ways they could detect us as soon as we dropped below lightspeed.

"Since we can't hide, we rely on surprise instead. We break out high above the ecliptic, aim directly for the inner system, then launch a scout boat filled with all the survey equipment it can carry. The boat will traverse the inhabited region of the system while *Promise* maneuvers laterally to keep on the outskirts. Once on the opposite side, *Promise* will rendezvous with the boat and take it aboard. After that, we study the data and come up with a plan for making contact."

"What makes you think the boat will survive long enough to make rendezvous again?"

"We agree that it's a risk," Chryse replied, "but it's one worth taking. PROM has analyzed the orbital mechanics and calculates that it will be virtually impossible to intercept a boat traveling at point nine lights at a high angle to the ecliptic."

"Have any of you considered that they may not try to intercept our boat? They may just shoot it down."

"An important datum in itself," Corzan Biedermann said.

Braedon glanced at the technologist with a sour look on his face, then turned back to Chryse. "Which boat did you have in mind?"

"*Siren Song*. It has the largest cargo capacity."

"And the crew?"

"Myself, a pilot, and someone to help with the equipment."

"You?"

"It was my idea, so I should be the one to execute it."

Braedon chewed his lower lip while considering Chryse's plan. The idea seemed a good one. The boat, moving with *Promise*'s speed following breakout, would be virtually impossible to catch in the few hours it would take to traverse the target system. Passing through the heart of the system, it would be able to observe the alien civilization close up. Such observations could prove invaluable later on. However, when dealing with aliens, there were no certainties. Whoever inhabited the target system—Star Travelers or some other race of FTL-capable aliens— might find it childishly simple to intercept the interloping scout boat. Or they might destroy it outright. And try as he would to be objective, a single thought kept intruding on Braedon's concentration:

Siren Song was Terra's boat!

"Breakout!"

"Give me a view as soon as the radiation storm subsides," Braedon said. Overhead, the radiation shields were closed. Around him, the bridge was bustling with activity.

"Will do, Robert." Three minutes later, Braedon's screen flashed to life and the shields rolled back into their recesses. The scene overhead was much the same as it had been on *Promise*'s approach to Sanctuary—a blue-shifted star and a relativistically distorted universe. On the screen, however, a small orange-white star lay centered in a field of black.

"Any planets yet?" he asked after a minute or so. In answer to his question, the star on his screen was replaced by a schematic that showed six small dots circling a central representation of the star.

"I make it two Jupiter-class gas giants, two smaller gas planets—Neptune-size—and two smaller stony orbs, close in. There are undoubtedly others I have not yet located."

"What about energy emissions?"

"None detected so far, Robert."

"None?"

"I am scanning each of the planetary bodies in turn. So far, I have detected neither electromagnetic radiation nor neutrino emissions. Perhaps I'm not looking in the proper locations."

"Keep searching, they have to be there."

Ten minutes later, PROM had some more distressing news. "I have completed my initial sky scan, Robert. I cannot find any of the normal indications of an advanced civilization. If they are here, they don't use alternating electrical current or any of the many variants of radio. If they are communicating, it is with tightly focused laser beams, or something similar. Nor are there any drive flares from mass-converter powered spacecraft, gravity waves from grav generators, or neutrino emissions from fusion or fission power sources."

"Could it be that they are so far ahead of us that we don't recognize their emissions?"

"Possible, I suppose. However, I also can't find any hypertracks in the sky."

"Are you positive about that?"

"Yes, Robert. The sky is empty of radiation sources."

Braedon lapsed into a state of concentration. The last of the hypertracks had disappeared while *Promise* was still twenty light-years out in space. That had been expected. But to actually be in the star system itself and find the sky devoid of the tracks of returning starships, that was a subject of major concern.

"Keep looking. Are we ready to launch *Siren Song*?"

"All is in readiness," the computer responded.

"Open hangar doors."

"Hangar doors coming open."

On his screen, Braedon watched the same scene that he had when the FTL cutter had launched itself into space. Only this time, the egg-shaped hull of a scout boat floated away from the giant steel flower petals of the hangar doors. While he watched, the doors began to close.

"Get me Chryse Haller."

Chryse's face appeared on Braedon's screen. Behind her, out-of-focus instruments showed in the background. "Report system status."

"Everything nominal, Commodore," Chryse said, glancing up at something out of the comm-unit camera's field of view. She glanced back. "I still think you should have allowed us to go along. Automatic control is all right for some things, but this voyage may require human initiative."

Braedon shook his head. "We've been through all this

before, Chryse. The flyby is too dangerous to risk a human crew. The boat goes in on automatic pilot as we agreed."

"Yes, sir."

"You may transfer control to the scout boat when ready."

"Transferring control now, sir."

"Very good. PROM!"

"Yes, Robert."

"Begin lateral maneuvering, maximum acceleration."

"Acceleration to begin in five seconds ... four ... three ... two ... one ... Acceleration!"

CHAPTER 25

Terra Braedon stood in the hangar bay on the empty expanse of deck that the FTL cutter had once occupied and gazed upward toward where *Siren Song* lay nestled in her docking frame. She was alone in the frigid bay, a diminutive form in a fur-lined parka, wrapped with long streamers of exhalation fog. The fog was highlighted by the harsh, blue-white illumination of a dozen spotlights mounted high on the segmented dome above her. She was so intent on examining the scout boat after its long dive through the system of the K0 sun that she was oblivious to the sound of footsteps behind her.

"How'd the old girl come through?" Jim Davidson asked from close beside her right ear. The unexpected voice caused Terra to jump in startled surprise.

She glanced at her copilot and said accusingly, "You shouldn't sneak up on a person like that."

"I wasn't sneaking. You were just too preoccupied to notice. A decistellar for your thoughts."

"I was thinking that *Siren Song* has looked better."

"That she has," Davidson agreed.

The scout boat's hull, once a smooth, unbroken ellipsoid, was now dotted with antennas, telescopes, and other less familiar sensor devices. Most had been welded into place, mounted on tripods constructed of thin-walled tube stock, or otherwise hung on the scout boat with little or no regard for aesthetics. To make matters worse, the job had been done in haste. *Siren Song*'s flanks bore the scars of a hundred careless passes by the cutting torches. Here and there, actual holes had been drilled through the hull to pass cables into the compartment within and then sloppily closed with silicone sealing compound.

Besides the manmade scars, the scout boat had also acquired a "weathered" look. The surface coating on its rounded prow had been worn away as though by sand blasting. The space around any star is filled with a thick, primordial soup—at least, in comparison with the pristine vacuum of the interstellar void. *Siren Song* had plunged into the system at nearly the speed of light. Particles from the stellar wind had scoured the boat's leading edge, baring the metal of the hull beneath the ablative surface coating.

"What say we go aboard and check the interior damage?" Davidson asked.

Terra shook her head. "No time. We're due in a briefing. The scientists are going to tell us what they found out."

Davidson shook his head and gestured toward the mutilated hull of the scout boat. "It had better be good to justify *that*!"

The briefing was originally scheduled for the wardroom, but had been moved to the messhall when it became apparent that seating would be a problem. Every officer, department head, and scientist aboard wanted to be present when the Landing Committee reported its findings. Interest was also keen among the ordinary spacers. Those off duty would watch via the ship's intercom; those on duty would view a recording of the briefing as soon as they came off watch. Terra and Davidson found a place near one side of the messhall. Terra noticed her father and Chryse Haller seated in the front row, as were Scholar Price, Professor Williams, and Javral Pere. Corzan Biedermann stood behind a podium in front of a wall-size holoscreen. Biedermann had been one of Terra's professors at the Alphan Academy for Astronautics. In those days, he had seemed a humorless, cold fish of a man; yet on the trip out from Earth, he had developed a reputation as a skilled raconteur. Terra wondered if the change weren't merely that he was now doing something that interested him.

Biedermann glanced out over his audience and said, "Please be seated, people!" in a clear, penetrating voice. When the buzz of conversation died away, he manipulated a control on the podium, causing the overhead lights to dim and the holoscreen to come to life.

"In the four days since our arrival in this system, we have been trying to learn everything possible about the star, its planets, and inhabitants. This is hardly news since most of you have been working watch-and-watch to assist in the effort. Eight hours ago, we finally managed to rendezvous with our errant unmanned scout boat after a long stern chase. We have spent the intervening time reviewing the boat's data. I would remind you that eight hours is not a long time to become an expert on an entire star system. Therefore, please consider what you are about to hear as preliminary—I repeat, *preliminary*!—information. I wouldn't stake my life on the accuracy of what I am about to say. Neither should you.

"Now, then, the facts as we know them: The star is an orange dwarf of the K0 spectral type. At thirty-five hundred degrees Kelvin, its surface temperature is significantly cooler than that of Sol or Procyon. Like all members of its class, it is rich in metals, with the calcium lines particularly strong in its spectrum. We have positively identified eleven major planetary bodies in the system, with indications of a possible twelfth. Of these, the second, third, and fourth are in a zone which we would consider habitable.

"First slide, please." The screen changed to show a single world centered against a black backdrop with a few stars sprinkled across it. The planet displayed a distinct crescent shape. "This is our best candidate for the home world of whatever race inhabits this system. It is the second world out from the star. The photo was taken by automatic cameras aboard the scout boat at a distance of forty million kilometers. The world is approximately the size of Earth and Alpha although somewhat colder. Next slide."

Biedermann continued his catalog of the planets of the K0 sun in the order of their likely habitability. The last three planetary bodies were little more than fuzzy dots on the screen. When he had finished, he turned to face his audience.

"So much for the local real estate. To discuss the inhabitants thereof, I'll turn the discussion over to Colin Williams."

The Solarian professor bounded up to the podium and accepted the screen control from Biedermann. It was a particularly humorless face that stared out over the expectant rows of expedition members.

"I'm afraid, ladies and gentlemen, that after four days of careful observation from the fringes of this system, and eight hours spent examining the scout-boat data, we are still unable to confirm that there *are* any inhabitants. The local equivalent of Space Guard certainly hasn't come out to investigate our arrival. Nor have we been able to detect any of the normal radiation emissions associated with an advanced technological civilization. If it weren't for the fact that more than two thousand starships seem to have departed this system over the last forty years, it would be easy to conclude that the place is uninhabited."

"Could they be hiding from us?" someone called from the back of the messhall.

Williams shook his head. "Highly unlikely. It took half a day for the photons and particles from our wake to reach the inner system. Even if they shut down all their industry the moment they detected us, we should have had a full day to observe their capabilities."

"What if those capabilities are so far beyond us that we don't recognize their emissions for what they are?" one of the Solarian scientists in the third row asked.

"It's possible," Williams agreed. In spite of his words, his tone was dubious. "Who's to say what scientific principles remain to be discovered? Having conceded the point, however, I must tell you that I don't believe it for a second. One of the prime tenets of science is that there are certain universal constants. The process of fusing hydrogen into helium emits neutrinos. That is true whether it happens deep within a star or inside a mass converter. When we fail to detect any artificial neutrino emissions from this system, it's easier to believe that there aren't any mass converters in operation here than the alternative, which is that the inhabitants have discovered a way to suppress neutrino emissions in the fusion process."

"So where do we go from here?" someone asked nervously.

"For that, I yield to the expedition commander."

Terra watched her father climb onto the rostrum and order the lighting returned to normal. He looked very tired. She knew that he'd been practically living on the bridge; she wondered if she should talk to him about getting more rest.

Braedon took his place behind the podium and began to speak. "Because of our lack of hard information regarding the locals, I've decided to take the ship into the system to investigate. I don't like going in blind, but I see no alternative. I'll keep you informed about our progress via the ship's annunciators. Are there any questions? If not, this briefing is at an end. Scout pilots, please remain for a few minutes!"

"Procyon's Promise to *Siren Song."*

Terra Braedon, encased in a bulky suit of space armor, stared at the dark-blue planet centered in a lightly populated starfield on the scout boat's main viewscreen. Also on the screen were readouts giving range and velocity data, as well as those that compared the boat's actual position with its computed flight plan. At the call from the distant controller aboard *Promise*, Terra reached out and keyed for the long-range communications channel.

"Siren Song. Go ahead, *Promise."*

"Less than twenty minutes to orbit, Terra. Anything to report?"

"Negative. We're just coming up on maximum range for the search radar now. Stand by."

Terra turned to her copilot and grinned. "They must be getting anxious. Check the aft cabin and see if there is anything they aren't telling us."

"Right," Jim Davidson said. Like Terra, he was clad in space armor. With the two of them suited up, the control cabin seemed even more cramped than usual. Terra heard the *click* that indicated he'd switched to another channel to talk privately with the technicians in *Siren Song's* aft cabin. Three of them were packed in among the various computers and instruments that processed the data stream from the hull instruments.

After half a minute, Davidson was back on the main circuit. "Technician Ramirez reports that you are getting it as fast as he is, *Promise*. He put it more colorfully, but that was the gist of his comment."

"Understood." It was obvious from the controller's tone that he, too, was feeling the heat from above. Terra smiled. She suspected that Chryse Haller had probably gnawed her manicure out of existence by this time. Even in an age of near-instantaneous communications, being on the scene was somehow less nerve wracking than waiting for reports to filter back up the chain of command.

The plan for exploring the K0 system was relatively straightforward. The starship had been headed out of the system at nearly light-speed when Robert Braedon decided to risk entering it to investigate the mystery of the missing inhabitants. It had taken three days to shed that velocity, and seven more to return to the system outskirts. When *Promise* had bent its orbit into the plane of the local planetary orbits, Braedon ordered all three scout boats out as insurance against unpleasant surprises. The plan called for two boats to guard the starship's flanks while the third preceded the starship toward the system's second planet.

With a forest of sensing gear already strung out across *Siren Song*'s hull, the choice for point boat had been obvious. And since *Siren* was Terra's boat, she had made sure that she and Jim Davidson were given the assignment. Her father hadn't liked her going into danger, but was a good enough commander not to use his influence to rearrange the duty roster.

Terra listened while the controller aboard *Procyon's Promise* checked with *Divine Wind* and *Caroline*, the other two scout boats. Both reported negative results as well. However, they were two million klicks farther from the target, so that wasn't surprising.

"I'm going to long-range search mode now," Ramirez reported from the aft cabin.

"Pipe it to the screen, Juan," Terra ordered.

"Will do. Stand by."

The telescopic view of the planet was ringed with a glowing green line as the radar confirmed its presence. Suddenly, the screen changed and a series of bright-green dots appeared in quick succession. Each was accompanied by a pale-violet arrow indicating velocity vector. As Terra watched, ten dots became a hundred, the hundred quickly multiplied into a thousand. The process continued until the planet was surrounded by two broad bands of green dots and violet arrows.

"Madre de Dios!" Ramirez exclaimed in Terra's headphones. "We have encountered more than twenty thousand contacts on the first sweep, and *they* all read out as *artifacts*!"

"We've got contacts!" Jim Davidson reported to *Procyon's Promise*.

"We see them" came the response.

"Looks like we've found our inhabitants," Terra said to the controller. "What are your instructions?"

A new voice answered after a two second communications lag. "Terra!" The voice belonged to her father.

"I'm receiving you, Commodore."

"Do you have any evidence of activity?"

"We're getting slight energy spillage from the contacts," Ramirez' second-in-command reported, "but still nothing from the planet below."

"Stand by," PROM's voice said. "We are going to give you a course change for a close pass by one of the contacts."

"Standing by, PROM," Terra reported.

There was a high-pitched whine on the communications circuits as the new course was passed from starship to scout boat. Simultaneously, the pale-red line on the main viewscreen showing *Siren's* projected orbit changed shape slightly.

After a dozen minutes of waiting and watching the now-cluttered screen, PROM's voice once more echoed in Terra's ears. "Three minutes to first contact. You'd best turn your cameras on."

In the aft cabin, the three technicians switched their recording gear to high speed, while Jim Davidson did the same for the main screen recorder.

After that, there was nothing to do but wait. The seconds passed with surprising rapidity, while on the screen, the dark-blue planet slowly expanded and began to slide to one side. Then it drifted off the screen entirely, leaving only the blackness of space and a shimmering galaxy of electronic contact markers. Terra called for maximum magnification and strained for her first sight of whatever it was that lay ahead of them.

"There!" Jim Davidson yelled.

Terra followed his pointing, gauntleted finger, but saw nothing. Then she too saw the glint of sunlight off metal. The contact grew in size with surprising rapidity. Terra reduced the screen mangification. Even so, it continued to grow alarmingly. Then, suddenly, it was upon them.

Terra managed to gain an impression of two spheres joined together by a central framework of girders before the object disappeared from the screen. She sat for long seconds, transfixed, before taking a deep breath and punching for the long range communication channel.

"Hello, *Promise*. We have positive identification."

"What is it?" Chryse Haller's excited voice asked.

"It's a Maker life probe!"

Silence followed Terra's revelation. For the span of a dozen heartbeats the only sound emanating from her earphones was the faint hissing of the far stars. At the end of that time, Robert Braedon asked, "Are you absolutely sure of that identification?"

Terra, recognizing the restrained excitement in her father's voice, turned to Jim Davidson, who was already punching commands into his lapboard. The viewscreen flashed, and the orbital object once again filled the forward quadrant with its bulk. Only this time, the image was stationary. There was no longer any need for Terra to rely on afterimage or impression. She scanned the object carefully, noting a myriad of details that she had missed during the original encounter. The object's shape was that of two framework spheres attached to both ends of a solid column of intricately woven beams. The bulky shape of a mass converter was clearly visible inside the larger of the spheres, while the smaller enclosed a jumble of complex mechanisms. At several points along the object's length, slender stalks jutted outward into space.

"There's no doubt at all," Terra reported. "It looks just like the old recordings of the probe that visited Earth."

"Okay, we've got a picture now. Stand by for further orders." For more than a minute there was silence on the comm circuits. Terra could imagine the hurried conference that was probably taking place on *Promise*'s bridge.

"Bet they ask us to go back for another pass," she said, speaking to Davidson on a private channel.

"No bet. I'll begin plotting a minimum elapsed time loop-back maneuver."

The order, when it came, was nothing like what Terra had expected.

"Hello, *Siren Song*," Braedon said. "You are hereby recalled. Stand by for new rendezvous coordinates."

Terra muttered a comment about overprotective fathers and began setting up the course that would take them back to the starship. She was still fuming two hours later when *Siren Song* was pulled aboard *Promise* in a net of tractor beams. Terra, Davidson, and the three techs were met by Lieutenant Carpenter, late of Space Guard Marines, now *Promise*'s Master-at-Arms.

"Your father asked me to conduct all of you to the wardroom, Miss Braedon," Carpenter said, saluting.

"What's up?" Terra asked.

"Strategy session. I don't know what you found out there, but things seem to be stirred up as a result."

The wardroom was occupied by Robert Braedon, Scholar Price, Chryse Haller, Colin Williams, Corzan Biedermann, and Braedon's yeoman-secretary. Terra and her people, still clad in vacsuits and carrying their helmets under their arms, were ushered to seats at the foot of the table.

"What's going on?" Terra asked her father as she unclipped the blood-oxygen sensor from her right earlobe. "Why did you pull us back?"

"We may have to run for open space," he said. "Your mother would never have spoken to me again if I were forced to leave you behind."

"Who's talking about running?"

"I may be if we get a few more surprises like that last one." Braedon turned to Ramirez and indicated the carrying case in the senior tech's hand. "Is that the data, Juan?"

"Yes, sir." Ramirez opened the case and handed a record cube to Braedon's yeoman-secretary, who inserted it into the cube reader lying in the middle of the wardroom table. "I took the time to consolidate the most interesting data into a single summary, Commodore. First photograph, Sven."

The clerk manipulated the cube reader and the orbital object flashed onto the bulkhead holoscreen. "As Terra reported, it appears to be a carbon copy of *our* life probe prior to the attack of 2066."

"Not quite," PROM said from the overhead. "There are a number of important differences. The proportions between the control sphere and drive sphere are different, and the overall dimensions are somewhat larger. There are also discrepancies in the way the fuel tanks are mounted and in the number and placement of sensor booms."

"But it *is* a life probe?" Terra asked.

"Obviously," PROM replied. "The differences may be due to evolutionary improvements in the design."

"Are you saying this probe is a newer model than the one which visited Earth?"

"A distinct possibility."

"What other data have you for us, Juan?" Braedon asked.

"Well, sir," Ramirez responded. "We were able to obtain some fairly good long-range views of other orbiting artifacts."

A different shape appeared on the screen. This one looked like a box kite, with eight small spheres mounted at the corners of a rectangular frame. With the range data from the scout boat's radar, PROM quickly superimposed dimensions on the figure. The "kite" was nearly a kilometer long and half that wide.

"Next."

The third figure was a single sphere. It had the same look about it as the life probe and the box kite. The black maw of an electromagnetic nozzle could be seen jutting from one side.

"Half a life probe?" someone guessed.

"No," PROM replied. "The mass is approximately the same as for the others. Merely a different form, I would think."

"Why would the Makers have constructed more than one kind?" Chryse asked.

"For the same reason we built more than one kind of starship for this expedition," Horace Price answered. "Form follows function. Maybe the box kite type is for short distances, the dumbbell shape for intermediate, and the sphere for very long range."

"More likely, they are equivalent designs from different eras or different manufacturers," Braedon said. "Considering that the Makers have been building life probes for two hundred thousand years, they've had plenty of time to tinker with the design."

The fourth shape was another box kite, while the fifth was different from anything they had seen yet. The sixth was another of the classic "dumbbell" shapes.

"But there are thousands of them out there. Surely the Makers wouldn't have sent so many probes to this one system," Terra said. "Which means..."

Braedon gazed at his daughter with a large grin on his face. "By The Promise, we've found them!"

CHAPTER 26

"Father of us all; Creator of the Universe and Man; Builder of Worlds and Suns. We, Your servants, are of many faiths. We worship You in many different ways. Some know You as Allah, others as Vishnu or Siva, still others call You Father of Christ, or God of Moses. We, who are nothing without your intercession, thank You for delivering us safely to this place, that we may properly honor our ancestors and our obligations. We pray that You will guide us in our dealings with our ancient benefactors. In the name of Saint George and Saint Francis, of Joseph Smith, and of Your Prophet, Mohammed.

"Amen."

Scout boat *Divine Wind* was chosen for the first photographic reconnaissance mission over the Maker planet. While the sensors of *Siren Song* watched intently from a hundred thousand kilometers overhead, *Divine Wind* whipped around the planet in a tight, hyperbolic orbit. Its path took it over the largest continent in the Southern Hemisphere, which long-range observation had identified as the site of one of a major planetary population center.

"Photographic mosaic in memory and I'm coming home," Zou Chou Ling, *Divine Wind*'s pilot, reported after five heart-stopping minutes spent just above the upper fringes of the planet's atmosphere. "No evidence of activity noted. No industrial emissions observed."

"Nothing here either," Terra Braedon reported from her position high above Zou's ship.

Zou began to transmit his data back to the starship via comm laser as his scout boat maneuvered for the long journey home. Even at maximum transmission rate, it took ten seconds for each high-resolution frame to be built up on the pseudosurface of a holoscreen. All over *Procyon's Promise*, small groups sat quietly together and watched in fascination as swiftly moving points of light painted views of an alien world.

One of the first things they noticed was that the second planet of the K0 sun was thoroughly civilized. The population center that had been the primary target of *Divine Wind*'s cameras turned out to be far larger than anyone had suspected. It covered half the continent, even spilling into the sea for a distance of a hundred kilometers at one point. The aerial view of the city was subtly different from a similar view of one of its human counterparts. Human cities tend to expand or contract in strict adherence to whatever economic conditions exist at the time. The result is a variegated look that is evident to even the casual observer.

The city on the screen had a look of *sameness* about it, as though it had been built in a single night, or in strict compliance to a master plan. Not that there weren't architectural variations among its individual components. There were, lots of them. Long, slender towers stood alongside squat domes; small boxlike structures were intermixed with airfoil-shaped skyscrapers; the clean lines of a glass rectangle stood next to a seemingly haphazard jumble of pyramids. But the variations seemed well mixed, with no obvious clustering of similar styles in any particular location. If there had once been a city center, the passage of time had erased all evidence of it. The Maker city was different from human cities in another way. It was crisscrossed by wide swaths of vegetation and open spaces—some paved, others left in parklike splendor.

Even though the city was breathtaking, the views that most excited the scientists aboard *Promise* were those taken far beyond its perimeter. Everywhere the cameras pointed, they found evidence of intelligent beings at work. The southern continent appeared to be a single, giant park. Rivers ran in straight lines across the countryside, occasionally disappearing into tunnels drilled through mountain ranges. Whole forests appeared to have been planted in careful, geometric patterns. Vegetation with markedly different characteristics grew side by side with no evidence of intrusion by either type into the other's habitat. Grasslands were contoured and planted with thousand-kilometer-long hedgerows to cut the force of the wind. All along the continent's coasts, vast bays and inlets appeared at too regular an interval to be natural. By their shapes, it was obvious that they had been dredged for the convenience of the Makers.

"I wonder if the whole planet is like this," Robert Braedon mused as he and Horace Price pored over scene after scene of idyllic beauty.

"Why not?" Price responded. "You can do a lot of gardening in a million years."

"PROM!"

"Yes, Robert."

"Any estimate on the population of that city yet?"

"Still insufficient data. More than one hundred million, but less than a billion, I should think."

Braedon whistled and returned to watching the data being displayed on the screen. Twenty minutes later, PROM spoke again.

"You had best study the frame coming in now, Robert."

Braedon reached out and manipulated the control that would return the holoscreen to realtime display. He and Price had slowly fallen behind in their studies as one or another found something that interested him and froze the display to study it more closely. A partial frame appeared on the holoscreen. It continued to build, until half a dozen seconds later, it was complete. The view was an extreme closeup of a small village surrounded by fields of purple vegetation. The village had been built around the perimeter of a perfectly circular lake with an island at its center. It was a common pattern for Maker villages, and one they had seen dozens of times before. Only this particular village was different from the others they had observed.

It was on fire.

What had happened was evident from the raw, black wound that cut through the vegetation at the upper left of the village. A billowing, white smoke plume flowed out of the frame at the lower right and confirmed their suspicions. A wildfire, pushed before the prevailing winds, had burned through the vegetation to the edge of town. It hadn't stopped there. Half the village was in flames. Even buildings on the edge of the small lake were ablaze.

"That's strange," Price said. "Even a backward place like First Landing has enough fire protection to prevent that from happening. You wouldn't think a race as old as the Makers would allow a forest fire to get started in the first place."

"Maybe they've had an equipment breakdown," Braedon said.

"If so, they've had quite a number," PROM replied. "Look at this."

The scene changed. This time they were looking down on a section of the megalopolis. A single tall tower stood in an open square, rising a thousand stories above the ground. Beside it, the rubble from what was obviously its twin lay collapsed in a heap. The collapse of the second tower had completely blocked a major thoroughfare. The pile of rubble expanded to fill the screen as PROM increased the magnification. As it did so, thick vegetation could clearly be seen poking up through broken building blocks.

"It fell down and no one seems to have made any attempt to clean it up," PROM said. "Then there is this."

The next view showed another part of the city on the seacoast. They were looking down on a harbor in which the shapes of several large ships were tied up to docks. At first, Braedon could see nothing wrong with the view. Then he noticed that one of the ships had a different appearance than the others.

"Zoom in on the one in the middle, PROM."

Once again, the view expanded to fill the screen. The reason that the ship in question had caught Braedon's eye was obvious. It had sunk at the dock, settling a few meters beneath clear, green waves. Its outline was still clearly visible, but softened by the intervening blanket of seawater.

"What do you make of all of this, PROM?" Price asked.

"I have spent the last several minutes scanning all data which we have received to this moment. From a distance, the city appears to be intact. And, indeed, it seems to be in an excellent state of repair. However, I have noted a number of discrepancies of the same class. I've seen roadways washed out, buildings with collapsed roofs, vegetation which has choked a variety of structures."

"Maybe their civilization has collapsed. That would certainly explain your observations."

"It would not explain another observation I have made, Robert. Or rather, one I have *not* made."

"Which is?"

"You will note that the city is crisscrossed with pathways for vehicular traffic. I have yet to see a single vehicle use them. The city was built for at least a hundred million Makers. Yet, of all the organisms I have seen on the planet's surface, I cannot positively identify any of them as being Makers. The most common animal type within the city appears to be something that fits the same ecological niche as terrestrial cattle. There are large herds of them grazing in the grasslands east of the city."

Price stroked his white hair. "Would the Makers be herbivores?"

"No. The basic layout of the major population center is too like that of a human city. That suggests beings who are omnivores. The few herbivorous races we know of all tend to be nomadic."

"What are you getting at?" Braedon asked.

"I think the city has been abandoned, Robert."

"Of course! That explains the starship wakes!" Aeneas Spatz muttered to no one in particular after studying frame after frame sent up from the orbiting scouts.

Colin Williams heard his assistant's comment and favored him with an irritated glance. There were dark circles under the chief scientist's eyes, the result of his having spent most of the previous two sleep periods staring into a workscreen. "What the hell are you talking about?"

"Obviously, the Makers have packed up and moved out of the system. That's what created the hyperwakes."

"A scientist should avoid jumping to conclusions at all times, Doctor Spatz."

"Nonsense..." Spatz said before remembering who he was speaking to. "Uh, what I mean, sir, is that it all fits! Don't you see! They were migrating. One of their probes finally came through for them and they decided to move to greener pastures. Hell, we weren't lucky in

stumbling across that flyway! When you consider how
many ships it must have taken to move the entire species,
this whole region of space must be crisscrossed with the
wakes of Maker starships."

Williams frowned and considered the younger man's
comment. "An intriguing theory, Doctor Spatz. However,
until you provide some solid evidence to back it up, it is
still only a theory."

"We've got the hypertracks! What more evidence do
you need?"

"As you yourself pointed out, a species-wide migration
would require millions of starships. Surely they didn't
build them out of hard vacuum. Where are the mines
where they obtained their metal? Where are the shipyards
where they built their fleet? Where are the spaceports
from which they launched their migration?"

"I'll get right on it," Spatz said, turning back to his
workscreen. He pondered a few seconds before starting
to code search parameters for PROM.

If charting the Maker world had been hard on Colin
Williams, it was doubly so on those who manned the scout
boats. Three boats weren't enough for everything that
had to be done. The pilots, copilots, and sensor operators
did their best, often spending eighteen hours at a stretch
strapped into their control couches. More often than not,
meals consisted of cold yeast concentrate and day-old
coffee; sleep was by rotation; and showers were non-
existent. The initial excitement at the prospect of exploring an alien world had quickly been replaced by a dogged
determination to get the job done.

As soon as the second planet was mapped to Braedon's
satisfaction, he gave *Divine Wind* and *Caroline* the task
of exploring the remaining planets in the system for signs
of the Maker civilization. With the departure of two-
thirds of the expedition's scouts, he grudgingly agreed to
use *Procyon's Promise* to observe the Maker world directly
and had PROM place the starship in a five-hundred-kilo-
meter-high equatorial orbit. Twelve hours later, he ordered
Siren Song back to the ship.

"What's up?" Terra asked.

"Modifications. We're going to dismount your sensor
gear."

"By The Promise, what for?"

"I'll explain when you come aboard. Now, stand by for coordinates."

Four hours later, Terra, Jim Davidson, and *Siren Song*'s three sensor techs climbed wearily down the ladder from the high docking cradle to the hangar deck. Chryse Haller was waiting for them at the airlock leading to the engineering spaces.

"What's going on?" Terra asked. "What can possibly be important enough to place us eight hours behind schedule?"

"I bring news. All your assigned tasks are hereby canceled. We've a new job for you after you're rested."

"How long?"

"A minimum of twelve hours, maybe a whole day," Chryse answered. "Depends on how long it takes to restore your boat's aerodynamic efficiency."

Terra stared at Chryse. Fatigue made her slow to react. "What's the job?"

"We've found a spaceport! We want you to check it out."

"We've found lots of spaceports."

"None that cover ten thousand square kilometers and which have facilities to service a thousand ships at a time. From the cradle dimensions, we estimate the average size to be about two kilometers in diameter."

Jim Davidson whistled softly. "That's a lot of tonnage!"

"Now comes the best part," Chryse answered. "One of the cradles is still occupied."

"Huh?"

"You heard me. We've located a Maker starship!"

CHAPTER 27

Terra Braedon and Jim Davidson sat in *Siren Song*'s control couches and listened to the first tenuous wisps of atmosphere keen against the hull. Before them, the main viewscreen displayed the limb of the Maker world, its gentle curve backlit by the system primary. The planet itself was black except for the occasional pinprick flash of lightning that marked the location of several widespread thunderstorms. The vast carpets of lights which mark the home of a technologically advanced species were absent.

"Funny we didn't notice that right away," Terra said.

"Notice what?" Jim glanced up from the navigation display.

"That the planet is pitch-black after the sun goes down. Artificial light is practically the first thing an intelligent species invents."

"Not if they're nocturnal, I'll bet."

Terra shook her head. "Intelligent owls wouldn't build all those glass walls and skylights. Nor would they orient their structures to catch the sun the way the Makers do."

"Maybe they're nocturnal sun worshipers."

Terra was about to reply when she realized that he was grinning. She made a face instead, following it with a short, pungent comment regarding what he could do with his nocturnal sun worshipers. She was about to loose another salvo when the hatch in the aft bulkhead opened and Chryse Haller stepped through. Like Terra and Dav-

idson, she was wearing a lightweight vacsuit whose folds
hung loose in the pressurized compartment. Her helmet
was hinged up and back, leaving her head free.

Terra glanced around at Chryse, catching a glimpse of
the main cabin through the open hatchway as she did so.
Siren Song had been stripped of its instrument consoles. In
their place were six passenger couches, five occupied by
vacsuit-clad figures staring at the planet on the cabin viewscreen. The other members of the first expedition to the
surface were Scholar Price, Engineer Gomez, and Aeneas
Spatz. Rounding out the eight member crew was a two-
Marine security detachment. Chryse closed the hatch
behind her.

"Excited?" she asked Terra.

"A little."

"A little? I can hardly sit still back there! I feel like a
school girl on her first date. Too bad I can't be more like
Horace Price. He just sits there, calmly enjoying the view.
How do you suppose he does it?"

"I've known Horace Price since I was a little girl,"
Terra said, "and I can assure you that he's far from calm
at this moment."

"He hides it well. How is it that your father let him
come along?"

"My father didn't have much choice in the matter. Oh,
he has the *legal* right to bar Horace Price from this mission, but he would never do so if Price insisted on coming
along. That old man did more to unravel the secret of the
stardrive than anyone alive. He practically built *Procyon's Promise* with his own two hands. He's earned the
right to be the first human to set foot on the Maker world."

"I'm not arguing the point," Chryse said, "just surprised that your father would take the risk."

"Well, *I'm* surprised he let *you* come!"

Chryse shrugged inside her suit. "I merely pointed out
that as chairman of the Landing Committee, I should be
on the scene in order to evaluate the situation at first
hand. I also noted that this expedition needs someone to
do the cooking, guard the ship, answer the radio, and
generally keep things organized while the rest of you are
clambering around inside strange machinery. Finally, I
threatened to pout all the way back to Earth if he refused
my generous offer."

"In other words, you used logic on him."

"Say what you will about my methods, young lady. They worked."

"Seventy-five kilometers altitude," Jim Davidson warned. "We could encounter buffeting in another minute or so."

"You'd best return to your seat and strap down," Terra said. "The artificial gravity in these boats is not helpful in turbulence."

Two minutes later they were approaching the major northern continent at an altitude of fifty thousand meters. It was early morning, local time, and the K0 star behind them cast an orange glow across the fluffy clouds below.

Terra disengaged the guidance computer, took hold of the manual controller, pushed forward, and placed the boat into a steep dive. She leveled out at an altitude of one thousand meters just as *Siren Song* crossed a coast of black sand on which purple waves crashed ashore in frothing orange breakers. "Recorders still on?"

"On and clicking away," Davidson confirmed.

"PROM, you there?"

"Still here, Terra."

"We're going to start our run for the spaceport. Turning, now!"

"I have you on the scope. Be careful!"

Everyone aboard the starship had recognized the necessity of sending an expedition down to the planet. The problem was how to do it safely? One faction, led by Javral Pere and Colin Williams — as usual — had argued vigorously for caution. For once they had found an ally in Robert Braedon. His concerns were twofold: First, if the Makers were anything like humans, they had left a lot of automatic machinery running when they abandoned their world. There was no telling what forty years of neglect had done to such machines, or what would happen to the first careless explorer who tried to use one. Secondly, and of greater concern, was the possibility that not all the Makers had abandoned the planet. The reaction of hold-outs to a boatload of aliens was something Braedon would have given a year's pay to know in advance.

Since neither concern could be answered from orbit, Terra's flight plan called for *Siren Song* to make close observations of several targets-of-opportunity before risk-

ing a landing at the Maker spaceport. The first such target
was to be one of the small villages. Terra's orders were
clear—having been spelled out both in writing and in a
blistering, private session with her father. At the first sign
of trouble, she was to climb for space as fast as the scout
boat would carry her.

"Smallville coming up," Jim Davidson said.

"Lock the nose camera straight ahead, then switch
your screen to starboard view."

"Done," Jim reported. On his half of the main viewscreen, the Maker countryside began to move laterally
past at blinding speed.

Terra nudged the manual controller to the right until
the cluster of buildings below was at the center of a wide,
sweeping turn. She studied the village while using it as a
guide point for the turn.

The layout was circular, with a dozen structures arrayed
more or less evenly about the perimeter of a central parklike expanse of vegetation. The buildings varied considerably in size, but were architecturally similar, something
like a mixture of neo-classical Greek and twenty-second
century Functionalist, with vaguely oriental decoration.

On their fifth circuit of the village, Terra asked, "Shall
we risk a hover?"

"Looks safe enough. Besides, we aren't going to learn
anything more hanging around up here."

Terra brought the scout boat out of its turn and pointed
its nose directly for the large open area at the center of the
village. She brought the boat to a halt three meters off the
ground, then initiated a slow, hovering turn to the right while
her eyes drank in the slow panorama on the viewscreen.

In front of them was a building with one glass wall—
or at least, something that looked like glass. In spite of a
thick coating of dust, she could see *Siren Song*'s reflection
as it hovered over a tangle of deep-purple plants with
scarlet growths which might or might not be flowers. Sunlight flooded into the interior through a skylight on the
roof, illuminating a number of tablelike objects.

"Eating establishment with a view of the park?" Jim
asked.

"Or art museum, or *sensie* palace, or maybe the local
courthouse," Terra replied. "Think we should set down
for a look?"

He shook his head. "Against orders, remember? No landing before the spaceport."

She sighed, but nodded. The orders made sense. With an entire world to explore, they would have to discipline their curiosity. If they stopped to investigate *everything*, they would never get anywhere. Terra continued to rotate the scout boat slowly. Below them, loose leaves and dust were stirred up where the grav field touched the ground.

"Stop!" Horace Price said from the overhead speaker. Terra immediately halted the boat's rotation.

"What is it, Horace?" she asked. Before Price could answer, her heart skipped a beat, and then began to thud against her rib cage. There was a sharp intake of breath from Jim Davidson.

At first she thought the figure was alive. Only after long seconds of study did she recognize the object for what it was.

The statue had once stood in the open air in the center of the park, but was now nearly drowned in purplish-red vines. It had been invisible from the air, but a gap in the vines now gave them a clear view—once their brains sorted out the patterns of light and dark beneath the canopy of growth. Terra's first impression was of a vaguely humanoid creature poised in a crouch. The being was biaxially symmetric, possessing a central, barrellike trunk which ended in two ambulatory appendages at the base. Two arms emerged from the round body where a human's shoulders would have been. Each possessed two elbows and an extra forearm, giving them considerable length and flexibility. Both terminated in a cluster of six grasping digits. The head was mounted directly to the barrel, with no evidence of a neck. Nor were there any eyes or ears; instead, the hemispherical skull was covered with scalelike features which might serve the function of either or both.

"Scholar Price, do you suppose that thing is a Maker?" Terra asked breathlessly.

"It will do until we find a better candidate" came the answer from the aft cabin.

"PROM, are you getting this picture?"

"I am."

"Does it look familiar?"

"How can it? I have no memory of the Makers."

The eight humans in the scout boat, and several hundred

more in orbit above, continued to stare at the statue for long minutes. Finally, Robert Braedon's voice issued from the speaker in *Siren Song*'s control cabin.

"You are falling behind schedule, Terra. Finish your sweep of the village, and get on to your next target."

"Yes, sir."

When they had finished the sweep of Smallville, Terra asked, "Everyone seen enough back there?"

No one objected. She pulled back on her controller and sent the scout boat climbing. When they had altitude, she set course for the large city to the southwest, then sent the boat leaping toward its next assigned survey site.

The city was *immense*!

Terra had known that it would be, of course. PROM had been careful to give her the raw statistics—250,000 square kilometers, two million separate structures, a population of between 100 million and a half billion Makers at its height. She could quote the numbers as well as anyone, but she hadn't really *understood* them. Not until she found herself flying over the horizon-to-horizon cityscape.

The first thing she noticed was that the buildings were all much larger than she had expected. In the photographs, she had mentally tagged them as being roughly the same size as the megastructures of New York City. Yet, compared to the buildings of the alien "Metropolis," New York's mammoths were minor doodles by a first-year student of architecture. One Maker structure alone had an area larger than Manhattan Island and was tall enough that Terra had to adjust *Siren Song*'s course to avoid crashing into it.

For more than an hour, the scout flew above and around such behemoths, across the vast prairies and parklands in between, and caught glimpses of a river that—in spite of being larger than the New Amazon on Alpha—was nearly roofed over by Maker bridges and other structures. Twice, they circled to watch herds of four-legged animals grazing where groundcars once rode.

Yet, with eight sets of eyes intently scanning every screen, they saw no sign that the Makers still lived in their city. Also, the signs of neglect were more evident than they had been from orbit. Not one of the massive structures was completely whole. Here and there, windows were broken but had not been repaired. The excrement of a variety of small, four-winged flyers stained the sides of needle-shaped towers like great, mottled waterfalls. A carpet of dead leaves lay in the lee of most buildings; and everywhere, the wild growth of the Makers' feral gardens struggled to gain a foothold on the sleek sides of sky-scrapers. Once the scout boat flew above a small water-course, the source of which appeared to be a break in the city's water system.

"This is depressing," Jim Davidson said after they'd been flying over the city for nearly ninety minutes. "How much longer are we going to survey this graveyard?"

"Not much longer," Terra said, glancing at the elapsed time indicator. "Let me check with the paying passengers." Terra switched the guidance computer back on-line, released the side controller, and stretched her aching left arm before activating the intercom. "Scholar Price."

"Yes, Terra?"

"It's been an hour and a half. Ready to call it quits on this phase?"

"Affirmative. I've seen more than enough of this city, thank you."

"Chryse?"

"Agreed! This place makes me feel humble. Too much of that could ruin a person."

"Engineer Gomez?"

"I came to see the ship, pilot. The sooner the better."

"Aeneas?"

"Ready, Terra."

"PROM?"

"I was about to suggest that you move on, also. You will need the remaining daylight at your next objective."

"Then it's unanimous." Terra keyed in the command which would send *Siren Song* on a high speed dash toward the spaceport.

At just under Mach One, the trip would take forty min-utes. Halfway to their destination, they encountered the blanket of clouds PROM had warned them to expect. With the ground below hidden by a layer of white, it was easy to imagine that they were on Earth or Alpha. Much of the unease which Terra had felt during the flight over the city began to dissipate. Finally, it was time to descend again.

Terra took the boat off autopilot and slowly dropped

toward the cloud layer while watching the instruments closely. Then the viewscreen was sheathed in white. They broke through the overcast and into a cold, gray day.

"My God, look at that!" Jim Davidson exclaimed.

Terra didn't have to ask him what he meant. The spaceport was nowhere as large as Metropolis, but it was just as impressive in a different way. Like the city, it was a place of wide-open spaces and huge buildings. They passed over one structure that seemed to be an immense hangar. Ten-story-high doors stood agape, revealing acres of empty floor. The plain on which the port had been built was covered with immense craters spaced in a perfect hexagonal pattern. The craters, presumably landing cradles for starships, were lined with heavy machinery. Domes of indeterminate size were positioned in the center of each group of landing cradles. Covered passages radiated outward from the buildings, stopping just short of the crater rims.

Terra sized up the system of landing cradles and debarkation buildings in a single glance. A close study of their intricacies would have to wait. Something far more interesting riveted her attention and that of everyone else onboard the scout boat.

In the distance, its base half buried and its top reaching nearly to the cloud layer above, was the starship. Like *Procyon's Promise*, it was a sphere. Around it, two dozen ramps led to airlocks, each large enough to hold a regiment of Space Guard Marines. A variety of mechanisms jutted from the hull, including a spire on the ship's prow.

"Horace!"

"I see it, Terra."

"What's the matter, you two?" Chryse Haller asked from the main cabin.

It took several seconds for Terra to find her voice. "Except for its size, Chryse, this ship looks just like those we found at First Landing!"

"Is that significant?"

"It tells us who it was that gave the Makers the stardrive."

"Of course!" Chryse exclaimed. "The Star Travelers must have encountered one of the Maker life probes and followed it home!"

CHAPTER 28

Events moved quickly after *Siren Song* touched down at the Maker spaceport. As Terra had explained to Chryse, a lifetime of accomplishment had earned Horace Price the honor of being first to set foot on the Maker world. Terra helped Price run through the suit safety checks before letting him enter the scout boat's airlock. Peering through the clear plastic bubble of the vacsuit's helmet as she helped him adjust his backpack, she was struck by how much he had aged since *Procyon's Promise* had entered the Maker system. Terra had heard that he was working too hard, but up until that moment, she hadn't realized the strain he'd been under since the accident with the stardrive.

"You should rest, Horace."

He smiled wanly. "I have worked all my life for this moment, Terra. I'm not about to sleep through it."

"Look at you! You're practically dead on your feet."

"I'll rest later. Now, young lady, are you ever going to finish whatever it is that you are doing back there?"

"Done," she said as she gave one of the harnesses a final tug. Terra helped him into the airlock, closed the inner door, then moved to the flight deck for a better view. The airlock warning indicator on the control board turned from green to red as she climbed into her control couch. A few seconds later, Price came into sight on the main viewscreen. He was descending the ramp leading from the airlock. He stepped gingerly onto the scarred surface of the spaceport. He walked a dozen paces toward the alien starship, stopped, gazed upward at the curved metal cliff towering over him, then slowly, awkwardly, got down on his knees.

"What's he doing?" Jim Davidson whispered.

Terra shushed him.

Scholar Price was silent for nearly two minutes. The only sound that emanated from the scout-boat speaker was the soft susurration of his breathing. At the end of that time, he climbed to his feet with difficulty and signaled for the rest of them to join him.

Twenty hours after the scout boat's landing, the physicians aboard *Procyon's Promise* decided that the planet's air was safe to breath. The ground party gladly exchanged their vacsuits for winter clothing and hiking boots. At the same time, they moved their base of operations from the cramped quarters inside the scout boat to several tents which they pitched outside. The atmosphere of the Maker world had a higher oxygen content than Earth, and its pressure was also higher. The oxygen-rich air brought forth an exhilaration that partially compensated for the planet's five percent greater than standard gravity and twenty-seven-hour day.

They spent the second day after landing poking around the base of the starship, seeking a way inside. The K0 star was just sinking below the horizon when they broke off their search and returned to camp.

"How long before we can get in, Gomez?" Aeneas Spatz asked over dinner.

The assistant engineer looked up from the scribbled notes he had been studying. "Tomorrow, maybe. The day after, for sure. The airlock mechanism appears straightforward enough. I just have to make sure that I'm not overlooking something subtle before I force it open."

True to his word, Gomez succeeded in prying open one of the starship's smaller airlocks on the third day. With a passageway open into the black interior of the ship, Gomez, Aeneas Spatz, and the two Marines lost no time in exploring the interior. Each man went in with two canteens, ten kilos of supplies, a respirator, a pistol, two flashlights, and an inertial tracker. The latter could be set to backtrack to the airlock entrance if anyone got lost or separated.

"It's the biggest goddamned thing I ever seen!" said Corporal Cibolo, the senior Marine guard, four hours later. "There must be room for ten million people in there!"

Aeneas Spatz quickly confirmed the corporal's observation. "The bunkrooms are designed to hold a thousand sleepers at a time. The messhalls are even bigger."

"How much did you see?" Price asked.

"We barely scratched the surface, Scholar. We managed to penetrate almost to the center of the ship. The deck we were on appears to be devoted entirely to living quarters. Gomez found several lifts leading to other decks, but they were inoperative. There are also emergency stairs, though I'd hate to face a kilometer-high climb in this gravity. At least, I'd hate to face it more than once."

"Not necessary," Gomez said in his slightly accented Standard. "The lift mechanisms are self-contained, sealed units. Once I get a power pod hooked into their circuits, we should be able to go up and down in style."

"Any sign of engine or control rooms?" Scholar Price asked.

"Negative," Gomez replied. "However, the whole center section of this deck is blocked off by a heavy bulkhead. I'll wager we find the stardrive behind that wall when we find a way around it."

The next day they learned that Robert Braedon had recalled *Divine Wind*, leaving *Caroline* with the dangerous and lonely job of mapping the rest of the Maker system. They learned of the decision when the scout boat touched down with supplies and eight new passengers—and orders for *Siren Song* to return to the starship. After Terra and Jim Davidson had docked their scout boat in *Promise*'s hangar bay, they found Chief Engineer Reickert and Colin Williams waiting with their kit bags, as well as a large pile of packing crates. Upon delivering their passengers and freight to the spaceport, they learned that Gomez had managed to get two lifts working and that Chryse Haller and Aeneas Spatz had discovered the starship's control room.

"You should have seen it!" Chryse told Terra later. "There were things like barber chairs all over, and horseshoe-shaped control panels wrapped around every one. To work all the buttons, a human would have to be built like a chimpanzee..."

"Or a Maker," Terra said, remembering the length of the arms on the statue they'd seen.

Two days later, Price and Reickert managed to patch into the ship's dormant computer system. Even though PROM knew nothing of the Makers, she was a descendant of the same technology that had built the starship's brain. Horace Price was of the opinion that all they need do to tap the starship's data banks was to link the two computers together. Hans Reickert was less sure, but willing to give it a try.

Once again, Terra and Jim Davidson found themselves ordered to orbit, this time to pick up the equipment that would provide the link. Once again they found a passenger waiting for them.

"Father!" Terra exclaimed. "What are *you* doing here?"

"I'm tired of reading reports about this starship. I want to see it with my own eyes."

"But is it safe for you to leave *Promise*? I mean, what if there's an emergency?"

"I can handle it from the ground just as easily as the bridge," he said.

"Glad to have you aboard, sir," Jim Davidson said. He took Braedon's kit bag and stored it in a locker. "It'll be another fifteen minutes or so before we're ready to launch. You can go forward and sit in one of the pilot's couches until we get our cargo loaded, if you like."

Braedon grinned. "That's the politest way anyone ever told me to get the hell out from underfoot, Mr. Davidson!"

"Yes, sir."

Braedon stretched and opened his eyes. Above him, green fabric flapped in a gentle breeze that bore with it alien smells mixed with the odor of frying bacon. He groped for the depolarizer on his sleeping bag, found it, and felt cool air swirl around his bare legs as a seam appeared in the fabric where none had existed previously. He threw back the covers, levered himself into sitting position, and regretted it immediately as every muscle in his body cried out in protest.

It was his own damned fault, of course. He had insisted that Aeneas Spatz show him *everything* aboard the Maker starship. For sixteen hours, they had trudged through compartment after compartment, until everything had become one continuous blur. They had visited the cavernous engine room with its generators the size of small mountains. They had walked between bone-dry tanks in the hydroponic gardens, crushed dessicated leaves in their hands to sniff their tart aroma. They had visited the living quarters and wondered at the lack of privacy: Were Makers naturally more communal than humans, or had the task of moving their entire race to some faroff star forced them to congregate in such concentrated masses? Finally, they had visited the control room high in the prow of the ship. There they found a work gang under Horace Price's supervision struggling to install the computer link between PROM and the starship.

"Are you sure there's something in there?" Braedon had asked, gesturing at the alien computer modules, as he tried to ignore the dull ache in his lower legs.

"There ought to be," Price had answered. "A similar set of data banks managed to store the probe's cargo of Maker knowledge for a hundred centuries."

"What about language?"

"Since PROM doesn't speak the Maker tongue, that could be a problem at first. However, I talked it over with her. PROM thinks she should be able to crack any code she encounters in relatively short order."

"How long before the link-up will be ready?"

"Another four hours, at least. You might as well go back to camp and have dinner, Robert. I'll radio for you as soon as we're all set."

"Right," Braedon had said. By the time he and Spatz returned to camp, however, he found that he was nearly ready to drop from exhaustion. He remembered eating a meal of hot stew, warm bread, and coffee; but after that ... nothing.

Braedon pulled on his clothes and then crawled from the tent. He stood up and stretched to get the kinks out. As he did so, he noted the height of the K0 sun above the horizon. It was already halfway to zenith.

"Good morning," Chryse Haller said to him when he walked into the mess tent. Braedon sat at a makeshift table that someone had constructed by laying a sheet of light alloy across two pieces of alien machinery of unknown function. Chryse stopped fussing with the dishwasher and poured him a cup of coffee instead.

"Why didn't someone wake me?"

"I wouldn't let them," she replied. "You fell asleep during dinner. Some of the men put you to bed. I figured that you needed your rest."

"I guess I did," he said, yawning. "How is the computer tie-in going?"

"I understand they finally got a hard link-up about midnight. Scholar Price bunked in the control room last night. I sent Sven Jorgenson up with food for his work party two hours ago. He hasn't come back yet."

Braedon took a sip of coffee, then said, "I'd better be getting up there."

"Not until you've had breakfast," Chryse replied. "How do you like your eggs?"

Braedon started to argue, then gave in. Nearly an hour later he pushed himself back from the table. "I didn't realize I was that hungry."

Chryse smiled and turned back to her stove. Braedon watched her work. A wild strand of hair fell down in her eyes. She absentmindedly brushed it out of the way. The gesture reminded him of Cecily. Braedon smiled as he remembered long-ago mornings when he would sit at the breakfast table back home and watch his wife move about the kitchen.

"What are you grinning about?"

Braedon glanced around in time to see Terra seat herself next to him.

"Just enjoying the morning and the company. What brings you here at this time of the morning?"

"I stopped by your tent, saw you were up, and took a chance that I'd find you here. I wanted to talk to you about Scholar Price."

"What about him?"

"I just left him up in the control room. He looks *ghastly*, Father! I don't think he slept more than a couple of hours last night, if that much. You may have to send him back up to the ship for a rest."

"You shouldn't worry about Horace. I've seen him work on a problem seventy-two hours straight, then be fresh as a terl after a good night's sleep."

"That was a lot of years ago. He's too old to push himself like that now."

"I agree," Chryse said. She had filled three coffee cups while Braedon and Terra talked, and sat down across from them. "You remember how tired you were yesterday, Robert. Think of how it must feel to be fifteen years older."

Braedon glanced at the two women and shook his head. "You have to understand. Horace Price is pushing himself because he *hasn't* very long to live. Oh, I don't mean that he's ill, or anything like that. He's in remarkably good shape for a man of sixty-six. He's been driving himself ever since the accident because there is so much to learn. Discovering all the secrets of this world will be the work of several lifetimes. Horace Price doesn't even have a single lifetime to devote to it."

"All the more reason why he shouldn't work himself into a premature grave," Terra said.

Braedon sighed and nodded. "I have to go up and check on progress. I'll talk to him about it."

"May I come along?" Chryse asked. "I haven't been out of this tent except to sleep in thirty-six hours."

"If you like," he replied, smiling.

Terra glanced at her father and at Chryse. She bit her lip, hesitated, then came to some inner decision. "I really should get back to work too. May I accompany you?"

Braedon gave his daughter a strange look, then nodded. "If you like."

Thus it was that the expedition commander, the camp cook, and their reluctant chaperone made their way through bright sunshine to the airlock that led into the interior of the Maker starship.

The journey from airlock to control room involved a ten-minute hike through darkened corridors lit by widely spaced glowtubes. Half a kilometer inside the ship, they came to a bank of lifts, two of which had been restored to operation. The familiar barrel shape of a terrestrial power unit squatted in one corner of the lift car and was connected to the alien machinery via several heavy cables. The acrid smell of ozone hung in the air, one of the power unit's normal by-products.

There was a brief surge of acceleration as Braedon activated the lift and a similar period of deceleration a few moments later. When the door opened, they found themselves facing another long corridor dimly lighted by

glowtubes. Braedon let Terra and Chryse lead the way
while he brought up the rear. As they marched along the
corridor, his sense of unease grew stronger. Something
about the old hulk caused the hairs on the back of his
neck to stand on end. It was the same feeling he'd experienced while watching transmissions from Terra's scout
boat during its long aerial tour of the Maker city. It was
the feeling of being watched, of trespassing where one
doesn't belong, an irrational fear that the rightful owners
will show up any minute to claim their property. Braedon
tried to shake the feeling as he followed his daughter
toward the control room. He was only partially successful.

Several hundred meters beyond the lift, they came to
an intersection of corridors. The guide path of human-
installed glowtubes turned to the right, while far to his
left, Braedon noticed a distant glow the color of daylight.

"What's down there?" he asked, pointing toward the
skyglow.

"That's the open access hatch where they installed the
high-gain antenna for the link-up," Terra said. "Remind
me to show it to you after you're through in the control
room. The view from up here is spectacular."

The control room was a cylindrical compartment nearly
a hundred meters in diameter. It was filled with horseshoe-
shaped control stations arranged in concentric rings about
a central dais. The arrangement was similar to that of the
control consoles on the bridge of *Procyon's Promise*. The
coincidence would have surprised Braedon if not for
the obvious fact that both human and Maker starships
were based on the same Star Traveler design.

The perimeter of the control room was lined with deck-
to-ceiling viewscreens. Other screens were inset into the
horseshoe-desks of the control stations. On Braedon's
previous visit, Reickert's technicians had been experi-
menting with the viewscreens, displaying a variety of interior and exterior views. Now, however, the large wall
screens were dark. On the far side of the compartment,
several scientists and technicians were intent on disman-
tling one of the control stations. In the center of the compartment, Horace Price sat at another station and read
glowing text from the screen of a human-style workscreen.

Braedon, with Chryse and Terra in tow, strode to the center of the compartment.

"How are things going, Horace?" he asked when he reached Price.

A pair of hollow, sunken eyes looked up at him briefly and then immediately returned to the screen. "Hello, Robert. Things are going well. PROM has cracked the Maker language and is nearly a quarter of the way through the ship's data banks."

"Any reason why she can't handle things for a few hours while you get some sleep?"

"I appreciate your concern, Robert, but I can't quit right now."

"Why not? What can you possibly be learning that is worth ruining your health?"

Price's laugh was shrill, with a touch of hysteria to it. "What am I learning? More than you can possibly imagine. For instance, in the last six hours, PROM and I have discovered the principle that makes FTL possible, and more. Do you remember Luigi Chiardi's theory that the I-mass must be somehow related to the stardrive because they represent the two universal mysteries of physics? He was right on target with that one!"

"Are you saying that you've learned the physical principles behind *both* the stardrive *and* the I-mass?"

"Principle, Robert. Singular. The stardrive and I-mass are two aspects of the same thing."

"Which is . . . ?"

Price laughed again. "The critical mistake everyone made was in misunderstanding the true nature of antimatter. Actually, it doesn't have a nature. Antimatter doesn't exist!"

CHAPTER 29

After a dozen seconds, Terra said, "That's silly, Horace! Of course, antimatter exists."

Price gazed at her as one does a favorite pupil who has nevertheless obtained the wrong answer on a quiz. "How do you know that, Terra? Because your schoolmasters told you so?"

"Well . . . yes."

Price sighed. "Never forget that schoolmasters are human too, young lady. In science, truth is a moving target. The knowledge of one generation is merely the jumping-off spot for the next generation's inquiries."

"Make your point, Horace," Braedon said.

Scholar Price turned to face his commander. If he was offended by the sharpness of Braedon's comment, he failed to show it. "In a moment, Robert. I have some ground-work to lay if you are to understand the full import of what I have discovered. Forgive me if I fall back to basics, but there is much to unlearn. Chryse, would you be so kind as to explain the concept of antimatter?"

Chryse looked sheepish. "I majored in business, Scholar. Physics wasn't high on my list of 'must' courses."

Price laughed. "Never mind. I will answer my own question. Conventional theory holds that for every kind of subatomic particle there is an antiparticle which possesses the same mass and spin, but with the opposite electrical charge. Thus, the antiparticle for the electron

270

is the positron, sometimes called the antielectron. The positron masses five-point-four-eight-eight times ten to the minus fourth Atomic Mass Units—exactly the same as the electron. It also has the same spin as the electron. However, as the name implies, the positron's charge is positive rather than negative.

"Likewise, the positively charged proton is complemented by the negatively charged antiproton. The neutron's antiparticle is the antineutron, and although both are electrically neutral, the two possess opposite magnetic moments. Since normal matter is composed of protons, neutrons, and electrons, it is a simple progression from particles and antiparticles to a form of matter composed entirely of antiprotons, antineutrons, and positrons. The name we have given to this form is *antimatter*.

"Because of the opposite electrical charges of the two forms, if they were ever to come into physical contact, both would be annihilated in a burst of pure energy. Indeed, the first antimatter observed by human beings was manufactured in particle accelerators. And since the process was both difficult and expensive, astronomers began to search the sky for signs that large quantities of antimatter existed in interstellar space.

"Of course, no such evidence was ever discovered. As far as the astronomers could see, the universe was totally devoid of antimatter. This negative result caused considerable consternation among the cosmologists of the time. By then, the Big Bang was well entrenched as *the* cosmological theory, and one of the inescapable consequences of the Big Bang was that both types of matter should have been created in equal quantities.

"The problem of the missing antimatter was resolved with the discovery of the I-mass early in the twenty-first century. Not only are I-masses composed entirely of antimatter, they are sufficiently numerous to account for all the missing mass in the universe. Also, there are good reasons to believe that the Big Bang left the two forms of matter well mixed, and by God, that's precisely how it has turned out! Luckily, the antimatter is all buried inside tiny black holes, thus insulating it from the normal matter and preventing a titanic explosion.

"If cosmologists had left well enough alone at that point, everyone would have been happy. However, they noted that black holes composed of normal matter tend to evaporate due to quantum mechanical effects. Yet antimatter black holes do not. Since the two forms react similarly in all other respects, the question arose as to why this should be. It's a question which has resisted solution for nearly four hundred years. That is, until now."

"And you know the answer?" Braedon asked.

Price smiled mirthlessly. "I've already told you. The fault lies in our theory of antimatter. There is no such thing as an antiparticle. Nor am I the first man to suggest such a possibility."

"What?"

"It's true. Ever hear of Richard Feynman?"

Braedon frowned. "No, should I have?"

"Possibly. He was a twentieth-century physicist who specialized in quantum mechanics, a late contemporary of Albert Einstein and a winner of the Nobel Prize back in the days when that meant something. He invented the Feynman diagrams often used in I-mass physics. I had PROM check the data banks, and Feynman appears to be the first person to suggest the true nature of antimatter. Simply put, Feynman's hypothesis was that the behavior of antiparticles can be explained if one assumes that they are standard particles *moving backward in time*!"

"Surely you can't be serious!" Terra exclaimed.

"I am very serious. Take the most elementary thing we know about them—that they possess an opposite electrical charge from the normal particles. How did we come to such a conclusion?"

"Easy," Terra said. "Put the two in a magnetic field and one will curve to the right, the other to the left."

"Precisely!" Price agreed. "If the electron follows a curved path to the right in a magnetic field and the positron follows an identical curve to the left, then they obviously have opposite charges. But wait! Doesn't such an analysis make an assumption regarding the particle's direction of travel? By definition, doesn't the starting point of a journey always predate its end? If the positron is actually an electron traveling backward in time, its starting and ending points must be exchanged end for end, and the particle curves to the right during its flight through the magnetic field, *just as the negatively charged electron does*! The concept is strange, but not particularly difficult. Think of a holomovie being projected backward."

Braedon's brow was furrowed in concentration as he stroked his chin. "An interesting theory. But how does it explain such things as pair production or matter/antimatter annihilation?"

"Quite easily," Price said. "For Chryse's benefit, pair production takes place when two high-energy photons collide. Both disappear and are replaced by an electron-positron pair with exactly the same energy state. Yet is it not equally valid to think of the electron/positron 'pair' as being a single electron (in this case, originally moving backward in time) which has been knocked forward by its collision with the photons? By the same token, the annihilation of matter with antimatter can be explained by the reverse process: a forward-moving electron which has reversed its direction in time. The conservation of energy and momentum would require it to emit a high-energy photon at the moment of reversal. To an outside observer, himself moving forward in time, it would appear as though the electron/positron pair had disappeared and been replaced by the photon."

Price paused to gauge his listeners' level of understanding before continuing. "All of this has merely been a pleasant intellectual exercise unless this new theory can explain some things that the old cannot. So, let's consider the effect of this new model of antimatter on current cosmological theories. Robert, please describe the best current guess as to the structure of the universe."

Braedon licked dry lips and hesitated. When Price had begun his explanation, Braedon had been skeptical. Now, however, he was unsure. It all sounded so logical, yet . . . He ordered his violently swirling thoughts and said, "Uh, there doesn't seem to be any doubt that the Big Bang actually happened. Everywhere we look in the sky, we see evidence of the primordial fireball in the three-degree Kelvin background radiation. The universe is also closed. That is, the gravitational attraction of all the matter in the universe is sufficiently strong that it will eventually overcome the momentum imparted by the Big Bang. One day, the universe will stop expanding and begin to fall in upon itself. At the end of the contraction phase, the galaxies will be crushed together into another Big Bang."

"Very good, Commodore! Let us take your hypothesis one step further. If this is truly an oscillating universe, then we live in a sort of trough between tidal waves. There are cosmic explosions in both our future and our past."

"Obviously," Braedon said.

"Try to visualize what such an event must be like. The universe explodes and matter is spewed across billions of light-years of space! It is also spewed forward in time to the next Big Bang. But remember Feynman's theory. If antimatter is normal matter moving backward in time, then the Big Bang in the future must be the source. There are two opposite currents of matter in the universe. One travels past to future and we perceive it as normal matter; the other travels future to past and appears as antimatter."

Chryse Haller, who had been following the discussion with some difficulty, frowned. "That still doesn't explain why all the antimatter ended up inside I-masses."

"It does if one assumes that the Big Bang futureward from here will be a particularly violent one," Price said. "The pressures and temperatures involved must be far in excess of that required for singularity formation. The Big Bang in the past was far less violent—as evidenced by the fact that it left vast quantities of 'normal matter' in the free state. And, since all the universe's physical laws are scrambled by each Big Bang, that also explains why I-masses don't follow exactly the same rules as normal matter black holes."

"What does all this have to do with the stardrive?" Terra asked.

Price leaned back in his chair and grinned. "Ah, leave it to the young to keep the objective firmly fixed in mind. Up until now, I haven't mentioned the principle which we know as entropy. Terra, will you do the honors?"

Terra shrugged. "Entropy is the measure of randomness in the universe. It always increases. In other words, things tend to run downhill."

Price nodded. "Is it not strange, then, that we are moving from a lesser explosion to one of greater violence? Is that not a case of the universe 'running uphill'? Can anyone see where I am heading?"

No one answered. Braedon's and Chryse's expressions, which had seconds earlier reflected some degree of understanding, once again displayed bafflement.

"The reason why faster-than-light travel is so difficult, people," Price said triumphantly, "is because no one understands the true nature of time. It isn't the antimatter that is going backward. It's us. We're the antimatter! That was the great breakthrough the Star Travelers made. They suddenly realized that time (as we measure it, at least) is a negative quantity. Without understanding that crucial fact, *FTL travel is impossible*!"

Scholar Price, his lined face alight with excitement, stared at Braedon and the two women. Braedon's expression showed the turmoil he felt at the sudden deluge of facts. Terra's face mirrored Price's as the sense of wonder overtook her. Chryse Haller looked thoughtful. Finally Braedon said:

"What does PROM think of this theory?"

"Why don't you ask her? She's been listening on the intercom the whole time."

"PROM?"

"Yes, Robert."

"Do you agreed with Horace's assessment?"

"Yes, indeed. My analysis of the starship's data banks is nearly thirty-percent complete. The sequence of theories which Scholar Price has detailed is well documented. The Makers were able to crack the FTL barrier only when they recognized that time is a negative."

"You mean when the Star Travelers pointed it out to them, don't you?"

The computer hesitated, something computers never do. When she spoke, her tone was cautious. "I didn't want to interrupt while Scholar Price was speaking. However, I have encountered a piece of data which I think you should see, Robert."

"What sort of data?"

"A photograph."

"Put it on the screen."

"It would be better to use one of the large peripheral viewscreens."

"Fine."

Across the control room, a wall-size viewscreen suddenly came to light. After a few seconds of multicolor static, a scene appeared. In the foreground several Makers were doing something incomprehensible. Behind them, in the background, were a ship and a large building. Something about the building drew Braedon's gaze. It took him a few moments to realize what he was seeing.

"That's the spaceport at First Landing! Look, there's Randall's Ridge behind it. What's the meaning of this, PROM?"

"The meaning is clear, Robert. I discovered this scene in the starship's data banks a few minutes ago. It clearly shows the exploration base at First Landing while it was still occupied."

"But that means..."

"That the Makers and the Star Travelers are one and the same," PROM agreed. "It would appear, Robert, that the Makers discovered the stardrive sometime before *Life Probe 53935* entered the solar system."

CHAPTER 30

A stiff breeze whipped across the concrete plain of the Maker spaceport and tugged at Robert Braedon's clothing and hair. The weather, clear and bright in the morning, had turned cold and gray in the afternoon. Braedon had barely noticed the change. The dark, scudding clouds matched his mood too well to intrude on his whirring thoughts. It had been four hours since he had departed camp. Most of that time he'd spent walking aimlessly, hands thrust deeply into pockets, head bowed against the wind.

Braedon glanced in the direction of the great spherical mountain that was the Maker starship. Even from five kilometers—the distance he had walked during his introspection—the ship was awe-inspiring. He let his gaze slide from the point where the great white hull split the overcast to the diminutive collection of tents at its base. Braedon frowned. In the middle distance between himself and the camp, a solitary figure strode purposefully across the plain in his direction. Despite the distance, he had no trouble recognizing Chryse Haller's distinctive walk.

"What brings you out here?" he asked ten minutes later when they had closed the gap between them.

"I was looking for you, of course. I have news. The doctor has Horace Price sedated and would like your permission to transport him up to *Promise* first thing in the morning."

"Permission granted. He can use *Siren Song*. That way, Terra will have something to do to take her mind off her troubles."

"Who is going to take your mind off *your* troubles?" Chryse asked.

"I don't have any troubles."

"Then why do you look as though you just had to shoot your pet dog?" Chryse gestured toward a small block-house a few hundred meters to their right. The spaceport plain was dotted with such structures. Although their function hadn't been positively identified, the most popular theory held that they were bunkers intended to protect delicate instruments against the weather. "Look, would you mind if we get out of this damned wind for a few minutes? I haven't felt anything on the right side of my face for the last half hour."

He reached up and touched her cheek. It was ice cold. "You should have worn a jacket with a weather hood," he said.

He took her arm and they walked quickly toward the bunker. It was featureless save for a single opening just large enough for a human being to enter on hands and knees. Chryse squatted down and peered into the interior. This bunker was empty, although it showed scars where equipment had once been rigged, then removed. Opposite the doorway, an open hatch and metal ladder led up to the roof. Gray light flooded through the opening, illuminating the interior.

Chryse led the way inside. Braedon followed, keeping an eye out for the local rodent-equivalents. Several expedition members had undergone involuntary cardiac-stress tests when the small, scaly animals had unexpectedly darted out of nooks and crannies.

Chryse sank down against one wall and patted the ground beside her. "Please, sit with me for a few minutes."

He joined her. They looked at each other without speaking for a long time. Chryse finally broke the silence.

"What's the matter with me, Robert?"

"I beg your pardon?"

"You heard me. There were four of us present in the control room this morning when PROM flashed that picture of First Landing on the screen. Shortly thereafter, Horace Price collapsed from nervous exhaustion, Terra went to her tent and refuses to come out, and you took off for the wilderness without saying a word to anyone. I seem to be the only one who didn't react as though PROM were announcing the end of the world. All I felt was a mild excitement at learning a fascinating new fact. What's wrong with me? Am I *that* obtuse?"

"You reacted as any Solarian would, Chryse."

"I would still like to know what I missed this morning."

Braedon sighed, and nodded. "We've spoken often enough about the differences between our two peoples, yet I wonder if we truly understand each other. You say that you were mildly excited when PROM placed that image on the screen. I have no doubt of that. In your life you have probably viewed hundreds of similar scenes from the data banks. And that is all they are to you—scenes, images on a screen, nothing more.

"But consider how we Alphans felt when we saw the Maker advance base on Alpha Canis Minoris VII. Those mountains in the background were *our* mountains. I have climbed their slopes, camped in the shadow of their peaks, made love to my wife amid their forests. That hangar behind the Makers was a building where Horace Price and I spent much of our adult lives. It's a place that I took Terra to see when she was barely old enough to walk. All of our lives we Alphans have been indoctrinated in the sanctity of The Promise.

"SURROGATE is our first teacher in school. He tells us stories of our ancestors who braved the rigors of interstellar space to keep The Promise. He tells us of the privations they suffered, of the times when there was too little food, of the children born deformed because of the high radiation levels aboard the starship, of the dozens who committed suicide because they couldn't adjust to the reality that they would never see Earth again.

"When we are older, our parents speak to us of The Founders and their great disappointment when they discovered Alpha deserted. They tell us of the hardships encountered in those first few decades, years when there was real doubt that humans would be able to survive on Alpha. We swell with pride when our fathers tell us of the proudest tradition of our people—that we never forgot our pledge.

"Think of the cost! For two hundred years we poured

our resources into understanding the estee record strip we dug out of their refuse dump. We built *Procyon's Promise* straining what little heavy industry we have to its limits. We braved danger and hardship to cross a thousand light-years of space. Finding this world cost us twenty-five good men and women, including the crew of the scout boat destroyed exploring the Sanctuary protostar. Ten generations of Alphans have given their lives to The Promise.

"And all of it was totally unnecessary!"

"What are you talking about?" Chryse asked. "Of course it was necessary."

"Didn't you hear PROM? The Makers discovered the stardrive long before the probe fell into the solar system. The wake the probe detected near Procyon came from a Maker starship! We've been on a three-century-long fool's errand!"

Chryse stared into his eyes for long seconds, then leaned close. She kissed him. It wasn't the kiss of a lover, but rather that of a compassionate friend. A dozen heartbeats passed before she broke off the embrace with a smile.

"Don't you see? Far from being wasted, your struggle has succeeded beyond your wildest dreams! You've undergone a test of strength, passed gloriously, and will now reap the rewards of victory."

"What rewards?" Braedon asked sourly.

"Why, the stardrive for one! Remember, if your ancestors hadn't taken *Pathfinder* to Procyon, *Homo sapiens* would now be as starbound as the other races of this galaxy. And what about all the life probes orbiting above our heads? Each of them carries the entire knowledge of a different alien species to add to our already existing stock of knowledge.

"By proving that humans can be trusted, your people have given our race the whole galaxy! You've made us heir-apparent to the Makers. From now on, it will be humanity which controls access to the stars. Any alien species which doesn't measure up to our standards will never be released from its cage."

"What of PROM's warning that a human interstellar empire would be self-destructive?" Braedon asked.

Chryse shrugged. "A problem, of course. However, I know people well enough to be confident that we won't hoard the secret. The lure of knowledge, adventure, and interstellar trade will be too great to maintain any kind of an embargo on the universe. We'll be hard pressed to keep adventurers and entrepreneurs out of the systems we find dangerous, let alone all of them!" Chryse got up, reached out, and pulled Braedon to his feet. "Come on. I'll show you a sure cure for what ails you!"

"Where are we going?"

"Up top!"

Climbing as quickly as she could find the too widely spaced rungs, Chryse swarmed up the ladder leading to the roof. Braedon followed as soon as she was through the hatch.

The wind was stronger than it had been on the ground. It plucked at them with cold fingers, pushing and tugging, as though to sweep their alien presence away. From the roof of the blockhouse, it was possible to see several of the craters that had served as docking cradles for the departed Maker fleet. Ten kilometers to their right, one of the massive structures that had been tentatively identified as a passenger-handling facility disappeared into the clouds.

"Look out there," Chryse said as she used one hand to sweep the horizon. "It's a brand-new world, a world that now belongs to us if we want it. Nor is it the only one. There are billions of habitable planets in the galaxy. How many of them are just waiting for someone to come along with the courage to claim them? Let's have no more talk of fool's errands, Commodore Braedon," Chryse said with mock severity as she snuggled close to him.

"You've given us an entire universe to explore. That should be enough accomplishment for any single lifetime!"

"We're ready, Father!"

Braedon glanced up from his work at the sound of his daughter's voice. Terra, resplendent in dress uniform, stood in front of the desk in his office.

"Is it that time already?" he asked.

"Yes, sir."

He sighed. Not for the first time, he wondered where the time had gone. Not just the minutes since he'd sat down to catch up on his reports before the ceremony that would mark the departure of *Procyon's Promise* from the Maker world; but the days, the months, the years of his life. He looked at Terra and wondered at what precise moment had the pigtailed urchin been transformed into a beautiful young woman. It seemed like only the day before yesterday that she had climbed into his lap to listen to the legends of Old Earth.

"I suppose we had best be off to the ceremony, then. Wouldn't do to have the expedition commander show up late for his own departure." Braedon rose from behind the desk and allowed Terra to help him slip into his own dress tunic. When she had sealed the last of his seams, he pulled her to him and kissed her gently on the forehead. "When we started on this trip, I never thought I'd be leaving you stranded on an alien world. I'm going to miss you."

"I'm going to miss you too," she said, her words muffled against his chest. When Braedon released her, he saw that she had tears in her eyes. She wiped them away with a sniffle. "Why do I get so emotional at times like this? It isn't as though you were going halfway across the universe. You'll be back in a month or so!"

"Less if I can help it," he said. "This ship is about to set a new speed record for the round trip between here and Sanctuary."

Terra laughed. "That shouldn't be too difficult. Don't hurry so much that you forget to bring the fleet back with you."

"No chance of that," he said. "Hopefully, Bill Tarns has managed to extricate *Golden Hind* from whatever trouble she got into at the Grelsho sun. I'll start sending the big freighters through as soon as we can strip Sanctuary and repack the equipment."

"We'll be waiting," Terra said. "With a hundred people in the ground party and with Chryse to organize things, we should begin to make good progress on our explorations of the Maker starship. By the time you get back with the fleet, we may even be ready to begin work on the spaceport itself. If there are any clues down there concerning where the Makers went, we'll find them, Father."

"I know you will," he said. "Still, no great loss if we come up empty handed this time. We'll run into them in our travels sooner or later. When we do, I wonder if they'll be interested in learning what happened to their lost life probe?"

"Of course they will. It was faithful to its duty, wasn't it?"

Braedon nodded. "Not a bad requiem for the probe . . . or anyone else, for that matter!"

About the Author

Michael McCollum was born in Phoenix, Arizona, in 1946 and is a graduate of Arizona State University, where he majored in aerospace propulsion and minored in nuclear engineering. He has been employed as an aerospace engineer since graduation and has worked on nearly every military and civilian aircraft in production today. At various times in his career, Mr. McCollum has also worked on the precursor to the Space Shuttle Main Engine, a nuclear valve to replace the one that failed at Three Mile Island, and a variety of guided missiles.

He began writing in 1974 and has been a regular contributor to *Analog Science Fiction*. He has also appeared in *Isaac Asimov's* and *Amazing*. *Procyon's Promise*, his third novel, is the sequel to *Life Probe*, which was published by Del Rey Books in 1983.

He is married to a lovely lady by the name of Catherine, and is the father of three children: Robert, Michael, and Elizabeth.